## An invitation . . .

She dropped her eyes. "No," she murmured. "It was real. I saw it. But what *was* it?"

What indeed? All the motions and movements of an afterlife, without there being anything particularly lifelike about it. Those whom she had seen had indeed interacted, brushed shoulders, stirred the dust of the streets, spoken—sometimes to her—and yet there was nothing about them that indicated that they were anything more than memories . . . disembodied remnants of past and present lives spun off to suck a little existence out of the borderlands between life and oblivion before, like dust devils on a hot day, they faltered, collapsed, faded. . . .

She opened her handbag, cupped the paper in the palm of her thin hand. The words stared up at her: *Come on in . . .*

*The water's fine.*

She felt fear again. There it was, waiting for her. For now, she could turn her back on it, leave it. She could lock the garden gate, put the semi-existent key in a safe-deposit box where no one would ever see it . . . if, indeed, anyone but she could ever see it in the first place. But later on, when she died . . . how could she escape?

Could one kill one's own soul?

# THE
# BORDERS
# OF LIFE

*G. A. Kathryns*

A ROC BOOK

ROC
Published by New American Library, a division of
Penguin Putnam Inc., 375 Hudson Street, New York, New York 10014, U.S.A.
Penguin Books Ltd, 27 Wrights Lane, London W8 5TZ, England
Penguin Books Australia Ltd, Ringwood, Victoria, Australia
Penguin Books Canada Ltd, 10 Alcorn Avenue, Toronto, Ontario, Canada M4V 3B2
Penguin Books (N.Z.) Ltd, 182–190 Wairau Road, Auckland 10, New Zealand

Penguin Books Ltd, Registered Offices:
Harmondsworth, Middlesex, England

First published by Roc, an imprint of New American Library,
a division of Penguin Putnam Inc.

First Printing, July 1999
10   9   8   7   6   5   4   3   2   1

*For those who have brought me
to my present condition*

# Author's Preface

Much is made of that elusive thing called "tradition." Some deify it, others hold it in contempt. Still others ignore it, having convinced themselves that their reinvention of the wheel is, in fact, the only legitimate version of the device that has ever existed.

Somewhere among the three points of this undesirable triangle is a middle way, one that respects what has gone before yet seeks at the same time to expand upon it, always giving just due and credit to the foundations upon which further construction is laid. This book attempts exactly this act of delicate balance, for those readers with cosmopolitan taste (or who were forced to suffer through some of the less pleasant aspects of high school English) will recognize, in my small, fictitious Mississippi county, echoes of the work of William Faulkner, whose Yoknapatawpha County lives and breathes in the pages of his novels and stories. While I cannot hope to equal (or even approach) the depth and substance of Faulkner's work, I can at least take from it inspiration and so create therefrom my own vision of dusty roads and clayey bottomlands, washing it with the stranger, "Kathryns-esque" colors that have been granted to my writer's palette and thereby, in my own small way, carrying on the branch of literature that Faulkner began. If "tradition" does indeed exist, it exists in just this way: in furtherance, not in novelty; in respect, not in worship; in humility, not in arrogance. My own Oktibushubee County is but a pleasant shadowbox to Faulkner's grand theater, and yet I have grown to love my little paint-and-cardboard construction, and to love also the people who make their lives—and their deaths—within its deliberately anachronistic boundaries. I hope that you, too, will find in its bittersweet roads and hollows something of the gleam of meaning that I have, in my writing of this book, caught just out of the corner of my writer's eye as I struggled forward in the shadow of the great man.

# A Note on the Language

We live in an age of intolerance, in which the terms "civil" and "civilized" are not only held in some contempt, but are, in some quarters, actually used as pejoratives. Peaceful dialogue has fallen by the proverbial wayside, and constructive discussion based upon rational thought has been reduced, by common usage, to shouting matches rooted in political and spiritual fanaticism. Ours is a time in which reaction and bigotry meet political correctness with all the vehemence of proton and antiproton, in which a book like Twain's *Huckleberry Finn* can be repeatedly challenged as to its fitness to remain on library shelves, in which art finds itself under pressure from both the left and the right to remain sanitized and safe and inoffensive in every way, shape, or form . . . to anyone and everyone. And then, too, we have an occasional bomb going off here and there.

And now I create a book guaranteed to cause a certain amount of controversy and consternation among those who would dictate what can and cannot be said in speech and in print. To them I will not respond, since any response would thereby dignify their intolerance and their coercion.

But to those who read my book with dismay—but, nonetheless, with open minds—I would remind them that this is a story set in the past, and that both the time and the characters with which I have peopled it speak not with my voice, but with their own tongues . . . from which come, at times, words we no longer think of as fitting or desirable, but which are, nonetheless, their words and their custom. To do other than allow them their own language would be falsehood, and falsehood I will not abide. Still, to those who are legitimately grieved by this aspect of my story, I humbly offer my apology and my hand with the prayer that, someday, there will be a world in which hurtful words have been utterly forgotten.

*You have taken east
from me, and west;
you have taken before
from me, and behind;
you have taken moon
and sun from me;
and great my fear
that you have taken
God from me.*

—Irish *Sean-nós* Song

# Chapter 1

Death was not what she was looking for, though she did not know it at the time.

The railroad station at Lee's Corners, like the library, like the city hall, like the power plant and even the new fire engine, was a product of the perennial and acrimonious rivalry between the town and what, to the nonlocal or perhaps objective observer, could easily have been its twin just across the county line, Magdalene: a bitterly polite, internecine war of status, appearance, and acquisition that had been waged for decades, even centuries. Yellow from paint and gray from weather, its high-backed wooden benches as comfortless when the agent turned the lights on for the northbound 3:05 (A.M.) from Biloxi as when he turned them off after the passing of the southbound 8:07 (P.M.) from Memphis, its windows powdered with clayey dust in dry weather and streaked with clayey mud in wet, the station had a rawboned, defiant, fist-in-the-air-and-jutted-chin sense of *ad hoc* vulgarity about it, as though it had been thrown together on a moment's notice not because Lee's Corners had needed it (it had not), but rather because word had arrived that Magdalene was building a railroad station, and, therefore, Lee's Corners not only had to have one first but had to have one that was bigger, better, and more expensive than Magdalene's, no matter how much bigger, better, or expensive Magdalene had originally planned for its own station to be.

Which was, actually, precisely the case.

Alma Montague, seventy-seven years old and waiting, remembered the station perfectly. Almost sixty years had passed since she had last seen it—from the window of a departing train—but it was much the same: still defiant, still shaking its fist at its Magdalene counterpart (which was, to be sure, shaking its fist right back at it), still a mixture of the tawdry, the vulgar, the *ad hoc* . . . an unchangeable feature of the town, to be removed or renovated only at the Last Trump. Or when Magdalene decided to make the corresponding change.

Alma herself, though, was not the same. She had left Lee's Corners with an angry spring in her step, but, human stuff being less sturdy than wood and brick, and considerably less renewable than dust or coats of paint, she had returned wrapped in shawls against the mild April weather, her joints twinging from the damp and from a miserable night spent on the train, her feet throbbing from . . .

. . . well, from age. Simple age. Millions of footsteps, the stupid, mechanical wear that was the result of bearing even a skinny female frame through so many years of locomotion.

*Funny,* she thought. *You treat a hundred patients for hemorrhoids and arthritis, and you watch them age and, sometimes, you watch them die, and there it is right in front of you: your future. But you miss it. You just miss it. It's someone else. You're safe in your white coat, and that stethoscope is hanging around your neck like a talisman of divine protection, and so you just keep missing it until, one day, you wake up, and now it's your hemorrhoids and your arthritis, and you're looking in the mirror and seeing those lines and wrinkles and knowing that it's not someone else this time, but* you, *and there's no protection for you, and so it all settles down to the tiresome business of just getting through another day until you finally—*

"Miz Montague?"

*But that's not it, is it? Not really. It all came years before the lines and the wrinkles and the parchment skin, years before the aches and the pains, years before you looked in the mirror and saw that it was you who was getting on. Years before. The outward form is just a confirmation of what already happened a long time ago.*

"Miz Montague?"

She looked up, feeling like a doddering old woman, hoping that her feelings were wrong. But there was the colored porter, standing before her with a bow and a smile that, ageless and fixed as the station itself, would not have appeared one jot different had she been a dewy-faced bride or a drummer from Memphis.

"The driver will be around with the car in a minute, ma'am," he said. "He's loading your baggage now."

"Thank you."

"Where shall I tell the driver he will be going, ma'am?"

Every syllable enunciated, every gesture a perfect expression of pleasant and genial goodwill . . . and she had seen the sign herself the day before, just at sunset, as the train had passed the limits—the limits that hardly warranted the term *municipal*—of some nameless village:

NIGGER . . . DON'T LET THE SUN SET ON YOUR HEAD

"Please tell him . . ."

She heard herself say *please*. It sounded, perhaps, a little too loud, a little too strained. She had been born here. She had spent the first eighteen years of her life here. But she was a stranger, a stranger from the North, and she knew the porter would see her for exactly that.

". . . that he'll be driving me up to Montague Mansion."

The porter's smile slipped for a moment, and his face actually registered puzzlement. "Montague Mansion, ma'am? I . . . I'm afraid . . . I don't right know where that is."

Alma smiled, nodded. She had expected it. "It's outside of town. The mansion. On the hill."

"Oh! The mansion! On the hill! I'm sorry, ma'am, it clean went—"

"No offense taken, I assure you," said Alma. "There's no reason for you to remember Montague Mansion. It's been deserted for years."

She gathered her shawl about herself and prepared to rise, hoping that she would eventually get used to the damp enough to shake the worst of the aches that had come upon her in Memphis. But her joints faltered for a moment, and that, coupled with a sudden commotion of footsteps that echoed along the arched ceiling, left her sitting on the bench.

Distracted for a moment from the damp and the aches, she straightened up and peered through the slanting sunlight and the hovering dust. There appeared to be more going on in the station this morning than the unnoticed return of a prodigal, for a number of people were moving—hurrying—toward one end of a train platform that usually felt nothing more remarkable than the tread of the livestock agent or the occasional drummer. Alma was first aware of a sallow youth with black hair, then of a parsnip-colored man, then of a matronly, middle-aged woman in furs and diamonds . . .

"That's Mrs. Gavin," the porter said in a voice that still betrayed nothing but genial goodwill, but Alma heard the distinctness—and the status—of the honorific. "She's the widow of Mr. Gavin, the banker." He paused as though the mention of the name would elicit some sign of recognition from Alma, but, as it did not, he continued. "She does appear to be enthusiastic about meeting her Magic today."

. . . and then Alma saw the young boy of perhaps six or seven years who had just gotten off the train in the company of the conductor. Before him the matronly woman, sweating and heaving in furs and diamonds, went down on her knees, and as she threw her arms about him, the parsnip-colored man (there was, Alma noticed, a parsnip-colored woman with him) looked on hostilely, and the sallow youth shrugged, pulled out a cigarette, and slouched against a nearby wall, smoking.

"My dear little boy!"

Yes, if the matronly woman was Mrs. Gavin, then Mrs. Gavin was indeed enthusiastic about meeting her . . . her . . .

What had the porter called him?

"My sweet little Magic!"

Alma stared. It was an outlandish name for a town like Lee's Corners, and it made the scene on the platform appear all the more grotesque and compelling, as though a clown had been found in the middle of Main Street with his throat cut.

The porter bowed and smiled again before he turned away. "I'll have the car up front for you in just a minute, Miz Montague."

"And did he have a good time? Did my sweet Magic have a lovely time after his mommy and daddy *sent him away* from me?"

Alma blinked. *Her* Magic? Whose Magic was he?

"Mr. and Mrs. Harlow?" the conductor was saying, his voice faint with the distance.

Mrs. Gavin continued to be enthusiastic. "My! Hasn't he gotten big since he was *sent away*! Just look at him!"

As one, the parsnip couple nodded and, after the husband had signed the conductor's receipt, advanced on the boy, who had been standing—who continued, despite the attentions of the stout woman, to stand—with lowered head, his eyes fixed on the floor five feet in front of him, his left hand in his jacket pocket, his right arm, hand, index finger extended almost spastically before him as he made short, choppy jabs into the empty air.

"I have so many things to show my dear little boy now that he's back! His room is all fixed up and waiting for him! Does he know that his parents forgot to tell me that he was coming home today?"

The parsnip man said something. Mrs. Gavin ignored him, bent closer to the boy.

"What's that, sweetie?" she said. "What are you saying?"

Alma saw the boy's lips moving. The jerks of his right hand and arm became, if anything, even more distinct.

"What?"

And then Mrs. Gavin apparently understood, for, as though startled, she looked up.

"Benny!"

The sallow youth's cigarette vanished instantly.

"Benny! I want to talk to you!"

Mr. and Mrs. Harlow grabbed the boy's arm and pulled him toward the side door.

Mrs. Gavin's fury—and attention—were fixed, for the moment, on the youth; but then she appeared to notice that Magic was no longer near her. With a cry, she rose, her stockings laddered, just in time to see Mr. and Mrs. Harlow—and Magic—vanishing through the side door of the station.

*"Sweetie!"*

And the porter was back, smiling, bowing: "Yo' car is here, Miz Montague."

"Montague Mansion?"

The taxi driver was as puzzled as the porter, and, lacking the porter's polished veneer, he showed it more overtly, squinting up his black face as though he were judging the flavor of a lemon. "Montague . . . Mansion?"

Alma, safely stowed and bundled into the backseat as though she were a porcelain figurine, allowed herself a smile that, for once, betokened genuine amusement instead of the wry despair that had taken her away from her life in the Northern city (*perhaps,* she thought, *away from life . . . period*) and brought her home to Lee's Corners. Doubtless, she would have to get used to this. For a little while, at least. Until the town realized just who she was and what she intended to do . . . and that she could easily make good her intentions. "The mansion," she said. "Up on the hill."

Out of the corner of her eye, she saw a battered green car pull out of a parking space and turn toward the street. A blurry face behind the glass, a jerking hand and index finger: Magic.

The driver squinted a bit more, then: "Oh! That!"

Alma nodded.

But he was not so easily convinced. "Oh, ma'am, what you want to be going up to that place for? Ain't no one lived there for years. It be half–fallin' down, and there's no lights even."

Alma just looked at him, appreciating her own smile, appreciating the despair held in abeyance for the time by this novel encounter.

"There's a good hotel downtown," he went on. "A presidential candidate stayed at it once, I hear. It's very nice. Let me take you there."

"The hotel?" Alma's smile broadened. "Now, when I was a girl, the only rumor about a presidential candidate was that he stopped at the train station."

The driver stared at her.

"And over in Magdalene, they were saying that he only stopped in the train station because his dog had to urinate."

The driver's mouth was open. "You . . ."

Alma settled back in the seat, hoping that she would get used to the damp quickly. Sixty years ago she would not have noticed that her feet did not reach the floor of the car, but now she did, and the pressure on her thighs was making her knees ache terribly. "I'm going up to Montague Mansion," she said. "I grew up there."

Astonishment fled from the driver, and his manner changed immediately. "You a Montague? Oh, ma'am, I'm sorry if I offended you."

"Nonsense," she responded. "You're only doing your job. What kind of a crazy woman wants to go up to a deserted mansion, anyway?"

*What kind, indeed?* she wondered silently . . . but she knew that crazy was an equivocation even to herself. Nonetheless, from the look on the driver's face, she judged that she had read his thoughts perfectly, and she answered her own question.

"We'll, *this* kind of crazy woman does, my man. So drive on. I'm going home."

"Home?"

"Home. As I said: I grew up there. And yes, I'm a Montague. In fact, as far as I know, and as far as the bank here knows, I'm the *last* Montague."

Still, the man hesitated, his face squinting up as though estimating whether the lemon in question had come from the north or the south side of the orchard. Alma let him squint: she had not only discovered that she had said far more than she had wanted to say, but she sensed that his hesitation was now not really a hesitation at all, but rather a slow digestion of unusual news.

She sat back in her seat, bundled in her shawls, her feet swinging above the floorboards. The last Montague. Coming home. Doubtless the news would be all over the town by evening. Doubtless, too, she would have visitors . . . but, then again, perhaps the disrepair of the house would keep them away. She hoped that it would. For a little while, at least. In any case, she did not intend that the house would remain in disrepair for long. Maybe she—

"Ma'am, you *sho* you—?"

She looked sharply at him. "What's your name, sir?"

He was abashed. "Why, ma'am, 'round here they just call me Uncle Buddy."

She held his eye for a moment longer, then allowed her face, old though it was, to soften into another smile. This time, though, the amusement was gone, and the despair was back: just one more interaction to add to her stock of interactions, one more sharp word, one more memory she could brood about while she lay, awake and restless, in her bed during the hours before sleep would grudgingly take her. But that was for her. For him, the smile was something else, and that, she supposed, was good. "*This* kind of crazy woman, Uncle Buddy," she said.

Her smile took the edge off her words—for him at least—and he turned to face the wheel. But as he was pulling away from the curb, he was cut off by a big DeSoto that seemed to come from nowhere. Dark and brilliantly shined, the car swerved in front of Buddy, forcing his foot onto the brake so hard that Alma was tossed about as though she were on a storm-swept boat.

The jostling ceased abruptly, and she reached up to resettle her hat. "That man ought to be arrested."

"That's no man, Miz Montague," said Buddy. "That there's Mrs. Gavin. The widow of the banker. She sho in an all-fired hurry 'bout something."

Alma watched as the big car swept up the street in a cloud of gleams and dust. She recalled that the Harlows' car had gone the same way. "She wants that little boy."

"Magic, you mean? You know 'bout Magic Harlow, ma'am?"

Alma looked away from the vanishing DeSoto, shook her head. "I know a little about children, ownership, property, and madness," she said. "So I suspect that yes, I know a little about Magic Harlow."

Puzzled again, Buddy looked at her over his shoulder.

She reached down deep, found another smile to display. "Take me home, Uncle Buddy."

* * *

The rivalry between Lee's Corners and Magdalene ran deep, and it was probably not surprising that, having attempted to outdo one another in the realm of public buildings, the two towns had also flirted briefly—and simultaneously—with a faddish liberalism that had eventually prompted Lee's Corners to demonstrate its superiority by electing, by scant majority, a Negro mayor just before the turn of the century. The mayor, however, enjoyed his office and stature for only two weeks before a party of hunters discovered his burnt body hanging by a set of trace chains in the forest (it was not hunting season, but then, the hunters had not bagged any game, so there was no technical illegality). Though the neck of the late mayor had plainly been broken and some signs of spurious mutilation (doubtless by forest animals) were present, the death, carefully considered by a grand jury, was officially ruled an accident, and the mayoral office was soon filled with another candidate.

Nevertheless, despite its ill luck with regard to public officials, the spirit of the town had been forever altered by that brief flirtation with political miscegenation, and while, for the most part, Lee's Corners conformed to the general ethos of the South, divisions between the races were a bit less well defined there than in other small towns (except, perhaps, in Magdalene, which had elected and similarly lost its own Negro mayor within days of the Lee's Corners entr'acte). And so, when Mr. Dark, quietly arrayed in his usual gray suit and, save for his complexion, looking as much like a respected businessman of the town as, say, Delphi M'Creed, who had owned the local hardware store for at least twenty years and who was a staunch member of Mr. Burke's Baptist congregation, walked into McCoy's Soda Shop and ordered his usual noontime dish of vanilla ice cream, there was little comment.

"That damn nigger. Every day—*every day*—he shows up just as cool as you please. He orders him his ice cream and then he eats it right out there in public. Just like a white man. Can you *believe* that?"

For the most part.

"Next thing you know—You listen to me, Sam! Don't you go daydreamin' on me when I'm talkin' to you or I'll learn you

summat you won't forget!—next thing you know he'll be givin'
the other niggers ideas, and they'll be puttin' on airs and such
trash, and then they'll be wanting to marry white girls."

Lindy Buck fantasized often about Negroes and white girls.
Perhaps it was because, womanless and solitary, he fantasized
often about white girls himself. The son of a hill-bred and self-
doctrined Presbyterian, he had, years before, come to Lee's
Corners looking for a congenial group with which to worship,
and, having been rejected by every single corporate group of
human congregants (including the Klan, which had found him
much too radical in his beliefs), had given up his search and
proceeded to found his own, one that, combining as it did minister and members into one individual, held enthusiastic and
self-righteous meetings at least four times an hour.

But, regardless of Lindy's religious sentiments or his fantasies about white girls (with or without Negro intervention),
his powers of observation were unimpeachable, and, indeed,
Mr. Dark, his checked suit, iridescent green tie, and maroon-
and-white shoes a blaring statement of Slagtown fashion, was
just then coming out of the soda shop with his dish of ice cream.
Apparently not only extraordinarily conscious of his appearance but outright reveling in it, the Negro displayed himself
grossly, his knees wide apart and his coat open to reveal his
bulging groin as he sat down at one of the sidewalk tables and
began shoveling voluptuous spoonfuls of the gleaming dessert
into the hole between his thick, blub lips.

Lindy's fury, as was the case every day, was mounting at the
sight. "I'll bet he's a pimp," he said. "Got houses in Memphis
and Biloxi. Comes through Lee's Corners just to show off." He
glanced at his companion. "And to try an' get other white women
to work for him."

Sam Libbeldoe, tall, thick, blond, and a little less than a congregation to Lindy's preaching (Lindy had learned all about
corporate worship) but a little more than an audience, knew his
cue. "He sho likes his ice cream. Huhuhuhuh!"

The two men were across the street from the soda shop,
lounging against the front of M'Creed's Hardware Store where
they lounged every day and where they would continue to

lounge until M'Creed himself came out and ran them off. But inside the soda shop, Willie McCoy—who had been promoted to tending the counter ever since Greta Harlow had, first, gotten herself with child, then, with complete disregard not only for her own reputation but for that of her family as well, insisted upon staying in town to have the child, and *then*, with even more disregard not only for herself and her family (including her son, Magic), but for the entire town, insisted upon killing herself—watched as the Negro in his gray suit and his polished black shoes ate his ice cream with a businessman's fastidious precision.

"That Mr. Dark," he said. "He's one of a kind. You'd jest about think he was white. He looks like a pro-fessional, that's what he looks like."

Willie's friend, looking up from the milk shake he had bought in lieu of the school's cafeteria lunch, examined the elegant man through the plate-glass window, his gaze resting only briefly on the pair of scruffy individuals slouched against the front of the hardware store. "But he's black."

"Well, yeah," said Willie. "But sometimes you jest think that he really *ought* to be white. Don't you?"

His friend went back to his milk shake. "Willie, yo' are one crazy son of a bitch."

"Well, he's a good *man*, ain't he?"

"Yeah. I guess so. For a Negro man."

Willie shrugged. That would have to do.

But Willie's friend was again looking out the plate-glass window at the black man who, dressed and groomed as he was, would not have been out of place in one of those skyscraper offices in New York City about which Willie and his friend had often heard. "Is that all he ever gets? A dish of ice cream?"

"*Vanilla* ice cream," said Willie. "Yep. That's all. No syrup. No nuts. No nothin'. Jest vanilla. And he always eats it outside unless it's raining. Been doing it for years now."

"That's funny."

"*What's* funny?"

Willie's friend went back to his shake with a smirk. "I woulda thought he'd like chocolate best."

"I asked him 'bout that once," said Willie, completely oblivious. "He told me that chocolate ice cream wasn't really chocolate. Said it was like colored trying to pass for white."

The friend stared. "He *said* that?"

"Sho."

But, across the street, the two slouching figures were in
motion, for Delphi M'Creed had indeed come out of his hardware store to inform Sam Libbeldoe that the walls of the store
did not need any support from his backside (the truth of which
was immediately and enthusiastically acknowledged by Sam
with one of his habitual and ratchetlike giggles) and to remind
Lindy Buck that he needed to get a crop in so that he could pay
his share—third and fourth—to the bank that was holding the
land in trust for whatever faceless and absentee landlord actually owned it.

"And you're probably just settin' there with your black heart
calling God's wrath down upon us all for not bendin' down to
your self-righteous Presbyterianism!" M'Creed finished up in a
shout that was more than fitting for a devout Baptist who was a
staunch pillar of Mr. Burke's congregation and who had even,
upon occasion, been known to speak in tongues. "*By the sweat
of thy brow thou shalt earn thy bread,* said the Lord, and you
don't heed that at all, do you? Now, when I was in the Rangers,
we had a name for people like—"

But then he fell silent, half because he appeared to come to
the conclusion that he had perhaps said too much, half because
the object of his exhortations was already stalking across the
street, widening the distance between himself and M'Creed
enough that the latter, staunch Baptist though he was, was unwilling to raise his voice enough to continue his sermon.

But having been on the receiving end of one of Delphi
M'Creed's public and full-throated sermons yet again, he—
Lindy Buck, that is—was now in search of someone to blame
for his misfortune. Actually, he had, with great satisfaction (it
was always good to have an excuse for what one wanted to do in
the first place), already settled the question of whom to blame,
and, disheveled, dirty, and determined, he had crossed Jefferson
Street to stand at the side of Mr. Dark's table, glowering down
at the simian-faced individual who was just then running his

tongue suggestively across the glistening surface of the remaining ice cream.

"Now look here, nigger. You've caused enough trouble in this town with your slate-brained, whore-minded shenanigans, and I want to see you out of here—You listenin' to me?—out of here for good. Startin' today!"

Mr. Dark looked up, his blub lips parting in an expression of mild and imbecilic surprise. "I beg yo' pardon, honky dude?"

Lindy had warmed up with his first words, and now he felt substantially moved. "You black-faced he-devil! You sprout from the sinful shoot of Cain! Comin' in here with your airs and your fancy clothes, running your hand up our women's skirts and violatin' their pulchritude, you—"

"Sorry about dat, ya' know?" said Mr. Dark. "Be ya' referrin' t' me?"

Undeterred, Lindy kept on. "Me and my friend here . . ." And, indeed, Sam had just then come trotting up, nodding enthusiastically. ". . . have been watchin' you. Every day."

"Yeah. We have. Huhuhuhuh!" Sam added.

"Sheeit," said Mr. Dark. "I'm sorry. Ya' know? Gots Ah given ya' offense in some way?"

"Lots! Huhuhuh!" said Sam.

But Lindy was building toward his climax, his voice rising, his callused hand lifting one grimed index finger into the air. "And we seen you. We seen you every day. And we gonna tell you, right out, that we're not gonna let our town—"

His words halted abruptly. Not because Mr. Dark had done or said anything, but because a hand had come down on his shoulder.

"Did you want somethin', Marshal?" said Lindy without looking around.

"Oh, nothin' much," said Abram MacDonnell, the town marshal. "Just a little peace and quiet. And when I saw you walk up to this colored gentleman here . . ." He nodded to the man in the black suit and broad-brimmed preacher's hat, the man who responded, quietly and deferentially, with a *God bless*. ". . . I knew I wasn't going to get much of either unless I stopped and had a little word with you."

"I wasn't doin' nothing," said Lindy. He glared at the Negro, who was now grinning with a self-satisfied air. "*Was* I?"

The blub lips grimaced at him, but the dark eyes glanced furtively back and forth. "T' be honest, Ah didn't dig some word ya' said. Sheeeiit," came the response.

At least, Lindy thought, he had taken some of the edge off Dark's obscene and complacent arrogance.

Behind Lindy, MacDonnell was nodding, his cold, gray eyes changing expression not in the slightest. "All right then. I guess you and Sam got something to do. Or maybe I'm mistaken?"

There was no mistake. Lindy was now recalling quite a number of things that he had to do.

"Lots! Huhuhuhuh!" said Sam.

"I guess you boys better go do it then," said the marshal, and as Lindy and Sam moved off, he turned again to Mr. Dark. "I reckon they've gone and spoiled your ice cream."

"Not at all," said Mr. Dark with a smile that was both gracious and humble. "A minor inconvenience, really, on such a glorious spring day."

For a moment, MacDonnell examined him, wondering again, like many people of the town, exactly what Dark did for a living. MacDonnell had no information or evidence that pointed in any particular direction, but he had privately decided that Dark was a preacher for some little Negro church back in the hills—one of those ministers who could turn from humble to thundering in a heartbeat, once a few Gospel verses came into play—and was therefore more than likely responsible for at least one or two fewer colored dice games or razor fights that he, MacDonnell, had to deal with every year. Which was, all in all, a very good thing.

"Don't you think so?" Dark was saying.

"Think?"

"The spring day. Simply glorious."

MacDonnell stood for a moment, then: "Sho," he said. "Why not?"

Mr. Dark rose. "Well," he said, "I have appointments to keep, and I must be on my way. God bless you, Marshal." A bow, a smile, and he was gone, his black suit a shadow on the sidewalk.

And, inside the soda shop, Willie McCoy was staring after the gray-suited man, planning on how to spend the five-dollar tip that had been slipped to him with a fatherly wink and a smile when money and ice cream (vanilla) were changing hands.

# Chapter 2

Had she thought about it—which she did not—Greta Harlow would have been unable to say exactly when she had stopped thinking or caring about Jimmy White. It had happened. To be sure it had happened. Somewhere between his last appearance in the soda shop—an appearance whose sole purpose had been to formalize the claim he had made upon her body not so much for himself as for the son with whom he had impregnated her and the tradition of such unwanted and unwarranted impregnations that had come down to him from his father and his grandfather . . . after which he had driven out of town and onto the highway and had been killed by a semitrailer—and the present, somewhere he had, as far as Greta was concerned, evaporated, his place taken and filled to capacity with that same son to whom she had, in the interim, given birth, as if the nature of the human psyche was such that it could not deal with a complete lack of obsession: having eradicated one, it must, consciously or not, locate and expand another.

And had she, intrigued by this sudden assignment of her rapist to the status of nonentity, attempted to analyze, by converging increments, the events that surrounded it, closing in on the instant of assignment itself as though subjecting the emotional content of a given number of months to a psychological calculus—which she did not—she still would have been unable to find the exact moment at which Jimmy White had left even the shadowy existence of memory and had instead become nothingness. To be sure, she might have narrowed the time frame: Jimmy had still been uppermost in her mind when she had served Mrs. Gavin a strawberry phosphate in the soda shop (and he could not have been otherwise, for it had been but a matter of a few hours since his last and final visit), and he had continued to be so when the childless matron had tacitly revealed the reason for her childlessness. And Jimmy had been equally the confluence of her emotions when she had, in effect, begun to retrace Mrs. Gavin's very steps: entering the town library and looking for a particular old book about herbs, kneeling on the cool, linoleum floor in the dark corner formed by a bookshelf and a rear wall while she paged through the antique plates, searching for the depiction of the herb—the weed—in question. And even when, after gathering the plant and preparing the poison that would release her from Jimmy's claim, still it was not the child who was important to her—not even as a burden, or as a mark of shame, or as, perhaps, a mere target of the abortifacient—but, rather Jimmy himself, young and swaggering, who had spread his seed across Oktibushubee County in the same violent manner as had his father and his grandfather, and who had laid claim not only to her as a vessel for the reincarnation of himself, but to the child within her as that very reincarnation made flesh.

But as though in rebellion against Jimmy (who, now dead under the wheels of a truck, could not protest her rebellion), she had not consumed the poison. Instead, she had, unexpectedly, claimed the child as her own.

Perhaps that was when it had happened. Jimmy, dead, belonged to the past, and his place had been taken—and more than taken—by the intruder within her, the intruder whom she made welcome, made, in fact, the focus of her existence, echoing in her psychology the single-minded, single-purposed dedication of her physical body's urge toward breed. And had she thought about it, she might have seen in the sudden upwelling of devotion that devolved upon the as-yet-unborn child with an almost religious intensity yet another echo, perhaps a reification: one of Jimmy himself and his gloating claim in the course of that last, brief meeting at the soda shop.

But she did not think about it. Her attention was too full of the child for her to have any time for considering his origins.

Yes: *his*. For she herself knew that, as Jimmy himself had promised, the child would be male, and she also knew that (again, as if in fulfillment of Jimmy's own prophecy) she would, in defiance of the Protestant and conservative foundations of the town, give him the name *Magic*.

And, in like manner, her attention was too full of Magic—*her* child, *her* welcomed intruder—for her to have any capacity for considering her reputation, her family, or her town; her defiance of convention in naming her child being therefore matched, overtopped, by her defiance of convention in general. But in this case it was not defiance: it was merely the acceptance of the inevitable ... no, it was complete obliviousness to the inevitable, for in her (entirely unconscious and unthought-of) rebellion against Jimmy, in her making Magic into the focus of her existence, she could but hardly notice when her mother's face closed toward her, or when her father ordered her out of the house. She noticed, true, when Mr. McCoy, who owned the soda shop where she worked, fired her (when she began to show), but she noticed only obliquely, even though the loss of her job meant that she could no longer afford the cheap room she had taken in Mildred Riddup's boardinghouse, even though the fact that she was now beginning to show meant that her days at the boardinghouse were numbered in any case (for Mildred Riddup was a respectable Christian woman, and though a respectable Christian woman might not notice gossip, she would certainly notice the swelling belly of an eighteen-year-old girl).

Perhaps, though, her obliviousness was justified. Or perhaps it was a testament to an irrationally acute trust in the same Providence that had, in bringing about her meeting with Mrs. Gavin in the soda shop, pressed her toward her defiance in the first place. Regardless, she had not been carrying her cardboard suitcase along the sidewalks of Lee's Corners—oblivious, too, to where she might be going or what she was going to do when the sun set—for more than two blocks when the dark DeSoto pulled up alongside her and Mrs. Gavin beckoned for her to get in.

Alma, too, was thinking about Magic, though she did not know (*could* not know) that, unlike Greta, who had left Mildred Riddup's house with a belly and a cardboard suitcase seven years before, she held no illusions or professed no mythology about the boy. She had, of course, seen him only briefly, and so there was hardly time to form even a vague impression outside of a jutted index finger and a jerking hand (And what *was* that all about? Was the child palsied?), and, true, Greta was essentially an untried girl, while Alma was an old woman: Alma had seen too much, both in and out of her doctor's office, to harbor much of anything by way of myth or illusions about anyone.

But like Greta, Alma's capacity for myth and illusion was innate, inborn, and perhaps her ability to so do away with myth and illusion in the greater part of her life rested upon the counterbalancing existence of a mythology that had flowed unbroken through nearly five decades of her existence, that had begun when she was an intern at the only hospital that had been willing enough or condescending enough to accept a woman graduate from a medical school . . . the school being, itself, the only one she had been able to find that would accept her for study in the first place.

How old would *he* be now? That was easy, for she marked his birthday every year, not with cake and candles, but inwardly, with a pang of regret and a shudder of memory at the gray, lifeless being that had come forth only reluctantly from a dead womb. But regardless of how his birthdays were commemorated, or what memories surrounded the event that had engendered them, there would have been almost fifty of them by now, and he would be thinking of retirement from whatever it was (strangely, she had never fixed upon an occupation for him) he did. He would be living up north—no bloodied nose against the Jim Crow wall for her boy—and the three children she had imagined for him would be, variously, starting married life, entering college, and attending a trade school.

Again, as she frequently did, she returned to the question of his work. Strange—yes, strange—that she had imagined his life in all details . . . save for that one. Perhaps he would be a minister . . .

The memory of shouted Bible verses and of a torrent of blood from a dying woman made her shudder yet again. "No," she murmured to herself. "Never a minister. He would know why. I would tell him why."

"Ma'am?"

She came out of her daydream, came back to the taxi and to the passing landscape of trees and cotton and corn that surrounded Lee's Corners. "I'm sorry, Uncle Buddy. I was just thinking about some old times."

"Old times be the best times, I always say, ma'am. Ain't no times at all like old times." His tone seemed to indicate that he believed his own words, but he glanced at her in the rearview mirror. "We always seem to remember them with a little more shine on them, though, don't we?"

Another smile from Alma, hideously artificial, one that was more than matched by the words that she did not believe: "We sure do, Uncle Buddy. Maybe that's what keeps us living: so that we can have more shiny old times to remember."

He pursed his lips. "Now, I never thought about it quite like that, ma'am, but I do believe you have a point."

She wondered whether either of them believed anything either of them had said.

Buddy drove on. Alma struggled to bring herself back to the present. She had thought that retirement from her practice and a departure from the Northern city would have left her memories behind . . . or at least dulled them. Instead, this returning to her ancestral home was freshening them, bringing them up renewed and in new guises. Magic Harlow had reminded her of the imaginary life she carried within herself, and this drive was taking her straight back not only to the house in which she had grown up, but to her departure from it and her reasons for that departure.

She had forgotten how far the house was from the town. When she had left at the age of eighteen, she had walked, thereby avoiding detection, physical interference, and, most likely (and at the very least) a repetition of the argument that she had both endured and participated in on an almost daily basis for at least a year. It had been a mile and a half from the mansion's front gate to the place where the taxi she had ordered the day before had been waiting, and at the time her excitement and apprehension had been such that that distance, as well as the much longer drive from that rendezvous to the train station, had appeared negligible. But now minutes passed, many minutes, and still the road wound into the hills above Lee's Corners, passing rutted lanes that led off to tenant plots and sharecropper farms that lay within what Alma vaguely recollected were once Montague lands.

Here were relics of past and present both: gates that had fallen down, broken wheels from broken surreys, curling twists of fan belts flung away and caught on barbed wire. And farther off, just glimpsed through dips in the embankment or between clumps of trees, were shacks—upright, leaning, half-collapsed—perhaps owned by their inhabitants, perhaps owned by no one save a bank that had foreclosed on someone seventy years before: unpainted, patched things kept together from year to year by nothing more than a kind of dogged bitterness upon the part of those who dwelled within, who, with bent backs and cracked, callused hands, wrenched a niggardly bounty out of the earth.

Uncle Buddy was now as cheerful as he had previously been puzzled, and he gaily pointed out sights and told stories that seemed to Alma to possess the vague familiarity of dreams, for in doing so he mentioned names that she remembered as having belonged to people from her childhood, people who were now dead or moved away or just . . . just gone in one way or another. Younger people bore the names now, younger people with their own lives and their own stories.

"Have your people been in Lee's Corners very long, Uncle Buddy?" she asked, not knowing whether she was disturbed or relieved to find her past so faded.

He shifted conversational gears as effortlessly as he did those of his cab. "Long and not so long, ma'am. My papa brought my mama to Lee's Corners 'bout thirty years ago because he thought it was safer for a good-lookin' black woman. The both came from Dutchman's Curve up there in the hills, and they were having some . . . uh . . . trouble back then."

Alma nodded. Buddy did not need to elaborate. His tone of voice had said everything, and she had not lived in the North so long that she had missed it.

" 'Fore then, we was always Dutchman's Curve people," he said. "Way long ago, my people belonged to the Scovilles up there."

"You must be related to the Haleys, then."

Buddy's face lit up. "Why, ma'am, you certainly are from

around here, ain't you? Yes, ma'am: Scovilles—black and white both—and Haleys do go back a ways, don't they?"

For a time, then, they chatted about families, and now the names that Alma heard—names still at once familiar and unfamiliar—seemed to reach out and lace themselves into the rocks and trees of Oktibushubee County, so intimately connected with the land that they seemed as much a physical feature of it as the curves of the road or the stands of hickory and gum and oak. And yet, even when the name Montague was mentioned, she felt unconnected with it. General Montague had fought in this battle and had died in that one, and Herbert Montague had homesteaded his land in ought-two, playing British interest off against Indian claim and securing for himself and his issue a swath of fertility where Tippah Creek met the Yallabusha River, and Peter Montague had built the mansion that, screened by immense beech trees, still stood, dilapidated (and, some said, haunted), on the hill overlooking the valley that held Lee's Corners.

*Haunted?* Alma wondered. *Why haunted? Oh. Oh, yes. Grandfather. Yes, of course they'd come to think it was haunted.*

But she felt unrelated to them all. She might have lost her blood as well as her accent in the deep freeze of the North.

"There it is, ma'am!"

Alma, musing on her grandfather and his books and his séances—and had it not been her grandfather who had encouraged her rebellion, even from the first?—looked up. "Uncle Buddy?"

"Oh, ma'am, I'm sorry. You just missed it. You could see the house through the trees."

The trees. Yes, she thought, they too were probably much bigger and far more spreading now, oak trees and family trees alike sending out new growth and new branches, hiding the house, hiding her past. But then, as Buddy's cab wound up a long rise, the road turned to dirt . . .

. . . and it all came back to her.

Suddenly, she was remembering, recognizing, and though her connection with the town and, indeed, the land as a whole was still seemingly abstract, ephemeral, she was seeing this last stretch of road, the one she had walked before sunrise sixty years ago, as something familiar, something seamlessly contiguous with her aged mental image without any particular sense of abruptness or incongruity.

She knew the road. She knew the trees. She could have asked Buddy to stop, stepped out of the car, and without hesitation laid her finger upon the very spot where her older brother had carved his initials on a thick trunk. She could have found the clearing where Grandfather had taken them for a picnic on her seventh birthday and where he had, to the mortification of her parents, encouraged her to take off her shoes and run wild through the grass. And there, too, just passing, was the old mulberry tree, rootless and stunted, that had burned itself into her thoughts and her memory when she, dressed in a fine white gown, pumps, and long gloves, had been driven by her father down this same road to attend the annual Gardenia Society Tea and Cotillion: at sixteen, a debutante and an adult.

She realized that she was sitting bolt upright as though an electric wire had been taped to her back. She forced herself back down. Debutante. Adult. And property, too.

*And who had Father already decided that I was going to marry? There was no escape for me. I would never have been allowed to make my own choice. I was, after all, a Montague.*

She shook her head. She had escaped after all. And then it occurred to her that, in referring to her family name and her heritage, she had, mentally—and, perhaps, accurately—used the past tense: *was.*

*Had it started even then? Didn't it wait for the hospital, for her . . . and for him?*

"Here's the house, Miz Montague."

Marshal Abram MacDonnell's office window looked out onto the intersection of Jefferson and DeWitt. Here, two relatively insignificant county highways, having dwindled into two streets of an otherwise insignificant town, converged and then went on: east–west, north–south. Two years ago, the town had installed a traffic signal at the corner, the argument being that if a minor Lee's Corners intersection like Duncan and Main had a stop sign, then Jefferson and DeWitt, both county highways, certainly warranted a light . . . particularly since Magdalene had recently installed one at an even *smaller* intersection; but as

far as MacDonnell had been able to tell, the signal had made little difference to the town besides making provision for a ready
source of municipal revenue . . . whenever MacDonnell and his
deputies decided to start writing up traffic citations for those
who ignored the signal. Which was just about everyone.

It was from the office window that MacDonnell had seen Lindy
Buck carom off Delphi M'Creed's sermon like a billiard ball
and head across the street toward Dark—causing MacDonnell
to grab his gun belt and coat on the way out of the office so that
he could get to the soda shop in time to prevent the collision—
and it was from the office window that he had seen not only Uncle Buddy's cab coming from the direction of the train station
and turning toward the hills (prompting MacDonnell to wonder
what or who could have prompted Buddy to do such a thing) but
also the unmistakable form of Sophonsiba Gavin's DeSoto rac-
ing in hot pursuit of John Harlow's old beater.

MacDonnell shrugged. Mrs. Gavin and the Harlows had
been going back and forth about Magic ever since Greta had . . .
well . . . died—

MacDonnell reached up, laid a hand on his mustache, and
very deliberately stroked the whiskers downward.

—and doubtless the boy would grow old and die himself before they would stop fighting over him. Praise the Lord they
hadn't taken it to court . . . though perhaps Mrs. Gavin was hoping that the Harlows would do exactly that, since the entire
situation leading up to Greta's death would certainly give her a
moral advantage in any kind of a legal battle, even leaving aside
the money that she had available to put into such a contest.

The marshal of Lee's Corners was small, thin, even wiry, and
his walrus mustache was the stuff of legend in a county full of
mostly clean-shaven men. Howie Amherst had once said that
MacDonnell probably *needed* that mustache in order to keep his
eyes from freezing the rest of his face so hard it would crack off—
which had elicited laughter from everyone save MacDonnell—
but, nonetheless, it was that very article that the marshal would
inevitably cover with his hand when deep in thought (as though,
continuing Howie's hypothesis, a certain coldness was good for
logic), and it was just as inevitable that he would cover it when
the subject of Greta Harlow came up.

He was at his desk with his hand still on his mustache when Otis York, the deputy, came down the flight of stairs from the small jail above and hung the big ring of keys on the peg near the door.

"Mornin', Marshal."

"It's afternoon."

"Afternoon, Marshal."

"Afternoon, Otis. You have any trouble up there?"

"Nope. That big nigger's gentle as a lamb."

"Amazing how he could kill his foreman in cold blood like that."

"It is, sholy."

"With a .45-caliber bullet."

"Sholy."

"Out of a .22-caliber gun."

"Sholy."

"You hear anything from the Frammis boys?"

"Nope. Beat Two's quiet. Leastwise the shurf ain't said nothin'."

MacDonnell sighed. "Bad sign."

"Real bad."

"They'll be here at midnight sho as death."

"Prolly."

MacDonnell still had his hand covering his mustache. "I saw Sophonsiba Gavin lightin' out after John and Alice Harlow a half an hour ago."

Otis laughed. "Oh, that."

MacDonnell's eyes were as cold as ever. "You want to tell me about it?"

"Magic Harlow came in on the 10:50 from Memphis," said Otis. "I guess Sophonsiba thought she was going to get first crack at him."

MacDonnell's eyes drifted back to the window, but his hand was still covering his mustache. "Sho. Why not?"

Otis's damp, pale face glistened like a fresh-cut slice of potato. "She carried on something fierce. Down on her knees and all. Sipsey Dewar's boy told me all about it."

"The porter?"

"That's right."

"Do you remember when Greta Harlow died?"

Otis stopped, stared at MacDonnell, and the marshal could almost hear the grinding as Otis laboriously shifted, reversed throttle, and backed up to the nearest switch. "Sho I do," he said after the necessary mechanics had been attended to. "I was there first. You remember that. I was on duty that night, and when Mildred Riddup called—"

"You got up to the Riddup place lickety-split."

There might—or might not—have been something more than usual in MacDonnell's voice. Otis blinked, reversed again, and looked for another switch, but behind him were miles and miles of straight track, and so, nonplussed, he remained motionless, steaming lightly.

"Sure I did," he said, letting out the excess pressure in a spurt of three words.

"Mmmm." MacDonnell leaned back in his chair, craned his neck a little, and caught sight of Lindy Buck moving along the street in the direction of his sharecropper holding outside of town—the opposite direction from the one taken by Dark. That was good. "Did Mildred mess everything up before you got there?"

"Mess everything up?"

"Did she go through everything? She doesn't have a lot of money, and so it'd be natural for her to . . ." MacDonnell shrugged by way of ending the sentence.

Otis closed his eyes, at once thinking and increasing the resemblance between his face and the slice of potato. "Well, she was running around like a horse with his gums full of saltpeter. Carrying on something terrible. But I told you about that back then."

"Tell me again."

Again, there might—or might not—have been something in MacDonnell's voice.

Otis shrugged. "Oh, going on like womenfolk do. Sayin' how she was a respectable Christian woman and nothing like that had ever happened to her before. Sayin' how she caught that nigger going out the back window not an hour before and gave him a behind full of buckshot and that she shoulda known right then and there that Greta Harlow was still nothing more than a whore and an abomination unto womanhood, but she thought that Sophonsiba Gavin had reformed her, but she shoulda known better because whores and abominations unto womanhood don't ever reform, as that nigger going out the back window could testify, that is, if you could peel every black behind in Oktibushubee County and look for buckshot until you found it so you could ask him. Sayin'—"

"Had she touched anything?"

"Lord, Abe, I couldn't tell. The room was a mess."

MacDonnell was nodding. "Sho it was. And there were probably clothes and rubbish you had to pull off her body in order to see whether she was really dead or not."

"No, Marshal. Like I told you back then, she was stark naked on top of a pile of dresses that looked like they came out of her suitcase. There was stuff all around her, but there wasn't nothing on top of her."

MacDonnell's eyes did not change expression. "Sho."

"It's been years, Marshal."

"Sho." MacDonnell looked out the window again. "It's been years. And Sophonsiba Gavin is still fightin' like a tomcat with a toothache over a boy that's no kin of hers."

Otis shrugged. "Seems like she made him kin, seein' how his momma's folk put her out."

"That's one way of saying it. And with Sophonsiba Gavin his momma had a place to call her own. And then she ran away from it." MacDonnell stood up. "It's your office, Otis. I'm going to make rounds, and I'm going to stop at the bank and see if they can send some dog-in-trousers out to make sure that Lindy Buck breaks his land instead of standing around on the corner preaching to himself. Or to Sam Libbeldoe. Same thing, I guess. I don't give a damn about Lindy, but he's got a mother and a sick sister that need that dollar's worth of flour and fatback he sends out to them twice a year. And you make sure the shotgun's cleaned for tonight. We'll have a devil of a time getting that boy out of here alive if the Frammis boys decide to make trouble. Which they sholy will. Chances are he just wants to go home, but home ain't safe for him anymore. He got a wife?"

"Yeah. Big tall woman with a gold tooth."

"Where is she?"

"Over in a boardinghouse, far side of Hewlitt, waitin' to take his body home."

MacDonnell was at the door. "We'll have to see what we can do."

Otis was nodding. "According to proper po-lice procedures."

MacDonnell smiled: the expression stopped just above his mustache. "Sho. Why not?"

# Chapter 3

"Don't you lie to me, Benny!"

Benny, sallow and young, shoved his hands in his pockets and assumed a posture of contrition. His eyes, however, made it plain that his thoughts were elsewhere. Anywhere.

"I'm not lyin'," he said, lying.

Mrs. Gavin was not unperceptive. "I told you to get rid of that gun, and you kept it, didn't you? And Magic saw it, didn't he? Or did you show it to him?"

Benny kept his hands in his pockets and his eyes . . . elsewhere. In truth, he cared very little about this old woman and her worries about guns and kiddy nutcases, but this old woman was surprisingly free with money (and though Benny had still not figured out *why* she was so free with it, he was quite willing to accept that she *was* free with it, just as he accepted that grass went into a cow and milk came out: one did not have to understand the interior mechanics of such matters in order to benefit from them), and as the kiddy nutcase was, for some reason, important to the old woman (who was surprisingly free with money), he continued to ape contrition.

"I'm *not* lyin'," he said again. Lying.

"I don't believe you."

"Suit yourself." This was a somewhat daring thing to say, but Benny had been with Mrs. Gavin for a couple of years now, and he knew, down to the last inch, just how far he could push her.

Mrs. Gavin put her hands on her hips in the manner of one who was lecturing a small child, even though Benny had hit his growth spurt a good year before and she had to look up at him.

The sound of distant hammering drifted into the otherwise silent room. Somewhere, one workman called to another. His voice was muffled: he might have been asking for a board, for nails, for the time, for anything.

"Benny," said Mrs. Gavin, abruptly shifting tactics, "you know that I love you, don't you?"

Benny was silent. He had heard all this before.

"Just like I love Tiffany and Magic, don't you?"

"Just like you loved the others?" Daring again, shaving that inch a little closer.

Mrs. Gavin turned half-away, rested her hand on the lacquered back of a chair. "It was time for them to go. They were grown-up. They were old."

As Mrs. Gavin was no longer looking directly at him, Benny took the opportunity to look directly at her. Old. Of course. Twenty-one years was old. Benny figured that he had a good six or seven years left to him . . . if he played his cards right. Then, too, he looked younger than he was (something that he had used to his advantage in Memphis and Nashville and Atlanta), so he might, he had decided, last even a bit longer than that. But if he wanted to last, he could not push it too much, so:

"Yeah," he said, "I guess they were."

"One eventually has to let one's children go, so that they can grow up and become adults. Look at Sam, for example. How grown-up he is. He would not have had that chance it I hadn't set him free. So, you see, I was doing him a favor."

Benny knew all about Sam Libbeldoe, saw him, in fact, almost every day: dirty and idle, lounging in front of M'Creed's Hardware, doing, essentially, nothing except the occasional day labor job that allowed him to pay the rent on the trash-filled shack he called his house . . . even though everyone else called it an abandoned stable on a vacant lot. But: "Yeah."

"Just like I'm doing a favor for little Magic by doing everything in my power to make sure that he has a good life, despite what John and Alice are trying to do."

"Yeah."

He was a little shocked at the tone of his own voice, and he hastened . . .

"Yeah."

. . . to improve upon it. Yes, he had indeed pushed it as far as he dared. Another word from him and he could well wind up back out on the streets, getting felt up by Peach Trees in the alleys of Biloxi or Memphis, or turning tricks in Atlanta.

"OK," he said. "I'm sorry. I'll get rid of the gun."

Meaning that he would find a different place to hide it.

More pounding from the distance. This month, the workmen were replacing the ceiling in the formal dining room so that it would match the floor they had replaced last month. Soon they would move on to the bedrooms upstairs, renewing them one by one until they were finished . . . at which time they would start on the downstairs rooms. Perhaps with the ceiling in the formal dining room.

"Really, Benny . . ." Mrs. Gavin came toward him, and Benny steeled himself. This was by far the most unpleasant part of these interviews.

Slowly, she lowered herself to her knees.

"You know I love you, Benny. And Magic and Tiffany, too. I only do these things for you. All of you."

Benny was looking elsewhere again, acutely conscious that Mrs. Gavin's position put her face right on a level with his crotch.

"You know that, don't you?" she said.

*What if he . . . ?*

"Yeah . . . yeah, I know."

*No. No, never.*

"And after what Magic was saying at the train station this morning, I simply had to bring this up with you."

Benny waited.

"He was talking about his pow-er again. You remember, don't you? How he goes on about his pow-er?"

"Yeah. Yeah, I remember."

How could he forget? *Pow-er* was Magic's most often used word, and anything that he could pick up and fashion—or imagine—into some kind of vague right angle was, in his mind, some kind of gun. Benny had even seen Magic bite a sandwich into the outline of a service automatic and plug Tiffany repeatedly from across the lunch table. And, if there were no objects, Magic would—as he had at the station that morning—turn to

his own hand. *My pow-er,* he would say. *My pow-er. Pow!*
*Pow! Pow!*

"He started after he saw that gun of yours. Do you remember? Before John and Alice sent him away?"

"Yeah. Yeah, I remember."

He also remembered how he had wanted to take that sandwich and shove it into the pinhead's face.

*Pow! Pow! Pow!*

The old woman was still on her knees in front of him, just like that skinny old fart in Atlanta that had, for crissakes, wanted him naked and *gilded* so that he—the fart—could worship him like an idol (he had gotten out of *that* one as quick as he could, and he had been months picking gold body paint out from under his fingernails). Benny kept his eyes carefully away from her face, knowing instinctively that, even blinded as she was by . . . by . . . by whatever it was that caused her to bring children into her house, ply them with money, ask nothing in return, and then, when they began to show signs of maturity, summarily toss them out on the street, she would, nonetheless, be able to see the combination of revulsion and contempt in his expression were he to look directly at her.

"Yeah," he said.

"He saw your gun, and he wanted one, too. And he called it a pow-er. And then John and Alice sent him away."

Passing by the folding doors that, open, gave into the main hall, a workman with a bundle of lath on his shoulder glanced into the room . . . then looked quickly away. In the distance, the pounding continued.

New. Everything in the house was new. Walls that had been put up a year before came down and were remade in new styles, new arrangements; carpeting that had been laid last summer was replaced with wood as the wood that had been installed at the same time was replaced with carpeting. In the two years that Benny had been with Mrs. Gavin, the roof and siding had been redone at least a half dozen times.

"Yeah. Yeah, they did."

"You don't want them to send him away again, do you?"

Benny wanted to scream at her that the stupid kid had been up north for the last three months, and that if the stupid kid was *still* going on about guns and pow-ers, it was most likely because someone had shown the stupid kid some heat up north. And even if the stupid kid *was* still hooked on the .38 Benny kept upstairs in the drawer with his underwear (that he had only seen because the stupid kid couldn't keep his hands out of *anything*), the fact that the stupid kid hadn't let go of it even after three months should be enough for anyone with any brains to figure out that Magic needed a shrink a lot more than he needed Mrs. Gavin's money or lifestyle or anything else.

But:

"Yeah . . ." he said. "I mean . . . I mean, *no*. I don't want them to send him away."

Mrs. Gavin, to his relief, heard exactly what she wanted to hear. "Please be a dear, then, Benny, and get rid of the gun."

"Yeah. Yeah, I'll get rid of it."

Again, Benny steeled himself. He knew what was coming.

Mrs. Gavin took hold of the hem of Benny's jacket, lifted it to her lips. "Bless you, Benny."

Benny said nothing. He simply waited. At least there was compensation for all of this.

Laboriously, Mrs. Gavin got to her feet, swaying unsteadily, then reached into the neckline of her blouse and extracted something from between her breasts. "I have something for you, Benny."

Benny waited.

Mrs. Gavin proffered the bill. Actually, Benny noticed, there were two bills.

"One for you, one for Tiffany," said Mrs. Gavin. "I want you both to have fun."

"Fun? Oh . . . oh, sure. Oh, yeah. We'll have fun."

"I'll give both of these to you. You'll make sure that Tiffany gets hers, won't you?"

Benny took the bills. Two twenties. "Tiffany? Oh, sure! Sure I will!"

"Just be sure you both have fun!"

"Fun. Yeah, sure. I'll have lots of fun." He was already folding the money, stuffing it into his pocket. "Tiffany, too. Yeah, we'll both have some fun. Sure we will."

\* \* \*

"Oh, dear . . ."

Here, with Montague Mansion itself before her, the sense of familiarity that Alma had felt on the road persisted, but it might well have been the familiarity experienced by a French farmer returning to the Somme . . . after the battle. Rising up beyond the wide, U-shaped drive that, though overgrown with weeds and grass, was still outlined by a procession of massive oaks, the house looked like a rheumy-eyed derelict who had found his park-bench slumber interrupted in the wee hours by the ungentle prod of a police billy club.

Mortar was crumbling. Wood siding was rotten . . . where it was not missing altogether. Windows . . .

What windows? There appeared to be no more glass in the Montague Mansion than in a Neanderthal cave.

The broad steps up to the verandah that spanned the front of the house were mostly missing, scavenged for building material or chopped up for firewood. The wide, double front doors to which they had once led were also missing . . . doubtless for the same reasons. And all this was, Alma knew, only a first-glance estimate, for wisteria and bougainvillea, as though making a determined bid to enshroud the entire house, had twined crazily across the entire façade, possibly hiding from view even greater horrors.

"Oh, dear . . ." she said again.

Uncle Buddy was obviously distressed. "Oh, ma'am," he said. "I shoulda told you about this. It been a long, long time since anybody lived here."

"I know," Alma said, her eyes still filled with the terribly crumbling, terribly familiar mansion. (Was that not her room up there on the second floor? Yes . . . yes it had to be. But was there even any way to get up to the second floor anymore? And what about the third floor?) "I'm the last Montague, Uncle Buddy. The house went to my father, of course, and then, since the boys were lost in the war and since I was a girl . . ."

She glanced at him. Uncle Buddy was nodding. There was nothing unusual in what she was saying, even though it was not the truth.

". . . and a black sheep at that . . ."

*That* was the truth. She saw Uncle Buddy blink and glance quickly at her.

". . . it went to a cousin. But he wouldn't live in it because he said it was tainted."

"Haunted, Miz Montague?"

Alma laughed, and this time, to her relief, there was something genuine about the expression, even to her own ears. "No, Uncle Buddy. Not haunted. Tainted. Cousin Wilfred was very religious—a Pastoral Quaker, and a serious student of the Bible—and some things my grandfather did here made him unwilling to live in the house. So . . ." She shrugged. "I'm not sure how long it's been deserted. Long enough, it seems."

"It been . . . oh . . . a good fifteen or twenty years, ma'am."

In truth, it looked more like a hundred and fifteen or a hundred and twenty. Alma supposed that, what with two dead sons and a daughter who was playing the whore up north (going to school, actually, and practicing medicine . . . but it was the same thing as far as he was concerned), her father had allowed the place to become run-down in the last years. After that, tenantless, the building was merely wood on the hoof for anyone who needed to patch a chicken coop or brew up fifty gallons of white whiskey in some nearby valley.

"I daresay," said Alma. "Well, if you'll get my bags out of the car—"

Buddy was horrified. "Ma'am! You not thinking of . . . of . . ."

"Staying here? Of course I'm staying here. This is my home." Alma smiled at Buddy's expression. Stay in a decaying, deserted house? Who but a madwoman would even consider such a thing! But there were all kinds of decay and desertion, and the house had every right to match the owner. Or maybe it was the other way around.

She put a hand to her face, feeling the aches, the old bones. Two of a kind. And yet she kept her voice cheerful when she spoke: one less thing to brood upon, to occupy her regrets as she lay in bed . . . or wherever . . . come nightfall.

"But that's an awfully long way for you to carry them, isn't it?" she said. "Why don't you drive up as far as the front steps? It doesn't look *too* bad, even with the weeds."

Alma sensed that Buddy was half of a mind to take her

straight back to town and deliver her up to whatever authorities were responsible for the care and maintenance of the feeble-minded and the deranged. But as though impelled either by her smiling insistence or by his own curiosity, he put the car back in gear and took her straight up to the front steps, the cab jouncing and bucking over the ruts and potholes in the drive and forcing its way through patches of waist-high weeds.

But if he drove to the front steps, and if he accompanied her up what was left of those steps (hovering near her, as though even her meager weight would collapse the half-rotten wood . . . and never mind what was supporting his near two hundred pounds), it was with the air of one who was only waiting for her to take a good enough look at the remains of the house to come to her senses and allow him to drive her to a comfortable hotel in town.

Alma, though, had no intention of coming to her senses. Nor had she any intention of telling Buddy that, compared with the room she had been forced, by a combination of gender and neg-ligible income (perhaps the two were related after all?), to in-habit after she had first arrived in the Northern city sixty years before—a room behind the basement furnace of a three-story walk-up in which the roar of the boiler would keep her awake half the night, a room in which, small as she was, she could hardly stand upright, in which the only light came from a bare bulb hanging from a bare cord in the middle of the bare ceiling—this house, though run-down and decayed, was luxurious, even palatial.

But it was probably good that she recalled that long-ago room behind the furnace, else, having passed through the gaping hole left by the missing double doors, she might have faltered at the sight of the interior of the house. The wide staircases that had once swept up so imperiously along either curving side of the entry hall were now no more than skeletal, toothless grins, the treads and most of the risers pried off, carted away, chopped up. From the domed ceiling hung the remains of what had once been a chandelier: sere and withered now, like the webby veins of a dry leaf. The floor—marble and inlaid—was intact . . . if one could discount water stains and dirt so thick that weeds were growing in places.

"Let's go on to the back of the house."

"Ma'am . . ."

She eyed him. "*I'm* going, Uncle Buddy. You can come . . . if you want."

He came.

Down the wide corridor, dark now with cobwebs and disuse. Lumps of what might have been furniture—once—loomed on either side, some shrouded in mildewed drop cloths that seemed to all but move in the half-light of the interior.

"Ma'am?"

"Yes, Buddy?"

"You *sho* this place ain't haunted?"

"Positive," she replied. "Grandfather had connections. He would never have tolerated it."

"Oh . . . OK, I—" He caught himself. "He had *connections*?"

Alma's grin was mirthless. "Come on. There are some back stairs that might have been missed."

"Miz Montague, you sholy ain't tellin' me that you're gonna go *upstairs*!"

"Only if I don't have to fly in order to do it, Uncle Buddy. I promise you that."

The corridor led them past shadowed storerooms that had long ago been gutted by rats—four-footed and two-footed—and into the kitchen. Dust. Refuse. A long metal table lay on its side against one wall. The big stove was covered with a thick layer of greasy dust.

Alma looked at the stove for a long time while Buddy fidgeted. Her father had brought that stove from Chicago when he, then a young, swaggering man, had inherited the house and become its master. It was ostentation and display, a symbol of Montague status in the valley below and beyond, and for and even beyond its time the stove had been a masterpiece of utility and technology both. Converted from wood-fired to gas-fired when gas had been brought to the house, it had been in use all the days that she remembered, and, almost as a point of honor for the house, it had been scoured into brilliance every Wednesday by the kitchen help. Now, filthy and unused—and filthy, as was evident, for some time before it had become unused—it told her much about her father's mental state during the last years that the mansion had been inhabited.

She suddenly turned away from the stove. Too suddenly. "The stairs are through that door," she whispered, pointing.

And, yes, the stairs were usable. Doubtless dating from the antebellum origins of the house, made of wrought iron and therefore too big and too heavy to pull out and take away (not to mention having no utility whatsoever in the patching of chicken coops or the firing of stills), they were indeed still extant.

Alma put her foot on the bottom tread.

"Ma'am . . ."

'Shhhh. This is my home, Buddy."

"The floors upstairs, ma'am . . . they might be rotten."

"Maybe. But the only way to find out is to go and see."

Buddy stood at the foot of the stairs as, leaning heavily on the railing, she mounted. He scratched his head. "You say you the black sheep of your family, ma'am?"

"Yes, Buddy," she called back from the shadowed stairwell. "I am."

"Well I sho can see why, if you don't mind me sayin' so."

And he followed her.

The stairs held. So did the second floor. Here the house looked in better shape . . . probably, Alma thought, because the scavengers would take first what was easiest to take. Dirt and broken glass lay about, certainly, but there looked to be little damage from water, and the doors were actually still on their hinges.

Experimentally, she pushed at one of the doors. It creaked open. She caught her breath.

It was her old room. Choosing (so she thought) at random, she had, of all the doors up here, picked this one. And not only was it her old room, but . . . but it really *was* her old room. Despite the passage of sixty years and the ravages of abandonment and neglect, the room was essentially as she had left it, with her bed covered with the ruffled spread her mother had made, her pictures on the wall, her dressing table . . .

"They kept it for me," she murmured. She pushed the door all the way open. It swung wide. Yes. Yes: dusty and bewebbed, but essentially just as it had been on the morning—distant now as only time can make distant—when she closed the door on it and turned her back on her Montague heritage and destiny. "They kept it. As though they were waiting . . ."

She put her hands to her face.

Buddy was all but wringing his hands. "Let me take you back to town, ma'am. You got no business prowling around here by yourself."

She wiped at her eyes. "I'm not by myself, Uncle Buddy. You're here, aren't you?"

She looked at the room again. Waiting for her. Perhaps the whole mansion had been waiting for her. And now . . . here she was. Old and tired and wanting nothing so much as a peace that would have bewildered her grandfather, who had so striven to prove that there was something beyond the Veil that, proof or no proof, he had come to believe it implicitly.

"Please bring my baggage up," she said. "I'll be staying here tonight." She halted his protest with a raised hand. "I mean it."

"But there might be—"

"I'll be perfectly safe, I assure you." She went to the window and looked out. The drive curved away down toward the road, the road she had taken through the whispering, morning mists of April . . . sixty years ago. "Grandfather had connections, after all. He wouldn't have it any other way."

The moon, full. The road, a streak of white, like the center-line of a highway painted down the blackness of spring-sown fields and idled ground alike. The night air was heavy, moist, partaking of and amplifying its own darkness. It *was* darkness: hanging heavy in the hollows of hills, flowing like water down ravines, gathering in wet bottomlands. Darkness like smoke. Darkness like the final closing of eyes.

His watch said 9:30.

Mr. Dark, his gray suit turned by the moonlight as black as the fields, as black as the air, as black as his skin, passed a hand across the lower part of his face, considering. Nine-thirty left him plenty of time to attend to his business in Beat Two and still be back in time to supervise his business in Lee's Corners. Or, rather, to supervise his *lack* of business in Lee's Corners, for aside from a relatively easy matter that he could with confidence leave to another, there was nothing in the town that demanded his presence. In fact, Marshal MacDonnell and Deputy York would be smuggling their prisoner and his wife out into York's own car about now, MacDonnell having telephoned ahead to friends in Surrey or Wayburn or Hyde or one of the hundred different hamlets and villages and towns sprinkled lightly across the hills of Oktibushubee and Kenniscoggin Counties. By three in the morning, York's car would arrive at the selected destination, and the prisoner—who was really no prisoner at all, unless one surrounded by such determined defenders could be considered a prisoner—and his wife would both be . . . somewhere else, blending into the Negro section of a town, or installed on some previously vacant stretch of farmland.

Mr. Dark chuckled. If the Frammis boys wanted trouble tonight, they would have to content themselves with discharging a few rounds of buckshot at the front of the jail . . . as if the weathered brick would even show it come morning.

Dark pushed on, his steps steady and even, his polished black shoes crunching along the unpaved road. Slowly, an inky point in the seemingly limitless stretch of moonlit white, he made his way up a hill, down into a hollow, up another hill. Somewhere ahead . . .

He would know the place when he saw it. He always did.

But as he topped a ridge, a light, distant and off to one side, caught his eye. It was not the light that Mr. Dark expected at his destination—that was much farther ahead—rather, it was a light that shone from a place that had been lightless for twenty years. Glimmering uneasily, as though produced by nothing more substantial than a lantern or a solitary candle, it wavered and danced from a distant hillside that overlooked the town of Lee's Corners, sometimes disappearing for many seconds at a time, but always reappearing, yellow and uncertain, like the light in the eyes of a dying man who looks up to see Death waiting for him.

Dark stopped where he was. He had business in a swampy hollow where a hut hugged a creek and the steam rising from a still was hidden, even in daylight, by the mists that gathered over the stagnant water; but it could wait for a moment. His schedule was flexible: he could afford to examine the light, to estimate its place and position, to draw his conclusions.

"She's early," he murmured at last, his voice shadowed and edgeless. "She's early. I'd thought perhaps the middle of the summer."

He looked ahead at the blank road, then back at the light; and again he passed a hand over his face, this time in the manner of a man with a hard task ahead of him.

"I'll have to get up there in the next couple weeks. Or maybe I'll give her a chance to settle in. That's what she wants, I'm sure of it: just to settle in. And she'll have a lot to do, too. Maybe I'll make it a month."

Almost absently, he was digging into the pocket of his vest, searching with his fingers for something that had been there for a long time, so long, in fact, that he had almost forgotten that it was there at all. So long that it seemed all but unnatural for him to grasp it between the tips of his index and middle fingers and draw it forth.

He held it up before his eyes. Two and one half inches of gleaming brass sparkled in the light, and on the grip, dark, was a a single letter, deeply etched: *M*.

# Chapter 4

It was always worst at night.

Alma herself was not exactly sure how she had persuaded Uncle Buddy to drive away from the abandoned wreck of Montague Mansion and leave her alone, with no electricity, no running water, and no food. Had she simply convinced him, unwittingly, that she was indeed a madwoman, and that he should flee rather than face contamination by some subtle agent of insanity? Or had she prevailed by direct order, unconsciously falling back on some familial and hereditary belief in what her father had insisted was the "basic, womanish, servile nature of the black race"?

She smiled into the shadows at the thought of her father's words . . . or perhaps she smiled at herself, who had heard the racism from the beginning but had not detected the hidden barb within the statement until, years later, it had pricked her—in spite of . . . or perhaps *because* of . . . the gowned and gloved and high-heeled inviolability of her Southern womanhood—at her first cotillion. Regardless, there was no more mirth in her expression than usual. Perhaps there was even less.

But, despite his protests, Buddy had left (though she had noticed that his cab had paused at the end of the drive for a long time before it finally disappeared into the falling shadows of evening), and she had turned away from the window, turned back into the house, to the cobwebs and the dirt, to the rust and the decay . . . to her memories of what had been . . . of what had been before yet more layers had been added to her regrets and her memories.

She had indeed lied to Buddy. There were no old, shiny memories; or, if there were, they were incapable of imparting any sense of enthusiasm for the continuing business of living. Alma had come to the conclusion long ago that their function— if they had a function, if in fact they existed at all—was that of an opiate: something to dull chronic pain, something to keep the patient tractable during the last days of a terminal illness. Dispensed with niggardly parsimony, too dilute to do much of anything save ensure that the patient did not squirm *too* much in the course of the final throes, they—opiates and memories both— allowed for maintenance only. Thriving was out of the question. Improvement was out of the question.

Montague Mansion had been built fifty years before the Civil War, but the house had continued to grow and change with each passing generation until, as though a fit of amnesia had set in, it had apparently been abandoned shortly after the death of Alma's father. Sprawling and involuted both, exhibiting, even, a sense of the *organic,* and now filled with darkness and the moldering relics of an old family, it seemed to Alma to be a fitting symbol of life—in general, her life—and so, knees aching with the unaccustomed damp and footsteps tapping faintly and uncertainly in the dust and dirt that covered the floor, she explored the corridors, passed through archways and along turnings, and probed into abandoned wings and deserted galleries as though searching for something that might perhaps tell her why, having ceased to hope, having found both memory and life to be mere dross and delusion, she had come back to Lee's Corners—to earliest memory, to beginning life—and what she hoped to find now that she had.

But she found only ghosts. Yes, the mansion was indeed haunted, but not in the sense that the local rumors suggested. Ghosts are, invariably, a part of one's personal luggage—imports or purchases are not necessary—and Alma was different, perhaps, only in that temperament or predisposition enabled her to declare the contents of her suitcase down to the last bottle of blood pressure pills and pair of socks. Conflict, failure, argument, mortification, despair: a well-furnished life had them all, and, wandering through the dark house, she found them rising within

her, called forth by fatigue, darkness, and the shifting shadows
cast by her lantern.

And what about *him*? What about the child of her imagination, who, born dead of a dead mother, still lived on in mind and
dream? Why, he was here, too, was he not? With his still-unknown
occupation and his fabricated mate and his imagined children?
Alma was here and, therefore, he was here: down this corridor,
and through this door into this darkness that held the delivery
room, the father standing over the bleeding mother like a red-
eyed bull looking for a place to plant his horns, forbidding either transfusion or intervention, booming out Bible verses as
woman and child died . . . and Alma herself, technically a doctor, but still a woman who dragged the tatters of her upbringing
behind her and who faltered before the threat of violence and
the justification of religion just long enough—

She turned away, slamming the door, but there was a flash of
phosphenes behind her clenched eyes . . . or maybe it was a
head of blond hair rounding the corner and vanishing even as
she looked.

Lantern in hand, she ran, stumbling, her shawls flapping like
moth wings.

More darkness. More dust. But in the receding cobwebby
shadows of the gallery she saw her, remembered that one touch,
that single meeting of eyes, that certain conscious and consciously simultaneous knowledge that went beyond any sexual
or emotional desire, that rendered both unnecessary (there being distilled in that glance and that knowledge the essence of attraction, courtship, consummation, and lives forever linked,
lives forever shared) : a love as forbidden as heroin, as deadly
as a hundred euthanizing drugs, as barren as stone.

But the knowledge had been simultaneous with the ending—
had, in fact, *been* the ending—and Alma had not seen her the
next day, nor the day after that; and a week later she had finally
heard that she had abruptly and without explanation left her position at the hospital. And later on she had heard that she had
married, that she had lived with a constant and external fidelity,
had borne children, had raised them . . . and had been beaten to
death in a marital argument turned violent.

But by then it had been long enough that Alma had not even grieved. Or maybe she had (for there she was, coming home to her house, wearing her suit and carrying her black case in her hand, and there she was . . . pausing . . . looking up at the house that was empty save for a woman who came in to clean and to cook), and had simply not realized that she was grieving, or that it was grief that so caused her to pause on her front walk, look up at that window, and wonder, just wonder, at how dark it was, at just how completely empty a house could look.

One touch. No, not even that. A pressure of one shoulder against another as they had conferred over a chart. Once. Only once.

And then she was gone, and Alma leaned against the wall, her head tipped back, breathing . . . just breathing . . . reminding herself that she was alive, and that the past was past, that ghosts were only ghosts. She was alive (yes, she supposed that she could still call it that), and the past was dead, and—

A scuttling froze her, and she shivered, realizing that she had come to the door of the room that had served her grandfather equally as library, study, office, and bedroom; realizing, too, that she had, when she had so imperiously sent Uncle Buddy away, ignored not only such common, ordinary things as food and water, but had forgotten about such common, ordinary things as rats.

But though rats might alarm her, they could not make her shiver. She had spent too many of the early years of her career working in ghetto hospitals and visiting tenement patients to be bothered by rats. No, it was the memories—and the implicit threat of memories made eternal—that so laid a cold hand on her.

But she pushed the door open anyway. The hinges creaked, and the light of the lantern fell into the shadows, splashing onto the dusty floor, up the sere and rotting curtains, into the yawning, empty fireplace.

Lantern held aloft, she stood in the doorway. Yes, there was the sofa on which her grandfather (the old man refusing, after his wife had died, the comfort of the bed he had once shared with her) had taken his nightly rest for the last half of his existence, its crushed-down cushions still grotesquely echoing the imprint of his body. And there, just visible through the door into the inner room, was the desk at which he had written his almost daily letters to his mediums (and, come summer nights, he would fetch them home from the railroad station and personally usher them up to the guest rooms, their white faces, male and female alike, all but interchangeable, their eyes blank and staring as though peering so fixedly and so single-mindedly through the Veil had taken away their power to see anything save the intangible . . . and, come night, the parlor would be filled with voices and raps, the sound of plucked guitar strings, and the tinny bark of trumpets). And there, closer, shelves rising from floor to ceiling and without a volume missing (as though her grandfather had, just a minute before, left the room after having been nagged by his daughter to excavate and neaten what she almost always referred to as "Father's pit"), was his library of Spiritualist tracts, encyclopedias, exegeses . . .

She lifted the lantern higher. No, not quite without a volume missing. Up on the second shelf from the top was a gap like an absent tooth. One book was gone.

Well, doubtless she would find it elsewhere. She was certain that the devout Baptists and Methodists who had plundered Montague Mansion for lumber and firewood would have had no interest whatsoever in heretical scribblings about séances, spirit communications, and life in the realms beyond the Veil, where the spiritual stuff that had once been human beings interacted in perfect concord and harmony, reuniting with loved ones, exchanging pleasantries with friends—

Another rustle . . . from the interior room. And . . . and something that sounded like a footstep.

"No!" she almost shouted. Angrily, she shoved the door all the way open and strode past the sofa and the bookcases and through the inner door.

Silence. The desk, the chair, the window: dusty, but essentially as she remembered them. No spectral visitant. No waiting haunt. Not even, to her infinite relief, a letter or a piece of paper on the desk top.

"No," she said, calmer now. "There's nothing. I live, and I die, and then I don't have to worry anymore. Because then it's over. There isn't anyone I have to talk to, anyone . . ." She choked, and the aches made her lean on the desk, leaving on the dusty surface handprints that were so thin as to be almost skeletal. But she forced herself to continue, as though her words were kind of reassuring litany: ". . . anyone I have to see again. No arguments. No messy decisions. No losses." She coughed: dust . . . dust and something else she would not admit. "Nothing. I'm just . . . smoke."

On the wall by the window, a reproduction of a painting. Böcklin's *Island of the Dead*. Her grandfather had owned it for as long as Alma could remember. Now, the old man gone, the painting remained. Alma's lantern poured yellow light over it: craggy island, enormous cypress trees, harbor wall . . . enigmatic boatman and even more enigmatic—almost terrifying—figure in white.

"I want to go there," he had said, pointing at it. "I want to go there when I'm done here, and I want to think for a long time. It looks like a good place for thinking."

Alma went up to it, examined it closely. Sun and wind and rain seemed not to have touched it. But: "Don't you understand, Grandfather?" she said. "I don't want a place to think. I don't want to think at all. I don't want anything. I just want—"

A sound: high, wailing, coming, seemingly, from a great distance. Alma stiffened as though once again an icy hand had touched her, as though she had only to turn around to see—

Defiantly, gritting her teeth, she turned. The sound continued, but it was coming not from any floating chunk of ectoplasm or shadowy, reaching specter, but from the glassless window. From far beyond the window, actually.

She went to the opening and leaned out, holding the lantern high as though by doing so she could pierce darkness and distance. But there was only the night like a moist, velvet drape, the faraway lights of Lee's Corners, and the sound: wailing, rising, falling.

She cocked her head, listening. It almost sounded like singing, but what kind of singing sounded like . . . like *that*?

She saw headlights coming up the driveway.

* * *

Abram MacDonnell parked the police car in front of the house, shut off the engine, looked at his watch, and gave himself five minutes. After that, he got out of the car, walked slowly up to the front door, and gave himself another minute, listening all the while to the voice that was crying, singing, lugubriously crooning:

"Jesus! Jesus! Jesus!"

And then he gave himself yet another minute . . . and, finally, knocked.

The door was flung open (the voice—continuing—growing louder) by a short man clad in trousers and an undershirt. His mottled, balding head resembled a rusting cannon ball.

"I'm . . . I mean, *we're* sure glad you're here, Sheriff—"

"I'm the marshal," said MacDonnell.

"Sure, sure." The man looked over his shoulder and into the interior of the house. "It's the sheriff, folks!"

"The marshal," MacDonnell corrected affably, though his eyes were, if anything, even colder than usual.

"Yeah . . . yeah . . . the marshal. Sure."

And all this time the voice continued: "Jesus! Jesus! Jesus!"

MacDonnell looked even more affable . . . if one could ignore his eyes. "And how is Old Abaijah?"

"Abaijah? Oh, you mean Dad. Yeah, he's OK. I guess."

MacDonnell was nodding. "I reckon you and your brothers and sisters have a considerable bit of work ahead of you. What with him on his way to dying and all."

"Yeah. Uh . . . yeah."

"Jesus! Jesus! Jesus!"

The balding man was leading MacDonnell back along a hallway. The voice was growing louder. "Listen, Sheriff—"

"Marshal."

"—she just came in through the front door like she owned the place. She waltzed into Dad's room and picked him up, and then she—"

"Who?" said MacDonnell. Affably.

"Well . . . well, *her.*"

"Jesus! Jesus! Jesus!"

They were passing a room just then, and MacDonnell glanced into it and caught a glimpse of at least a half dozen faces—male

and female both—that looked like muffins out of the same pan
that had produced his guide. There was a table there (it was the
dining room) and legal papers lay open and unsealed on the
table.

"Your pa was a rich man," he remarked.

The balding man followed his gaze, then grabbed the handles
of the folding doors and quickly pulled them shut.

"Jesus! Jesus! Jesus!"

"If you say so," he said.

MacDonnell did not reply.

"You've got to arrest her!"

MacDonnell reached up, adjusted his hat. "Her?"

The balding man stood for a moment, stunned. "Yes! *Her!*"
He pointed down the corridor.

"Jesus! Jesus! Jesus!"

MacDonnell was feeling very affable. He had known Abaijah
extremely well—the old man had, in his younger days, made a
point of teaching the boys of the town, MacDonnell included,
how to spit, swear, and chew—and knew to the penny just how
much Abaijah had despised his children.

So: "Her?"

"That . . . that . . . that *woman*."

MacDonnell yawned. He did not know this man, he did not
know his name, he knew nothing about him save that he was
one of a half dozen or so sons and daughters who, after having
had no communication with Abaijah for years, had simultaneously boiled out of Memphis and descended upon Lee's Corners
scant hours after the old man had taken to what was generally
considered to be his deathbed. They had laid claim to his house,
ejected his doctor, dismissed his cook, read his mail, rifled his
safe, made his decisions, and kept him isolated from his friends.

"Jesus! Jesus! Jesus!"

But MacDonnell knew Anger Modestie extremely well, and
though her methods were sometimes excessive—though perfectly appropriate, he reflected, in this particular case—he
could not himself say with any certainty that he did not want to
see her dark face above him as his own eyes were closing for the
last time.

"Jesus! Jesus! Jesus!"

Of course, he reflected, he would probably not have any say in the matter. Anger had her ways, and it was usually best to go along with them.

"The one with the big carpetbag?" he said after another yawn.

The balding man nodded agitatedly. "Yeah. Yeah. That one."

"Jesus! Jesus! Jesus!"

"And the red purse, too?"

"Yeah."

"And the hat. With . . ."

"Jesus! Jesus! Jesus!"

". . . with flowers?"

"Yeah. Yeah, her."

MacDonnell unbuttoned the flap of his shirt pocket and extracted a notebook. "Well, then," he said slowly, "if you'll just go ahead and give me a description . . ."

"Jesus! Jesus! Je—!"

The voice cut off as though a tap had been turned. MacDonnell kept his eyes on the balding man and let the silence lengthen before he spoke again. "You got any idea of her height and weight?"

The door at the end of the hall opened, and if the balding man had intended to give MacDonnell any kind of description at all of the woman who then appeared, he would have had his work cut out for him, for her body was encased in such a fantastic assortment of castoffs, hand-me-downs, rags, and necklaces that any estimation as to its shape or displacement could, by necessity, be nothing more than a vague guess. Even her race was uncertain and indistinct, for her flat, weatherworn face leaned no more toward black or white than did an old leather purse. Stumping on what might—or might not—have been short legs, she came up the hall as, MacDonnell knew, she had gone down it: in the manner of a pile driver dropping or a bulldozer tossing aside everything in its path.

Old Abaijah's children had never stood a chance.

"Abaijah been all attended to, Anger?" he said as she passed.

"Ah been deathin' ma babies since you was in diapers, Marshal," she said as she passed (not even looking at him). "And Ah ain't never lost a one. Abaijah be in the arms of Jesus now, and in the bosom of Abraham and the saints."

"God bless him, then," said MacDonnell. "You have a good night, Anger."

"And you, too, Marshal. And you pray to Jesus that he'll receive you in heaven when you die."

"I always do, Anger, " said MacDonnell.

"Ah know you do," came the reply as she rounded the corner. A moment later, the front door banged open and banged closed.

The balding man was staring after her. "That's . . . that's her!" He turned to MacDonnell, pointing down the hall. "That was her! Arrest her!"

MacDonnell busied himself with opening his notebook and digging a pencil out of his pocket. "I reckon you'd best look in on your dad. He's dead."

The balding man stared.

"Was anyone in there with him besides Anger?"

The balding man spluttered. "Besides *her*? Why would anyone be—?"

"Sho," said MacDonnell, who had seen what was obviously Abaijah's will lying open and, from the look of it, thoroughly read on the dining room table. "Why not?"

In the distance, he heard a shotgun go off: the pocked bricks of the jail had just been pocked a little more. He looked at his watch. Otis and the colored couple would be well out of range of the Frammis boys by now, and about an hour away from their destination.

"Now, about that description," he said.

Though the origin of the voice remained a mystery, Alma went downstairs to discover that the headlights belonged to Uncle Buddy's cab. "I'm sorry, ma'am," he was saying through the driver's side window before he had even come to a stop. "I—I mean, *we*—just couldn't leave you alone up here all by yourself."

Still half-caught in memory, and still unsettled by the voice (yes, there it was, still wailing faintly behind the sound of the automobile engine), she was dismayed: entanglements. She had been thought about, discussed. Here were more memories, even now, being formed. And what room would she find *them* in?

"I . . . I said I'd be fine, Uncle Buddy."

"Sho you said you'd be fine, and I believe you, ma'am.

"But it just ain't right that you go to bed without any supper, and Lucy—she's my wife—she felt the same way."

He had stopped by now at the base of what remained of the broad, front stairs, and when he shut off the engine and got out, Alma could see that he was carrying a basket.

Now she was thoroughly aghast. "Oh, Buddy! She shouldn't have!"

"Shouldn't have, ma'am? What kind of Christian folks are we that we're going to let a woman sleep in an empty house with an empty stomach? Ain't no saints smile at that!"

"But . . . but I'm sure your wife has better things to do!"

He was already carrying the basket up the stairs, picking his way by moonlight across the half-rotten expanse as though he were negotiating a minefield. "Ain't no better thing to do than feed a person, I always say."

Alma was following him up the steps. "But—"

" 'Sides, she got time these days, since she's not cookin' for Abaijah Jones no more."

"Abaijah Jones? Wait . . . I knew Abaijah . . ."

And, in the silence left behind by yet another upsurge of thoughts about her past and the people she had known—people who were now old, perhaps dying, perhaps dead—there came, clearly, the distant, crooning cry.

Shawls flying, Alma whirled on the steps. "Dear God, what *is* that?"

Buddy was at the top of the flight. He turned around and, one hand still holding the basket, reached out with the other to help Alma up to the porch. "That's old Anger," he explained. "She be singing somebody to Jesus."

"Singing someone? To . . . to Jesus?"

"That's what she does, ma'am. She been deathin' folks for the last ten years. She just showed up one day, and there she was."

The crooning wail rose and fell, then suddenly ended.

"That's it," said Buddy. "I bet that was Abaijah who just passed on."

"D-deathing folks?" Alma looked back into the dark distance.

"She say we got midwives to birth babies," said Buddy, "but she say we ain't got no one to death people. Midwives and doctors see folks into the world, and Anger Modestie sees folks out. She come in and she holds whoever be dying, and she sings them out. Sings them to Jesus."

"Doesn't anyone . . . object?"

"Nome. Or even if they do, they don't say nothing, and they don't try to keep her out any more than they'd try to stop a river by holding up their hands." He chuckled. "Moses mighta done it, but no one since. And, anyway, Moses never knew Anger Modestie."

Alma was still horrified. She tried to imagine a scene involving Anger Modestie at the hospital where she had worked, and found, with little surprise, that she could not. "What about the person who's dying? Don't they—"

Buddy had turned for the front door. "They usually smiling when they go, ma'am," he said. "I can't blame them, neither. Someone holding your hand straight to Jesus? Why, there ain't no finer thing I can think of."

He led her back to the kitchen and, by the light of Alma's lantern, righted the metal table, wiped it down with a rag, and set the basket on it. True to his words, the basket proved to be full of food: fried chicken, biscuits, a tub of gravy, collard greens, banana pudding. And, to top it off, a thermos of coffee and a jug of water.

"Some for tonight, some for morning," Buddy explained as he lifted out the last two.

"Buddy, I'm . . . I'm touched." Alma found that, indeed, there was a lump in her throat that defied memory and disinclination both. "That you and your wife would go to all this trouble for me is . . . is . . ."

"Shucks," said Buddy. "Colored folks always been taking care of white folks. 'Specially when those white folks want to go and do things like staying in houses that ain't fit for them."

Alma blushed, feeling the blood prickling in her sere cheeks. "You hardly know me, Uncle Buddy."

He smiled. "Been a long time since we had a Montague in Lee's Corners. Least we can do is welcome you back."

She found a smile to return in spite of herself. "That's very kind of you."

"Kindness is why we're here, Miz Alma." She heard, distinctly, his shift to the honorific and first name. "And it looks to me like you gonna need quite a bit of kindness if you gonna stay up here."

The thought struck her as so funny that she laughed out loud. "Here? As it is? Oh, Uncle Buddy! I didn't come all the way back to Lee's Corners to stay in a run-down house!"

He looked at her, and she read his thoughts: *Well, you sho picked a good enough way to start.*

"Not at all," she continued. "I'm going to restore it."

"Restore it?"

"My furniture and the rest of my things are coming down after me. Before it all gets here, though, I hope to have the windows finished and the walls patched and the floors repaired." She saw his look. "No. Not by myself. I'll be hiring men from the town. With any luck at all, I'll have Montague Mansion looking fit for living in by summer."

She saw him look up and around, and she followed his gaze. Cobwebs, dust, dirt . . . broken this, rotted that.

"I'm a Montague, Buddy," she said. "It will be done."

"Well now, you sho do *sound* like a Montague, Miz Alma. Leastwise, as much as I've heard about Montagues." He fumbled into the dark shadows that lay out of reach of the lantern's light and came up with a chair, which he wiped down and set before the table. "Now you go ahead and eat," he said. "If you gonna do what you say you gonna do, you gonna need a full tummy and a good night's sleep."

She saw doubt suddenly cross his face.

"I brought a sleeping bag, Uncle Buddy."

"Oh, Lord, Miz Alma! You gonna sleep on the *floor*?"

Sleep she did. And, indeed, on the floor. But her sleep in that lonely place was fitful and broken, and, toward dawn, she dreamed that she was being rocked in the arms of a woman who was crooning, singing, crying out the Jesus should take her into His bosom, that all the saints should welcome her home, and that her place in Paradise should be made ready; and Alma woke up screaming, for she wanted none of it.

# Chapter 5

"What's he saying?"

Alice Harlow shrugged. The light of the bare bulb above the kitchen table was not responsible for the peaked look about her, nor was the lateness of the hour (or, rather, the earliness—for the clock gave but three hours before the dawn). It was habitual fatigue that had so marked her, that had, by fitful nights just such as this, turned her thin and dry and bleached; and, wrapped in a threadbare bathrobe, her mousy hair turned to plastered list-lessness by stubborn traces of the day's short-order grease, she looked at her husband and saw a mirror of herself: thin, dry, bleached. Only the grease was missing.

"I think you can guess," she said.

John Harlow was angry. "What got him started again?"

Alice pulled the front edges of her robe closer together. The night was not cold: she huddled only against her husband's in-effectual blast. "He didn't get started again," she said. "He never left off."

Where Alice had long ago surrendered to the monotony of these nights (and had maintained her capitulation even while Magic was up north with her sister), John still raged against it. "It was that bitch."

"Maybe to begin with. I don't know." Alice looked at the clock. Soon she would have to get up and wash the short-order grease out of her hair in preparation for a new coat to be laid down in the course of the day: truckers coming and truckers go-ing, all of them wanting eggs, wanting hamburgers, wanting pie, wanting something to drink, the kerosene grill hissing in front of her and the waves of heat and grease baking into her skin whatever expression she happened to be wearing just as a kiln might fix a glaze on raw clay.

But it was the same expression every day: the same resignation that had as its foundation the memory of Greta's back receding footstep by footstep, growing smaller as, with her cardboard suitcase in her hand and her old teddy bear under her arm, she went down the street and away from the house while her father, a thin, vertical line of outraged masculinity, stood in the doorway, his jaw clenched with the vicious, muttered words that were still seeping from between his teeth even as his daughter—no, not his daughter: he had denied her, denied her loudly, denied her repeatedly, denied her with his fist—vanished around the corner.

They had seen her only once more. At the hospital. The doctor had lifted the sheet just long enough for them to make the identification. Everyone had known who she was, though. Everyone had known who she was and who her parents were . . .

. . . and they had known about her boy, too.

"What do you mean *to begin with*?" he demanded. "You saw her at the station. Came in running. Someone told her about Magic coming back, and she was right there. *Right there*. She *knew*."

She was not inclined to argue. "I guess so."

He looked at her. Then: "Can you trust that sister of yours?"

She lifted her head. "Don't you dare say that!"

"Say what?"

"Don't you dare talk about my sister that way!"

"I didn't *say* anything about your sister. I was just asking if—"

"I know what you were asking. You were asking if Marcy's been talking to Mrs. Gavin."

"No, I didn't. I just asked—"

"I *know* what you asked!"

Silence. They stared at one another across the table, the light of the bare bulb gleaming dully on wood that had once, in better days, been varnished, but which was now a bare, crazy roadmap of scratches, nicks, dents. Dimly, they heard a sound from the upstairs bedroom. It had been there all along, though—plosiving through the floor, throughout the entire house—since a half an hour after Magic had been put to bed.

"He's saying it, isn't he?" said John. It sounded almost like an accusation.

"That's what woke me up," said Alice.

"That's what woke me up, too." He rose, wavering with fatigue, wavering with impotence, wavering with a poverty that had lasted now for three years and showed no sign of doing anything but deepening. But his eyes were on the ceiling, as though he were staring through the flaking paint and falling plaster and holding in his eyes the image of his grandson. "It's like one of those damned Chinese water tortures. Doesn't he ever say anything else?"

"He—"

"For crissake, he's seven years old! He ought to be saying something besides *pow-er, pow-er, pow-er* and pretending to shoot everybody and everything. He's got to start school this fall! What's he going to do in school with his *pow-er, pow-er, pow-er*? They'll think he's crazy!"

Alice was listless. She did not respond to his words. "Marcy said he was doing it up there, too."

"Yeah," he said, "and that Gavin bitch probably gave him his own gun."

Alice was silent.

"I wouldn't be a bit surprised if she did. She can give him anything, can't she? She's got all the money in the whole town in that bank her husband owned, doesn't she? If she wants our grandson, she can just buy him, can't she?"

John's voice rose, high-pitched and righteous, its edge honed by the loss of his daughter, sharpened by the knowledge that, even in his own estimation, the claims of Mrs. Gavin upon Magic were, in many ways, justified, stemming as they did not so much from money (though money was indeed involved: it was money that gave Mrs. Gavin a big house with extra bedrooms and a standing in the town sufficient to shield an unwed mother from at least *open* societal disapproval) but from her unabashed—even eager—willingness to support not only Greta during her pregnancy but, afterwards, Greta and Magic both, filling the role first of doting grandmother and then, after Greta's death, moving quickly to usurp, in addition, the very title of *mother*, catching it even as it fell from Greta's lifeless, black-and-blue hands.

*"Can't she?"* He thumped his fist on the table. "We're poor, and she's rich. What boy in his right mind—?"

"She has money," Alice admitted.

"—wouldn't want to stay with her? What boy wouldn't want a gun of his own?"

"I don't think she gave him a gun. She's not the sort."

"Well, what sort is she, then?"

She was used to his outbursts, and though she might take hold of her bathrobe and draw the garment tighter about her thin shoulders, she was not speechless, for it was the monotony of these nights that gripped her more than the arguments and vestigial discussions that occurred in the course of them.

"Shhh . . . you'll wake him."

"He ain't awake *now*?"

"No. He says it in his sleep."

"I—"

"Would you rather have him say it while he's awake?"

"Dammit, he *says* it when he's awake! He says it when he's eating, when he's playing . . . he says it all the time!"

It was true. Alice lapsed back into silence.

"We got to get him away from here."

Alice only looked at him.

But John's eyes were on the ceiling again. "We got to. We *got* to!"

Alice shook her head. "She'd find us just like she found out where Magic was up north—"

"And her sending him all that trash while he was up there. Marcy's boys probably thought it was Christmas for everybody but them, and—"

"—and just like she found out when he was coming back—"

"—prob'ly pestered Marcy and Don half to death with wanting the same things."

"—so she could meet him at the station."

"Bribing him! That's what she's—"

"Shhh."

Silence. Silence . . . and that sound: a soft, plosive conso-
nant, repeating. And repeating.

"That's what she's doing."

"He doesn't seem to care for her," she offered.

"He doesn't seem to care for *us*."

Silence again.

Finally: "So she'd know, and she'd track us down," said Alice. "And then she'd probably bring in her lawyers."

"To take our grandson away from us. *Our* grandson." Still
standing, he leaned across the table, leaned over the form of his
wife, who sat plucking ineffectually at the edges of her robe.
*"Ours!"*

"She's got a claim," she reminded him.

Again he turned accusing. "So, you want to just hand him
over? So he can be hers? So he can grow up to be like that goon
who's always hanging around in front of M'Creed's with Lindy
Buck?"

"I didn't say that."

"Yes, you did."

"No, I didn't."

And still, above them, drifting down, that sound.

"I want to fight her," he said. His hands were gripping the
edge of the table. "I want to fight her like a man. I want to have
it out with her. I want to get a good lawyer, like that fellow over
in Jefferson who tied those Wyott's Crossing devils into knots.
Someone like *him*. Then I'd show her a thing or two."

Alice fell silent again.

"Trying to take our grandson away from us. Bribing him. She
probably tells him to call her *mamma* when he's over there. Got
a big house, and a room all to himself, and everything a boy could
want. And those . . . those *kids* she keeps over there. You ever
seen the way that boy of hers . . . what's his name . . . ?"

"Benny."

"Yeah. Benny. You ever seen the way he looks at you?"

Alice bent her head, staring at the table. Yes, she had seen.
She had seen more often than John could imagine. "You'd need
money to fight her," she said at last. "We don't have any money."

John flinched at the reminder. "Shutup!"

Silence again. Off in the distance, though—in the far dis-

tance: outside, somewhere across a range of hills, perhaps two—
something stirred. More a feeling than a sound, it swept across
the countryside, across Lee's Corners, across the house, rattling
the panes of glass in the windows before it rushed on.

John looked up, went to the window, shoved aside the muslin
curtains. "What's that?"

Dulled by the hour, dulled by life, Alice did not look up.
"Thunder, maybe."

"Can't be thunder. The sky's clear."

Alice shrugged. Less than two hours, and she would have to
wash the grease out of her hair.


Deputy Otis York was anxious to get home. For one thing, he
was tired (it was, after all, getting considerably on toward
dawn), for another, the piece of skullduggery in which he had
participated that night was not at all to his taste, and he wanted
to put it behind him as quickly as he could.

And so, rather than returning the same way he had gone—via
unobtrusive and circuitous back roads and indirect byways that
had added at least an hour to his outbound travel time—he took
as direct a route as possible across the moonlit darkness of Oktibushubee County, leaving the paved highways only when experience told him that a dirt thoroughfare would shorten his trip,
crossing hills, swooping through valleys, rattling along deep-
rutted passages whose existence only he, the marshal, the sheriff, and inhabitants within a radius of one mile knew of, even
cutting directly across Beat Two . . . which was probably safe,
since if the Frammis boys were not still unloading buckshot
into the front of the jail (which was quite possible), they were
probably residing *in* that jail (which was even more possible) or
drinking themselves into a stupor in some cove in the hills (in
which case they were Sheriff Hayes's problem).

So, very much ill at ease with the bad business behind him
and looking forward to a few hours of sleep and (maybe) a little
tumble with his wife before he had to be back at the office, he
drove on, not thinking of anything in particular until, as he
skirted the marshy border of a hollow so shrouded in mist that it
looked like a soup plate full of clouds, the sky suddenly lit up
from one horizon to the other, the soup plate turned into a

foamy geyser, and a tremendous *BOOM* rushed over the land like a downhill freight train that had lost its brakes, sending frightened birds blundering into the air, deafening Otis for the better part of a minute, and dazzling his eyes long enough that he nearly sent his car straight into a patch of quicksand.

Greta knew (and perhaps she had always known, intuiting with a woman's instinctive surety, intuiting without any consciousness of intuiting because such consciousness is, by society's tacit agreement, buried deep . . . for the simple reason that human beings could no longer continue to coexist in any orderly fashion were it not) that Mrs. Gavin's childlessness was not natural, that it was, in fact, by design rather than by chance, for the unspoken confidences that had passed between the old woman and the young one in the soda shop on that last day of July had not been in one direction only. No, Mrs. Gavin had—intuitively—seen Greta's situation and had, by her own experience, offered a remedy; but Greta had—intuitively—seen Mrs. Gavin's situation, too, and the knowledge of what the childless matron had done had bubbled up into consciousness, never to be buried again.

It was simple, really: these herbs, boiled in this way, and drunk in this amount, and that was it. Shame could be hidden then, or, as Greta (intuiting again without being aware of intuiting) knew was the case with Mrs. Gavin, the inconvenience and trouble of children could be avoided . . . as could the proprietary claim upon a woman who has had children by the man who got them on her (impregnation forever reassigning the status of her flesh from autonomous and independent to that of personal incubator). Mr. Gavin had, before his death, been the banker of the town—from a financial point of view he had, indeed, *been* the town—and Mrs. Gavin had, apparently, determined from the beginning that there would be at least *one* thing in Lee's Corners that he could not call his, even if she had to make that thing her own body.

Why she had come to that decision after marrying him (or why she had married him after coming to that decision) puzzled Greta, but it puzzled her even more when, Mrs. Gavin having turned, in effect, so completely around in her attitude toward children that she accepted not only a girl of eighteen (technically a child, though the swollen belly of that child doubtless provided some argument against that categorization) into her house, she subsequently turned even farther around and accepted, with considerable enthusiasm, in fact, the infant offspring of that girl . . . along with all the concomitant feedings, diaper changes, squalling, and general carryings-on that went with the presence of a baby.

*Maybe it's because he's not hers,* Greta thought. *Maybe it's different when you can play with it and then give it back. He's not hers, and she didn't have to carry him, and she didn't give her husband the satisfaction of a baby of his own. Maybe that's it.*

And those were her thoughts for some time. But as the weeks after the birth stretched into months, she started to sense something else, something that was again, at least at first, an intuition that was denied access to consciousness (in this case not for societal preservation but for individual survival) save as a general sense of unease. She did notice, though, that Mrs. Gavin became more and more in the habit of taking Magic off with her when she went visiting or shopping or driving, sometimes keeping him for so long that Greta had to suffer through painfully swollen breasts for several hours before Mrs. Gavin brought the baby home and—reluctantly, even grudgingly—returned him to his mother.

Mother. Perhaps that was it. Greta suddenly began to wonder who Magic's mother really was. To be sure, she had birthed the boy, but as she was eating and sleeping in Mrs. Gavin's house, taking Mrs. Gavin's money, living by Mrs. Gavin's goodwill, and being shielded from the opinions of the town by Mrs. Gavin's social standing, so she became aware of a kind of subtle pressure, one that was slowly inching her toward the status of a nonentity, a shadowy figure who, though having provided the generative organ that had made Magic, was now no more and no more thought-of than that organ.

Greta had the run of the house, money, and protection, but it began to dawn on her that she did not have Magic, that, somehow, the ownership of the boy—birth ownership, mother ownership— had been transferred to Mrs. Gavin. She noticed the birthstone ring that the older woman now wore—amethyst: Magic's birth-stone—and when Mrs. Gavin appeared wearing a gold necklace that said *World's Best Mother,* Greta became, in spite of her best efforts, overtly distraught enough that the older woman actually refrained from wearing the article for some weeks . . . though she gradually insinuated it back into her day-to-day wardrobe.

And it grew worse. Greta found herself dreading the day when Magic would be weaned, when he would begin drinking from a child's cup and making his first forays into solid food, for then the last link with her physical being would be broken: freed from the need to return Magic to her, Mrs. Gavin could arm herself with bottles and jars of food and take him away for as long as she wanted to, leaving Greta alone . . . and forgotten.

"You're mine," she said to Magic as she put him to bed one night. "I'm your momma. You know that, don't you? *I'm* your momma? Magic? You *know,* don't you?"

Magic just gurgled, and, extending the index finger of his chubby right hand, jabbed it at her. He was smiling.


Noon at the soda shop.

Willie McCoy had been serving up midday dishes of vanilla ice cream to Mr. Dark for several years, and the black man's habits were so precise that the dish was already waiting for him when he came through the door. As usual, he was wearing a trim, gray suit, and his shoes were polished so brightly that they reflected the big plate-glass windows—reversed and in miniature—with exquisite perfection.

"The usual, Mr. Dark?"

"Always the usual, Willie," said Mr. Dark. "My word, if I ever ate something other than vanilla ice cream, what would become of us all?"

His smile was almost fatherly, and Willie was reminded of what he had said to his friend the day before. But he realized that he had been wrong. Mr. Dark ought *not* to have been white. Not at all. He was—as perfectly as his shoes were perfectly shiny—black, and that was very much a perfect thing.

"Here's your ice cream, Mr. Dark."

"Thank you, Willie," said Mr. Dark, and he reached inside his coat and extracted his wallet.

The action reminded Willie of that five-dollar tip. It had been a magnificent tip, quite excessive by any standards, and now it was all but embarrassing to him. Perhaps Mr. Dark had made a mistake?

"Uh . . . Mr. Dark . . ." he ventured, honesty getting the better of him. "About . . . uh . . . about . . ."

Mr. Dark handed him a bill, took his change. "I always say, Willie, that if a man finds that heaven's gold has gone and fallen in his pocket, then he should thank heaven and not ask why." And he gave Willie a wink and handed him another tip.

Willie took it but did not look at it. He could tell by the feel that it was considerably less than five dollars, but then Mr. Dark's tips were always changing. Willie would not have been overly surprised had Mr. Dark, one fine day, offered him nothing more than a penny . . . or a live chicken . . . or even an automobile. That was exactly, he realized, what Mr. Dark was like. And, like the shine of his shoes or the color of his skin, that was perfect, too.

And Mr. Dark was still smiling at him.

"Did you hear about the explosion last night?" said Willie in the manner of a young man who has discovered that his thoughts have betrayed him into philosophy (bad) or sensitivity (worse).

Mr. Dark picked up the dish of ice cream. "The explosion?"

"Earl Hogback's still blew up. Earl blew up, too."

"Really?" Mr. Dark looked grieved and thoughtful both. "I think I might know Earl Hogback. Is he the one who lives in that bottom out in Beat Two?"

"That's the one. 'Cept it's *was* and *lived* now. Sheriff Hayes said he musta fallen asleep while doing something and left a valve or something closed. We heard the explosion all the way here in town."

"Bless my soul," said Mr. Dark in his quiet way. "That's really something. Earl Hogback, you say. How awful."

Willie, now distanced from any potential accusations regarding philosophy or sensitivity, warmed to his subject. "There was hardly anything left of Earl. I mean, when the still went up, it jest took him with it. Sheriff Hayes said there were pieces of Earl hangin' off the bushes."

Mr. Dark, his ice cream starting to melt in his dish, shook his head. "Terrible. Terrible. Earl could have been someone, but instead he kept brewing up that brain damage he called whiskey. I'm sure everyone told him it would be the death of him, but I'm just as sure no one expected it would end like that."

"It was really something, though."

Mr. Dark nodded somberly. "I'm sure it was. Well, may the good Lord have mercy on his soul, Willie, and may we all hope for that same mercy."

"Yessir."

And Mr. Dark turned for the door. It was a sunny day, and he always ate his vanilla ice cream outside when it was sunny. At the door, though, he was nearly run into—run *over* maybe—by a big man in blue coveralls who was just then coming in.

"I beg your pardon, sir," said Mr. Dark, bowing, smiling, and moving out of the way.

The big man—a stranger in Lee's Corners—only glanced at the colored field hand as though wondering why he had not moved out of the way faster, and Willie noticed that a telephone company truck was parked at the curb in front of the soda shop.

The big man strode up to the counter, leaving Mr. Dark to contend with the heavy, plate-glass door that was now swinging closed right in his face.

"Gimme a Coke with lots of ice, boy," said the big man, "and you got any idea where a place called Montague Mansion is?"

Willie—who did not in the least like to be called *boy*—filled a glass with as little ice as he could call *lots* with a straight face. "Montague Mansion? Never heard of the place." In fact, he had not. But even if he had, he doubted that he would have told the big man about it.

"Well, I just drove all the way over from Magdalene—"

"Figures," Willie muttered to himself. He pulled one handle for syrup and then another for soda and presented the big man with his drink.

"—and I'm supposed to put a telephone line in up there. But nobody can tell me where the godforsaken place is."

Mr. Dark was still standing at the door, ice-cream dish in hand. "I beg your pardon," he said.

"And so how am I supposed to put in a godforsaken telephone line if they don't give me any godforsaken directions?"

The big man took up the glass, emptied it with two swallows, and belched loudly.

"Ah be axin' yo to pardon me, sah," said Mr. Dark.

The big man turned around and examined him. "You talkin' to me, boy?"

"Dat's what Ah be doin', yes indeedy," said the Negro, shuffling his heavy brogans on the checkerboard floor. "Montague Mansion's done be aut in da hills outside o' town. Ib'n yo take Highway 15 east, dere's a little dirt rhad jest past Quincy's. Den yo' can go rhait up dere."

The big man stared at Mr. Dark. Then: "Much obliged."

Mr. Dark bobbed his head, smiling and backing up through the door. "Yo' berry welcome, sah."

The driver was still staring at him as, outside, he sat down at one of the sidewalk tables and began to spoon up his ice cream in small, precise mouthfuls, leaning far forward, as though his filthy canvas overalls and threadbare shirt needed shielding from even the most minuscule stray drops of the dessert.

The big man finally swung back to Willie. "Is that right? I never trusted his kind."

Willie found himself bristling. "I've never known Mr. Dark to steer anybody wrong."

"*Mr.* Dark?" The driver glanced back at the broken-down sharecropper. "Yeah. Sure. Whatever you say." He flipped a dime onto the counter. "Well, thanks for the Coke, kid."

And without looking again at Willie—*or* at Mr. Dark—he went outside, climbed into his truck, and drove away in the direction of Highway 15.

Willie put the dime in the cash register, picked up a rag, and gave the counter a surly wipe as his father came in from the back room.

"Mr. Dark get his treat?" said Mr. McCoy as he peered through the plate-glass windows.

"Yup."

Mr. McCoy nodded and hooked his thumbs through his suspenders. "I'll tell you, Willie, that's one man who knows how to wear a suit. Black or white, any man who can look that good is—"

He fell very silent very quickly. Willie looked up, followed his gaze.

"What you been doing in here all morning, Willie?" his father said sternly. "That floor is a fright."

"I mopped it when I opened up, Pop. Honest."

"Well, maybe you did," said his father, "but maybe you better mop it again. Look at that mud. Looks like an army's been tromping through here."

Willie looked at the infinitesimal flecks of mud that had not been there five minutes previously. "Bottom mud," he said without thinking.

"Bottom mud?" His father looked again. "Good Lord, you're right! Now, where'd *that* come from?"

"There was a fellow come in here from Magdalene," said Willie as he turned to get the mop and the bucket. "I'll bet he left it."

"Magdalene, eh?" said his father. "I wouldn't be at all surprised."

# Chapter 6

That was the way it started, and the telephone, arranged for by Alma even before she had left her life in the Northern city—left in order to return to something that approximated home . . . until such time as the need for any home would be forever beyond her—the telephone allowed it to continue.

Calls went out to the contractors of Lee's Corners and of Memphis (and even, occasionally, to those of Magdalene: Alma had no patience with prejudice or parochialism), and plumbers and electricians who had expected a summer of nothing more remarkable than an occasional clogged drain or blown fuse found themselves in great—and profitable—demand.

Suddenly, amid the clatter of hammers and the odor of cleaning solvents, Montague Mansion gave a shudder, shook off the dust and decay of twenty years, and began to live again. Layers of dirt and dust came up off of walnut and marble floors. Spiderwebs came down from corners. Old plaster came off walls and new plaster went on. Windows were removed, cleaned, painted, refitted with glass, and rehung. Wisteria and bougainvillea were forcibly evicted from their tyrannical possession of the outer walls and convinced (through the Draconian application of clippers) to remain in their allotted areas. Where stairs and railings had been taken away, new ones were fitted: the wide descents to the entry hall spread their wings once again, and no longer did Alma have to use the iron steps from the kitchen in order to reach the second floor.

The lights came on during the second week, and the plumbing was functional a few days later. The water from the tap ran red with rust for a good hour and a half once pressure came up, but it cleared shortly thereafter . . . and tasted just as bad as Alma remembered it had tasted sixty years before.

Crates and boxes of all sorts, brought by a steady stream of delivery trucks (and now it seemed to Willie McCoy that he was giving directions five and six times a day to men in coveralls whose first words upon entering the soda shop were, "Where the hell is Montague Mansion?" . . . after which, to his relief, they usually did order a soda or an ice-cream cone), arrived from as far away as New York City, divulging, upon being opened, chandeliers, lamps, sinks, toilets, and modern appliances. A specialist from St. Louis appeared one day and began the laborious process of piping arabesques and foliage ornaments onto blank, fresh ceilings and walls, clambering about on high scaffolding for six and seven hours a day with something that looked like a giant pastry bag in her hands.

"You're doing this for your children?" she asked Alma as they examined her day's production of plaster vines, flowers, and medallions.

"I have no children," said Alma.

"For your heirs, then?" said the specialist, whose enthusiasm, like her long black hair, tended to escape its tight confines at inopportune moments. "How wonderful! To restore a lovely old place like this when you yourself can't possibly expect to live in it for more than—"

"I have no heirs."

The specialist blinked at Alma through enormous round spectacles. "None?"

"None."

"Then . . . why . . . ?"

"That rose is particularly magnificent," said Alma, walking away . . . and glad that her knees were letting her do so with steadiness this afternoon. "Thank you. You're doing such a wonderful job. I'll see you tomorrow."

Hall by hall, floor by floor, wing by wing, the transformation and awakening spread as crews of men labored through the lengthening days, emptying rooms, cleaning them up, setting them to rights; and the very heart of the house—the kitchen— fairly blossomed under the care of Uncle Buddy's wife, Lucy

(Alma knew an opportunity when it arrived in a basket of chicken, gravy, biscuits, and collard greens): the stove emerged from beneath its coating of grime, and meals were both on time and extremely good.

But that was only the house. The grounds, alas, looked to be a considerably larger and longer project, for they had been so neglected that what soil had not been eroded away or baked into brick by years of rain and sun was so thoroughly overgrown by brambles and creepers that Alma wondered on more than one occasion whether she should make some inquiries as to whether the Army Corps of Engineers might like to give itself a real challenge.

With the state of the house growing increasingly secure and updated, she spent much time walking through what had once been gardens and landscaped plantings, poking into undergrowth and peering into ditches and rank fields as though she were trying to look into the past, into the lush lawns and bright flower beds of her childhood. Clad in khaki trousers and a canvas shirt and a pith helmet, her joints slowly loosening as they acclimated to the sodden air, she pushed through fields of waist-high grass that had once been close-cropped, edged aside mats of brier in a vain attempt to discover lost roses (they *had* to be in there somewhere!), and gingerly lowered herself into some of the shallower of the ravines cut by decades of heavy rains. Everywhere she found the same neglect and ruin, and, day by day, she grew more crestfallen. She would have to start from scratch, and while houses were easy to clean, paint, and renovate, such was not the case with gardens: landscaping needed time to look its best, to mature, to grow and be guided into shape, and she did not have—did not, really, *want* to have—that kind of time.

Enter Isaac with shovel and bucket.

He was a black man with a furrowed face that could have been just about any age, depending on what kind of weather or abuse one postulated, and Alma reflected that, if nothing else, his appearance at her back door amply demonstrated that the news of a Montague's return to the ancestral home had spread throughout the town . . .

"I hear you need a gardener, ma'am," he said. "I'm that."

"Are you from Lee's Corners?"

"I been around."

. . . or perhaps even farther than that.

"But where are you . . . ah . . . from?"

"I been around."

Perhaps, being a gardener, he considered himself a citizen of the world, free from anything so paltry or puerile as a specific birthplace or residence.

"You . . . ?"

"I been around. Ma'am."

And the *ma'am* was, she judged, more of a formal termination to the line of questioning than anything else, stuck on because he guessed that she expected it to be there rather than from any inclination or need on his own part.

Still: "Do you have . . . ah . . . references?"

He looked at her over a nose that was much too thin for a black man. Alma noticed then that his eyes were gray. "I been around."

"Around?" she said.

"Around. When you want me to start?"

"Do you drive?"

"Well as any man. You want that, too?"

"Upon occasion." Alma smiled, relieved that her last question had not met with yet another iteration of *I been around.* "I often don't feel like driving myself anymore."

He nodded: curt, precise, proud. "Suits me down to the ground, ma'am. You want to go anywhere, you give me fifteen minutes to wash my face and change my shirt, and I'll get you wherever you name and bring you back safe."

She tried once more. "Are you . . . living in town?"

The gray eyes did not change expression in the slightest. "I been around."

But she understood. "There is a back bedroom off the kitchen. It will be yours."

"Suits me down to the ground." He had left his tools just outside the back door, and now he looked as though he wanted them in his hands, wanted dirt before him, wanted a bare-root plant at his side. He looked full of appetite, but not for food or for sex or for any of the other such things that drive a man and shoulder one another aside in an effort to be first at the chance to cause his downfall. No: something else.

"What you pay?" he asked almost as an afterthought. And, again, almost as an afterthought: "Ma'am."

She named a figure. It was generous. For a moment, he looked at her suspiciously. And then he accepted.

Something else, indeed. Within a week, there was a broad swath of flowers blooming along the curve of the overgrown drive. It was his notice to the earth itself: *I'm here. Y'all is gonna grow, turn green, and make flowers. Understand?*

A few days later, Alma, too, had a figure named to her, and though her reaction partook in no way of suspicion, it was strongly expressive of incredulity.

"Surely there's been some mistake," she said.

The man from the bank shook his head. "Nope. It's true as it can be. But up until now, you understand, we didn't know where you were . . . or even if you were still alive."

He did not notice that Alma's eyes flickered. Alma, in fact, did not notice it herself.

"Far as we knew," the man, whose name was Snatcher, went on, "your cousin, Wilfred, was the last in the Montague line. But the terms he put in his trust weren't exactly the most clear that any of us had ever seen, so our board of directors in Chicago decided to hold the accounts and the real property for the statutory period. In case someone showed up to make a claim."

"And if no one had showed up?"

"Well . . . then, the state would have claimed it. That's what the statutes say." Snatcher looked up at the ceiling (clean, painted, decorated), at the walls (papered), and at the floor (gleaming). "I imagine they would have taken it over as one of those historical sites they're always going on about."

"I doubt it, given the condition it was in when I arrived," said Alma. "It wanted a wrecking ball in the worst way. But I'll keep that in mind for the future."

"You think your heirs would go along with that?"

Here was someone else asking about heirs . . . about continuance. And why not? What was the first thing one asked of any woman old enough to have breasts? *How many children do you have?* She had herself asked—and had *been* asked—the question a thousand times: standard procedure, taught in medical school. *The entirety of the female metabolic organism*—(Oh, he had been a pompous ass! And at an eight o'clock lecture no less!)—*is occupied with a physiological imperative toward the production of offspring.*

And Alma, recalling once again how she, gowned and gloved, had been driven to her first cotillion by her father . . . like a prize heifer taken to market . . . fixed him with her gaze. "I have no heirs."

And Snatcher looked just as puzzled as had the specialist from St. Louis. "Then you're doing all this for . . . for . . ." He fell silent, looking for a word.

"Whimsy?" offered Alma. "The hell of it?" She saw his eyes widen at the use of the unladylike word and was rather pleased with herself. "Not at all. I'm keeping myself comfortable. For the next few years, I intend to have a lovely house and lovely gardens, and perhaps I can find enough in them to keep me reasonably busy and reasonably entertained for that length of time."

Snatcher was nodding.

"And then I can die and be done with it."

Her open admission made him blink. "Ah . . . yes. Sholy."

She was tired. She had been tramping through the undergrowth like a young girl again, and her old bones were protesting. She wanted to have a cup of tea and lie down. "Is there anything else, Mr. Snatcher?"

He cleared his throat. "Well, actually, yes. I really ought to acquaint you a little with the extent of the Montague lands in this area. They've shrunk a little over the years—what hasn't!—but they're still out there, and you really ought to know what you've got."

He opened his briefcase, took out a sheaf of papers.

"If it's no trouble for you, ma'am."

Alma pressed her lips together, but: "No trouble at all, I assure you, Mr. Snatcher. I was just about to blowtorch the south forty . . . but it can wait a little longer."

He was opening the sheaf, but he froze. "Blow—"

"Blowtorch. I always like to lay waste to a bit of land before lunch. I find it . . . relaxing."

"Uh . . . yes. Sholy." He spread the papers on the table. "Just a . . . a very few minutes of your time, then, Miz Montague."

It was more than a few minutes, but it was really not very long. But as Alma examined the deeds, maps, and records that Snatcher displayed, she felt her incredulity returning stronger than ever. Beyond establishing a vague sort of trust to keep Montague properties from evaporating into the possession of the state, Cousin Wilfred had done nothing with either the considerable amounts of land or the considerable sums of money. Everything had sat idle since her father's death.

"We leased some of the acreage out to tenant farmers," Mr. Snatcher explained in response to her unspoken question. "It seemed like a good idea—no one was complaining about it, sholy, and it's kept the land workable."

"Yes, that's fine." Alma riffled through some statements. "I'm quite surprised and . . . and . . . well . . . elated at this."

Surprised, yes. Elated, no. The last part of her statement was another bald-faced lie. Before she had left the Northern city, she had carefully added up her savings and her investments, and she had planned out a series of expenditures that would completely restore the house and grounds while leaving her just enough to get comfortably through what she expected to be the rest of her life. She had allowed herself a little extra, too: she had no intention of being caught a few months short.

Of course, she reflected, if she were indeed caught short, there were certainly ways around *that*.

But all this money. And all this land. And both—and particularly the latter, considering the tenant farmers—firmly entwined with the lives of other people. Well, she reflected, she would be gone soon enough, then she would have no use or concern for money *or* for land, and whether a tenant had a Montague or a bank or a state government for a landlord, it would be all the same.

But the situation rankled her nonetheless. She had left the Northern city to escape from ties and demands and interactions and entanglements, from all the dreary business and interpersonal sludge that made up what was cynically called life until grief or boredom or both finally collapsed the whole structure into a rotting corpse. And yet here they were—ties, demands, interactions, and entanglements alike—following her. And . . . and, in fact, she herself had added to them! Voluntarily! She had hired Lucy, and now she had taken on Isaac, too. And Lucy had children and a husband, and Isaac . . .

"Miz Montague?"

. . . well, doubtless Isaac had someone. Somewhere. He had, after all, been around.

"Miz Montague?"

She realized that she had been staring off into space, the past—and the present—rising up and enveloping her. She cleared her throat, turned to Mr. Snatcher. "I'm fine, thank you," she said. "Just a bit overheated. I'm not used to the weather yet, I suppose, after that icebox where I used to live."

Lucy appeared from the kitchen, anticipating the need before Alma had even thought of it. "The iced tea is ready, Miz Alma."

"Thank you, Lucy. Could you bring it in, then, please?"

And if Mr. Snatcher was startled by Alma's *please,* he hid it very well.

Alma watched him drive away a little later, her feelings unsettled, mixed. Always entanglements. Always *more* entanglements. She should have known that they would be waiting for her here, just as they had been waiting for her in the Northern city. She had thought that the relative isolation of Montague Mansion would keep her safe from them, but she should have known about *that,* too. Simply by living—by continuing to live—she was subject to them. How much more, then, was she in their thrall by being a Montague, and by having come home?

Had she really thought to escape the town? Really? After driving Delphi M'Creed and his clerk half-crazy with contractors' requests for materials and supplies? After establishing a link with Lee's Corners by virtue of having a telephone, by sending Lucy to shop for groceries . . . by simply *being* within the communal knowledge of the townsfolk?

Had she really expected to be a Montague in Montague Mansion, and to be a *hermit*?

And now there was the bank, and now there was money and lands. Tenants. Rents.

She put her hands to her head and felt the fevered, protesting heat of her brow. She did not want it. She did not want any of it. And, in fact, she supposed that she could, after all, leave most of it to the bank. But they—the tenants—would know, nonetheless. She would have a name. For some, she might even have a face: a young face, a face from sixty years ago. Little Ammy Montague . . . come home after sixty years . . . living up in the big house.

The heat was suddenly oppressive. Or maybe it was not the heat after all. But she was turning back into the house when movement caught her eye and made her pause. A car was coming up the long drive to the house. A police car.

"Who?"

Oddly enough, it could have been said of Lindy Buck that he was enamored of flowers. Perhaps this was because of his work: laboring eight to ten hours a day (and sometimes more) behind the back end of a mule could not but make one somewhat protective of the results of that labor, and so Lindy, who farmed cotton, was, to say the least, interested in the well-being of the creamy white cotton flowers when they opened, for it was those flowers that would form the bolls, and those bolls that would pay his rent.

"That's right. Montague," said Snatcher. (He was standing beside the big black car that the bank had probably given him, that could not but remind Lindy over and over by its very presence that he himself had no car . . . had nothing, in fact, save a house he did not own and a mule and tools that were hardly worth owning in the first place.)

"Montague?"

And so perhaps Lindy could be forgiven for the rampant cross-fertilization that went on between his concerns about flowers and his near-constant concerns about women—white women—for as the cotton flowers rose and waved and dangled, opening their dewy, scented throats and inviting pollination, and as they were thereby vulnerable to intrusions of a more sinister kind—the long-nosed weevils insinuating themselves and their bastard young into the otherwise pristine crop, turning it rank with devoured seeds and mangled fibers and reducing it to blackened ruin—so did the pure, pale, pristine thighs of white women, dangling beneath their skirts, waving and chafing chubbily against one another with a fragrant moistness, exhibit a certain explicit vulnerability to the dark, erectile probosces of the opportunistic, Negroid violators who (in Lindy's mind) were all but intolerably exemplified by the vulgar presence and barely concealed genital displays of the pimp who had the audacity to eat ice cream every day at the white folks' soda shop.

"Alma Montague."

The mule farted loudly. Lindy glared at it and whapped it with his hat. "Shaddup."

But if such violators (of both species) were the general objects of Lindy's vitriolic fantasies and hatreds, so much more so were those white women who, assured (by his continuous and vigilant protection) of their innate purity, cast both purity and protection away and willingly yielded to the intrusion, allowing their creamy, nectared sanctity to be polluted with noxious (and unutterably fertile) secretions in exchange for the personal degradation of limitless orgasmic pleasure.

He glared at the man from the bank.

"Alma Montague?"

"She's the—"

The mule farted again.

"I know who she is. She's that dried-up, pasty-faced nigger lover who came down from up north and is doin' all that carryin' on up on the hill." Inspired not only by his standard imaginings but by his instinctive dislike of outsiders, Lindy warmed rapidly to his subject. "First thing she did was spend the night with that cab driver. Then she got his wife up there, too. Now she's got some white nigger who calls hisself a gardener. Don't you be denyin' it, Snatcher. Everyone knows all 'bout it. Why, I'll tell you, I can outgarden anyone like that with one hand behind my back, but I'll bet she's right satisfied with *his* gardenin', 'cause it ain't any furrows in the *ground* that he's plowin' up, I'll tell you that for a fact. Why, I bet she lets him—"

Mr. Snatcher was already backing up toward his car. "Well, that's all between you and her," he said quickly. "I've got no opinion on that at all. I just came to tell you that you're farming her land."

"*Her* land?" Lindy was stunned. "*Her* land? This here's the *bank's* land! Always has been, always will be!"

"Held in trust for the Montague estate," said Mr. Snatcher, who was climbing behind the wheel. "Has been from the beginning. We'll take care of the details for as long as she wants us to, sholy, but that's still her land you're farming."

"Montague land?" Lindy's voice rose to a yelp. "A nigger lover and a shameless hussy of a fornicator? She's got a share in my life? She's poking her nigger-lovin' hands into my livelihood? That's . . . that's . . . that's an abomination! That's what it is! An abomination! Lord have mercy! Fornication! And she's got her fingers in my land!"

Mr. Snatcher slammed the door as he started the engine and engaged the gearshift. With a brief grinding and then a loud roar, the black car began to move off down the road, and if he tried very hard, Snatcher could almost ignore the voice that was rising behind him, following his car and the cloud of dust that it trailed:

"Abomination and fornication! Bitchery! A Jezebel! That's what she is! A nigger-lovin' Jezebel!"

She had been six years old when God had called her.

Most people, she thought later on, would not have recognized it as a call; but then, most people were prideful and stiff-necked, and would expect a call to come in a flash of light, or with some kind of vision. But such things were for the apostles and the prophets. For little, humble people like herself, the call from God would necessarily be equally humble, a figurative tap on the shoulder that would go unnoticed by many. But Anger noticed, even when she was six.

"Yo' ain't et your corn bread, girl," her mother had said.

"No, Ma, I ain't."

Her mother had been a stern woman, a churchgoing woman for whom the tenets of her Baptist faith included giving the white folk what they obviously wanted, giving to God what was rightfully His, and feeding her children. If love were involved in the situation, it was obviously classified as optional: God's love would have to do for all.

"Yo' sassin' me, girl?"

"No, Ma. I was jus' 'bout to eat it."

"Well, get to it, then. I want to wash up, and I ain't got all day. And yo' don't, either. Yo' got to help me weed the vegeble patch."

"Yes, Ma." And little Anger, six years old and just then called by God, had stuffed her face with the molasses-sweetened corn bread with a relish that would have made her mother smile— had her mother ever smiled—though in truth she was so full of that calling that she felt there was hardly room inside of her for anything, least of all a piece of corn bread only slightly smaller than the state of Iowa.

It was nothing she could talk about at first, of course. Regardless of calls by God, she had to be a little girl for the time being, else she could not fulfill that call. (And besides, the Bible was very clear about things like boasting, and boasting was what Anger would herself have considered any sort of mention or admission.) And so, though her mother probably noticed that her daughter grew more solemn from that day forth, and her pastor probably noticed that Anger did not participate quite so wholeheartedly in the hymn singing that filled the little church on Sunday mornings, neither of them were aware of much of a change in the girl's outward demeanor. And Anger herself would have said (had she been willing to say . . . which she was not) that her solemnity and reticence were because she was "saving it up" for later.

What "it" was, she did not know, and in any case "later" did not come until she was eighteen and about to be married to a fine man from the church. Clad in the muslin wedding dress that her mother had, without a trace of a smile, stitched together from scratch, she was on the way to her wedding, was, in fact, actually stepping from the hired surrey to the bare patch of dirt in front of the church when "it" revealed itself, and when "later" became "now" . . . and she knew it without a doubt, just as she had known without a doubt that she had been called twelve years before.

And she turned from the church and from her wedding and from the fine man, and she crossed the street to a little house that was, really, hardly more than a shack with so many weeds growing in the yard that it was hard to tell where the vegetables were, and, without knocking and without asking any more than a thunderstorm or a tornado or a hurricane knocks or asks, she pushed in through the front door that dangled cockeyed from one hinge, pushed past the family members who were gathered around the back bedroom, and, sitting down on the bed, took the dying man in her arms and began to sing.

And, oh, what songs came out of her, welling up as though from some bright, secret place within her soul that human beings and all their vanities and dust could never touch, that place that God had put into her when he had called her! Sometimes low and crooning, sometimes with a cold wail that reached up to rend the sky open so that a rising soul might find its way to the heavenly realm unimpeded, Anger Modestie sang; and it was indeed as though she were a thunderstorm or a tornado or a hurricane, a force so great that mortal men and women instinctively knew better than to stick their noses into its business, for those who had come to the bedside of the dying man fell back and let her alone as she, holding him in her arms, sang on and on until, with the slightest of trembles, his spirit rose up and she placed him straight into the arms of the Lord Himself.

That had been the first time. Since then—husbandless, childless—she had wandered back roads and country ways, stopping where she was needed . . . where she *knew* she was needed. God saw to it that she knew, and God saw to it, too, that she had what she herself needed until the time came when she was called to a bedside to birth a soul into Jesus.

She had come to Lee's Corners ten years ago, and she had often looked at the old, abandoned mansion on the hillside above the town. She had spent a rainy night or two in its shelter, but more often she had watched it from afar as it had decayed, seeing in its gradual dissolution a visible parable about mortal life and vanity that end but in death.

And when the old woman came from the North and took possession of the mansion and made it shine gloriously with paint and electric light, Anger Modestie saw only a furtherance of the parable: the mansion, like the mortal body, reborn into a second, resplendent life beyond death.

But there was more there. More. Anger could not say exactly why (for the ways of God were mysterious, as they always were, and receiving His call at the age of six and then not saying

anything about it or acting upon it for twelve years had taught
her a good deal about patience and acceptance of those ways),
but she found that she was looking up at that mansion—or at
least, the place that she reckoned the mansion would be if she
could see it through the summery trees and the folds of the
hills—an awful lot these days.

# Chapter 7

Alma Montague was not at all what MacDonnell had expected. But, then again, he had driven up to the mansion not knowing exactly *what* to expect. He decided, though, that, had he actually expected something in particular, Alma Montague would certainly not have been it. Far from being, as his father had once described her, the shrewish bluestocking who had stormed away from her wealthy but restrictive family, the last Montague was a small, prim-but-kindly-looking woman who appeared to be in her seventies (*late* seventies, MacDonnell considered, mentally adding up dates and years), and who, if she dressed in a man's shirt and trousers, appeared to do so not because she was attempting to prove anything about equality or some such rubbish, but because she had things to do that required shirts and trousers.

But along with MacDonnell's arithmetical exercises with dates and years came the recollection that Alma Montague had been a doctor—one of some prominence—before she had returned to the comparative obscurity of her hometown, and it occurred to him that she had doubtless seen things that he himself might view with distinct unease . . . though the way Greta Harlow had looked there on the floor in Mildred Riddup's boarding-house might have given even a seasoned lawman from the north side of Chicago a certain queasiness. Why, Otis, who had been first at the scene, had looked like a—

Why was he thinking about Otis? Or about Greta, for that matter?

MacDonnell passed a hand over his mustache but dropped it

to his side quickly enough. "This ain't police business, Miz Montague," he said affably. "This ain't even official. I just come to welcome you back to Lee's Corners and to see if you need anything. You've been up here in this big house all alone for a couple months now, and . . . well . . . I guess you can say we're all a little curious down below there."

He smiled, but even *he* felt the expression stop just north of his mustache. To his relief, though, Alma (who, he was absolutely sure, saw the smile stop right where it did) was willing to play along with the charade, and with a bright, cordial smile, she swung the door wide (she answered her own doors, he noticed) and invited him in directly.

If the exterior of the house—cleaned and repaired and looking very much like something out of a movie—had impressed him (and it had), the interior went well beyond that, and despite himself, MacDonnell was tipped forcibly from impressed into awestruck. Alma Montague, he realized (though he should never have forgotten, since his father had told him all about the Montagues' money as well as about some of their excesses), was a wealthy woman: the interior had been, if anything, even more carefully refurbished than the exterior, and it exhibited a masterful taste that was obviously the product of age and breeding both.

And yet Alma Montague was as affable as MacDonnell himself was attempting to be, giving the marshal no impression at all—as was most assuredly not the case with the other moneyed house within the municipal boundaries—that he had entered sacred precincts in which he was merely tolerated. No: Alma was open and frank, seemed genuinely pleased to see him, and was obviously inclined to take MacDonnell's reason for being there—a casual, informal, friendly visit—at face value.

Which MacDonnell himself could not.

Exactly why he could not was puzzling him, though, and it annoyed him that he did not know his own reasons for making this visit. Still, he was used to discovering the illicit motivations and secrets of those who wished to keep them hidden, and he had invariably found that, given time, such things revealed themselves despite even the best and most frantic efforts to conceal them. MacDonnell resolved, then, to allow himself the same opportunity to blunder into a confession, and so he accepted Alma's subsequent offers of iced tea, lunch, and a tour of the house and the grounds with the same perfect equanimity as he sensed Alma made them in the first place.

"Well," Alma was saying as she led him along the walk that paralleled the side of the house, "I'm afraid that the gardens aren't much of a match for the house at all. They were neglected for so long." She sighed, surveying the unruly growth. "Do you have any idea what happened, Marshal?"

The question was forthright, honest. MacDonnell shrugged. "My daddy told me a few things before he died, and I saw some of them myself. Your grandfather passed on—" He looked at her. "Have you been out to the graves?"

Alma started, then visibly blushed. "Ah . . . no, Marshal. I've been remiss, haven't I?"

He tried hard not to think anything of the omission. "Well, they're out in the town cemetery. On the west side near the creek. I'll show you where they are, if you want. Just give the word, and you'll have yourself an official police escort." He winked, but, to his dismay, felt his eyes just as cold as ever.

"Thank you," she said. "I'd be greatly obliged."

MacDonnell found himself charmed by a charming woman. He hardly minded that he did not know his reasons for being here this afternoon. "Well, your grandfather passed on, and your father just kind of . . . well, he let the place go a bit."

"That was after the war?"

"Yes. After that. I 'magine he was done in a bit by his sons dying."

Alma was looking out across the briers and tall grass. "And by a daughter deserting him."

MacDonnell said nothing. It was the first thing she had said that bordered in the slightest on the personal.

"Did Wilfred ever even *look* at the house?"

"Wilfred?"

"My cousin. He inherited the house from my father."

MacDonnell considered for a moment, striving pointedly to avoid considering questions of desertion and inheritance. "There was a fellow came down on the Memphis train about ten years ago. Didn't say anything to no one 'cept the cab driver he picked up at the station. Cabbie drove him out Highway 15—toward the mansion, that is—and then drove him back. The fellow got on a train that evening, headed back to Memphis."

"Did you see him?"

"Nope. Driver—that would have been Blackleg Pete, Dewart Trowley's boy, passed on about five years ago—said he was a tall, skinny one, with glasses and a funny hat."

Alma remembered Dewart Trowley. He had owned one of the last livery stables in the town. Another name from the past, another passing. Even his son was gone. She shook her head. "I suppose it could have been Wilfred."

MacDonnell nodded and discovered to his chagrin that his hands were in his pockets. He extracted them.

"But thanks to Isaac, the grounds are beginning to perk up," Alma said with a distinct change of subject.

*Perk up* would not have been MacDonnell's choice of phrase to describe the narrow paths that Alma's gardener had forced through the matted grass and vines, but he supposed that it was as good as any.

"Sometimes I think it's a lost cause, though."

MacDonnell felt a pang rise from (still) unknown origins. "I sho hope you ain't thinking of going back up north because of a few little thornbushes, Miz Montague."

"Not at all, Marshal. I've come home for good." She stopped, pulled off her pith helmet, gazed up at a sky that was almost too blue to be believed. "There's nothing for me up north anymore. Just ghosts."

She stared at the sky a little longer than MacDonnell expected.

"And it's nice to be at home in a place that's quiet."

"Oh," said MacDonnell, "we have our to-do's down here just like they do in the big cities."

And then, suddenly, he knew why he had come up to Montague Mansion. No, it was *not* just because he had wanted to be sociable. MacDonnell did not believe in just being sociable. He did not believe in *just* being anything. Since his father had laid down his badge and MacDonnell had picked it up (some jobs in Lee's Corners were as hereditary as the status of Venice's *gondolieri*), he had seen enough to be purged of every confidence in human nature save an unshakable belief in its depth. It was not even a matter of suspecting duplicity: he had gotten through that in the first three years, and had come to believe that if there was duplicity in the world, it was a duplicity that came from denying the depth, the hidden workings, and the unconscious motives that would eventually—given time, given patience—announce themselves . . . just as his own reasons for this visit had finally risen to the surface enough to be recognized.

He cleared his throat. He was not a subtle man . . . unless subtlety lay in a self-control so great that even the sight of a straight flush on a first deal would not produce the slightest physiological indication of its presence.

Alma Montague: wealthy to begin with, and even more wealthy now that Snatcher and the boys at the bank had dusted off the old records. Owned half the valley, perhaps. Did not have to worry about money. Did not have to worry about *anything*. And, as a by-product of all that, incorruptible and incorruptibly objective.

"There was that suicide a few years back, for instance," he said . . . affably. "Put the whole town in an uproar."

She stopped looking at the sky and looked at him. MacDonnell was acutely conscious of the old, faded eyes coming to rest on his face, and he suddenly wondered how much of his own brand of subtlety was possessed by Alma Montague.

"Are you talking about Greta Harlow?" she said.

Straight flush, ace high. It made no difference. "Well, now, I'll be doggoned," he said. "How on earth have you been hearing 'bout all the skeletons in our closet when you've been all taken up with rebuilding a house?"

A silence a fraction of a second longer than MacDonnell thought quite natural. But that was all right. He expected that. Anything else, and he would have branded Alma Montague a fool. A wealthy fool, to be sure, but a fool nonetheless. "Oh," she said, "Lucy has been letting me know about things. And, of course, there was that scene at the train station when I first arrived."

"Scene?"

"I believe it was Sophonsiba Gavin and Magic Harlow and Magic's grandparents." Alma was bending over a waist-high patch of brier that seemed bent on attaching itself not only to the side of the house but to her trousers as well. "Mrs. Gavin wants Magic."

Regardless of the cards, MacDonnell refused to count his money at the table. "A lot of folks see her point."

"Yes . . . I suppose so."

And there was a sense of detachment about Alma's words that gave MacDonnell hope.

"You heard the . . . details about Greta, then?"

Having succeeded in freeing her trousers, Alma straightened up. "About her baby, or about how she died?"

Honesty seemed the best policy. "About how she died."

"Yes. Lucy told me." Alma smiled. In the bright sunlight, the expression looked thin, sere, bleached. "Given her flair for the dramatic, she could easily find a place as a camp counselor on ghost-story night."

MacDonnell smiled back, partly at the image Alma conjured up, partly to mask the meaning of his next words. "You're a doctor, Miz Montague—"

"I *was* a doctor, Marshal. I've retired."

He could not read her tone, but: "Well, all right. But you *were* a doctor . . . and in a big city. You ever hear of anything like that? Someone beatin' themselves to death?"

"Are you asking for my professional opinion regarding Greta Harlow?"

He could read her face no more than he could her tone. "Well, I reckon so."

Above them rose the south wall of the house, and it bounced the sunlight straight down onto this section of derelict garden, turning it into an outdoor furnace. Alma lifted her head into the glare, looked up at the wall, the windows. The contrast between the order of the restored house and the chaotic insanity of the overgrown garden could not have been better exemplified, MacDonnell thought . . . but where did Alma Montague fit in? A bridge between them? Or a lit match in a fireworks factory?

She finally shrugged. "I never saw anything like it up north," she said. "But that doesn't mean that it isn't possible. I heard once about some Russian prisoner who was going to be tried for something. He beat his own brains out on the floor of his cell."

"So you're saying . . . ?"

"It could be done," said Alma. "One would have to be insane to do it, but one would have to be insane to contemplate suicide in the—"

She stopped, stared. Then, finally:

"One would have to be insane to do it," she said with an effort . . . as though she had forced herself to continue her thought. "And . . . and it would be very difficult to strike a critical blow, so the damage would have to be cumulative. In other words, death would be . . ." She stared again. At something that was not there. ". . . slow and agonizing."

MacDonnell nodded, but his gesture indicated more surety of understanding than, given Alma's behavior, he actually felt.

"In other words," she said, "insane."

MacDonnell nodded again, wondering whether he should raise or call.

But Alma looked directly at him. "You're suspecting foul play?"

MacDonnell opened his mouth without knowing exactly what he was going to say. It was a fatal lack of foresight, but Alma saved him.

"You could always exhume the body," she said. "Forensic medicine can do some fairly amazing things."

Now MacDonnell smiled in spite of himself. That forensic medicine could do some fairly amazing things, he would grant willingly. But he would also grant that money could do even more than that. "I'm afraid there ain't no body to exhume, Miz Montague. Greta Harlow was cremated."

"I see. Orders of her family?"

"Orders of Sophonsiba Gavin."

Alma blinked. "But she wasn't related to Greta!"

MacDonnell turned half away so as not to confront her with the frost that he was feeling more keenly than ever. "That's 'bout the size of it," he said. "Not related at all. Not related to Magic, neither." He shrugged, looked up at the gleaming, restored house. "It sure looks like if you got a problem in this sorry old world, you just throw some money at it, and things get done."

Alma followed his gaze. "Yes," she said. "Yes. I imagine so.

Fortunately or unfortunately, though, some things aren't particularly responsive to money."

"Some things?" MacDonnell avoided looking at her.

Alma gestured. "Briers and brambles don't give a hoot about
money."

MacDonnell nodded. He was entirely unsure as to whether
Alma had gotten his point or not.

"Could we . . ." Alma looked at herself, shrugged. "Could we
look at those graves this afternoon, Marshal?"

He touched the brim of his hat. "My pleasure, Miz Montague."

The road to the cemetery took them through the middle of
town, and as though doing his part to bring Alma up-to-date on
news of her old home, MacDonnell pointed out farms and
buildings and told stories about them—about how, in that field,
Whitey Nilbick had blown himself up with a stick of dynamite,
or how a fellow had come down from Little Rock and had
opened a second movie theater last summer . . . only to be run
out of town once everyone had found out what kind of movies
he had intended to show, or how, at this very spot, seven years
ago, Jimmy White had made his last reckless turn out onto the
highway (and MacDonnell was, at that moment, making the
same turn . . . though a bit more carefully than had Jimmy
White) and had found himself facing the business end of a
semitrailer.

Up until then, Alma had been content to be silent, looking
without comment at the objects of MacDonnell's stories, examining the people they passed on their way through the center of
town. She wondered at the faces she saw, at the thought of what
childhood friend or acquaintance might have sired or borne
them; but the mention of Jimmy White brought her thoughts
back to MacDonnell's words.

"White," she said. "I know that name."

"His father was Vinty White."

"Vinty. Yes, I remember Vinty. We all used to call him Squirt."

MacDonnell laughed. "Oh, mercy! The industrial power of
Oktibushubee County: Squirt White!"

"He always talked about putting a mill in the forest. Did he
ever do that?"

"Couldn't, Miz Montague. Quicksand's thick as squirrels out there. You could put a mill down one day and by morning there wouldn't be a trace of it."

"And how is Vinty?"

"We haven't seen much of him since Jimmy died." MacDonnell accelerated onto the highway. "Kind of went into seclusion. It was like all the air was let out of him when he lost his son. His only . . ." The marshal paused, then shook his head. "Well, his only *recognized* child." He cleared his throat and went on. "Vinty White put a lot of belief into that boy. It was like he saw him as kind of a . . . younger version of himself." He glanced at Alma. "Though, to be perfectly frank, Miz Montague, there's an awful lot of folk in Oktibushubee County look a little more than middlin' like Vinty White."

It was not news to Alma. "He was that way when I knew him," she said.

MacDonnell's eyebrows went up. "He was, eh?"

Alma gave him a cold glance. "I'll have you know, Marshal, that Vinty White had two broken ribs."

"He did?"

"Yes. He did. I put them there."

"Hmmmm." MacDonnell was suddenly very intent on his driving.

Alma went back to the landscape. Now *there* was a memory she would be glad to leave. Though doubt had been growing within her ever since she had seen the look on her father's face as he had driven her to the cotillion—something a little less than proprietary, but something considerably more than fatherly— the dance had, to outward appearances, been picture-perfect, something to lay away and dream on like ribbons or pressed flowers. But then Vinty White, as though personifying the existence and destiny that, she had realized only that night (little gullible fool!), had been planned out for her from her first breath, had grabbed her in the upstairs hallway, wrestled with her, and, as though intent upon examining in detail the goods that had been brought to market, actually gotten as far as putting his fingers into—

She shuddered and blinked herself back to old age. Just one more memory—and, to be sure, not the worst—that she would be done with soon enough. The house and the grounds would keep her occupied for a while (she supposed there were some advantages to the time it would take to restore the gardens), and then . . . nothing and no one. Blessed oblivion, loving annihilation.

The automobile passed through the cemetery gates and onto quiet roads. Headstones all around, family plots and monuments shaded by trees.

"The Montague plot is up there on the—"

"I remember," said Alma.

The car stopped. Alma got out. There were stones for each family member, and one central, granite obelisk that bore the single name: MONTAGUE.

Some of the stones she remembered, others she did not. She found her father and her mother side by side: a condition in which she could not recall them having occupied in life. She found her brothers in graves like twin beds: womanless, adolescent, lovely.

And over on the Hawkins side of the plot were her mother's mother and father, their relationship the exact converse of her parents', for where John and Harriet Montague had gone through their lives like two tangential circles, Walter and Sinta Hawkins had been separated early on by the latter's death, and the former had dedicated his life to bridging the gap between their conditions. Hence her grandfather's library, his constant correspondence, the comings and goings of mediums throughout the long summers, the séances and the knocks and raps and cacophony of musical instruments played by unseen hands.

Alma bent, touched the single stone that covered them both. "Did you find her, Grandfather?" she whispered. "Was she waiting? I hope so . . . for your sake."

But she bent her head. If he had found her, then what did that say about her own hopes? Would she, then, find new entanglements, meet new people, become involved in new interactions, new situations . . . be forced to learn all the little social niceties that applied to the dead?

Her eyes ached. Perhaps she could just . . . could just . . . slip out the back way when no one was looking, taking French leave . . . into nothingness.

When she wiped her eyes, though, she found herself looking at her grandfather's half of the stone. There was an open book carved deeply there, and on the pages the words *Blithe Spirit*.

She was reminded of the volume missing from the old man's bookshelf. It had not yet turned up, even with all the cleaning and rummaging about. Perhaps, then, he had lent it to someone who had kept it after he had died. Perhaps it had been lost or destroyed. Perhaps—and she would not have been surprised, so devoted he had been to his books—he had ordered it buried with him.

She reached down, put her hand on the book. *Blithe Spirit*. A fond wish? "I do hope you found her, Grandfather," she whispered. "And I'm sure she was as radiant as she was on the day you married her. Please . . ."

She choked, but she struggled on.

". . . please put in a word for me. Tell them to just let me go. I'm tired, and I just want it all to end."

She stood up, and as she did, she noticed that at the edge of the plot, on the Montague side, there was space for one more grave.

Silent as she had been on the way to the cemetery, she was even more so during the trip back to the mansion, and MacDonnell, obviously mistaking her silence for some variant on grief, did not try to make conversation. But as the police car slowed in order to make the turn from one road to another, Alma, looking out the window and back into the past, thinking about that empty grave waiting for her as though her family had left the front door unlocked and a room ready for her return, found herself abruptly staring into a square, squinting face that was itself staring back across a limp strand of barbed wire—staring with an intensity and a vehemence—*anger* was the word that came to her unbidden—that not only snapped her out of her thoughts but left her speechless for a quarter of a minute.

"Who . . . who was that?" she managed, as MacDonnell (who had not noticed her discomfiture) was leaving the turning behind.

"Who, ma'am?"

"That . . . that man back there. Behind the barbed-wire fence."

"Oh." He glanced over his shoulder. "That's Lindy Buck. I hear he's one of your tenants."

"*My* tenants?" Alma hardly wanted to entertain the thought.

" 'Cording to Snatcher from the bank, that's your land he's been farming for the last five years."

Alma found that her forehead had beaded with sweat. She pulled a handkerchief out of her purse and dabbed at the moisture. "He . . . he doesn't seem all too happy about it."

MacDonnell made a motion of his head as though to dislodge a fly. "Don't pay no attention to him, Miz Montague. He's just a nigger."

Alma blinked, not only at MacDonnell's casual racism but at the utter incongruity of his statement. "A nigger?" she blurted. "Marshal, the man I saw was white. Distinctly white."

He was unfazed. "Yep. That's what Lindy thinks, too. But under it all, he's just a nigger."

He must have felt Alma's look, for he glanced at her for a moment before returning his eyes to the road. "Miz Montague, far as I'm concerned, there are white folk, and there are colored folk, and some of 'em are good, and some of 'em are bad, and some of 'em are mixed around . . . just like folks always are. And then there's niggers, and it don't matter a bit if those niggers are white or colored. They're niggers whichever. And Lindy Buck's one of 'em. A nigger straight to the core."

He drove her the rest of the way home, then, and he saw her to her door. With a tip of his hat and a "good evening, ma'am," he got into the police car and motored slowly down the drive toward the dirt road that would take him back to town.

"The workmen have all left for the day, Miz Montague," said Lucy as she came in. "And I have supper waitin' for you."

"Thank you, Lucy. I appreciate it. I hope I'm not too late."

"You right on time, Miz Montague," said Lucy. She smiled. "You remember, don't you? Your time is my time?"

Alma smiled in return, and Lucy turned to go back to the kitchen. "Lucy."

"Yes'm?"

"Do you know Marshal MacDonnell?"

"Yes'm."

"What's he like?"

"Oh, he's a good man, Miz Montague. Next to my Buddy, he's the best I know."

Her own question had brought her back to the one asked by MacDonnell. About Greta Harlow. And why had he asked it? She had no doubt why he had asked it. "That's what I thought. Thank you, Lucy."

"My pleasure, ma'am."

And Lucy had just reentered the kitchen when there was a knock at the front door. Half-expecting that MacDonnell had returned for one reason or another, Alma swung the heavy door open. But it was a black man who stood on her porch, a tall black man wearing a fine gray suit. His shoes gleamed and there was a dapper air about him.

"Miss Montague?"

"Yes . . . ah . . . sir."

He smiled, bowed: courtly and elegant. "My name is Dark, ma'am. Your grandfather left something for you, and I'm very sorry for not having brought it earlier. The time, however, seemed inappropriate. Until now."

His teeth, white. His manner, cultivated. He looked like a college professor. Or a businessman with a string of oil wells behind him. But he was at her door, and he was reaching into his vest pocket, extracting something, offering it to her.

Alma took it almost without thinking. It was as though his very offering of it was an intrinsic and unrefusable demand that she take it. She must have had it in her hand for several seconds before she realized it was there and looked at it.

"A key?" she said.

"Yes, ma'am. To the garden."

"Garden? What garden?"

"The garden with the gazebo."

Alma blinked at the key, then at Mr. Dark. "But I don't have a garden with a gazebo! I've been all over the entire grounds, and there's nothing but—"

"Oh," he said, "it's there. You just haven't found it. Because you haven't had the key. But you have it now." Another smile. "So you will."

She stared at him.

"Just one thing. Please don't use the back gate of the garden.

If you must go out, climb over the stile. That will be ever so much better."

"Mr. Dark, I . . . I assure you, at my age, I don't intend on climbing over *anything*."

"All the better, ma'am. Good night, then."

Smiling, bowing, infinitely dapper in his dark gray suit and his polished black shoes, he stepped back, nodded to her, then turned and, descending the steps, vanished into the shadows of the growing evening.

# Chapter 8

It had been Mr. G's right to expect children, just as it had been his right to demand a nightly use of her body that would, under most circumstances, have resulted in the eventual production of such drooling, defecating, micturating, vomiting offspring as he had desired her to bear, to raise, and to clean up after.

Hallowed as those rights were by the Bible, by her minister, and by the pronouncements of her society, she had agreed to them, and she had therefore allowed Mr. G the nightly use of her body—moist armpits, dripping orifices, clammy sheets, and all—but she had reserved one right for herself: the prevention of the almost inevitable outcome of those uses, the right to be free of the production of children with their whining, their excretions, and their incessant, selfish demands upon the watery fluids of her mammae.

"And did you find it interesting to work at Miss Montague's house, Sam?"

"Miss Montague is real nice, Mom. She brought us sandwiches at lunchtime, and she let us go out and look around in the yard when we didn't have anything to do. But we were awful busy all the time. I mean, we were *really* busy. Huhuhuh!"

"What was she—"

"A-and, guess what, Mom?"

"—like?"

"Mom? Mom? Guess what?"

"What?"

"She had someone buy her a new car in town. It's newer than yours. It's all black and shiny, and the colored man who drives it said it can go real fast. He said he had it up to a hundred miles 'n hour on the dirt road that goes up to the house! A *hundred* miles an hour! But he doesn't let Miss Montague see him do that! Huhuhuh!"

"Sam, the road up to the house is dirt and winds so badly that Miss Montague's driver would have difficulty going even thirty-five miles an hour."

"Honest! He said he did a hundred! Well, maybe ninety. But it was *almost* a hundred miles an hour, and that ain't bad for a big car like that. Huhuhuh! And . . . and, Mom?"

"Yes, Sam?"

But after years had gone by, she had come to understand that although Mr. G had the right to expect children, he was really not overly disappointed when they did not appear, nor was he inclined to take issue with her about the matter so long as she both submitted to the outrages he committed upon her and did not make an issue of the outrages he committed elsewhere; which was fine with her, even considering the occasional infirmities that he brought back with him, infirmities that, in any case, would be cured quickly enough by Dr. Wyatt (who would ask no questions because Mr. G owned the bank in which Dr. Wyatt—and everyone else, for that matter—kept his money).

And eventually Mr. G even stopped the nightly outrages . . . at least upon *her.* He was still active enough up in the Negro district of Memphis, but, with the passage of years, he had come to find her aging body to be a less-than-desirable receptacle for his heaves and his squirts and his drips, preferring something young and resilient and without bags or wrinkles . . . which was also fine with her. And so, while he was away up in Memphis, she could keep the bed clean, the sheets smooth and cool and spotless, and she could sleep alone with only one pillow exactly centered at the head of the mattress. Then, too, she could regard the women she saw in town—women who were not so nicely dressed as she, women who were accompanied by squalling, dirty children with *stuff* hanging from their noses and chocolate ground under the nails of their sticky fingers—with a certain aloof smugness. And it was only right that she could, for *they* were covered with the drips and spatters of their world's omnipresent infantile secretions, while *she* was clean and trimmed, her hair done every week at the beauty shop and her clothes fresh every day. And even when Mr. G was at home and insisted (as was his right, she supposed, though she had her own rights, too . . . not that she had ever told him about them) on sleeping in her bed, even when the cleanliness of her sheets was thereby marred by his dribbling and his sweat and his body hair, she did not mind overmuch, since he did not now force his attentions upon her; and in any case he would eventually go back up to Memphis, up to Beale and Fourth, and she would, once again, be alone in her clean house and her clean bed.

"A-and guess what? She's got these . . . these big rooms in the house. They've got like . . . like these stone floors? They're real old. *Real* old. Huhuhuh! And, Mom? Mom? She told me to be careful of them because they were *three hundred years old.*"

"Sam, Montague Mansion itself isn't even half that old!"

"That's what she said! Three hundred years. A-and I could tell that they came from some . . . some *castle* or something like that, 'cause I know all about castles and stuff. Huhuhuh! They were *real* old. A lot older than Gavin House!"

"Yes, dear. And Miss Montague?"

"She really liked me, Mom. She *really* liked me!"

"Of course she would like you, Sam. You're a very likable boy."

"A-and, Mom? Mom? Guess what?"

"What, dear?"

"Miss Montague told me to come back because she has some other stuff that needs to be done."

"Did she ask the rest of the crew also, dear?"

"Well, yeah. Huhuhuh!"

"So Miss Montague looks to be staying in the house?"

And finally Mr. G died, and she did not have to worry about any of it anymore. The sweat and hair were gone from the house, the bed was clean—one pillow, centered, the sheets white and spotless and tucked smoothly in at the corners—and she was always nicely dressed in clean, inviolate clothes. And it could have gone on like that until she reached the complete inviolability of her own grave but for Greta Harlow.

Perhaps it was that Greta had always struck her as such a

neat, clean young woman, one who exhibited none of the over-ripe grease that clung to other postadolescent female bodies like a fleshy glaze. Perhaps it was that her father was an employee at Mr. G's bank. Perhaps it was that, as was the case with herself until she had become too old for Mr. G to be interested, Greta's outrage had been forced upon her. For whatever reason, when she had, in the soda shop, instinctively understood what had happened to Greta and (with a vividness perhaps amplified by her own aging body) sensed the filth reaching out to take her, she was moved to reveal indirectly to the girl what she had not previously revealed to anyone else, opening to her the same escape that she had herself used over and over again during the years of her marriage.

And yet, to her surprise, Greta had not taken the opportunity to deny Jimmy White's outrage. She had, in fact, accepted it, even embraced it; and as the days passed, as she began to swell, as she drew ever nearer to the sweating and the secreting and the gushing forth, she seemed proud of, even dedicated to, the maintenance and endurance of her condition.

"Oh, yeah! Huhuhuh! And she's got lots of money. *Lots* of it. She's got gold plates, and . . . and gold faucets in all the bathrooms, and she's even got a . . . a gold toothbrush! A-and, Mom? Wanna know something else? Mom?"

"What is it, Sam?"

"She gave . . . she gave me a hundred dollars!"

"Yes, Sam. So you're going back up there?"

"Well . . . maybe. Huhuhuh!"

"Maybe? I thought you said the crew was going back to Montague Mansion."

"Well, yeah. They are. Huhuhuh!"

"You quit your job with the crew, didn't you?"

"I . . ."

"Sam . . ."

"I . . . I had to, Mom! They all started actin' like jerks! They all . . ."

"Sam, you have to do something with your life. You just can't go on all the time hanging around with Lindy Buck. He has his own work to do in any case. You have to make something of yourself."

"I guess so."

That was, she knew, the reason for it. That was the cause of her awakening one morning in her tidy, spotless bed with the single pillow still exactly centered at the head of the mattress to find that she hated it all. Her house was old. Her life was old. Her very body was old . . . and she could feel it decaying about her even as she rose from a bed that now resembled nothing more than a slab of marble in a mortuary.

There was not a trace of youth or renewal in any of it. The house was still and sterile, her body worn-out with the burden first of endured intimacy and then of offspring denied. There was no continuance, no hope, no future . . . and she had spent that day and the next day after that and the next day after that curled in a ball in her spotless bed, her arms wrapped round her knees, her eyes wide and staring as she contemplated the decay that was not only around her but *in* her, decay having possessed her more intimately than any probing erection.

By day, she stared at the backs of her hands, seeing the liver spots and the wrinkles and the flaccid skin that were the emblems of the vibrant rot triumphing within her. By night, she struggled with cerements and with the mingled and close-pressed odors of embalming fluid and packed earth seeping into the airless precincts of her closed coffin. Her limbs, invisible in the darkness, slowly liquefied, staining the clean, white sheets with fluids infinitely more abhorrent than any male secretions; her bare skull stared with empty sockets into blackness . . . and, come morning, when she saw her fleshed hands again, she could not believe in either their reality or their honesty.

"You know I still give you money because I care about you, Sam, and because I'll always care about you. But I just can't keep giving you money. You have to learn how to stick with a job."

"I will!"

"Sam, you *always* say that."

"I've got a job."

"Really, Sam? Where are you working?"

"Well, I mean I'm talkin' with someone 'bout it. But he says I got a real good chance to get it."

"Sam . . ."

"He did! That's what he said! A-and, guess what, Mom? It's a great job. I'll be in charge of an entire crew all by myself, and that ain't bad!"

"Yes, Sam."

"A-and, you wanna know something?"

"Here is money, Sam. Just don't give any to Lindy. He has to earn his own way. Just like you."

"Thanks, Mom!"

"And you say that Miss Montague is rich?"

"Oh, yeah! She's real rich! Huhuhuh! She was a doctor and all, and so she had a lot of money, and then the man from the bank came and told her that she had even more money. Told her all about it. And then Marshal MacDonnell came when we were paintin' the upstairs bedroom, a-and Miss Montague liked the way I painted so much that she gave me a *hundred* dollars, and she told him—"

"Marshall MacDonnell? What did he come to see Miss Montague about?"

"—and guess what? She—"

"Sam? What did the marshal want?"

She began to watch Greta after that, parking her car so that she had a view of the girl's front door, or strolling casually within sight of her window, or stopping—spontaneously—for a strawberry phosphate while she still worked at the soda shop; and as the weeks passed, she observed Greta thickening and swelling, Greta putting on flesh, Greta slimed with the grease of pregnancy. But where before all these would have repulsed her, now, embodying as they did the distinct and tactile opposite of the withering age and death that so obsessed her, they were for her a promise of youth, of the physical, biological continuance for which she was suddenly yearning even as she sought, with workmen and lumber and paint, to remake her own house into something else, something new, something that did not smell of death.

"I heard them through the window, Mom. He was asking her about Greta. Huhuhuh! But, anyway, Miss Montague *really* liked me, and she said I could come back anytime I wanted."

"Sam! Sam . . . you must listen to me. What . . ."

"Huhuhuh!"

". . . what sort of things about Greta did the marshal ask Miss Montague? Did Miss Montague know Greta?"

"No, Mom. But . . . but, Mom? Wanna know something else?"

"Sam, are you *sure* you did everything the way I told you to do it? That night?"

"Sure! Huhuhuh!"

"Did you make sure that everything was done correctly when you were through? Did you look at the list I gave you?"

"Huhuhuh!"

"Did you *burn* the list like I told you to do?"

"I think so."

"*Sam!* Did you?"

"Sure. Sure I did! Huhuhuh!"

"Sam . . . you know I love you . . ."

"Huhuhuh!"

And then, one day, she saw Greta, her belly now distinctly protruding, leaving Mildred Riddup's boardinghouse with her cardboard suitcase in her hand.

Alma had been dreaming of the past again . . . and of the future.

For a long time, her dreams had, at least, been fairly predictable, like the familiar ache of an old compound fracture or the pull of a scar. Interactions, entanglements, disappointments, embarrassments . . . all of a life's minor and inconsequential failures and uncertainties that, at the time of their commission or omission, seem so trivial—and even in retrospect appear not worth considering—but which, accreting over the years, gradually build into a deep and chronic regret that no amount of rationalization can banish: this was the stuff that slid between the covers like an unwelcome lover as Alma lay asleep.

But now, added to the past was the future, for even though she had sought to flee from it, the future had caught up with her in Lee's Corners. Snatcher had found her with his assurances of unwanted money and undesired land. And MacDonnell had found her with his cryptic (and perhaps not-so-cryptic) questions. And, even at the beginning, Buddy had found her and had taken it upon himself to protect her. And it went on and on— each new entanglement and interaction an occasion for error, for mistakes . . . or, simply, for the increasing weight of personal history, of cumulative past—and it *would* go on and on just like that, straight through this life and on into the next, where she would have new faces to learn, new preferences to assimilate, new subjects to avoid and social mores to attend to so as not to outrage anyone . . . and so on for eternity.

And when she awoke, she was thinking again of the boy . . . the dead boy who lived his fabricated life within her imagination. She lay with her eyes unclosed for several minutes, staring at the white ceiling of her room while the growing light filled the house as water might fill a cup, listening to the very faint sounds that told her that Lucy had already arrived and was making breakfast, that Isaac was already shoveling earth in preparation for another planting.

And she thought: *He is waking up now. He is lying beside his wife. He is unclosing his eyes and looking at the light grow in just this way as his wife rises sleepily and goes to make him breakfast. And his children are grown up and some have children of their own. And they have their own lives. And all these things—light, wife, children, breakfast—he is thinking about at this very moment.*

But that was his life. This was hers. She rose and stretched, wincing as her old joints gave up eight hours' worth of accumulated stiffness, and then she dressed (reaching now by habit for the canvas trousers and shirt in which she inspected the ruins of the once-beautiful grounds of the estate) and went downstairs. And, yes, Lucy had breakfast ready, and, yes, Isaac had already eaten his corn bread and milk and coffee and was at work in the garden . . .

She stopped short at the foot of the stairs. The garden. The garden with the gazebo. Mr. Dark.

In her pocket was the key.

She reached in and withdrew it. Short and brass, its grip was engraved deeply with the letter *M.* Montague, of course. But . . . but *what* garden?

She ate in the kitchen with the key lying on the table beside her plate. Lucy silently kept her coffee cup refilled . . . and just as silently stared hard at her when she did not finish what Lucy considered to be a proper amount of food for an elderly woman who insisted upon tramping about her grounds like a man.

Alma noticed neither the filling nor the stares: she was caught up in the key, trying to think of what it might fit. She had already dismissed the idea of a garden as such—either Isaac or she herself would have stumbled upon a garden by now, particularly if it was marked with such a distinctive structure as a gazebo—but she had personally overseen most of the renovations in the house, and to the best of her knowledge there was no lock in the entire mansion that looked even remotely as though it would receive the key.

"Lucy?"

"Yes'm."

"Do you have any idea what this key might fit?"

"What key, ma'am?"

It was Alma's turn to stare. Lucy was looking at the table—where Alma's finger was indicating the key lying not two inches from her plate—but her expression was such that Alma herself looked back to the table to make sure that there was indeed a key there.

Alma held it up. "*This* key, Lucy."

Lucy's expression did not change. "Ah . . . well, ma'am, I'm afraid I ain't got no idea about that key there."

She did not have to say it. Alma had read her face. Lucy did not see the key at all.

Alma looked again at the key. Unmistakably solid, unmistakably brass. Unmistakably in her hand. I'm sorry, Lucy," she said, shoving it back into her pocket. "It was a rather stupid joke."

Lucy smiled, obviously relieved at being freed from participation in so exotic an interchange. Emancipation was decades in the past, but in accordance with the Byzantine code of race relations that governed this part of the country, the colored help was still supposed to humor their masters. "Yes'm." And, by way of changing the subject: "Would you like more coffee, ma'am?"

The key in Alma's pocket seemed suddenly to measure at least one by three feet and weigh in at a good fifty pounds. Unconsciously, she covered it with her hand. "No, thank you, Lucy.

I have some things to do outside, and I want to get right to them."

"Yes'm." And, still with that sense of relief, Lucy began to clear away.

But Alma was barely outside before the key was out of her pocket and in her hand again. Palpable. Real. And yet just as real had been Lucy's half-bewildered, half-terrified look.

She held it up to the sun, weighed it in her hand, even went so far as to close her eyes and drop it on her foot, convinced that something made entirely of hallucination could not but fail in some crucial physical aspect. But the key remained solid and convincing.

And he had said his name was Dark. Who . . . ?

She found Isaac with a shovel in his hands, a hole at his feet, and a rosebush at his side. "Mornin', ma'am."

"Isaac, you've been all over these grounds, haven't you?"

"I been around," came the cautious reply.

It would have to do. "Have you seen a gazebo anywhere?"

"A gazebo, ma'am? I don't reckon I quite know what a gazebo is."

"It's like a little . . . ah . . . like a little house. With open sides."

"No, ma'am. Ain't seen nothin' like that."

"Have you noticed a locked garden?"

"No, ma'am."

"Or a gate."

"No, ma'am."

She had the key in her hand, and she could not help looking at it. "I don't have a key in my hand, do I?"

Isaac eyed her warily. "No, ma'am. I should say you don't."

Alma nodded. "Thank you, Isaac."

"My pleasure, ma'am."

She turned away from him, turned back to the house. The mansion rose up, white, formal, and patrician, but its foundations lay in a wasteland of thorns and dust. Isaac could count on job security: he would be laboring for years in order to regain control of the grounds.

She started back up the path he had hacked out of the overgrowth that, here on the north side of the house, was taller than a

man's head. ("It's tall," he had said, "but I'll larn it. It gonna
know who's boss here 'fore I'm through.") Green walls rose up
on either side of Alma, entirely eclipsing her view of the house,
and here in the shadow that was not broken by sunlight even at
the height of noon, the air was thick and muggy.

And then she rounded a turning of the path to find that she
was staring at a wooden gate she had never seen before.

Her stomach tightened, and she felt faint. She had walked
this path a hundred times over the last two months, going to and
from the house, into and out of the grounds, and this gate had
not been here. It was possible, of course, that Isaac had recently
cleared away an additional foot or two of vine at this point,
widening the path and thereby revealing what had been previously hidden, but the surrounding stalks and branches and ten-
drils showed no signs of any recent hacking, and Isaac himself
had said that he knew of no gate.

Her eyes had, of their own accord, gone to the latch. There
was a lock there. It would take the key. She knew it would take
the key.

Consciously, deliberately, she forced herself to breathe, forced
her stomach to unclench. She had seen things in medical school
that had sickened her. She had controlled herself. She had seen
even worse things in the hospital. She had managed. She was
not about to allow an oaken gate to do to her what the sight of
severed legs, splintered bones, and the gelatinous looseness of
exposed organs had not. With a sense of defiance, therefore (the
same defiance with which she had braved her grandfather's old
room), she pulled out the key and inserted it into the lock.

There was no resistance. The mechanism turned like oil, and
the gate swung open on iron hinges with only a scrape of dried
brier that fell away from its purchase on the wood.

Cool air puffed out at her. She heard water splashing, caught
the scent of magnolia and wisteria. She stepped forward, and
her shoe came down not on dry, baked earth nor even on a layer
of dead and withered leaves, but on lush grass.

Grass, yes. Grass and flowers. Juniper bushes and boxwood
topiary rose up on either side of her, and a few feet away was a
marble railing, entwined with rambling roses, that curved out
and away to the left, then curled back into view from the right to

frame a pair of brickwork steps. And within the encircling railing was the fountain, the magnolia tree, and (yes, she knew it)
the gazebo.

Seeking to reassure herself, she turned back to the gate.
There it was, standing open, and through it she could see the
heat and the dryness of a garden gone to ruin. But here in the
middle of that ruination, preserved in luxury as though lovingly
tended and maintained on a daily basis, was a garden that would
not have been out of place on a picture postcard from England.
The gazebo, wooden-latticed and copper-roofed, the marble
fountain, plashing clear water from top dish to bottom dish, the
brickwork walk, patched with moss and bordered by grass, that
led from the steps to the gazebo itself . . . and then there was the
magnolia tree, as studded with flowers as a birthday cake might
be with candles, rising beside and overtopping the gazebo,
shading the copper roof and its twining wisteria with fragrant
branches.

Still with that sense of defiance—though that sense was
rapidly becoming ever more muted—Alma took the two brick
steps and passed through the gap in the marble railing. Now the
gazebo lay open before her, neat as a doll's house model. Within,
facing her, she saw a bench that ran around three of the six
sides, and on the bench . . .

"No."

She stood, steadying herself on the lower dish of the fountain. She smelled the moisture, felt the cool, wet spray on
her hand.

"No. That's . . . that's not possible."

But she went forward anyway. Three steps took her into the
small structure, and another three took her across the brick floor
to the bench on the far side, but for a moment, as though unwilling to confront what was there, she stood looking out at the
wisteria-framed view. The marble railing did indeed lap all the
way around the gazebo and its little garden, and there in the back
was a wrought-iron gate, closed and, from the look of it, locked.
Beside it, though, built against the railing, was a set of steps
that led up and over.

She remembered Mr. Dark's words. *Please don't use the back gate of the garden,* he had said. *If you must go out, climb over the stile.*

Beyond the iron gate, the landscape rolled away, low hills against a dark sky, neither hills nor sky partaking in the slightest of anything that could ever have been produced by Oktibushubee County. The sunlight out there was veiled, hesitant, and Alma shivered and looked away . . . only to find that her eyes came to rest on the hat and the book that lay on the bench before her.

She picked up the hat and examined it, but she did not have to. She knew already that it was her grandfather's hat. She had seen him wearing it many, many times before she had left her family. Before he had died.

And the book . . .

*Blithe Spirit.* By Joinaud. It had her grandfather's name on the flyleaf, and, like the hat, it showed not a sign of having been exposed to the elements for what could not have been less than four decades.

# Chapter 9

Like his father, like his very name (given to him before he was born . . . given to him perhaps in that moment of epiphany when his mother, even then holding the poison cup in her hand, had rejected it), he was magic, but more than that, infinitely more, rooted in the very biological fact of his gestation, he was *hers*.

But that ownership was under assault—obviously so, painfully so—and Mrs. Gavin continued her slow encroachments on Magic with a passive insidiousness that would have made Greta protest . . . had there been anything definite to protest about. But nothing Mrs. Gavin did was particularly out of the ordinary, and, in fact, Mrs. Gavin could herself protest (and often did) that she had only the most laudable of intentions regarding both Magic and Greta. Magic, she said on more than one occasion, certainly deserved to be in the company of someone who not only loved him so much but was also in a position to provide him with social, financial, and educational opportunities he would not otherwise have; and Greta very much deserved to be relieved of the drudgery of motherhood every now and then, so that she could occasionally do what she wanted to do rather than what Magic demanded of her . . . though it appeared to Greta that she must have been more than deserving of such consideration, seeing how Mrs. Gavin seemed determined to surfeit her on it.

But outwardly laudable though Mrs. Gavin's intentions were, they had the inevitable effect of separating the son from the mother. Now that Magic was weaned, it was exactly as Greta had feared: days would go by during which she would hardly see her boy at all, and when she did see him, she noticed (as only a mother would) that there would pass across his infant face a momentary look of confusion, as if he were for a moment having to make a conscious effort to distinguish between his biological mother and the woman who was rapidly monopolizing his emotions.

Moreover—and perhaps more tellingly—Greta sensed a general sentiment arising in the town, one that seemingly endorsed and validated Mrs. Gavin's appropriation. Perhaps Greta's loss of respectability (shielded though she was from its most extreme consequences by, yes, Mrs. Gavin herself) was such that the price of mere toleration in the community was the ceding of her son to another; or perhaps it was more that Magic was so habitually in the company of the older woman that it was simply natural for the townsfolk to associate him not with Greta but with the individual from whom he appeared to be deriving most of his nurture. Regardless, the sentiment was real and, once recognized, quite compelling: even Greta caught herself wondering at times whether the pregnancy and the trauma of birth she had experienced were actual memories or mere fabrications on her part; and then she realized one day that she possessed no outward sign of motherhood. She had a room to herself without crib or toys or child's clothing in it; she had clothing of her own that seemed more appropriate for a twelve-year-old girl than for a woman—and a mother at that—of twenty; she had not even a copy of Magic's birth certificate.

She did have money, but it was not long before she discovered that while Mrs. Gavin was certainly willing to supply her with enough cash for herself, funds sufficient for the additional support and maintenance of Magic—whether Greta desired to take the boy to a movie or simply to buy him an ice cream cone—were simply not there; and so, even on those increasingly infrequent occasions when Greta actually had the physical company of her son, she had nothing with which to entertain him save the abundant toys that Mrs. Gavin had bought for him, and no place in which to interact with him save ... Mrs. Gavin's house.

"You're both as dear to me as my own children," Mrs.

Gavin exclaimed over dinner one day. "You and Magic *are* my children."

And Greta stared at the plate upon which she had been absently moving food since it had been set before her. And so she was Mrs. Gavin's daughter? And then what? Did that then make her Magic's *sister*?

Her plate crashed to the floor.

Mrs. Gavin was looking at her. "Oh, well. Accidents happen," she said cheerfully, as the servants moved to clean up the mess.

"Yes, Mummy," said Greta, and if Mrs. Gavin noticed her tone, she did not mention it.

One day, before anyone else was up, Greta took Magic, filled a suitcase with his tiny suits and her own childish frocks, and left the house just as dawn was graying in the east. Walking for two hours, she made it to the railroad station just in time for the northbound train to Memphis. But she did not board. She could not board. She did not have enough money for tickets for both herself and her son. In fact, she had already known that she did not have enough money when she had picked up the sleepy Magic from his crib, when she had packed the suitcase, when she had walked from Gavin House all the way to town.

She waited on the bench with Magic, watched the train come, watched the train go. And then she walked back to Gavin House. Mrs. Gavin pretended not to have noticed her absence; and, after she had bathed Magic, she took him off for shopping and visiting, leaving Greta in her room, staring out the window.

"Afternoon, Marshal."

"It's morning, Otis."

"Mornin', Marshal."

MacDonnell stood in the doorway of the office with his hand resting on his mustache, mentally running over the day's schedule. He was back from patrol, so Otis would be leaving in a few minutes to take the next shift in the car. Later on, about three o'clock, he himself would have to ask Anna Watson to come in and answer the telephone while he strolled over to the courthouse, where Judge Dewey would ask him a few pertinent questions before sentencing the Frammis boys to ten days in the jail for disturbing the peace with no less than twenty-five rounds of 12-gauge buckshot . . . diligently applied, round by round, to the front of that very jail.

But he was not really thinking about his schedule. No. That was just something for his brain to do while his thoughts—those imponderable parts of a man that will go off and do whatever they choose to do whenever they choose to do it, leaving him utterly flabbergasted when, at the end of a lengthy and conscious cogitation regarding, say, chickens, he actually finds that he has come to a definite resolution about having sex with his wife that night—revolved very slowly and evenly around Otis and the death of Greta Harlow.

MacDonnell noticed that his hand was still resting on his mustache. He also noticed that Otis was looking uncomfortable.

But it seemed to MacDonnell that Otis had been looking uncomfortable an awful lot in the course of the last few years. And when was it that he had bought that new car? When? Before or after Greta had killed herself? After maybe? MacDonnell decided that while he was over at the courthouse that afternoon, he would check the automobile registration that Otis had filed. Which would, of course, tell him exactly nothing, but . . . then again . . .

Otis was looking even more uncomfortable.

"Anything wrong?" MacDonnell said, dropping his hand from his mustache.

Otis looked relieved. "Nothing happenin' 'round here at all. Place is dead quiet."

MacDonnell nodded. "The car's yours. I gassed it up 'fore I brought it back, so you're all set. You might want to check over at the loading dock by M'Creed's store. There's a big colored fellah with a truck over there, and I saw Lindy Buck heading that way a while back."

Otis reached into the desk drawer and took out his holster. "Lindy Buck's got too much time on his hands."

"Cotton's that way. Break your back putting it in, and break your back taking it out . . . and not much in between."

"Wish he'd take up a hobby . . . like drinkin' or something."

"Sho be nice, wouldn't it?"

And if Greta had indeed beaten herself to death, what had she beaten herself *with*, anyway? No one had ever found *anything*.

"Sho would." Otis nodded and rose, reaching for his hat. "Oh, yeah. You got a message come in a little while ago . . ." He picked up a piece of paper and squinted at it. "That Montague woman called. Wanted to know if you knew a Mr. Dark." He looked up. "I guess she means *our* Mr. Dark."

MacDonnell found that his hand was on his mustache again. He patiently pulled it away and looked at his watch. "He's probably eatin' his ice cream at McCoy's right now."

Or had she, like the Russian prisoner Alma had mentioned, merely used whatever was at hand: dresser, bed frame, walls, floor . . . ?

Insane.

"You might want to call her back first thing," Otis was saying. "She sounded all in a flutter."

"In a flutter?" Now *that* was a puzzler. Something must have been seriously wrong for a woman like Alma Montague to be in a flutter. And, even leaving aside any question of flutters, what connection could there be between her and Dark?

But if Greta had been killed, who would have killed her? Mildred Riddup had chased a Negro out of her back window an hour before Greta's body had been found, but Mildred had also talked to Greta *after* discharging a double load of buckshot at the retreating black behind . . . and had told her that she had best get her *own* behind out of the boardinghouse by noon the following day.

And about an hour later, Greta was dead.

"Yeah, in a flutter."

And between Alma Montague's message and Greta Harlow's death, MacDonnell found that he was feeling very much like a man who had been informed that he had just eaten a bad batch of potato salad.

But he lifted his head suddenly, dropping his hand (again) from his mustache. "What's that?"

Otis also had lifted his head. "Must be Sophie Ellis's jalopy. It always backfires like that."

MacDonnell was already turning for the door. "That ain't backfiring. Them's shots."

\* \* \*

He was a big man—what Lindy Buck would have called . . .
*did* call, in fact . . . a "big buck nigger"—and he had come to
Lee's Corners at the wheel of a semitrailer with Michigan plates
and a load of parts that Delphi M'Creed had ordered to make up
for the depredations on his warehouse caused by Alma Montague's renovations. Easily six-foot-five, with a breadth across
his bare chest that gave the impression of a very dark cinder-
block wall, he had spent an hour unloading crates and bundles
and kegs of such a size and heft that even one of them would
have obviously been quite enough to buckle the knees of any
one (or even two) of the loiterers who had gathered behind
M'Creed's store to watch a black man and stranger lift enormous weights without any indication of strain beyond a few
beads of sweat on his forehead.

They watched, true, but they said nothing, for something
about his demeanor put any thought of question or comment
straight out of their heads, and there was a darkness about the
stranger's eyes that went beyond any matter of color, that spoke
eloquently of danger.

In silence, he labored. In silence, they watched.

"Have you checked in at the sheriff's office, *boy*?"

Well, almost in silence.

Up until then, Lindy Buck had stayed in his usual place in
front of the hardware store, muttering a continuous commen-
tary about why he was poor, about why he was justified before
God, about why he was saved, about why it was unjust that niggers had money, about why—unlike some nigger-loving, liberal whores from up north that had decided to invade Lee's
Corners with their particular brand of Northern, liberal, nigger-
loving—*he* always voted to keep them in their place, about why
it was his duty to inform those who were not saved about exactly why they were not, and so on.

And in there with all his words, winding through his mono-
logue and inextricably mixed with it like the marbling in a layer
cake, was the ever-present and irrefutable (in Lindy's opinion)
axiom that the white race was the natural and born master of the
black race, and that all the problems that were currently beset-
ting the country in general and the state in particular and Lee's

Corners in even more particular stemmed from the irrefutable
(in Lindy's opinion) fact that the governments of all three levels
had become lax in their attention to reaffirming that axiom and
that mastery.

And, beside him, Sam Libbeldoe, seemingly entranced by
the mere existence of someone who appeared to possess not one
particle of doubt as to the rightness of his opinions, could add
no more than an occasional,

"Uh-huh!"

Or its virtual reverse:

"Huhuhuh!"

It was that lack of doubt that made Lindy what he was, and
it was perhaps only a twist of Fate—or a favor of Divine
Providence—that caused him to be chopping cotton and muttering to himself in Lee's Corners rather than fomenting geno-
cide in some other part of the world, for if no one in Lee's
Corners listened to him, if he was almost universally shunned
by the townsfolk, it was not so much because of his square face
and his squint and his habitual ill temper. No, it was because of
that very lack of doubt, that utter and flawless conviction, for
those qualities could not but make all but the dullest of his lis-
teners afraid that, given time and opportunity, his ravings could
remake their own mild little thoughts into his own image, infect
them with his certainty, and force them to march, lock step, to
his tune. It was the fear—or the fascination—that the sane invariably demonstrate toward the mad, for madness carries with
it the ring of sureness that nothing that is of sanity can ever
know, for sanity implies choice and uncertainty, while madness
knows only the blind impulse of prophetic knowledge.

So it was with Lindy: when he was under the spell of his beliefs, he was invariably transfigured by them to the extent that
even his squint became a confirmation of his rightness, and his
sometimes-throaty, sometimes-whiny muttering could easily
seem the *sotto voce* murmurings of secret truths.

Or at least they seemed so to Sam Libbeldoe, who continued
with his unheard and reversible comments until Lindy fell sufficiently under his own spell to stalk to the back of the hardware
store and challenge the Negro truck driver . . . who, for all the
response he demonstrated, did not appear to hear the challenge

at all. Rather, he continued, without apparent strain, to lift the unspeakably heavy crates and boxes out of the back of the truck and deposit them on the loading dock, where, sweating and straining with the weight, John Harlow and a group of fellow day laborers took over and carried them into M'Creed's warehouse.

"You hear me, boy? You get your unrighteous, godforsaken black butt over to Sheriff Hayes and you let him know you're in his county!"

Still, the big black man said nothing, continued to unload.

Lindy did not stop there, though, and as John Harlow, his crew, and the loiterers listened (and it was a good thing that M'Creed was inside, attending to the storage of the delivered items, for Lindy's own agitation was as nothing to the ire that the devout Baptist would have demonstrated had he heard Lindy—the unredeemed and redeemable Presbyterian—taking it on himself to determine what was righteous or unrighteous, godforsaken or not), Lindy continued, his rhetorical flow of compounded and increasingly mismatched pejoratives steadily swelling as he realized more and more fully just how completely the "buck nigger" was ignoring him. Still, anyone who was watching carefully would have noticed that the darkness about the truck driver's eyes was, with each passing minute of Lindy's harangue, growing darker . . . and that there were a few additional beads of sweat on his forehead than could have been accounted for, given previous evidence, by the lifting of heavy weights.

But Lindy was not watching carefully. He was, in fact, not watching at all, for he was caught up in the same sort of compulsion that makes a man faced with a stubborn nail simply hit that nail harder and with increasingly larger hammers rather than take the time to find out that directly below the tip of that nail is a steel rivet the size of a baby's fist. Given the driver's apparent obliviousness to his words, Lindy was becoming utterly consumed not just with the urge to humiliate the black man by forcing him to acknowledge in some way (even by flat refusal) the order to report to the sheriff, but with the absolute *need* to realize that very humiliation, even if it meant that he himself had to escort the black man to the sheriff. The escorting looking more and more unlikely, however, given the size difference between the two men, Lindy had switched to simple verbal abuse; and as John Harlow and his crew went in and out of the warehouse at the back of the hardware store, they heard Lindy's speech reduced to stroboscopic details:

"And God said . . . the chosen people were allowed to subjugate . . . and it says in the Bible that . . . slew Onan because he did a . . . it just stands to reason . . . you slack-jawed, coal-souled niggers are all the same . . . makes perfect sense to me . . . and God put the mark of Cain on . . . there's masters and there's slaves . . ."

And all the while the darkness about the driver's eyes deepened . . . causing a number of townsfolk who had gathered to see the big, out-of-town semitrailer with the Michigan license plates to recall that there were some pretty rough cities up there in Michigan, and to think that it might possibly be a good idea to get Lindy away from the back of M'Creed's Hardware Store before something unfortunate happened that would make the burnt Negro mayor and the trace chains and the mutilation seem like one of Mr. Burke's Sunday school picnics in comparison; but since Lindy was by now practically shouting his philosophy into the driver's ear, no one could bring himself to intervene simply because he did not want to get that close to either of them.

Eventually, though, the truck was empty, and the driver reached up and slammed down the metal tambour door with a violence that made everyone flinch just as Delphi M'Creed appeared on the loading dock with the manifest in his hand.

"Says here," said M'Creed, "that you brought ten kegs of nails. There's eleven in there."

"Keep the change," said the driver.

M'Creed pursed his lips. If there was anything that Delphi M'Creed hated more than someone owing him, it was him owing someone else. "I'll cut a check."

"Account won't balance," said the driver.

And Lindy was still going on (though he had at least reduced his volume to a violent mutter when M'Creed had appeared):

". . . duty of the white race . . . subhuman sexual drives . . . doc-u-men-ted fact that brains are smaller in . . ."

"I'll call ahead," said M'Creed.

"Suit yourself," said the driver.

"Won't take but a minute," said M'Creed, who, occupied with the problem, did not notice Lindy as he turned and went back into the store.

And Lindy went on, louder now that M'Creed was back in the store:

". . . white women in particular . . . it just goes to show . . ."

By now, it was near noon, but no one had left for lunch. Everyone, including John Harlow and his crew, was waiting for something to happen. But the driver just stood there like a larger-than-life basalt statue of some African god with Lindy beside him like a putto afterthought.

". . . and another thing . . ."

M'Creed bustled out with a check in his hand. He gave it to the driver. The driver reached into the cab of the truck and took out a clipboard. He put the check in the clipboard, scrawled a receipt, and handed it to M'Creed. M'Creed squinted at the piece of paper, nodded, said . . .

"Afternoon. Drive careful, y'heah?"

. . . and went back into the warehouse. The driver tossed the clipboard into the cab, reached behind the seat, produced a chrome-plated pistol, and put two bullets into Lindy's chest. Lindy looked surprised, fell to the ground, and lay there like an empty flour sack while the driver swung up behind the wheel of the truck, started the engine, and drove away. And it all happened so smoothly and naturally that the truck was around the corner and out of sight—and, just possibly, all the way out on the highway and heading for Memphis and the state border—before anyone there at the back of M'Creed's Hardware Store ever thought about such things as license plates, telephones, Marshal MacDonnell, Sheriff Hayes . . .

. . . or even about Lindy himself.

Alma did not wait for MacDonnell to return her call. Instead, she took the wheel of her own car and drove into town herself, trusting that her motoring abilities had not become altogether atrophied over the course of a few months.

She heard the muffled pops as she turned onto Jefferson Street, and, having heard a few too many shots during the time she had lived in back of a boiler room, she had no doubt as to what they were. And though she, once a doctor, turned her automobile in the direction of the sounds and ignored the stoplight (which was perfectly all right, since no one who lived in Lee's Corners paid much attention to it in any case), she privately admitted that the idea of saving a life was only partly on her mind.

But when she reached the rear of M'Creed's Hardware Store, the truck driver had already left. Only M'Creed, the work crew, and a few loiterers were there, and all of them were milling around over the crumpled form of Lindy Buck, who lay, eyes open and bewildered, staring at the very blue sky. Some were shouting for the doctor, some were shouting for the marshal, and others were of the opinion that calling the sheriff would be very much the best thing to do . . . but all this, of course, did nothing for Lindy, who, throughout the milling and the shouting alike, was *still* lying there on the ground, staring at the sky out of a face that had turned the color of clay.

MacDonnell and the questions about Mr. Dark could wait: Alma stopped the big car, fumbled for the parking brake, and got out. But before she could even swing the door closed, Mr. Dark had come sprinting around the corner, tie flapping, coattails waving, and polished shoes winking. Without pausing to ask questions, he dropped to his knees beside Lindy and, as Alma approached, popped the bigot's mouth open and cleared his windway of the plug of tobacco that had gotten lodged there when the bullets struck. After listening a moment to Lindy's chest, Mr. Dark pressed down—hard—on his sternum twice, then cupped his lips over Lindy's and blew a chestful of air into him.

The effect was instantaneous. Lindy, still bleeding from the two holes in his chest, came to himself and began shouting weakly about "queer niggers." As the color returned to his face, he feebly tried to shove Mr. Dark away, but Alma herself was at his side by then, and she took hold of his hands and held them down.

"Lie still, Mr. Buck," she said, and there was enough of the old medical authority in her voice that he did as he was told.

"His heart and breathing had stopped, Miss Montague," explained Mr. Dark. "Something had to be done."

"To be expected, really," said Alma. She was already unbuttoning Lindy's shirt. "That was quite amazing, though. I've never seen anything like that before."

"Oh, just something I picked up . . . in . . . ah . . . China. Yes, I picked it up in China."

Lindy struggled. "You whorish Jezebel! Git your hands . . . !"

"Be quiet, Mr. Buck. I'm trying to save your life."

"And the Lord said that woman should be subservient . . . !"

"Mr. Buck," Mr. Dark said, flapping his blub lips in such a lascivious way that Lindy could not help but shudder, "yo' plez be calmin' down dere. Dere's no tellin' where dose bullets be, and yo' could be hurtin' yo'self."

"You can't talk to me like that!"

"Tak to yo' laik whut, honkey boy?" said Mr. Dark, running a very large tongue over his very large, very pale lips.

"He needs to be taken to hospital," said Alma, examining the wounds and giving up on any direct communication with Lindy.

"Agreed," said Mr. Dark. "Your car, perhaps? We can stretch him out on the backseat."

"Queer! That's what you are! Queer! You put your filthy nigger lips—!"

Alma frowned. "Is the hospital in Lee's Corners equipped for this kind of trauma?"

"Most of the time we go to Doc Wyatt," came a voice. "Nearest big hospital is over in Jefferson."

The man who had spoken was standing over them, and Alma recognized him as the parsnip man from the railroad station: John Harlow. Lindy's chest was bare by then, his wounds gaping in the noon sunlight, and Alma was mildly surprised that Harlow seemed able to look on the results of the pistol shots without blenching; but then she recalled that he had probably once looked on the body of his daughter. Compared to what MacDonnell had hinted at regarding Greta's death, two bullet holes and a bit of blood were, doubtless, as nothing.

MacDonnell. Mr. Dark. And here was Mr. Dark at her side.

"He'll need to go there," said Alma, dragging her thoughts back to the matter at hand. "He's bleeding internally."

Another voice. Fussy. Peremptory. "Now, now, now . . . what's this? Oh, my goodness. Let's take a look at you, Lindy."

Alma looked up to see a man only a few years younger than herself. He was carrying a medical bag.

"Alma Montague," she said by way of introduction. "I'm a doctor. This man has received multiple bullet wounds, with possible perforation of the—"

"And what have you gotten into now, Lindy?" said the man, without giving any sign that he had heard her. He dropped to one knee and opened his bag. "Looks like you picked on some-one a little big for you, eh?"

Alma tried again. "I believe he needs to go to the Jefferson Hospital. Those bullets need to come out."

"Oh, my-my," said the man, examining Lindy and com-pletely—and pointedly—ignoring Alma. "We'll have to have you up to my office right away." He looked up at Harlow and the work crew. "Y'all want to carry Lindy here over to my of-fice? And someone call Miss Elsie. I'm going to need some help."

"I'm a doctor," Alma repeated, trying yet once more. "I'm available."

The man fixed her with a severe glare through steel-rimmed spectacles. "Young lady, medicine is serious business. You really ought to leave it in the hands of professionals. Someone could have gotten hurt here if I hadn't come along. Seriously hurt."

He might just as well have slapped her. Alma blinked. De-cades out of medical school, a lucrative practice behind her, and yet the sting of the mockery she had endured as a student (And had they, teacher and fellow student alike, cowed her? Was that why she had wilted so readily before the Bible-shouting father and his hemorrhaging wife . . . wilted just long enough for both woman and child to die?) was still as fresh as ever. "Yes," she said. "Of course. Professionals." But she saw that MacDonnell and his deputy had both appeared at the edge of the dirt lot be-hind the hardware store, and the sight of the marshal jogged her memory. "Thank you for informing me of that. I'm sure that you're infinitely more qualified than I, Doctor, whether for the treatment of gunshot wounds . . . or for the determination of suicide by self-inflicted beating."

She did not know why she had said it—perhaps it was but a

wild urge for retaliation against the voices and mockery of both the past and the present—but the effect was gratifying . . . and, at the same time, disturbing. The doctor flinched visibly, and though he gave her another severe look before he busied himself with organizing the men who would carry Lindy to his office, it was a look that was more than a little touched with what Alma suspected was fear.

# Chapter 10

John Harlow came home for lunch that day with the urge to tell what had happened at M'Creed's Hardware Store, and in the manner of a man who, though technically a grandfather, was trying—with a mixture of defiance, humiliation, and outright rage—to fill the role of father to a boy whom town sympathy and the tacit manipulations of a wealthy woman were attempting to take away from him (which made him all the more determined to cling tenaciously to that role), he wanted to tell it first to Magic, to impress the boy with the crotch hitch and swagger of his close encounter with near-lethal force. In fact, he had it all planned out: what he would say, how he would say it. "Two bullets! Just like that!" And he would extend his finger in imitation of a pistol barrel, and then he would—

No. He would do nothing of the sort. Magic was already obsessed with guns. It had been months since he had returned from up north, and still almost the only thing out of his mouth was *Pow-er! Pow-er!*, and still almost his only gesture was that spastic, jabbing imitation of a pistol. And John Harlow stood at the end of the cracked walkway that led to the clapboard house he shared with his wife and his grandson—the clapboard house that was covered with powdering and mildewing paint, that was much smaller and much inferior to the house he had shared with his wife and his daughter when he had worked at Mr. Gavin's bank—and he felt not only the hot, deflated anger of a male who, set to display his vicarious status, finds instead his servility thrust into his face and is thereby forced to creep away, fawning and impotent, but also the abject sense of half terror, half rage that can only be felt by a man who has been bested, publicly and humiliatingly, by an enemy against whom he cannot legitimately fight.

But, as it was, when he went up the walkway to his house, walking (shuffling, he thought, with that servility that had become instinctive, that made him rage all the more against that which was forever beyond his rage) past the rotting picket fence and the clumps of sun-seared hollyhocks and the parched remains of blue flax that had been neglected to death because there was never enough time now for anything except trying to earn a little more money that never was enough to begin with and never went far enough as it was, Magic was not at home. His room was empty, his toys and his clothes left behind.

It was always like this. The boy would be out playing—if standing with fists balled save for thumbs and index fingers could be called playing—or would be looking out through the front window as though expecting exactly what would happen (And perhaps he was indeed expecting it. How far had she gone in her bribery? What had she given him, promised him, showed him so as to better and more effectively and more thoroughly turn his affections away from his kin?), and the dark automobile would pull up. An open door, a beckoning hand, and Magic would be gone. No warning. No word. No explanation.

It had happened, he supposed, just that way the first time, three days after he and Alice had found that Greta's body had been cremated without their permission. Magic had been in the yard one instant, and then he had been gone. For a week, they had searched frantically for him, enduring daily the scorn of the townsfolk, who, in a hundred different ways, made it known with no misunderstanding whatsoever exactly what they thought of people who would allow their daughter to become pregnant out of wedlock, reject their daughter for having so become pregnant, allow their daughter to kill herself and leave her illegitimate offspring for another to raise, and then attempt to lay claim to that offspring and take him away from one who had infinitely more right to raise him than themselves. To be sure, MacDonnell, the town marshal, had assisted their search without so much as a raised eyebrow, and had even gone so far as to contact the FBI and the police departments in Memphis and

Biloxi and Jefferson. And, in fact, it had been MacDonnell who had at last located Magic at Gavin House . . . where he was staying—quite willingly—with Sophonsiba Gavin.

It became clear then. And it was clear, too, that there was nothing John and Alice could do save submit. And when, at the end of another two weeks, Magic simply reappeared in their front yard without any explanation or warning, there was still nothing they could do save submit.

And so a new regimen came into their lives, one that had all the earmarks of regularity and enforced compliance without overtly demonstrating either of those qualities; and though over the weeks and the months they became accustomed to it, inwardly they fought it and fought their own capitulation to it with undiminishing fury. Magic was there. And then he was not there. Sophonsiba Gavin came for him when she wanted him and took him away to a world of money and toys and attention that John and Alice could never hope of even dimly echoing, much less equaling or surpassing. And when convenience or conscience told her that she was, for the moment, done with Magic, she would bring him back to the cheap, mildewed house of his mother's parents, back to his ten-cent toys and his threadbare room and the adults who had the temerity to claim him as kindred.

Silently, John Harlow stood in the middle of Magic's room, prodding with his toe at one of the tin playthings that lay tumbled on the threadbare rug. "If I had money," he found himself saying, "I'd fight you. I'd show you what happens to someone who takes a man's grandson away from him."

But he did not have money. Not anymore. Even when he had worked for the bank, he had not brought home the kind of money it would take to keep Sophonsiba Gavin away from Magic . . . even assuming for a minute that Judge Dewey or a jury of citizens from Lee's Corners would find in favor of people who allowed their daughter to birth a bastard and then kill herself. But now, a mere laborer who carried unspeakably heavy crates into warehouses—or dug trenches, or cleaned out cesspools, or did any of a hundred things depending on the need of the day—he could not even afford one of the steel construction kits with which (he was sure) Mrs. Gavin was plying Magic . . . when she was not (he was sure) plying him with guns.

But, indeed: by what right did he, having so proudly disowned his defiled daughter, thereafter claim so stubbornly the son produced by that defilement? He had watched Greta leave his house with her suitcase and her teddy bear, and with that dark rejoicing that is so much the mark of the human, he had been confident, even smug at having accomplished something that he knew could not be, in the long run, other than deadly. And over the following months and years, as the news that Greta had moved first into Mildred Riddup's boardinghouse and then into Sophonsiba Gavin's mansion had filtered back to him, he had remained steadfast in that confidence, that smugness, that secret joy that came close to forcing a smile to his lips when he contemplated the futility of the conditions he had created, that stemmed from his knowledge—unadmitted, as is always the case with such things, hidden from himself save for flickering intimation and consciously denied all the more fiercely for that—that he had, by his own words and actions, destroyed not only himself, but his daughter and his wife, too; and it was perhaps a further mark of the existence and the illicitness of that pleasure that he now coveted Magic with the same lustless passion with which a man craves a woman when he craves her not as an object of pleasure or even as a sexual toy, but as a thing to be owned, controlled, made subject to himself.

A step behind him. "It was a slow day," said Alice Harlow. "I left early. I heard you come in."

He did not turn around. "Did you see—"

"He was gone when I got home."

His fists were clenched. Greta was gone. But he would have Magic. "You could have stopped her."

"Nobody can stop her."

Now he whirled on her. *"You could have stopped her, goddammit!"*

She just looked at him.

"But you're out all the time, aren't you? You got that job."

He was accusing her, but she did not respond.

"I'm here now," she said.

"And you left when we need every dollar you can bring in."

"It wasn't my idea. They sent me home."

He looked down at the floor, and now it seemed to him that every particle of his penury was staring him in the face in the form of cheap, painted tin and bent windup keys. Every particle that allowed Magic to be taken away. Every particle that denied him a chance or even a hope of possessing him save at the whim and pleasure of another. "We can't afford for you to leave early."

"It wasn't my idea," she repeated.

The whim and pleasure of another. And Sophonsiba Gavin was beyond his reach. He did not recall what he shouted at his wife, but he punctuated it with a fist.

"Nigger lips!"

"Now, Lindy," said Dr. Wyatt, "you really ought to know better than to go around picking fights with strangers. Colored folks from around here, why, they *know* you, and they're likely to put up with just about anything you can think of because of that; but when you go and start something with a body from out of town, you're just as likely to get something you don't expect, if you follow my drift."

"Nigger lips!"

His chest swathed in thick layers of gauze and tape, Lindy sat on the edge of one of the two beds in the tiny hospital ward that Wyatt kept adjacent to his office. The other bed was empty, for the ward was more of a formality than anything else: as John Harlow had explained to Alma, anyone requiring complete care went to the big hospital in Jefferson, where the latest equipment—and lots of it—was available.

"Take that big nigger you tangled with this afternoon, for instance," Wyatt continued as though paying no attention at all to Lindy's murmured exclamations. (In fact, he was filling a large hypodermic syringe at that moment, and so intent was he on the level of the fluid within the glass tube that a bomb might have gone off next door without eliciting much more of a response from him than: "Well, I do declare: that's spoiled my proportions!") "He was from up north, and he just don't *know* you. Understand?"

"Nigger lips!"

But, though Wyatt's ward might have been nothing more than a formality, it demonstrated no dearth of the latest equipment itself, and had Alma visited it (a highly unlikely event, given what she had heard from—and what she had said to—Wyatt), she would have recognized several rather expensive pieces of medical apparatus standing ready along the wall . . . much more expensive apparatus, in fact, than a small-town doctor could, under normal circumstances, afford.

"And since he don't *know* you," Wyatt continued, baring Lindy's arm for the needle, "he was just as likely to pull out that gun and do what he did as he was to do anything else. And he could have killed you right dead if that second bullet hadn't broken up before it reached your ol' ticker. Now say you understand me, won't you, Lindy?"

"Nigger lips!"

Lindy, for his part, was essentially unconscious of either Wyatt's words or the needle which was even then being inserted into the large muscle in his upper arm, for his thoughts were full of recollections of Mr. Dark's simian face gibbering above him, and, worse, the smothering, fleshly pneumatic sensation of the colored man's protuberant lips being forcibly juxtaposed upon his own. And right there in front of God and man alike! And while Lindy had for a while been unable to decide whether he was more outraged by Dark's blatant violation of the sanctity of his white Presbyterian lips or by the complete inaction of the workers on the loading dock who watched that violation in progress and did not lift a finger to intervene, he had, with characteristic finality and self-righteousness, come down firmly on the side of the former, for he had reached the conclusion that the laborers' inaction could not but have been a natural and understandable by-product of the same outraged shock at the oscular miscegenation taking place right before their very eyes as had afflicted himself at the time, a shock that had even gone some distance toward eclipsing the pain of the two bullet holes in his chest.

"Not that your heart ain't immune to li'l ol' things like lead bullets, being as it's got all the feeling of a brick," Wyatt went on cheerfully as he withdrew the needle and checked his patient's pulse, "but all the same you were in a heap of trouble there, Lindy. It took me quite a while to get those bullets out, and one of 'em still ain't *all* out, owing to it broke up when it saw it was heading straight for that flinty ol' heart of yours."

"Nigger lips!"

In fact, so great was Lindy's distress at his oral violation that he had forgotten almost entirely about the first cause of the entire episode: the Michigan truck driver who had finally responded to verbal abuse in a fashion much different from Lindy's expectations. (And, for that matter, so great was the general astonishment at what had happened behind the hardware store that no one who had witnessed the shooting had as yet thought to report it to the state patrol or even to Sheriff Hayes, which left the truck driver with his empty truck and his check from M'Creed and his doubly discharged revolver speeding north along the highway to Memphis, more than likely only ten or fifteen minutes from the state line by now . . . all of which was, as aforesaid, completely lost on Lindy, who was infinitely more preoccupied with the sexual overtones of the perceived assault than he was with the bare facts regarding the almost offhanded and mechanical insertion of leaden projectiles into his thorax.)

"Now the X-ray says you'll be just fine," Wyatt rambled on, entirely oblivious to Lindy's obsession because anyone who had lived in Lee's Corners for longer than a week knew all about Lindy's obsessions, and Wyatt, who had lived in Lee's Corners for considerably longer than a week—and who had apparently found it very profitable to live in Lee's Corners . . . if the medical apparatus he had in his small hospital ward were any indication—had, over the years, treated him for everything from black eyes to bruises to an occasional broken bone occasioned by encounters similar to the one that had resulted in his latest visit. "There ain't one chance in a million that the piece or two I had to leave in there are going to give you any problem for the rest of your entire, godforsaken life, but all the same you really ought to get down on your knees and thank God for His saving your sorry ol' hide, and you ought not to go picking fights with strange niggers. You understand that?"

"Nigger lips!"

Wyatt sighed and put the syringe into the tray for the sterilizer.

Once Lindy got an idea into his head, there was no more chance of getting it out than there was of a mule learning to juggle.

A knock came to the door.

"Come on the hell in!" said Wyatt with the same cheerful abstraction with which he had ordered Alma away from Lindy. (And if the thought of Alma and what she had said to him bobbed to the surface of his cerebral lake and sent ripples spreading across its normally placid surface, his frown was but momentary and inward.)

The door opened and MacDonnell poked his head in. "How's the patient?"

"Nigger lips!"

Wyatt wiped his hands on a towel. "Oh, he'll do. Not quite fit as a fiddle, but he'll do. Needs rest, though." He bent until he was looking into Lindy's face. "You hear me, Lindy? You need rest! When I let you out of here tomorrow—and God damn it, it's going to *be* tomorrow or my name ain't Edward C. Wyatt!—you go home to that shack of yours and you lie down and you stay down for a week. I'll ask Sipsey Dewar to come in and cook for you for that long, and mind you don't say one word to her about . . . about . . . about anything! And I don't want to see you up and running around town or even lounging around in front of M'Creed's for seven days! Seven whole days! You got that?"

"Nigger lips!"

"You're a good Presbyterian—for whatever that's worth—and so I'm damned sho you know how to count to seven. *And on the seventh day He rested.* And you make damn sure you rest *for all seven*! You understand?"

"Nigger lips!"

MacDonnell was leaning against the wall by the door, arms folded, glacial eyes examining the room. And even Wyatt felt a trace of their chill when he looked up and noticed that MacDonnell's cold gaze was resting for a little longer than might have been expected on the equipment standing ready against the wall.

"Took Miss Elsie and me a powerful long time to get those bullets out, Marshall," he said. "Good thing we had everything we needed right here."

MacDonnell nodded. "Good thing," he said. Affably. Your patient got time for a little talk?"

"Nigger lips!"

"Depends on what you want to talk about, Marshal," said Wyatt. "He's kind of running on one track right now."

MacDonnell nodded. "Sho. But I reckon I can throw a switch somewhere and get him onto another."

Wyatt looked at him for a few seconds.

MacDonnell just smiled. "Alone."

"Nipper lips!"

"Don't worry," said MacDonnell. "I won't harm a hair of his head."

His frown having surfaced—not a lot, but enough to be noticed by someone like MacDonnell—Wyatt washed his hands at the white sink in the corner.

"I noticed you had a little talk with Alma Montague," said MacDonnell pleasantly. "I 'magine you had some professional things to say. She was quite a d—"

"That girl?" Wyatt interrupted. "She really ought to know better than mess with a seriously wounded man without training."

MacDonnell stopped with his mouth half-open like a man standing in front of a bear's den who has heard something in the forest *behind* him that sounds much more interesting than any bear; and, after a moment, he contented himself with, "Really?"

"Sick to death herself, too. I never did see the like."

"Sick?"

"Terrible sick," said Wyatt, scrubbing away. "A strong breeze could take her soul right up. I wouldn't be surprised if a little cold brought her down."

"She seemed strong enough to me," said MacDonnell.

"Well, you're asking a doctor's opinion, Marshal, and that's what you're getting. I pray I won't see the day, but it I'm ever called to her bedside, I fear I'll only be there for the end."

MacDonnell's mouth was half-open again, but, yes, he looked as though he was hearing something decidedly more interesting than even the biggest bear he could imagine, and so, silently, he turned . . . and went in search of other prey. "Fragile things, people."

"It's the lot of mortal man, Marshal."

"Nipper lips!"

Both the lawman and the doctor looked, as one, at Lindy, who, naked from the waist up aside from bandages, was still sitting on the edge of the narrow bed. He was staring off into space, eyes wide, lips pursed as though ready to receive, once more, that blub, pneumatic touch.

"That Dark," said MacDonnell. "Knew just what to do. Brought him right around."

"What *did* he do?"

"Something he learned in China, someone said."

"China?" Wyatt was incredulous. "I wouldn't expect that drunken wastrel to get much further than the county welfare office. What was he doing in China?"

"Been all over, I 'magine," said MacDonnell. "Maybe he was in the service." He smiled affably at Wyatt. "Alone."

"Suit yourself. Train's only got one track, though, I think."

And Wyatt dried his hands, pulled on his coat, and left the room. The door closing made a hollow sound that echoed off the bare walls and the checked linoleum floor and the expensive medical equipment that stood around the walls, and MacDonnell tried to remember the last time he had stood in this room. When the expensive equipment had not been there. Four . . . five years ago? He would have to think hard about that when he had a chance.

"Afternoon, Lindy," he said affably.

"Nigger lips!"

"You and I have got to have a little talk, Lindy," said MacDonnell.

"*Nig*ger lips!"

Smiling that affable smile that stopped just north of his mustache, MacDonnell moved in front of Lindy, took him gently by the chin, and altered the orientation of his head until he was looking directly into the marshal's glacially gray eyes. "I said, *You and I have got to have a little talk, Lindy,*" he said. Affably.

Lindy appeared suddenly to be able to see a bit more than Mr. Dark's blub lips. But what he saw made his face darken and his lower lip curve in the direction of a sour pout. "Don't you be forcin' me, Marshal. I heard you promise the doctor that you wouldn't hurt me. Now—"

"I'll call Ed in here this instant if you want," MacDonnell said. "He can give you a good going-over, and he can sign a statement that I haven't hurt you at all."

Lindy attempted to look away. MacDonnell's grip tightened. Not much. Just enough.

"As I'm sho you'll agree."

"What do you want to talk about?"

"You."

"Me?"

"Yup."

"What about me?"

Now that he had the mule's attention, MacDonnell dispensed with the two-by-four, dropping his hand and folding his arms. "All sorts of things about you, Lindy. About how you seem to make it your partic'lar business in life to stir up trouble with every colored man and woman within thirty miles of Lee's Corners. About how you were talkin' to Jim Frammis until he made life so miserable at that mill he runs for Vinty White that someone shot him—"

"Was that tall nigger done it. The one that run off."

"Wasn't any tall nigger about it, Lindy. Man who shot that Frammis boy couldn't have stood more than five-foot-five. But you didn't waste any time before you went and started spreading the word about that tall nigger and his .45, did you? And now there's three or four pounds of buckshot in the front of the jail."

"Maybe he was kneeling down."

"Sho. And maybe he had a magic hat like you read about in some of those fairy tales." And MacDonnell stood there, just stood there, for what must have been at least three minutes. Not long if one is doing something, but when one is sitting up on a narrow bed in a doctor's ward with a couple of freshly closed holes in one's chest, it cannot but seem an eternity, and Lindy was not immune to the effect. About a minute into the treatment, he started to squirm. At two minutes he was more than uncomfortable. Nevertheless, MacDonnell counted—slowly— to one hundred and eighty before he spoke again.

"I don't know what I'm going to do with you, Lindy Buck, but I know what I'd *like* to do with you. I'd *like* to tie your feet to a couple of those cannon balls that we keep digging out of Sol Armstid's north field and throw you in the reservoir. And if I wasn't sho I'd poison most of Oktibushubee County with the seepage, I believe I'd do just that."

Lindy dropped his eyes, looked at the floor. MacDonnell let him.

"All I can say is that it was a good thing for your mother and your sister that Doc Wyatt got to you as quick as he did today. Notice I don't say that it was a good thing for *you,* because I don't give a good God-damn about you, but you got two women up in the hills that get a skinflint's dole of dollar's worth of food from you twice a year, and I know they'd miss it if it stopped comin'."

Lindy was still looking at the floor, but the semi-pout he had demonstrated at the beginning of the interview had vanished, to be replaced by a noticeable clenching of his jaw. And had Mac-Donnell looked (he did), he would have noticed (he did) that Lindy's fists were clenched.

"You have been one damned piece of trouble after another ever since you dragged your sorry behind into Lee's Corners and started looking for a place to squat like a dog that's aiming to wet down a lamppost." MacDonnell told himself that it was somewhat uncharitable of him to act this way toward a man who had been so close to death so recently, but uncharitable or not, it was necessary, and so he continued. "Now, I been toleratin' you in this town since you ain't caused *too* much trouble in the past, but this is the end, Lindy Buck. This is sholy the end. From now on, you so much as look funny at any of the colored folk around here, and I'll get together with Sheriff Hayes and run you out of the county so fast you'll think you're in two places at once."

Lindy suddenly looked up at him, his eyes hot. "You're forgettin' it was *me* that was shot."

"And the way you were carrying on," said MacDonnell, "if I'd a-been there, I just might have offered to reload the pistol. If a man can't see that running around causing trouble is going to get him killed one of these fine days, then he don't deserve to be alive."

"That all you wanted to say?" Lindy was defiant, but Mac-Donnell read that his defiance stemmed more from bravado than from courage.

"That's all I wanted to say," said the marshal. "And you just remember that. One toe over the line, and I'll have you in handcuffs and on the first train to Memphis with a one-way ticket. And don't you even *think* about coming back if I do. You hear me?"

Lindy stared at the floor.

MacDonnell planted himself directly in front of Lindy and glared at the top of his head until the cold forced the wounded man to look up.

"I said, *You hear me?*"

"Yeah," said Lindy. "I hear you."

"And you goddamn well better hear me real good." MacDonnell crossed the room and threw open the door . . . and he had to bend just a little to pat Dr. Wyatt on the head since Wyatt was right there on the other side of the door with his ear pressed against the keyhole. "Just like Doc Wyatt heard me real good."

But Lindy was not looking at him or at Wyatt. He had gone back to staring, jaw clenched, at the checked linoleum floor.

# Chapter 11

"Mr. Dark!"

After the loading-dock crew had carried the still-bleeding Lindy Buck away to Dr. Wyatt's office, the black man had brushed the dirt off his trousers, bowed gracefully to her as though she were the first debutante at the Gardenia Society Tea and Cotillion (and she *had* been first debutante: her father driving her down to town in a carriage all white and gilt and polish . . . though the crimson trim on the wheels was, perhaps, prophetic of the conflict that was to come), smiled, and, with a murmured "Good day, ma'am," had turned to make his way up the street.

Bowing, smiling: as elegant as he had been the night he had appeared at Alma's front door to give her the brass key. But the key was the reason she had driven herself into town, and (one thing leading to another, as always) it had been the reason she had once again blundered into further entanglements with the people of Lee's Corners—first Lindy Buck, and now Dr. Wyatt—when all she wanted, really, was to have it all end . . . forever.

And so, in spite of her plans, in spite of the resolutions that had taken her away from her practice, away from her life in the Northern city—the plans and resolutions that, fully executed and implemented, would have turned her into a hermit for a greater or (as she profoundly hoped) lesser period of time—she found herself trotting after Mr. Dark, whose long legs took him down the street as though he were in a hurry to get someplace, which was more than likely because he looked like nothing so much as a businessman, someone who had come down from Memphis or even from New York on some abstruse errand that had something to do with money and lots of it.

"Mr. Dark!"

He stopped, turned around. "Miss Montague?"

She caught up with him, finding to her chagrin that she was tottering almost breathlessly on her old legs. "Excuse me," she panted. "I really hadn't expected . . ."

Gallantly, he offered his arm. "There are many things in the world we don't expect, Miss Montague. But, then, if we have old folks to get a little dizzy, we have young folks to give them someone to lean on, don't we?"

The two halves of his statement appeared to be connected in some way, though Alma was not exactly sure how. Nonetheless, she accepted his arm, and, after a bit—after she had caught her breath—they set off together down the street. She was not sure where they were going, but it seemed better at present to at least give the impression of a destination, and so she suffered herself to be guided away from the hardware store and out onto DeWitt.

"China?" she said, by way of saying something.

"China, ma'am?"

"You said you learned that . . . that breath thing . . . in China."

He laughed. "Did I? I can't recall now that I quite remember *where* I learned it. It might have been in China."

"You've traveled, then."

"I've been all over, ma'am."

"Are you from Lee's Corners?"

"I reckon I'm from just about everywhere, Miss Montague. I can't think of a square inch of this good old world that hasn't seen my shadow in one way or another."

And he was smiling, and his youthful, black face seemed as sunny as the day; but something about the tone of his voice—too much conviction, maybe, too much *entirely justified* conviction—made Alma pause in her thoughts. Everywhere? He had been *everywhere*? But he was just a baby, too young to have noticed the futility of interaction, too young to have become weary of entanglements, of the fraud of living . . . too young, in fact (and it suddenly dawned on her), even to have received that brass key from her grandfather's hand.

Which brought her straight back to the original question, albeit with some additional complications. "Ah . . . Mr. Dark . . . about that key."

"Key?"

She frowned at him.

"Oh!" he said. "Oh, *that* key!"

"Yes," she said. "*That* key. Would you mind telling me—"

But she broke off in mid-sentence, for the impossibility and absurdity had suddenly fallen on her like a brick wall. She had run after Mr. Dark, calling his name for all of Lee's Corners to hear, and he had waited politely for her, and now she was going to ask him about a key that only existed when someone else was not looking at it, and about a garden that was both utterly impossible and very real (at least to her) . . . both of which she had planned to discuss as though they were the most illogical (or perhaps logical) things in the world, when it was infinitely more likely that the sun had addled her brain, that senility was creeping up on her a little faster than she had estimated, and that the garden had—as was usually the case with gardens—been there all along, and only a foolish old woman who was journeying toward death much more slowly than she wanted could believe, if only for a moment, anything other than that.

"Ah . . ." she said. ". . . ah . . ."

But . . . the key . . .

"The key your grandfather wanted you to have?" he said, setting off once again with Alma still leaning on his arm.

"Yes, that one," she said, thinking quickly in order to come up with something she could say that was . . . different . . . from what she had intended on saying originally. "Now, you can't be much more than thirty, and Grandfather died over forty years ago, so he couldn't possibly have given it to you."

"Ah," said Mr. Dark, "but I never said that he gave it to me. I said that he wanted you to have it. I myself am simply the humble intermediary for his wishes."

And he smiled again, and it seemed to Alma that she had never in her life seen such a smile, for it appeared to partake equally of both joy and sorrow: an infinitely pure, infinitely perfect melding of the bitter and the sweet that left the two inextricably wedded, as though there would never, *could* never, be one without some hint—and maybe much more than a hint: a perfectly equal proportion, in fact—of the other, no matter how unalloyed the emotion might appear to be. Bittersweet: indeed, his expression might well have defined that term succinctly, quintessentially, and forever, speaking for all times and all places the essential nature of the human.

"And the garden?" she found herself asking before she could stop herself, completely undoing everything she had accomplished with her clever dodge a half minute before.

"Your grandfather's garden? Why, Miss Montague, it's a lovely garden, isn't it? I do believe the old man spent many hours in that gazebo, reading."

"Reading *Blithe Spirit*," Alma murmured, feeling a little helpless at the turn the conversation had taken.

"Indeed," said Mr. Dark. "Just that. It was his favorite book." She looked at him hard.

"As I heard the story," he added quickly. A moment of deliberation, which Alma sensed was a tad contrived, then: "It's one of the great Spiritualist classics. Isn't it?"

"Mr. Dark," she found herself saying, "you're not being entirely honest with me."

"I'm being as honest as I can, Miss Montague."

"And what does that mean?" she said sharply . . . but professionalism and breeding both tackled her on the spot, and: "Oh, dear," she said. "That's terribly rude of me. I'm sorry, Mr. Dark. I hardly know you. I've no right to speak to you in such a fashion."

He only smiled again. "I assure you, Miss Montague, there is absolutely no offense taken."

Like everything else about him, his assurance was honest and forthright: he might have been a knight out of an old book.

There was not a shred of the unctuous oiliness that Alma had seen some black men exude when speaking to white women, nor was there the ever-cheerful façade of the properly social-ized colored male. No: Dark was complete unto himself, and if he said something, he meant it, and that was that.

And Alma's heart fluttered.

Right there on the sidewalk, just a little past Webster's Feed and Grain, she stopped short, and, wide-eyed, pressed a hand to her chest.

"Are you not well, ma'am?"

Again, a brick wall had fallen on her, but now it was a brick wall of an entirely different sort. She continued to stand, eyes fixed forward, hand to her chest. "Oh . . . my . . ."

"Ma'am?"

"I'm . . . fine, Mr. Dark. It's just that I . . . ah . . . I just . . . thought of something. Something I hadn't thought about in a long time."

"Old memories?" he asked, smiling. "Happy memories, I hope?"

"I don't have any—" Again, she caught herself on the verge of blurting out something best kept darkling and private. "Not memories, Mr. Dark." She smiled ruefully, feeling the emotion sliding toward the inevitable despair. "It's just that . . . that I can't think of a single old woman I've ever met who didn't want to be young again."

"You?" he said. "Old? Nonsense!" And he took her hand and placed it back on his arm; and together they set off down the street once more.

"What you did to Lindy Buck, Mr. Dark?" she said, by way of changing the subject to something that was not quite so . . . uncomfortable. "I mean . . . was that wise?"

"Wise?"

"You being colored and he being the way he is. He's likely to resent it."

He shrugged: perfect equanimity. "I suppose it's up to him. I had to do what I had to do."

"I'm rather surprised that you put yourself in his way like that."

Mr. Dark shrugged again. This was plainly a subject that he found uncomfortable. Modesty? Alma could not guess.

"It wasn't his time, ma'am," he said. "I knew it wasn't his time. If he chooses to resent me because I saved his life for later . . . well . . . it won't be the first time he's done that."

*Saved his life for later.* She wondered at his turn of phrase. "You're a strange man, Mr. Dark."

He stopped. They had reached the edge of town, and, ahead of them, DeWitt turned from street into county highway, and the highway stretched away in broad, sweeping curves that followed the contours of the land, rising into the hills to the northeast, up toward the headwaters of the Tippah as, oppositely, it unreeled behind them, descending into the flatlands and the deeper, darker bottoms of the southwest, down to the deepflowing Tallahatchie and the ponderous lap and laving of the Mississippi itself. And Alma recalled that afternoon, months past now, when she, looking out of the window of Uncle Buddy's cab, had suddenly remembered the road that led up to Montague Mansion, remembered the hills, remembered even the very trees that surrounded the house, and had felt the intimate, tactile experience of them welling up within her. A Montague she was, born in this place and to this land, and by that birth and by every single one of her memories and her experiences—the very memories and experiences that, collectively, had come to weigh her down with the burden of living—established in the rightness of being here.

It was the hoary old Southern mystique, she supposed, but like a worn corduroy jumper or a much-beloved cotton blouse, it was well known, comfortable, and it fit like no other garment she could imagine, having been warped and wefted upon her soul by virtue of the one having been made concomitantly with the other. And perhaps that was it: perhaps she had come to Lee's Corners and to her family home in order to regain that essential sense of placeness that she had, over the years, and with the bustle of the Northern city and her lucrative practice within it, lost. Oh, death was in there, too, but if one was going to die—and she wanted to die—then one might as well be comfortable about it, particularly after a lifetime of pricks and cuts and the increasing cold ache of undiminished regret. She could do worse than make her passing while she was wearing that jumper and that blouse, and she could do much worse than wearing them in Oktibushubee County, with its heat, its mists, its one-bale tenant farms, and its thick, clinging mud that seemed to put its mark into the hearts of its inhabitants– -white and black alike—like a smudged fingerprint on a windowpane.

"Yes," said Mr. Dark. "I suppose I am."

"It wasn't China, was it?"

"No, it wasn't."

"Where, then?"

"I'm sorry, Miss Montague. I'm afraid I'm not allowed to discuss that."

His tone was suddenly formal. She looked at him, surprised.

But he smiled again—that once-in-a-lifetime, warm, genuine, infinite-joy-and-infinite-pain-all-mixed-up-together smile—and he bowed to her as though she were a great lady.

"I'll take you back to your car, ma'am," he said.

But as though the connection she had with this place had, in its upwelling insistence upon its rights, brought with it some of the old Montague steel—the steel that had won the land from Indian and Englishman alike, that had built the house, that had preserved it through the years of carnage and carpetbaggers— she would not be put off: "You won't tell me about the garden, then."

He seemed genuinely sympathetic. But, then, he seemed— no: he *was*—genuine about everything. "Ma'am, I *can't* tell you about the garden."

"So it's not my imagination, then. There *is*—"

"I can't tell you that, either."

"Well," she demanded, "what *can* you tell—?" But again she caught herself. It seemed that if she were going to lay claim to Montague steel, she had also to accept the limitations of female gentility that went with it.

Yes, she remembered it now. Part and parcel of her family and her family's destiny—or, at least, the destiny her family had planned for her—it was, at root, the reason she had run away, for in that moment of groping epiphany at her first cotillion, she had seen through it, had been revolted by it. And yet, now, like the memories and the interactions that generated them, it had caught up with her. And so: "Oh, my," she said, "there I go again. I seem to have an infinite capacity for the boorish today."

But Mr. Dark was gracious still. "No offense, I'm sure, ma'am."

She tried again. "What about that back gate?"

Worried now. Obviously so. "Oh, ma'am, I asked you not to use it, if you do recall."

"It's locked." She was searching his face, looking for a reaction, looking for something that would tell her . . . tell her something.

But she was disappointed. "Good." He smiled . . . no, he positively beamed. "I was afraid for a moment that Walter—"

And now it was his turn to catch himself.

"I'm sorry, Miss Alma," he said. "I really do have to take you back to your car now."

She smiled at his lapse into a colored man's familiarity. "So you can avoid my other questions, Mr. Dark?"

"Well . . . yes." She blinked at his discomfiting honesty (that was, actually, nothing less than what she had come to expect of him), but he turned and took her hands in his. "It was your grandfather's private garden, Miss Alma," he said softly, remaining with the more intimate form of address. "He spent a good deal of time there toward the end of his life, and he loved it greatly. Beyond that, ma'am, you'll have to go see for yourself."

"You can't tell me?"

"I'm not allowed to."

Alma looked at him for some time. A dark automobile passed by, turned onto the highway. Within it: a puffy, matronly face; an intent child with a spastic hand and a murmuring mouth.

"Use the stile steps, Miss Alma," said Mr. Dark. "Don't use the back gate. And please . . . please be careful."

She blinked. "Is there something out there I need to be careful of?"

He shook his head. "Only yourself, Miss Alma. Only yourself."

\* \* \*

She drove herself home that afternoon, parking the car directly in front of the astonished Isaac and putting the keys into his hand before she climbed the steps to the front door. Lucy was waiting for her with a little silver tray in her hand. There was a calling card on the tray.

"Mrs. Gavin came by when you were out," she explained. "I told her you weren't here, and she left this." She nodded at the card. "I'm sorry, ma'am. I hope I did right. I never worked in a grand house before."

Alma picked up the card. *Sophonsiba Gavin.* "Don't worry about it at all, Lucy. As I'm sure you've noticed, I don't stand on grand ceremony at all." And now she was thinking half about Mr. Dark and half about Sophonsiba Gavin and the web of entanglements that surrounded the woman. And yet a part of her was amused by the card: she had not known Sophonsiba Gavin in her youth. The woman was, as far as Alma could tell, a wife brought in from someplace else by Ellis Gavin's trophy-hunting son . . .

"As randy as Vinty White," she murmured. "I remember now."

"Ma'am?"

"Nothing at all, Lucy," she said, laying aside the involuntary shudder as quickly as she could. "As I said, I don't stand on grand ceremony. You did the right thing."

"Kind of funny, ma'am, that Mrs. Gavin'd be calling on *you.*"

"Lucy?"

"Should be t'other way around, far as I can tell."

"Hmmm . . . yes. I suppose so."

. . . and her time in Lee's Corners was, therefore, relatively inconsequential compared to that of the Montagues, her claim upon the locale infinitely less. With regard to matters of status, then, Lucy was right: it was Alma's privilege and place to take the initiative. How completely inappropriate for Mrs. Gavin to have come calling.

"Well, thank you, Lucy; I'll handle it from here." But Sophonsiba Gavin was only half of what was on Alma's mind, and that half was now rapidly losing ground. "Oh, wait a moment, please. Could you pack up a cold dinner in a basket for me? I have some . . . things to do this afternoon, and I might not be back until after dark."

"Yes'm." And Lucy was off to the kitchen.

Still, Alma stood looking at the card absently, even though her mind was already running along a different, darker track. "I've been remiss," she said to herself. "But, still . . . this tells me quite a bit about Mrs. Gavin. No, excuse me: about *my dear Sophonsiba*."

She would need something frilly in which to make the call, she supposed. (And *she* would be the one to make the call, not any upstart money-by-marriage vulgaroo from up north.) And a new handbag. And white pumps. And—

"Will sandwiches be all right, ma'am?" came Lucy's voice from the kitchen. "I can fry up some chicken, but it won't be cold."

"Sandwiches will be perfect, Lucy. Use your own judgment." Alma set the card aside—time enough for that later—and reached into her handbag for the key. It was, as she expected, there: very solid, quite palpable, and completely imperceptible to anyone else. Save Mr. Dark.

*And please be careful.*

Her stomach clenched at the thought that she was going someplace where she had to be careful, even leaving aside the question of what *only yourself* meant . . . which she sensed that she knew (her stomach clenching all the more when she considered that Mr. Dark apparently knew, too); but a few minutes later, dinner basket in hand and a flashlight stuck in her belt, she was rounding the corner of the mansion, heading for the garden gate.

The gate was still there, as palpable as the key, as undeniable as her own flesh. And Isaac and even Lucy had, doubtless, passed it a dozen times that day: passed its tall, oak-and-iron presence, passed its massive gateposts that looked as though they had each been hewn out of an entire one-hundred-and-fifty-year-old yew trunk, passed its lock that waited expectantly for the key in her pocket.

And it surprised her that she was so calm about it all. She was, she believed, going to a place that had no truck with the threadbare and scrabbling existence of the material world, a place that her grandfather (if she could trust (and she did) Mr. Dark's word) had known intimately, a place that (and now her stomach was clenching again, hard) promised something that she did not want, that she—desiring as she did more than anything to turn to the Great Conductor, thank Him earnestly, and with that wry despair that had been with her for so many years she had lost count of them, courteously return His ticket to him and walk away from the Train and into the absolute annihilation of the Night—utterly and desperately wanted to reject.

She examined the outside of the gate that could not be, surprised that she could believe in something that was not medicine, that was not physical, that smacked so much of the apported trumpets and roses that her grandfather had spoken of so excitedly. Perhaps she was indeed growing old, growing doddering. Would she soon, then, take to collecting little plastic statues of Jesus? Gathering bunches of silk violets into bouquets to hang about her room (yes, she had taken it back, refurbished and redecorated, but it was nonetheless the same room in which she had spent the first eighteen years of her life) with its spinster bed and its window open to the warm Mississippi night full of the sounds of crickets and frogs and Anger Modestie's crooning? Having herself driven into town every week in hat and shawl and cameos and pearls . . . ?

But she could not dismiss it so easily. She was not doddering. And if she had any doubts, why, here was the gate, the gate she was opening at this very moment, the gate that gave onto the path bordered by flowers, that let her into the garden with the plashing fountain and the marble railing and the gazebo standing in the middle of it all: mahogany-pillared, copper-roofed, wisteria-covered, shaded by the magnolia tree that (she did not doubt) was as covered with blooms in January as it was now in July.

The hat and the book were still lying on the bench within, unblemished, untouched, as though her grandfather had left them there not five minutes before, ambling off to pluck a rose for little Ammy, his favorite grandchild, or called off on some errand—

Montague business, perhaps—that required his presence—but only for a moment. He would be back soon enough.

His favorite grandchild picked up the hat. He would not be back. He would never be back. She had, in fact, only heard of his death months after it had occurred, notified by her father only indirectly: via a staid, impersonal letter from Wilfred that had been full of thee's, thy's, and Quaker bluntness.

Odd: in comparison, her father's death seemed more or less an afterthought. It was her grandfather's passing that had mattered, as though the spirit of the house had not resided in the patriarchally descended Montague who had sired her, but in a virtual import: a Hawkins from across the county line, an outsider. And yet it had been her grandfather's death that had wrenched Montague Mansion away from itself and turned it into a soulless collection of wood, plaster, and metal: her father's subsequent neglect of the house had been merely a confirmation of what had already happened.

She turned the hat over and over in her hands, remembering it, remembering what it had looked like on his head, remembering how it had bobbed just beneath her chin as he had carried her piggyback through the forest beyond the drive during those long-ago days before she had grown up and seen what being grown-up meant, before the despair had settled in . . . and as she did so, something slipped out from where it had been tucked within the band: a small card, perhaps two inches by one. It fluttered to the bench, and she saw the flash of blue ink on one side.

She bent, picked it up. Six words in her grandfather's handwriting stared at her from the whiteness of the unsoiled card:

*Come on in. The water's fine.*

She looked up: beyond the gazebo, beyond the locked gate to the rear of the garden. Bracken-covered hills, a dark and uncertain sky. She was sure that some kind of storm was imminent. And yet there was light on the hills, and, far off, there seemed to be a touch of gold.

But another touch of gold—much closer—caught her eye. Beyond the locked gate, just on the other side of a high hedge, someone was passing by, and though Alma could see no more than the top of a blond head, and though she knew that blond head had, years ago, crumbled into dust, she had no doubt about who it was.

She opened her mouth to call out, but then she recalled that she had never known her name. Even after the touch that had passed between them (or, perhaps, because of it), she had never attempted to learn it. And when word of her death at the hands of her husband had come to her, it had come without details. Just a nurse who used to work here once. Dead. The blonde. *You remember, don't you?*

And so Alma had no words with which to call out to one who had been her lifelong beloved, even though it seemed to her that she *must* call out to her, the blond head whisking along on the far side of the hedge, drawing away now.

She was gripping one of the pillars, leaning out. "I . . . I . . ."

There must have been a turning out there, for the blond head suddenly vanished.

Alma was still gripping the pillar, still leaning out. "Please," she mumbled, feeling old, helpless. "Please . . . come back . . ."

But there was no more movement out beyond the hedge, and the hills were still dark, the light fading as she watched. She leaned her head against the warm mahogany, staring out past the railing and the hedge, her heart laboring with what she had seen, with what she wanted. In her hand, the card with her grandfather's handwriting was growing damp, wrinkled, and she finally came to herself enough to notice.

She lifted it, smoothing it out between thumbs and forefingers.

*Come on in. The water's fine.*

Almost with a sob, then, she put the card back into the hatband, put the hat on her head, picked up her dinner basket, and turned for the doorway of the gazebo. But she did not take the flowered path back to the oak-and-iron gate that would return her to Montague Mansion. Instead, she picked her way through the bushes and flowers along the side of the gazebo (there were stepping-stones, she noticed—she should have guessed that there would be: her grandfather would have had it no other way), working her way around to the back, to the locked gate, to the stile steps that led up and over the railing, to the dark lands that lay beyond.

# Chapter 12

The trips to Memphis were a sop, something to keep her pacified, something to prevent her tacit and simmering rebellion from boiling over, at least in Gavin House, and Greta knew it. Clad in her girlish frocks, she would board the train in the morning—*without* Magic (for Mrs. Gavin would have him that day, as she had him almost every day, the time allotted for Greta to interact with her son shortening week by week as the older woman vested herself increasingly with the tacit but quasi-legitimized title of *mother*)—and she would settle in, looking out the window at the all-but-empty station (for though Mrs. Gavin was happy to drop her off, she would not stay to see the train depart, for she had things to do . . . with Magic; nor did it seem at all remarkable to Greta that, though Magic was growing out of pliable infancy and into the beginnings of a strangely withdrawn and silent childhood, Mrs. Gavin always managed to find something to do with him) as the baggage was loaded and the conductors and the engineers carried on in whatever arcane language allowed them to convey to one another the intricacies of the workings of a railroad. And then the last call would be given, the final announcement made, the whistle blown for the last time in a definitive hoot, and the train would be off, rolling toward Memphis.

And Greta might well have been a child again, a blondheaded, sweet-faced niece going off to visit a maiden aunt in the big city. And, in truth, she looked the part. And she knew she looked it. And, inwardly and almost without knowledge (for her anger had become so ingrained that she could not have suppressed it even had she wanted to, and yet it had become a matter of survival for her to keep it suppressed . . . and therefore it had to be hidden even from herself), she cursed her appearance: the childish dress, the ribbons in her hair, the patent leather, flat shoes that were all she was allowed to wear when she should, by right, have had at least one or two pairs of heels like a woman who had—as she had—passed her majority.

Yes, these excursions were a sop: a movie, perhaps, or some shopping (there was a dollar in her tiny purse . . . but what could a dollar buy that an adult woman would have any use for?), perhaps a stroll in the park with other . . . children. But they were a little more than a sop, too, for Greta saw plainly that Mrs. Gavin was managing matters in such a way that she, Greta, was ever more removed from the sight of the town and from any association with Magic. She lived, in effect, in isolation, and while, under some circumstances, this might have been excused as being for her protection, Greta had no such illusions about what was happening now.

Had she not been ensnared, she would have been somewhere else by now—in Biloxi, in Memphis . . . or perhaps farther north: Philadelphia maybe, or New York—and she would doubtless be holding down some menial job, keeping Magic at her side while she scrubbed other people's floors or did their laundry. But the job did not matter. Not at all: it was Magic and the possession of Magic that had come to define Greta, and had she left Lee's Corners at the beginning of her pregnancy, her relationship to him would be beyond question. But escape now seemed well out of her reach, for, having accepted Mrs. Gavin's help for years, she now was enmeshed too firmly in that help and threatened too much by the potential loss of Magic to break free alone.

Alone. That, she finally realized, was the problem. She was alone. Oh, she had Mrs. Gavin, but it was Mrs. Gavin who had engineered her isolation in the first place. No, if she was to escape, if she was to escape *with Magic,* then she would have to find someone who would protect her and support her . . . at least until she could free herself from Mrs. Gavin.

Greta's trips to Memphis, therefore, began to acquire other agendas, and if Mrs. Gavin noticed that she was less sullen when she stepped out onto the sidewalk in front of the railway station and leaned back in through the open door of the car to kiss Magic good-bye (Magic, for his part, seemingly oblivious to kisses and even words from Greta and Mrs. Gavin alike), she perhaps put it down to childish whim, or, at the very least, to resignation. But Mrs. Gavin was wrong: Greta was less sullen because, in fact, she was more hopeful, and she was more hopeful because Memphis was now less of a sop and more of an opportunity. She was twenty-one years old, and she was as reasonably attractive as any woman of her years, and now she was going to Memphis in order to find a protector.

As it was, though, he found her.


"Tch!"

Tiffany sighed and looked up at the ceiling, by now not even noticing the crystal chandelier that hung over the dining-room table because she had become so used to the constant displays of Gavin House that such things as chandeliers, mahogany tables, silver flatware, and fine china were no longer luxury but mere commonplaces. Even the plaster florals that, for some reason, Mrs. Gavin had recently taken it into her head to have piped onto the white ceilings had lost their novelty and had settled into a kind of stale elegance as easily forgettable as a porcelain dog.

When she thought about it at all, which was not very often, Tiffany supposed that she should at least try to keep herself from getting too used to such things, for as her stay in Gavin House had come out of nowhere, it could go back to nowhere very quickly . . . as she well knew, having seen it go back to nowhere for several young people who Mrs. Gavin had decided did not look quite so young anymore (though in some instances Tiffany was quite thankful for those departures, especially that of the one called Sam, for he had constantly laughed in that strange, giggling way, and he had always . . . *stared* . . . at her in a manner that had made her want to avoid being in the same room with him for longer than it took to get from one door to the other).

Not that Tiffany minded being stared at a little, which was why she found the clothes she had to wear while she stayed in

Gavin House—ruffled and frilly and with too many ribbons and bows for a girl who had a couple of breasts worth looking at— more than a little annoying. Tiffany liked her garments on the tight side, so that people could *see* her breasts and her waist and her flat belly. She liked the snugness of cloth against her skin, enjoyed the dimpled indentation of a tight skirt across her groin, relished the feeling of gathered-in, contained fullness provided by a good bra and a low-cut blouse. But life in Nashville had been hard, and she had endured a little too much of what she did not like (which had made her all the more eager to avoid Samson's gaze) to object too loudly—or, in fact, at all—to the child's clothing that Mrs. Gavin insisted she wear.

She had caught on quickly enough, of course, and now, approaching eighteen, she was using elastic bandages on her breasts so that they would not show quite so much. And she was using a few on her waist, too, so that it would not look as though it curved in . . . at least not quite so much. She kept her face bare of makeup—not that she was allowed makeup in Gavin House in any case—and her hair long and parted down the middle, or else gathered up in back save for a few long curls drooping artlessly and girlishly about her face . . . all to keep those telltale signs of physical maturity from shouting their existence too loudly in Mrs. Gavin's ear.

Tiffany had been adapting since she was old enough to know that something was wanted of her . . . and probably even before that, for girl children are quick to understand what is desired of them, and they give it so willingly that by the time consciousness infects them, the habit is so ingrained that they no longer realize that they are giving at all. And, therefore, though much of what Mrs. Gavin wanted ran counter to Tiffany's expectations, Tiffany, used to adapting, was willing to give it . . . in exchange for new clothes (and never mind what they looked like), a fine house, money in her little, child's purse, and movies as often as she wanted. She was, indeed, rather surprised that no one had asked her for sex, but when she thought about it (which was not very often) she supposed that she really ought to count her blessings. Giving sex was tedious work—one really *had* to be somebody else most of the time—and, under the present circumstances, she was perfectly willing to ignore the entire subject.

But what she was finding more and more difficult to ignore was this . . . this . . . this *kid* Mrs. Gavin insisted upon keeping around, and tonight the cooks had forgotten (how many times had she told them, had Mrs. Gavin told them, had, for God's sake, even *Benny* told them?) to remove the bone from his T-bone steak.

And, indeed, having quickly gnawed the blisteringly hot meat from the bone, Magic was, even now, waving it around, jabbing it at everyone in the room.

"Pow! Pow! Pow! This is my pow-er! Mine!"

"Yes, dear," said Mrs. Gavin from across the table. She looked at Benny. Benny looked at . . . something else.

"Benny . . ." said Mrs. Gavin.

"I got rid of it," he said quickly. A little too quickly, Tiffany thought, but Mrs. Gavin did not appear to catch it.

"I told you . . ."

"I said I got rid of it! OK?"

"Pow! Pow! Pow!"

Magic was now pointing the bone at Mrs. Gavin.

"It's not nice to point bones at people, sweetheart," said the older woman with great patience.

"It's my pow-er! My pow-er!"

Daggers at Benny. Benny was still looking . . . elsewhere. That had its advantages, Tiffany knew. It meant that, after dinner, Benny would probably sneak off behind the servants' rooms in order to settle his nerves with a cigarette, and if she followed him there, she could probably bum one off him. It was annoying to have to hide everything all the time, but a cigarette with Benny behind the servants' rooms was a lot better than no cigarettes at all.

"Pow! Pow!"

Mrs. Gavin signed to James, the tall butler. The black man— it was hard to tell where his livery left off and his skin began, so dark was he—stepped forward, reached over Magic's shoulder, and removed the bone.

Magic stared at his hand for a moment.

*One,* Tiffany counted inwardly. *Two. Three* . . .

And then Magic started to scream.

"Tch!" Tiffany cast her eyes up at the ceiling once again. "That's it. Now he's gonna be going on for hours."

"What would you have me do, sweetheart?" said Mrs. Gavin . . . with less patience.

"Oh . . ." Tiffany had overstepped her boundaries, and she scrambled to compensate. "Let him have it back, I guess. He wasn't bothering *me*."

She caught the amused look from Benny. When they met behind the servants' rooms, she would probably hear about how she needed to rub the brown stains off her nose.

"Besides," she said, "since he's got all the meat off, he's finished his dinner. I guess. So he can take the bone outside if he wants."

Mrs. Gavin looked at her for a long moment, then signed to James again. The tall man stepped forward . . . and the bone was back in Magic's hand.

His screams stopped instantly, and just as instantly his "Pow! Pow! Pow!" started up once more.

"Benny, you—"

"I said I got rid of it!"

Benny's sallowness was gone, replaced by a fine rose flush.

"Magic," said Mrs. Gavin, "you may go."

Still jabbing his bone excitedly, Magic was out of his chair in a moment. But before he left the room, he paused before James, who was standing with his back a precise six inches from the wall, his spine ramrod straight, his eyes looking directly ahead, his hands clasped behind him.

Magic pointed the bone. "Pow!" he said.

James did not move. It was not his business to move.

"Pow!"

James still did not move.

"POW!" And, as hard as he could, Magic rammed the bone straight into James's crotch. Black as he was, James turned faintly gray, and his eyes suddenly looked glassy. But he did not budge.

*"POW!"* And Magic rammed the bone home once again. This time, though, Benny was on him in a moment, and in an-

other moment the sallow youth had half dragged Magic out of the room.

"James," said Mrs. Gavin, "you'd like to freshen up, I'm sure."

"Yes'm."

"You may go. Tell Edith to attend to us until you're ready to come back."

"Yes'm."

And, walking stiffly, James made his way out through the kitchen door.

Benny returned in another minute, dusting his hands. "He's outside in the garden, Mommy."

Mrs. Gavin looked at him. "With the . . ."

"With the bone," said Benny cheerfully, though Tiffany noticed that it sounded forced.

Mrs. Gavin only looked at him. "With his pow-er, Benny. Yes?"

Benny sat down, looked down at his plate.

Tiffany knew what was going on, and she knew also that Benny had not gotten rid of the pistol at all: he had merely hidden it deeper in one of his drawers, inside a wooden box. Nor was this any temporary provision, for Benny had no more intention of disposing of the pistol than he had of disposing of his own manhood . . . which was, as Tiffany knew—and as she was sure that Mrs. Gavin knew also—growing on him. In the last few months, in fact, Benny had begun to demonstrate some remarkable signs of maturity, and even when he had protested that he had gotten rid of the pistol, he had done so in a voice that, despite barely suppressed cracks and squeaks, was, nonetheless, tending toward lower registers.

"Yes," said Benny.

"Can we finish dinner now?" said Tiffany with just the right girlish lilt to her voice. "I think it would be nice if we finished dinner now."

"I got rid of it," said Benny. "I did. Magic won't ever see it again."

"Can we . . . ?"

"Shut up!" said Benny, whirling on her.

"Children! Children!" said Mrs. Gavin. "We can have a nice dinner together, can't we?"

"Yeah," said Benny. "A nice dinner. This is a good steak, Mommy."

Mrs. Gavin beamed. "Thank you, Benny. You know I always want the best for my little sweethearts."

Faintly, from the French doors that opened onto the garden, Tiffany could hear a voice: "Pow! Pow! Pow!"

She shifted. The bandages around her breasts seemed very tight this evening, so tight that she could hardly breathe, and the wrappings around her waist felt as though they were about ready to smother her. She wished that her body would just hurry up and make up its mind how big and how small it wanted to be so she could figure out how to cope with it. If she could just get through this dinner, she could loosen the wraps a little, and then she could find Benny behind the servants' rooms and have a smoke. After that thing with poor James—stupid, moronic brat!—they both needed to settle their nerves.

"Pow! Pow! Pow!"

He was an old man with a face that spoke of years and decades and then more years and more decades following a furrow behind the back end of a mule with nothing to look forward to save a to-morrow containing more furrows and more of the same back end of the same mule.

But he was sitting on the warped and weathered porch of a one-room shack, tipped back in his chair with a steel-stringed guitar that looked as though it had been, quite early on, flung out into the road and driven over by a morning's worth of traffic, taken in, put back together with spit, piano wire, and maybe a wad or two of chewing gum, played a bit, then flung back out and left to season under the rolling rubber of a hundred cars and trucks before being brought in and fixed up once again . . . now to be pressed to his belly while one hand scratched at the strings and the other ran the neck of an old wine bottle up and down in quavering blue notes and slides that flowed as pungently and smooth as the syrupy water of the Mississippi itself.

And he was singing—if a rasping drone as unintelligible as a cicada's rattle could be called singing—a compilation, it seemed, of old, half-forgotten blues, bawdy folk songs, and an occasional field holler thrown in, all swapping around and mixing up and making one another sound not better but less distinct, as though any part or fraction of his vocalizations could be interchanged with any other part without anybody being particularly able to notice.

But he stopped singing when he saw Alma, and his hands fell away from the strings. "Why, how do, ma'am? And what brings you this way on this fine morning?"

Alma shaded her old eyes up at a sky that did not look much like morning . . . or any other time of the day, for that matter. Muted and dark, almost-but-not-quite oppressive, it nonetheless emitted a kind of diffuse, shadowless radiance that mimicked daylight. It was not night, to be sure, but it was certainly not morning, either. Or, at least, nothing that Alma would call morning.

But to the man on the porch, it seemed, it was indeed morning, and a fine one, too; and he smiled with all the geniality that his cracked-leather sack of a face could contain.

"I'm . . ." And there, for a moment, Alma stopped. Why *was* she here on this fine . . . whatever? Since she had climbed the stile, found a passage through the hedge, and set off down the road (following, but not really hoping—hope had died long ago—to find that blond head out of her past), she had lost track. Or maybe her action—decided upon on the spur of the moment, made on the basis of emotion rather than logic, rooted in the words (or, rather, the *omissions*) of Mr. Dark—had possessed no real reason or aim beyond proving to herself that this place in which she now stood did not exist.

For a moment, her body rebelled against her, tugging from within in a desperate attempt at flight from a realm where it sensed, with something beyond instinct, something deeper, more palpable and material than instinct, that flesh and blood had no business. But as she had denied it when it had begged for sleep during the thirty-hour, doctor-on-duty shifts of her internship, so she denied it now. She would stay. She would continue. And though she did not yet know why it was so important that she look upon what she had previously thought unthinkable, look she would.

On her head, her grandfather's hat and its invitatory note mocked her.

"I'm out for a stroll, Uncle," she said. "I'm a stranger in these parts."

"Oh, a blind man in a hoodwink coulda seen that, ma'am," the man said. " 'Course you a stranger. Ain't none but strangers come here carryin' a dinner basket."

It was the opening Alma had wanted . . . or perhaps the one she had feared. "What . . . *are* these parts, Uncle? Where am I?"

"I'm sorry, ma'am. I'm afraid I'm not allowed to discuss that," came the reply so promptly and formally that Alma blinked.

"You're not?" she blurted.

"Not what, ma'am?" said the man, back to smiling genially . . . as though he had not heard what he himself had just said.

"Ah . . ." Alma looked up and down the road. It continued on in much the same way as it had begun: more or less straight, but not quite; fairly flat, but not too much; bearing off into the . . .

East? West? North? South? She had no idea. The land was rolling . . . a little. There had been no signs, and there was no sun to tell her the directions. Just the muted, incandescent sky and the shadowless light over all.

"How long have you lived here, Uncle?" she said.

"Lived here, ma'am?" He smiled all the more, his hands straying to his guitar as though they would play it with no volition on his part at all.

"I'm sorry. How long have you *been* here, then?"

He smiled on and on. "Oh, I been here, I reckon, 'bout as long as I can remember."

It was a singularly useless answer as far as Alma was concerned. "Is there a town nearby?"

"Lee's Corners be over that hill, ma'am."

Alma shook her head. "Lee's Corners can't possibly be that close. Montague Mansion is fifteen miles out of town, and I haven't been walking any more than fifteen minutes."

"Be just over that hill, ma'am." Still the big smile. "Maybe you be walkin' faster than you think?"

She looked ahead to the hill. "Maybe. I suppose it's possible." She tried again, hoping. "Where did you say I was?"

Again the reply came, prompt and formal. "I'm sorry, ma'am. I'm afraid I'm not allowed to discuss that."

Alma nodded. "Just so. Thank you, Uncle."

"Be my pleasure, ma'am. You keep a sharp eye on yo'self, you hear?"

Alma smiled thinly. "I've kept a sharp eye on myself for seventy-seven years, Uncle. I'm not about to stop now."

It was his turn to blink . . . and then he looked at her for a long time. "Seventy-seven years, ma'am? Oh, I am sorry 'bout that."

"One gets used to it," she said as she turned away in the direction of the low hill that, like the other hills she had seen, climbed, and descended since she had taken this brooding, rutless road, was so low that it hardly warranted being called a hill at all. Nevertheless, it did block the view ahead, and so perhaps the designation was not completely unwarranted.

As she made her way up the slope, though, a thought occurred to her: that man with the guitar . . . he had looked almost familiar. But when she turned around, both he and his shack were gone, and he suddenly was one with all the faces of her life . . . the faces she had seen retreating into the past, heading off into other places, the faces she had known, recognized, gained insight from a moment too late: a lover lost, a child stillborn, a blond head that had passed by and taken a turning into invisibility.

Perhaps that was why he had seemed so familiar: because he would be passed by, because he would be unrecognized until it was too late to recover him. The aborted interchange, the stillbirth of recognition, was, after almost eight decades, so much a part of her existence that it had come to possess its own familiarity and its own custom.

Of course. Why should it be any different here? And perhaps therein, too, lay her belated recognition. He had put a face to her despair and her fear, for he had shown her that no matter which side of the border between life and death she stood upon, nothing would change. The burden of simple continuance, with all its failings and its disappointments—and its constant remembrance of both—would dog her from one world to the next.

She pulled off her grandfather's hat and felt in the band for the little card.

*Come on in. The water's fine.*

There it was. Blue ink. The unutterable curse of her grandfather's confidence and promise.

"No," she murmured. "I don't want it. I don't want the water, fine or otherwise."

And then she knew why she was here. She might have followed the blond head, but she did not want to find the woman it represented. She might have had thoughts of the dead child, but she did not want to see him. But that was not it, either. She did indeed want to find them both, but she wanted to find them in order to prove to herself that, contrary to her grandfather's beliefs— contrary, in fact, to the existence of the garden, to the presence of the book, to the note that the old man had somehow contrived to leave for her—there was no water. She wanted to demonstrate to herself without room for question or doubt that if there was something here—wherever here was—then it was something that was not life . . . nor even death. It was something else. It *had to be* something else.

Had to be. Something else. Memory, desire . . . anything that was not a continuance of personality and consciousness.

Alma stood in the shadowless light, her knees throbbing with age and unaccustomed exertion. Yes, seventy-seven years was a long time. But it was nothing, really, to be sorry about. What was the grief of it was the thought that all one had to look forward to at the end of seventy-seven years—or seventy-eight, or seventy-nine, or eighty—was . . . more of the same. Just more of the same. And no: one never got used to it. Ever.

She put the card back in the hatband, but she heard footsteps, and she looked up to find a young woman with a child in her arms climbing the hill. She was obviously the child's mother, but she seemed ridiculously young to have given birth . . . until Alma looked closer and saw that, though her garments were childish, there was a mature body within them.

Alma was half of a mind to speak to her, but as it appeared that the young woman did not see her, she remained silent.

Slowly, doggedly, as though wading into an unseen swamp, the young woman came toward her, passed her, went up and over the hill, disappeared behind it.

But the child had been looking back, and like the old man on the porch of the house, he had looked familiar, but Alma could not place him. Who else had she missed, ignored, not noticed for just a moment too long?

"Memory," she said to herself. "It's just memory. It's all just memory." But she was already trotting up the hill, her breath tightening in her chest, her eyes straining at the seam of earth and sky sinking before her as if she would see through it to whatever lay beyond.

She saw soon enough, though, and it did not surprise her at all—it was to be expected, really—that the young woman and the child were gone. Instead, the road stretched off and down the hill into a valley surrounded by forested hills. There, smoky with the exhalations of the coal-fired power plant, dusty with unpaved streets, filled with a mishmash of automobiles and buggies, houses she remembered from her childhood and houses that had been torn down a decade ago, was Lee's Corners.

She started down the hill.

# Chapter 13

Lee's Corners—at least, *this* Lee's Corners: the Lee's Corners that was *here* . . . wherever here was—might have bustled. There were certainly enough people in it, certainly enough vehicles on its streets, certainly enough activity in its shops. But it did not bustle, for bustling implies spark and verve, and neither of those qualities applied to what Alma saw or sensed in the town. This Lee's Corners, muted as the sky above it, moved in a kind of a subdued glide, like a patch of fog on a glassy ocean; and on its streets Confederate uniforms mixed somnambulistically with celluloid collars and narrow ties, just as hoopskirts mingled with flapper fashions and shirtdresses. Buggies and surreys held their languid and accepting ground alongside motorcars, while, to either side, buildings she had once known faded in and out from behind contemporary façades and gaslights flickered uncertainly within the nimbus of incandescent bulbs, one changing into the other and back in the time it took to tell a minute.

No one noticed her. No one, it seemed, noticed much of anything. Bows and smiles, doors opening and closing, an occasional automobile horn or the jingle of a shop bell: the sounds and actions of life without there being anything more to them than sound and action. And above it all hung the sky and its brooding incandescence: the shadowless light that suffused even the narrowest alleyway with tremulous brilliance and scrubbed away even the faintest vestige of Alma's shadow as she walked down the street, rubbing shoulders with the dead, breathing their air, leaving her footprints in the dust that was marked with the tracks of their shoes and boots.

She knew they were dead, and yet . . . and yet doubt followed her down the street, for not even the most outré prophesies of her grandfather's books had allowed for such an admixture of existences, nor had they intimated the sullen but bright skies and the foglike movement of the town. This might well have been a dream, with bits and pieces of memory and unconscious happenstance thrown together willy-nilly, jumbled past and present, fantasy and reality vying with one another in outrageousness.

Reality? Memory?

Alma stopped, bent, picked up a toy horse that a child had dropped, offered it to the tiny hand. Wide eyes, a snatch, and the horse and the child were both gone, fading into the fading façade of Jamison's Drugstore . . . or was it McCoy's Soda Shop? Alma shaded her eyes against the shadowless light and peered at the sign, but she could not make it out. The letters wavered before her. The outlines of the building, even its apparent location, rippled back and forth between one and the other with the disoriented liminality of a freighter's loom. Nevertheless, with her grandfather's hat on her head and her dinner basket on her arm, she followed the child, entered the building through a door whose fastening changed from handle to knob to latch even while her hand was closed about it, and sat down at the marble counter beside Abaijah Jones, who had been buried weeks ago.

"Afternoon, Abaijah," she said.

"Howdy, Alma. You've come home, I see."

"I arrived in April, Abaijah."

"April." He was drinking coffee and eating pie. "April. That's a nice word. April."

She peered at his face. His flesh was sound, his eyes clear. No animate and rotting corpses here. But he was staring off and up at the shelves above the soda machines and the spigots and the sink, and the chrome and the mirrors and the lights reflected on his thick glasses.

"April." He might have been turning a caramel over and over in his mouth.

"How long have you been here, Abaijah?" she asked.

He smiled. "Been here as long as I can remember, Alma."

She nodded, remembering the black man at the roadside shack. "Yes. Yes, I imagine so."

"You're looking well."

He was not looking at her, but: "Thank you. It's been a while, hasn't it?"

"Been a long time. A long, long time."

"It's nice to be remembered." She bent her gray head, looked at her hands, at the liver spots and the wrinkles and the knuckles left knobby by seventy-seven years of decrease. And what perceptible, qualitative difference was there between her living hands and the hands of Abaijah? Or of the child who had snatched the carved horse? None that she could see. None that was meaningful.

Again, the panicked tug from her flesh nearly overwhelmed her and sent her stumbling away from the counter, out the door, back toward the stile steps that would take her . . . back. But she remained where she was: making small talk with the dead.

"Any news?" she said.

"No news here in Lee's Corners, Alma. Always about the same in this place."

She had to try. "And what . . . what *is* this place, Abaijah?"

"I'm sorry, Alma. I'm afraid I'm not allowed to discuss that."

She had been expecting that exact response, and so she nodded again and ordered coffee from the busty woman behind the counter. The cup came, warm and fragrant, but the liquid had no taste. Or maybe, she reflected, it had taste only to those who belonged here. It might be. It could be. But that theory assumed that this place was real, that it was neither dream nor memory, but another state of existence entirely. And she did not want to believe that.

"You've been here . . . as long as you can remember, Abaijah?"

"Long as I can remember, Alma," he said, and he was still not looking at her. The chrome and the mirrors and the lights gleamed on his glasses.

She kept her eyes away from him. "How long do you reckon that is?"

"I'm sorry, Alma. I'm afraid I'm—"

"Not allowed to discuss that. Yes, Abaijah. I know." She

sighed, looked at her hands again. "Forgive me for troubling you."

"No trouble at all, Alma."

"How is your wife?"

"Oh, she's fine."

"And my brothers?"

"They're fine, too. Just fine. Everybody's just fine."

She forced herself not to ask about her grandfather or her parents. She sipped at the tasteless coffee, shook her head, put the cup aside, and leaned toward Abaijah. She did not know. She had to try. "Are you . . . happy?"

For the better part of a minute he did not reply, and Alma was afraid that she was going to hear, once again, the formal, formulaic response. But Abaijah blinked up at the chrome and the mirrors and the lights. "Happy," he said at last. "That's a nice word. Happy."

And when he said it, he did indeed look happy. And so Alma nodded at him once more, mustered a smile. "You take care, Abaijah."

"You too, Alma. See you again sometime."

With another forced smile for the busty woman behind the counter, Alma left a dime for her coffee and went back out to the street.

The dead. Yes, they were all here. Moving, speaking—

She saw Marshal MacDonnell's police car suddenly round the corner, pass a buggy that she was sure could not have existed any later than 1850, and ease up to the intersection. Almost without thinking, she waved frantically and ran for the curbside, almost colliding with someone in uniform.

Craggy features towered over her. A smile. "Do be careful, ma'am. I do believe you might do yourself an injury if you insist upon carryin' on that way."

She recognized him from a life-sized statue that had stood over a grave in the cemetery. "Uh . . . thank you. Sir."

"My pleasure, ma'am." A twinkle of blue eyes, a lifting of a hat, and he was gone . . .

. . . and MacDonnell's car was pulling past.

She turned to the street. "Marshal!" she almost screamed.

And there he was. Mustache. Cold gray eyes. The motor purred as he shifted to neutral, leaned across the seat, and rolled down the passenger-side window. "How are you, Miz Montague?"

"I'd be a lot better if I knew where I was."

She had spoken before she had thought, and the gray eyes examined her, puzzled. "You're in Lee's Corners, Miz Montague. At the corner of Jefferson and DeWitt." A glance, evaluating. "Do you need a ride home?"

Perfectly natural, perfectly at ease. And yet . . . something was wrong. No, not with MacDonnell. This . . . this *place* was wrong. "What is this place, Marshal?"

"I'm sorry, ma'am. I'm afraid I'm not allowed to discuss that."

As she had expected.

"Thank you, Marshal," she said. "I can find my way back just fine."

A nod. "You just let me know if I can be of service."

Memory? Or reality? "Yes," she said. "Yes. Of course. Thank you."

"My pleasure, ma'am."

And he rolled up the window and pulled away from the curb, weaving carefully among carriages and Model-T's and horses, taking the corner smoothly.

Gliding, moving through the actions of life, the town went through its motions about her as she, in turn, glided and moved through the town, wandering as aimlessly as if it were she who was the shade, returned now to visit the scenes of youth and life and, perhaps, even optimism. Streets and sidewalks—cobbled, dust, wood, and concrete—passed beneath her feet, and still about her she saw the gestures, the muted, social intercourse that at once echoed, mocked, and beckoned to her, continuing here beyond the borders of life as though it had never ended, summing the past and the dead—and, seemingly, the living and the present, too—into a drifting, inescapable whole.

Perhaps, she thought as she came to a stop on yet another street that hovered somewhere between the familiarity of memory and the recognition of reality, one had to be dead in order to understand the how or the why of it all . . . but the revulsion that arose from that thought nearly sent her to her knees.

She did not want understanding from death. She did not want anything from death save annihilation, oblivion. And yet about her, clinging to some kind of shadowy, lingering existence, were interactions of a sort, commerce of a sort. She saw money change hands in the warm interior of a bakery. She saw couples chatting in the park. And what else was there? Fornication between shades in the back rooms of the hotel? Letters gone astray at the post office? Misunderstandings? Mistakes? Lovers' quarrels? Eyes that met, exchanged a lifetime, and then parted forever? Infants doubly, trebly stillborn because of a minute's pause?

She found a bench and sat down. In the branches of the chinaberry tree above her head, birds twittered softly, purposelessly. Across the street, at the old railway station, the young woman she had seen on the hill came out, descended the steps with her child in her arms, and paced slowly toward the edge of town.

"It's just a dream," she said. Her eyes were aching, her vision blurring. "Please . . . it has to be just a dream."

Lindy Buck was no better a patient than he was a Presbyterian, and if he stayed in bed at all, it was not because Dr. Wyatt had told him to, but because the pain of his wounds made doing anything else inconceivable. Outwardly compliant but inwardly raging—at his injuries, at the stupidity of an ignorant nigger truck driver who could not even kill a man with *two* bullets at point-blank range, at Delphi M'Creed for allowing such stupidity to deliver goods to his store, at Alma Montague for having the gall to open his shirt in public even though she was as polluted as it was possible for a white woman to be, at Dr. Wyatt himself for having forced him to submit to a lecture when everyone in town knew that, just like everyone else in town (save, to be sure, Lindy Buck), Wyatt was a craven, unrepentant sinner who would, without a doubt, be cast into the unquenchable flames on Judgment Day—Lindy lay on his thin mattress, gasping in the heat that glared down at him from the lath and tar-paper roof of his house, listening helplessly to the rattle and clank as Sipsey Dewar (who, because of Dr. Wyatt's request, had come in without so much as a by-your-leave from Lindy himself) fixed his dinner in the battered, dented, unwashed pots and pans Lindy had been using (and not washing) since he had come to Lee's Corners and bought them, with much complaining about their cost, at the hardware store owned by the godless Delphi M'Creed (who, like the rest of the town, would be right there beside Wyatt on Judgment Day).

But all this was as nothing compared to the deep and profound fury that welled up from Lindy's soul when he considered (as he did often) Mr. Dark's brazen and physical intrusion into his life and his person. It was not a matter of judgment, it was a matter of honor, and Lindy would not, *could* not allow such an action to stand without some kind of response.

"I be fryin' you up some chicken, Mr. Buck," came Sipsey's cracked voice. "Doctor Wyatt said you needed that pro-teen stuff."

Lindy did not reply, for his anger called either for screams or for silence; and Sipsey must have decided that he was sleeping and that she should therefore leave him alone, for she did not speak again, making no sound at all, in fact, save for the inevitable rattles and clanks of kitchen work ... which suited Lindy just fine, for it allowed him to be alone with his pain and his outrage, to dwell deeply and without interruption on the remembered sensation of his violation: Dark's dribbling, blub lips pressed firmly down on his own, and ... and ... and had there perhaps been an exploratory flick or two of a nigger tongue in there somewhere? By God, yes! Dark had used the bloody incapacitation of his victim in order to satisfy his own depraved, sexual lusts!

Lindy felt cold, then hot, and then cold once more. Yes, it had happened. It had happened to *him*. That flick of a tongue. That breath, reeking of the brown odor of Negro, forced down into him as though to impregnate him with black spawn. It was one thing for a mother and father to prostitute their daughter (and they had got what was coming to them) or for that daughter to give herself over to the life of a whore-slave to a fast-talking nigger from Nashville (and she had got what was coming to *her,* too), but it was something else entirely for a degenerate like Dark to force himself on a wounded man.

And Lindy knew that there could be but one answer to such a gross liberty.

He was hot now. Very hot. And the sunlight falling on his shack had nothing to do with it, for it was an inner fire that made the sweat bead up on his forehead and trickle down the sides of his face as his eyes, open, stared at the hot roof as though he would rise up and punch a hole through it. But then he recalled MacDonnell's warning, and he suddenly grew cold again, and his belly tightened up into a knot that had nothing to do with pain or hunger (and why was that damned colored woman taking so long with that chicken?), for he knew MacDonnell well enough to know that the marshal was quite serious about it. Not that Lindy thought for an instant that MacDonnell would send him out of town in handcuffs, but he knew that the marshal was capable of just about anything short of that, for he knew with a loiterer's eyewitness conviction about the prisoners who had been whisked out of the jail before the lynch mobs could gather, about the unofficial searches that MacDonnell made of warehouses and homes and fields—not breaking and entry, really, and not even entry: just the stopping of the police car and a cold, gray examination from eyes that saw a bit too much for anybody's comfort—and about the owners of bad-whiskey stills who had just vanished from the vicinity of the town (and, in some cases, from the vicinity of Oktibushubee County entirely). And so Lindy knew also, with that same accuracy and conviction, that MacDonnell would make good his word, and that, at his whim and pleasure, somehow, *somehow,* he would dispossess Lindy of his place in the town and send him on his way, never to return.

Now, it crossed Lindy's mind that perhaps such a turn of events might, in the end, be justified, for it would let a godless town of bitchery and abomination (and that Montague woman was but the last and the worst of the lot) plunge headlong into perdition without even the faint hope of salvation embodied by Lindy himself. But the outrage of having his actions dictated to him by a such a sinner as MacDonnell made him turn hot once again, and once again the sweat began rolling down the sides of his face. To think that MacDonnell had possessed the gall to threaten him . . . and particularly after Wyatt had possessed the gall to lecture him . . . and particularly after Dark had—

It was too much for Lindy to bear, but bear it he had to, for he was too weak and in too much pain to get up. At most, he could clench his fists as he continued with his inward rage at the godless heathens of the town in general . . . and MacDonnell and Wyatt and Dark in particular. And Dark *most* in particular, for Lindy's rage, redoubled by Wyatt's admonishments and MacDonnell's warning, was instantly reflected straight back onto Dark.

And he knew what he had to do.

But there was MacDonnell.

Cold again.

But Dark . . .

Hot again.

Sipsey's rattles in the kitchen continued as Lindy's fists clenched even harder and his eyes stared up at the hot roof. It would take planning. It could not be anything thrown together like some dice-game, razor-fight, cut-and-run nigger like Dark would do. It had to be a white man's plan and a white man's revenge, and it did not matter how long it took to put together and carry through just so long as it *was* put together and it *was* carried through. It might take weeks. It might take months. But it *would* happen. Lindy would see that it did.


"Hello, Lucy."

The cook turned around with a gasp. "Miz Montague! I sholy wasn't expectin' you! You ain't gonna stay out, then?"

"I'm not going to . . . what?"

"Did you want supper, then, ma'am?"

Alma looked at the dinner basket that was still on her arm, then at the kitchen clock. Yet another characteristic of the garden and the lands beyond: no more than a few minutes had passed since she had set off for the garden gate. "There's no sense in you fixing anything else tonight, Lucy," she said, keeping the tremor out of her voice with the same force of will with which she had kept her body from fleeing the company of the dead. "Just lay a plate on the kitchen table and I'll eat what you

put in the basket. Buddy will be coming by soon, and you might
as well go home a little early and be with your man."

Lucy could not conceal her smile. "Yes'm."

But Alma was looking toward the window. *Be with your man.*
Couples. Coupling. And, in the Northern city, the empty house
she had returned to night after night. She had followed a blond
head into another world, but she had never seen the woman to
whom that head had belonged. Had she merely been mistaken?
Had the head been no more than a lure?

Weary, too weary to remain standing, she sat down at the
kitchen table and took off her grandfather's hat. "Lucy . . ."
Again, she had to think, to phrase the question in such a way
that she would not be thought deranged. "About . . . this hat . . ."

Lucy had turned around with plate and silverware in her
hands, and Alma could tell from her eyes that, yes, she could
see the hat. It was not her imagination, then. It was not a dream.
At least, it was not wholly a dream.

"What about the hat, ma'am?"

"How old would you say it is?"

"Oh, ma'am, it looks too new to be that old. But it's an old
style."

Alma nodded, felt in the band for the note. "Yes. It's old. It
belonged to my grandfather."

Lucy moved to set the plate and silverware before her.
Numbly, Alma watched her deft, brown hands. "He must've
taken real good care of it, ma'am."

"I believe he did, Lucy. Yes." Alma laid the hat aside, looked
at the paper in her hand.

*Come on in. The water's fine.*

From outside, through the open windows, came the sound of
an automobile engine. "Don't worry about the dishes," said
Alma. "I'll take care of them. You hurry home with Buddy."

A look from Lucy. Alma knew it well.

"Or," she added, "if you want me to leave the dishes for you
tomorrow, that's perfectly all right."

Lucy, assured of her absolute dominion in the kitchen, smiled. "Yes'm. Thank you."

"No problem at all. I'll see you in the morning, then. You have a good night."

"Night, ma'am."

And with a *tap-tap* of light shoes, Lucy was off to fetch her purse and her coat. Alma heard the door open and shut. More distantly, she heard snoring: Isaac was in his back bedroom, already asleep. He invariably rose with the sun to attend to the grounds.

The grounds that contained the garden.

The sound of a car door opening, closing, and Buddy's engine faded into summer's lingering daylight. Alma ate, surprised that she could be so hungry while being so tired that it was an effort to move her hand to grasp a sandwich. But even though she had been beyond the bournes of life long enough for her biology to have had every reason to expect her to be asleep, it was not physical fatigue that so afflicted her; it was, rather, intellectual weariness . . . or, perhaps emotional. The titanic labor of holding within her single ability to believe two mutually exclusive possibilities had told heavily upon her—was still telling—and her mind was on the verge of collapsing on its figurative face.

What should she do? What *could* she do? There was no way out for her: faced as she was with the utter destruction of her hopes regarding the afterlife . . . no, better: faced as she was with the absolute *uncertainty* of her hopes regarding the afterlife, there seemed to be no choices left to her but madness and death . . . which were, she reflected, no choices at all, for madness would make a torment of the remainder of her life, and death would possibly lead her straight into the torment of unending existence.

She dropped the remains of the sandwich back onto the plate, pushed herself to her feet, and put the plate and the rest of the food into the icebox. With what fragments of objectivity she had left, she recognized that she was caught in an endless loop of thoughts. The only thing to do, then, was to sleep.

Her steps and her mind were both teetering as she went out to the front hall to take the stairs up to her bedroom, but on the side table by the front door, she saw the visiting card still lying on its silver tray, and as she paused at the first tread with one hand on the banister to steady herself, she picked it up, read it . . .

*Sophonsiba Gavin*

. . . and put it back down. Yet something else she had to do in order to hold up her part of the motions of existence, yet another entanglement in this life of entanglements that threatened to be only a rehearsal for the more complex entanglements of the next.

She shook off the thought, for she simply could not contemplate it any longer without weeping or collapsing. Come morning, then, she would shop for something appropriate for a visit . . . which she intended to make herself: she was not about to allow Sophonsiba Gavin to claim the status of initiating the call again. If there was calling to be done, it was the Montague who would do it.

But as she pulled herself up the stairs, one by one, weary beyond all her previous conceptions of weariness, the card and the name on it brought back a recollection of the glimpse of Sophonsiba Gavin she had caught at the railroad station when she had first returned to Lee's Corners: the childless but matronly woman on her knees, embracing the enigmatic Magic Harlow.

And then she remembered. The hill. The young woman climbing up it with a child in her arms, and the child looking back as the mother, unseeing, passed Alma on her way into a Lee's Corners that could only exist on the far side of the Veil.

Alma stood still, her hand tightening on the banister. No. It could not exist even there. It *could* not. Because that would mean . . .

But even in the midst of the whirl of her denial, she remembered the woman, and she remembered the child, and she remembered also the tantalizing familiarity that had hovered about the boy's features. And now she knew the reason for that familiarity.

\* \* \*

There might have been some women in Lee's Corners who might have been proud to sport a black eye in public and so indicate to the town that their husbands were still willing to hit them and that they were still capable of giving them reason to, but Alice Harlow was not one of them. Quiet to begin with—quiet when she had watched her husband eject her daughter from her house, quiet when her grandson continued to drift farther and farther from her reach, quiet when her husband had been laid off at the bank, forcing them to sell the big, fine house and buy the small, shabby one—she now became quieter still, and John Harlow had to endure, right alongside a silent supper of bacon ends and beans and corn bread, that discolored eye silently staring at him (even though she herself was not) across the greasy plates.

In return, John Harlow became quieter himself, but regardless of what motivated or was contained by Alice's silence, his own was an impulse and a crucible for a growing, brooding rage that, as though given form and substance by his very wordlessness and no longer liable to dissipation by verbal or physical outbursts—whether at his wife or at the empty air—now grew dark and potent.

He did not feel guilt for having maimed his wife. That action appeared to him to be merely incidental: but one more sign of the hold the rich woman maintained on his life, touching now not only his blood and his kin but his very self. And if his silence was giving his rage impulse and form, then, glared at by that black eye (though Alice's gaze was anywhere but on her husband), his thereby increasing knowledge of the depth of his personal violation was giving it potent fodder on which to batten, for he found himself clutching at doorframes and window frames as he passed them, grasping bedpost and table alike in order to keep himself from turning his back on his wife and his home, walking through the falling evening, and storming Gavin House.

And, after supper, he lay beside Alice in the darkness, listening to her breathe, sensing the angry swelling of her eye. But still, the fact of her injury did not trouble him as much as the reason that he had inflicted it upon her; and he felt his chest lifting and heaving with each breath, felt his ribs expanding as he sucked down the heavy bottomland air made all the heavier by the lingering odors of supper's cheap bacon and cheaper beans, felt his body strain as it struggled to contain the facts, the inescapable facts, of Sophonsiba Gavin and her will and her wealth.

And now he did not even think *if I had money,* not because it was self-evident that he did not have money and would never have money, nor because he had thought about it enough so that the vein of thought was exhausted, but rather because his silence had, in the night, become so dogged, so all-pervasive, that there was not even room for the kind of conscious thought that takes the form of inwardly spoken words. Words were beyond him. Instead, he had visions, visions more felt than seen, and in the darkness of the bedroom he shared with his wife, just down the hall from the bedroom—empty tonight—that Magic used when he was allowed (allowed!) to stay with them, as he felt the heaving of his chest and allowed the silence to wrap itself ever closer about his rage, giving it shape, compressing it, it seemed to him that he could . . . *would* make those visions real.

# Chapter 14

"Mornin', Marshal."

"It's afternoon, Otis."

"Afternoon, Marshal."

Once again, MacDonnell stood in the doorway of the office, having completed his morning rounds, but this time he made a point of not laying his hand on his mustache and not looking overly hard at Otis. Yes, that car that Otis and his wife had been driving for the last few years had shown up shortly after Greta's death had been ruled a suicide, and MacDonnell had done a little more checking this morning—a few casual questions here and there, a few telephone calls—and had discovered that Ed Wyatt's medical equipment had arrived shortly after that. Such a prosperous town, Lee's Corners. Why, a man could never tell when a windfall of one sort or another was going to run up behind him on the street and tackle him like one of those college football players.

He wanted to ask Otis a number of questions, but he was not at all sure he wanted to hear the answers to them. Otis was a good deputy—responsible, didn't smoke, didn't chew, didn't even drink—and if, as MacDonnell suspected, he had demonstrated a failing in the past, he certainly made up for it in other ways.

But *this* failing . . .

The telephone jingled.

MacDonnell glanced at Otis, reached over, and picked it up. "MacDonnell," he said into the mouthpiece. He listened for a moment, then put the handset back on the hook. "Sipsey Dewar.

She says Lindy Buck's turned into quite a lamb. Says he's stayin' in bed just like he ought to."

Otis, his slice-of-potato face a little paler than usual this morning, nodded. "Looks like we won't have to worry about him for a while."

"I won't stop worrying about that piece of trouble until he's dead or across the county line," said MacDonnell. "If he's lying still, it means he's thinkin' about something. If he's moving around, it means he's done thinkin' about it and has lit out to do it. There just ain't no way around him."

"Sounds like you just about got him pegged, Marshal."

"It's my job, Otis."

Otis yawned. "Maybe you ought to let go of somethin' now and then," he said. "Lindy ain't doing nothin' for now. So you ain't got to bother about him. I declare: you never take your teeth out of nothing. You're worse'n a bulldog sometimes."

"Maybe I am," said MacDonnell . . . who had no intention of changing in the slightest.

"Take that Greta Harlow case," said Otis . . . but the deputy suddenly appeared to realize what he was saying and stopped as though a plug of tobacco had lodged in his windpipe.

Since Otis did not chew, MacDonnell was sure that Otis's silence had nothing to do with tobacco. "Sho. What about it?"

"Nothin'," said Otis a little too quickly. "It's . . . just a good example. You're still going over and over it in your head, and it's been years now."

"It's my head, Otis."

"Sho. Well . . ." The deputy rose, reached for his gun belt. "Guess it's my turn, huh?"

MacDonnell found that his hand was on his mustache. Chagrined, he removed it and shoved it into his pocket. "You remember Magic Harlow, don't you, Otis?"

"Sho." But, again, the response came a little too quickly.

MacDonnell did not want to ask Otis, but Otis was the only one he *could* ask. That was the problem with small towns: there were only so many doors you could knock on when you wanted something, and so it did not take much to make sure nobody answered any of them. "When you got to Mildred Riddup's boardinghouse that night—"

"What night?"

"The night you found Greta."

Otis's slice-of-potato face had turned even paler, was now approaching dead white. "Oh. Oh, that. Sho. What about it?"

"When you got there, where was Magic?"

"Magic?"

"That's who I'm talkin' about, Otis."

"I didn't see him nowhere," said the deputy. "Didn't he turn up at Sophonsiba Gavin's house? Didn't she say he was there all along?"

"Sho," said MacDonnell. "That's what she said."

"Who?"

"Sophonsiba Gavin."

"Well, that's right then," said Otis. "Greta just went off with that quadroon fella she'd taken up with, shacked up with him at Mildred Riddup's until Mildred ran him out, and left Magic with Sophonsiba Gavin. Where he belonged."

"Did he?"

"Did he what?"

"Belong there?"

"Lord, Marshal. She'd practically signed him over to Sophonsiba!"

"Maybe," said MacDonnell. "But don't it strike you as a little peculiar that a girl'll go on and move heaven and earth to raise a child out of wedlock, and then just . . . sign him over to someone else?"

Otis chewed on the words for a time. "Well, sho. I guess you're right."

"What *did* you find at Mildred Riddup's boardinghouse, Otis?"

"Find? Well, I found Greta, and—"

But Otis looked up and found that MacDonnell's cold, gray gaze was on him.

"Besides Greta," said MacDonnell. "What did Sophonsiba Gavin ask you nicely—just as sweet as pie—to get rid of?"

Otis just sat there. MacDonnell saw it. MacDonnell saw that Otis saw that he saw it.

"Come on, Otis," he said.

"It was a stick," the deputy said finally.

"What kind of stick?"

" 'Bout three feet long. Inch thick or so. Looked like oak. Looked like an axe handle, in fact."

"You think that's what it was?"

"Prob'ly."

"C'mon, Otis. You know an axe handle when you see one."

"Yeah. Yeah, it was an axe handle."

It struck MacDonnell as the height of absurdity that he had to grill his own deputy in such a way, but he persisted. "Anything funny about it?"

"Funny?"

"Dammit, Otis, you know what I mean. Funny. Scrapes. Scars. Blood. Hair."

"No, Marshal. It looked brand-new. It looked like it had come straight out of M'Creed's store."

Otis was sweating, but MacDonnell knew that he was telling the truth. *"Nothin'?"*

"Nothin' at all, Marshal."

"Was it wet?"

"Marshal?"

*"Damnation! Had someone washed it?"*

Otis stared at MacDonnell's outburst and looked as though he were about to melt, right there on the spot, but, almost unwillingly, he shook his head. "It wasn't damp. Not a mark on it. Price tag was still stuck to it, too."

Which was the damnedest and most unexpected thing that MacDonnell was ready—or, rather, not ready—to hear. Otis was telling the truth (he was sweating too much to be doing anything else), and Otis knew enough about axe handles and blood to know whether there was some of the latter on one of the former, just as he knew when a piece of wood was wet or dry. But why would Sophonsiba Gavin ask a police deputy to get rid of a brand-new axe handle?

It made no sense. None at all. MacDonnell, deflated now because something—he did not know what—had fluttered away just out of his grasp . . . or maybe it had never really been anywhere near him at all, jerked a thumb at the door.

"Go make your rounds, Otis."

\* \* \*

There he was, life-size, his craggy features carved out of the finest Carrara marble. He wore no hat as he stood above his grave, and Alma could see that he was balding; but though, in addition, the fingers of his outstretched right hand were missing, there was a sense of command and honor even in the stumps, and neither lack of hair nor lack of fingers appeared to lessen his stature in the slightest.

*Do be careful, ma'am,* he had said to her. *I do believe you might do yourself an injury if you insist upon carrying on that way.*

Yes, she had seen him, spoken to him, been touched by him . . . but now, standing, like his statue, in the bright sunlight of the cemetery, she was not sure whether she could sanely ascribe that interaction to anything but hallucination or dream. No, it was not that she was not sure. She simply did not want to; and if there was any uncertainty involved, it stemmed from her fear that she would have to.

## WILLIAM CUTHBERT FALLINGSWORTH
### 1821–1865

She dropped her eyes. "No," she murmured. "It was real. I saw it. But what *was* it?"

What indeed? All the motions and movements of an afterlife, without there being anything particularly lifelike about it. Those whom she had seen had indeed interacted, brushed shoulders, stirred the dust of the streets, spoken—sometimes to her—and yet there was nothing about them that indicated that they were anything more than memories . . . disembodied remnants of past and present lives spun off to suck a little existence out of the borderlands between life and oblivion before, like dust devils on a hot day, they faltered, collapsed, faded.

For a moment, she tried to remember whether the fingers of the hand with which he had lifted his hat to her had been missing. But she sensed that it would not matter whether they had been missing or not. His own memory would have supplied them if hers had not, and reality would at least offer the meager benefits of a few fingers to one who trod its streets.

She turned away from the memorial, walked back to her car,

and got in. "Back to town, please, Isaac," she said. "There's a dress shop on Duncan Street." She smiled. "Mind the stop sign. It's hidden in the bushes."

Isaac's head was straight as an obelisk at the top of his spine, and his hair was cut close. For a moment, she idly wondered whether he had a military background, but his "I been around" was as inevitable an answer to any questions of that sort as the "I'm sorry . . . I'm afraid I'm not allowed to discuss that" that she had heard on the far side of . . .

. . . of what?

She looked out the window as the cemetery slipped behind the car, pointedly ignoring the Montague marker. *Blithe Spirit* was back on the shelves of her grandfather's library now, the books—not a volume missing—arranged, dusted, precisely aligned; and the old man's hat was in the closet. The note, though . . .

She opened her handbag, cupped the paper in the palm of her thin hand. The words stared up at her: *Come on in . . .*

"Thank you, Grandfather," she said. "But I don't want to come in. I just want to . . . to . . ."

"Ma'am?"

She saw his unnervingly gray eyes in the rearview mirror. She had spoken a bit too loud. "I'm just being senile, Isaac," she said. "Don't mind me."

"Yes, ma'am."

*The water's fine.*

She felt the fear again. There it was, waiting for her. For now, she could turn her back on it, leave it. She could lock the garden gate, put the semi-existent key in a safe-deposit box where no one would ever see it . . . if, indeed, anyone but she could ever see it in the first place. But later on, though, when she died . . . how could she escape?

Could one kill one's own soul?

"Memory . . . please . . . let it be—"

"Ma'am?"

His gray eyes once again, quizzical. "Hmmm?" she said. "Oh, yes: the dress shop, Isaac."

Isaac's head, buzzed and straight, did not waver. "Yes, ma'am."

"Don't worry," said Alma. "I won't make you go in. There's

a lunch counter across the way. You can buy yourself some coffee and pie."

Isaac's head did not move, but Alma sensed relief. "Yes, ma'am."

Whatever Isaac's background, he was an expert driver, and in front of the dress shop he slid the big automobile into a parking space that Alma was sure would have required, under normal circumstances, a large application of grease. The tall Negro was out and around to the rear passenger door in a twinkling, and he opened it with a bow. "Here we are, ma'am."

She could easily see Isaac swinging the door wide for a colonel in front of a building housing an important intelligence center. "Were you ever in the military, Isaac?"

"I been around."

"Yes," she said. "Of course. Thank you, Isaac. I'll be fine now. Go get your pie and coffee."

He bowed, and she had a vision of him saluting—though he did not salute—before he turned away.

Alma turned, too—toward the dress shop—but in doing so she almost bumped into a strange woman a few inches shorter even than herself, a woman clad in a fantastic assortment of rags and scarves and castoffs of what must have been a hundred different styles and ages. One hand clutched a shapeless red shoulder bag to her side; from the other dangled a carpetbag large enough to have comfortably held a small child. Her face, though, creased up into a thousand smiling wrinkles of various depths and shapes when she saw Alma, and with a bobbing of her head that set the flowers on her hat nodding frantically, she said, "God bless you, ma'am!"

Alma recognized her from the descriptions she had heard. "You must be Anger Modestie," she said. And for once she was glad that her first years as a doctor had been spent in a run-down hospital on the edge of an impoverished section of the city, for at least half the patients she had seen at that time had been what the staff had referred to as "characters." Fully at ease with interacting with such strange apparitions, then, she could offer her hand with complete equanimity. "I'm Alma Montague."

Anger took her hand, pumped it wildly. "Pleased. Pleased. *Pleased* t' meet you, Alma."

The use of her first name was unusual, but Alma shrugged it off. Doubtless one who habitually held the dead and dying in her arms could not bring herself to participate in the flummery of social propriety.

"The pleasure's mine," she said.

"They's the same!" exclaimed Anger.

"The same? They?"

Anger set down her bags, held up her left hand as though it were a tablet, and used her right index finger as though it were a pencil with which to underline imaginary words. "Anger Modestie"—a stroke for each stress—"and Alma Montague." Another stroke for each stress.

Alma felt a twinge of unease. "We have the same initials, don't we?"

"And the same numb'r o' syl'bles." Anger nodded. "That's a fact. It means we connexted."

Alma considered . . . then, finally, nodded. How, she supposed, could it be otherwise? She had stepped into a realm of dead spirits or partially living memories. And Anger Modestie had taken it upon herself to escort those spirits there . . . or at least to foster those memories.

"I suppose so," she said.

"Ah!" said Anger. "You see, then!"

"See?" Alma was a little afraid. Did this woman . . . *know*?

"You see the connexton!"

She saw, indeed. She saw too well. "Yes."

"When it's yo' time, Ah'll take yo' to Jesus, darlin'. Yo' can be sho o' that."

Alma nodded pensively. "I'll need help, I imagine."

"Oh, don't you let that worry you none. We all needs help gettin' to Jesus."

And then Anger stood there, looking at her expectantly. Alma could not fathom what she was waiting for.

"Anger? Did you want something?"

"You wanna ask me anythin'?"

"Ask you . . . what?"

"Anythin' . . . 'bout anythin'."

"No . . . no, I don't think so."

"Don't you worry none, honey."

"Thank you, Anger. God bless you."

"God bless you, too, Alma."

And, feeling Anger's expectant gaze still on her, Alma entered the dress shop.

This shop had not existed when she had left Lee's Corners, but she had been in it a hundred times before, for it was like any other dress shop in any other city, Southern or Northern, white or colored. The same sense of adornment and anatomy as day-to-day business, the same loose, female mixture of purity, glands, and sweat. Racks of clothing, shelves of accessories, second-hand mannequins in impossible postures wearing garments for which there was no utilitarian purpose beyond the furthering of the illusion of utilitarian purpose.

"I'm going to be paying a call," Alma announced to the young clerk who, mincing on high heels as if they really were usable footwear and did not make her feet swell in the slightest, approached her. But Alma paused for a moment, smiled wryly. *Paying* a call. Yes. How apropos. "I need something suitable."

The shop was the same, but the floor plans were always different, and the clerk guided her first to one wall rack of what she thought, from Alma's khaki trousers and shirt, to be *suitable,* and then, prodded gently by Alma, to another . . . of what Alma considered suitable.

Fifty years of white blouse and navy blue wool suit had given Alma simple tastes, and though the day before she had muttered to herself about frills and ribbons, she opted for something considerably less complex. Nonetheless, she was calculating: the outfit spoke of money—lots of money, old money—and of a comfort with it that did not give a second's thought to even the idea of display.

"I'll need two inches off this hem," said Alma. "It comes of being a dwarf."

The clerk giggled . . . and there was a simper lurking in the background that Alma found distressing. "We can do that. We have a woman who does alterations for us. But . . . well . . . it will take some time."

Alma blinked, then swept the room with her eyes. Yes . . . yes, in spite of obvious efforts to hide it, parts of the store looked quite bare, as though the shop's stock had been selectively depleted.

"It's the Gardenia Society Cotillion," the clerk explained. "You haven't heard . . . ?"

"I think someone once mentioned it in my hearing," Alma said. But she could not help but wonder: was there a cotillion in that . . . other place? And at it did sixteen-year-old girls in white gowns and long gloves who had passed away in some old folks' home take the hands of gallant soldiers who had fallen with the gray cloth of their tunics stained with red blood and the mud of Tupelo?

She looked up suddenly. Was this shop there, too? And what faded in and out from behind it? Which was the butterfly, which the philosopher?

"Ma'am?"

"The Gardenia Society," said Alma. "Yes, that's coming up in September, isn't it?"

"Yes, ma'am." That simper, still. "All the ladies of the town have been getting ready for it for weeks now, and our seamstress is just buried. I'm afraid it'll be at least two weeks before she can do your alterations."

"Don't be afraid," said Alma, and she might have been addressing herself, for she felt the despair rising again. So much to be afraid of . . . and even death would not end the fear! "There are much worse things in the world than waiting two weeks for a hemline to be taken up. As it is, though, I sewed my own clothes for years, so I think I can be trusted take up a hem all by myself."

"Oh, ma'am—"

Alma stilled the protest with a gesture . . . and not a little of the old Montague imperiousness. "I need this for today. I have a call to make."

"Very well, then, ma'am."

"And I'll be paying cash."

The clerk blinked. Alma's reckoning was not at all a small one.

Alma smiled again. Yes . . . so much to be afraid of. "You do take cash . . . don't you?"

"Why . . . ah . . . yes!"

"Very well, then."

But as Alma was counting out bills, the confiding nature of women took hold of the clerk, and she rattled gaily on about this year's cotillion, last year's cotillion, the fashionable corsages, and how she remembered *her* first cotillion as well as she remembered her first pair of heels.

"I remember mine, too," said Alma in an attempt to stifle both the clerk and her own thoughts about fear and eternity.

"Yours, ma'am?"

"I was born in Lee's Corners," said Alma. "And when I was sixteen, my father drove me to my first cotillion in a surrey."

"A surrey? You mean . . . with . . . with horses?"

Alma nearly laughed. "Yes, dear. With horses."

"Oh, goodness! I had no idea that you were that—" But the clerk caught herself and blushed.

Alma smiled.

"I mean," said the clerk, flustered, "when Anger Modestie spoke to you, I thought, surely . . . ah . . ."

Alma saw her confusion, understood its source. "You thought that she couldn't have been interested in me as anything but a . . . prospective client?"

The clerk just stared at her, but there was nothing much left to say, and, in any case, Alma was feeling a chill.

Forever. It might be forever. It *could* be forever. This shop. Lee's Corners. Her life. Everything.

Her hand shook as though palsied when she handed the money to the clerk, and it was still shaking when the clerk gave her the receipt and her bundled purchases.

"Will there be anything else, ma'am?"

"Ah . . . no . . . this will be all, thank you."

"Will we be seeing you at the cotillion?"

"I . . ." Alma looked out past the display window. Anger Modestie was still in front of the store. She was still clutching her carpetbag and her purse, and the flowers on her hat were still bobbing with each turn of her head. She appeared not to be waiting for anything or anyone, and yet she appeared to have some definite purpose for being where she was.

"Not until I know," Alma murmured. "Not until then." But aloud, to the clerk: "Maybe," she said. "But maybe not. It's best for the old folks to get out of the way and let the youngsters have a little fun now and again, if you ask me."

"Mrs. Gavin is the president of the Gardenia Society. I'm sure she'd . . ."

"What a funny coincidence," said Alma much more brightly than she felt. "I'm going to see dear Sophonsiba . . . just this afternoon!"

And without waiting for the clerk to say anything more, she turned and groped for the door like a blind thing until she found the knob and let herself out.

"Yo' find what yo' wanted in there, Alma?" Anger called to her.

"Yes," said Alma. "Thank you."

"Yo' going to that cotillion?"

"I've not been invited."

"Oh, honey, they sellin' tickets!" Big smile.

Alma approached her. "Anger," she said, feeling the despair cutting into her, forcing her to ask the question. *Not until then.* "You take people to Jesus . . . don't you?"

"Why, Alma, that's my one and only business in this here world," said Anger. "I been doin' it all my life, and I 'spect I'll be doin' it in one way or 'nother even after I up an' die."

Even after. And what, Alma wondered, was planned for herself? Would she have a practice? Would she see patients? Would she watch again and again as a lover walked away, as a father prevented a transfusion long enough to—

*Stop!* she shouted inwardly. *Stop it!*

"You asked me if I had a question for you," she said. "I do."

"Figured that out the second I laid eyes on yo'."

Almost furtively, Alma looked up and down the street, then sidled closer to the strange woman. "Anger . . . when you take them to Jesus . . . do you ever . . . do you ever see what's on the other side?"

Anger looked at her, and Alma felt a cold terror that the formal, formulaic response she had heard so often in that . . . that *other* Lee's Corners was about to be repeated here, in this world, on the mundanity of a sunny town street.

But Anger just smiled. "The livin' got no business peekin' over there," she said. "And Lord Jesus, he keeps an eye on things and don't let no one get by without his say-so. I takes 'em up to the gate, and I hands 'em in, but Lord Jesus, he say *Anger, yo' keep your eyes offen what's in here,* and I say back *Yes, Lord, I do that 'cause yo' the boss.*"

"So you don't know."

"No one knows aforn they git over there, Alma."

"Yes, Anger." Alma looked away. Across the street, through the glass dimly, she saw Isaac rising from his seat at the diner counter, saw him laying down money—as she had laid down a dime in that other place—saw him start for the door. "Thank you, Anger."

"I be there for yo', Alma."

"Yes," said Alma. "I guess so."

# Chapter 15

And when Otis had left, MacDonnell was alone in the office with a phone he knew would not be ringing anytime soon . . . leaving him, therefore, with more time to think than he really wanted, with a shadow of a theory about Greta Harlow's death (that had, with the presence, or rather, the *newness* of an axe handle, been thoroughly cut to ribbons), and with his persistent, gut-level rejection of the idea that suicide could be committed by a self-inflicted beating.

But while he was looking at the phone, hoping that it would ring and thereby save him from his fuguing thoughts, he suddenly remembered Alma Montague's message from the day before. The one about Dark. Otis had said that she had sounded agitated, but though she had certainly looked intent and focused when MacDonnell had seen her behind M'Creed's Hardware Store, she had not appeared to be particularly agitated. But then, MacDonnell reflected, she had been a doctor with a wounded man in front of her at the time, and more than likely professionalism had been in charge.

Agitated? What could agitate a woman like Alma Montague? Had Sophonsiba Gavin gotten at her somehow? Or maybe she was *trying* to get at her?

MacDonnell was already reaching for the phone.

Alma laid down the skirt that she had just finished hemming and, as was her custom, answered the telephone herself.

It was MacDonnell, but though the marshal was, justifiably enough, returning her call from the day before—had it really only been one day?—any desire Alma might have once had to ask him about Mr. Dark had been left as far behind as the dime she had laid on the counter of Jamison's Drugstore . . . over there.

And as the marshal was speaking, she felt the chill again. Yes, she had left a dime over there. A small part of the real world. A small part of herself. And would that tasteless coffee that she had sipped at the counter beside Abaijah Jones drag her, like Persephone and her pomegranate seeds, back to that realm of darkling radiance again and again?

She came to herself just in time to catch the drift of MacDonnell's question.

"Oh . . . it was . . ." Did she want to say it? Did she want to say *anything*? "Oh, nothing really, Marshal. It's just that Mr. Dark came by the other night with something that . . . that belonged to my grandfather. That was all. But he left before . . . before I could find out where he lived. I wanted to thank him."

She sounded insincere even to her own ears. She could imagine how she sounded to MacDonnell.

"Dark . . ." he said. "Well, I 'magine I'm not surprised that he'd come by with something for you," said the marshal after a pause that was only slightly too long for Alma's comfort. "He's prob'ly the most honest man in Lee's Corners. Leastwise *I* think so. If he had something that was yours, you can bet your bottom dollar he'd bring it to you. But he don't care much for thank-you's. That just don't seem to be his way."

Another pause. Alma realized, too late, that she had left a hole in her excuse big enough for another question.

"But you saw him yesterday, didn't you, Miz Montague?" said MacDonnell, speedily filling the vacancy. "I'm sure you thanked him then."

Blushing furiously, Alma nodded as though she could thereby convince herself. "Yes. Yes, I did. Thank you, Marshal."

"My pleasure, ma'am."

And now it was her own turn to pause just a little too long for her comfort. "Good-bye, then."

"G'bye."

And Alma was left listening to the dial tone for a good ten seconds before she came to herself enough to put the handset down.

\* \* \*

"Sam . . . I need you t' do summat for me."

Lindy had called, and Sam had come. The big, blond, crew-cutted man stood beside the bed, his head nearly brushing the ceiling beams and his cloth cap—the same one he had been wearing when he had first appeared on the streets of Lee's Corners after Sophonsiba Gavin had finished with him—in his hand.

Lindy, still flat on his back, watched him out of narrowed eyes as he breathed the hot air and felt the tightness of the scar tissue growing in his chest. If a night and a day had not let him up from his bed for longer than it took him to half crawl, half stagger to his outhouse and back, neither had it changed his mind about Dark in the slightest. But, in thinking the matter through, he had come to the conclusion that he would need help in order to execute the righteous plan that had been taking shape inside his righteous head. And so he had asked Sipsey Dewar—no, he had *told* Sipsey Dewar: in Lindy's opinion, one never *asked* niggers to do anything—to tell Sam that he wanted to see him.

"Well, if you need it," said Sam, "I guess you need it, then. Huhuhuh!"

"Siddown, Sam."

There were no chairs in Lindy's house. Sam pulled up a dusty crate with a faded label that indicated it might have once held oranges. Or maybe peaches. Or lemons. Something, at least, vaguely round and pale. But even turned on its end, the crate was lower than a chair, and in order to lower his hams sufficiently, Sam's legs had to fold beneath him, leaving his knees spread to reveal the sweat stains around the crotch of his unwashed pants (and too well was Lindy reminded of Dark's thinly veiled genital displays outside McCoy's Soda Shop) and his long arms draped over his thighs, his hands and his cloth cap dangling like some outlandish reproductive organ.

Again, with a twinge, Lindy was reminded of Dark. And that reminded him of Dark's lips. And *that* reminded him of Dark's probing, inquisitive tongue. "I needs you to do summat for me."

"You said that. Huhuhuh!"

"I know I did. Don't you be tellin' me what I said and what I didn't say."

Grinning, Sam sat on the crate, his cap dangling from his dangling hands.

"Kin I trust you, Sam?"

"Sho! Huhuhuh!"

It was no more than Sam's way. To agree with everything that was said to him. To reply with whatever he sensed that his querist wanted . . . whether his later actions validated his response or not. But Lindy was used to that.

"Kin I trust you to do . . . summat for me?"

"Sho! Huhuhuh!"

"Maybe summat . . . that's not what you might o'dinarly do?"

Sam was still grinning, and something about his grin made Lindy wonder whether Sam had already done something that was not what he would ordinarily do. But Lindy, searching his memories, could think of nothing.

"I done a lot you might not know 'bout. Huhuhuh!"

Still grinning.

Lindy looked at him. "Well, sho . . ." he said after a time. "But I got summat else for you to do."

"Sho! Huhuhuh!"

"First, you gotta go up to Memphis and buy me a couple straight razors."

Sam's mouth fell slack, and he blinked slowly at Lindy. "Why?"

"Don't you be askin' me why! You said you'd do summat for me. Now is you or ain't you willing to do it?"

"Sho! I'm always willing! Huhuhuh!"

"You go up there behind my stove. That top brick is loose. There's five dollars and some change behind it. You take that money, and you buy yo'self a train ticket up to Memphis, and you buy those razors, and you come back here and give them to me."

"Sho. Huhuhuh!" Sam had resumed his grinning. "Then what we gonna do?"

"Don't you worry 'bout that yet."

And still Sam's grin made Lindy uneasy. What *had* Sam done? Anything? Or was he simply grinning because, in his dim, desperate-to-please way, he wanted Lindy to believe that he had done . . . something, and that therefore he was someone to be reckoned with, someone who could manage the difficult and exacting task of buying a round-trip ticket and two straight razors.

But Lindy, worrying suddenly that there was something about Sam that he did not know, was moved to speak again. "You ever seen niggers fight, Sam?"

Sam just grinned, nodded.

"What d'they use to fight, Sam?"

"I seen 'em use razors. Huhuhuh!"

"Razors kin cut a man up pretty bad, can't they?"

"Sho! Razors cut someone up better'n anything! Huhuhuh!"

In the stifling heat and half-light of the house that was empty save for Sam and himself (for he had sent Sipsey away), Lindy examined Sam as though he were running a thumb across the edge of the rusty, gripless strip of sheet steel he used for a kitchen knife. "You ever kill a man, Sam?"

He knew that Sam had not, but, to his surprise:

"Mmmmaybe," said the big man. "Maybe not."

And he was still grinning.

Lindy's eyes opened all the way. "You know what it's like?"

"I mmmmmight."

The nervous giggle had vanished from Sam's speech. Lindy wondered what it meant, but he knew—he *knew*—that Sam had never killed anyone. Suddenly, he was awash in doubt. Had he made a mistake in talking to Sam at all? But no: he would lead, and Sam would follow. There was no question about that.

"You go get me those razors," he said. "And mind you: you don't let no one from Lee's Corners see you. Then you and me gonna talk some more."

The . . . other . . . Lee's Corners shimmered at the edge of memory as Isaac drove Alma through the town on the way out to Gavin House. Buildings passed—the soda shop, the hardware store, the dress shop where she had bought the clothing she was now wearing . . . and had spoken to Anger Modestie— and all of them swirled together in the back of her mind with those of the Lee's Corners that existed beyond the stile steps, one peeking out from behind the other like a reflection in a pond mixed up with the sight of a face peering up from below.

She shuddered at the thought. Whose face was peering up?
And was it alive or dead?

She turned away from it, taking up, by way of defense, something more familiar: what was . . . he . . . doing? His wife cleaning
or mending or perhaps at the market, his children at school . . .
but no, not during the summer. They would be at their summer
jobs, then; and the eldest, who had children of his own, would
be going about his own affairs. But what about *him*? Where was
he? Out of what office window did he look, resting his mind
from the figures and papers before him? Or did he hold a ham-
mer and saw: a skilled carpenter? Or a mason? Or . . . ?

She struggled with the thought, but no clear picture came to
her; and it struck her again, more forcefully this time, that
through all the years of imagining a life and a family for him,
she had always been unclear on this point. It was as though his
life itself—imaginary though it was—was resisting her, refusing to conform to any employment, mundane or lucrative, that
she created for him, opting instead for its own path, one that she
had as yet not hit upon, one that she was, therefore, unable to
imagine.

But as he was, in fact, dead, so, perhaps, in that other place,
he did indeed have his own life, incomprehensible as it might
by nature be to her. If memories could persist even without a
mind to contain them, nurture them, and give them form, then
perhaps they could carry on their own existence in some vague
and untroubled way: growing up, interacting with other memories from other places and times, mixing as she had seen old
uniforms and carriages mixing with contemporary suits and automobiles on the streets of the Lee's Corners beyond the stile
steps.

But unconscious. Completely unconscious. The semblance
of people and things: no more. They would by necessity be but
reflections of the living, mere shapes and sounds that would go
through their remembered motions for a time, grow fainter, and
at last disperse. There were no spectral and monolithic islands
where one went to ponder the meaning of one's accumulated
years of heartbreak. There was no community of dead and de-
parted spirits, mingling in cloying conviviality. There were

only echoes. Only echoes of the ringing hammers and tears of life, echoes that reflected off the obsidian walls of oblivion.

Or so she hoped. Or so she desperately wanted to believe. He was dead. And that blond head she had looked after during its long walk down the hospital corridor until it reached a turning and disappeared—just as it had disappeared around some turning in the world beyond the stile steps—that blond head had long ago crumbled into dust, along with everything that had made it individual, conscious, self-aware. But what if it were otherwise? Even now, tucked into an inner pocket of her handbag, her grandfather's words, reaching back from beyond the grave, mocked her determination to relegate the dead to complete unknowingness.

"Gavin House, ma'am."

Isaac's voice startled her, and she looked up to see that, yes, she had contemplated away the remainder of the drive, and the car was now rolling up the wide driveway toward the house.

It was as big and white as Montague Mansion, but even though the latter had been so restored and renovated that less than a quarter of the exposed plaster and wood dated any farther back than a few months, it still retained a sense of ancient solidity about it that was not shared by the obviously more modern (in spite of its attempt to ape the antebellum style) Gavin House; and this difference was only exacerbated by the presence of scaffolding across one wing, raw plaster and brickwork, and crews of workmen coming and going from a side entrance.

Alma recalled what she had heard from the contractors who had brought their crews to Montague Mansion. At the time, she had discounted their tales of the constant changes at Gavin House as mere exaggeration, and even when the restoration specialist from St. Louis had announced that she and her pastry bags of plaster had been hired for another job in Lee's Corners, Alma still had not given credence to the implication. But here it was, and now she found herself believing everything. Yes, from the look of it, Gavin House was a serpent that shed its skin not once a year, but every week . . . perhaps even every day. Struck by a lightning bolt and reduced to cinders, it would, by virtue of the accumulated momentum of the perpetual construction, doubtless reappear the next morning, as new as ever . . . and still with something *else* being changed, swapped, altered, or remade once again.

There were two construction trucks parked a respectful distance from the front steps, but Isaac pulled in and stopped directly before the house. In a twinkling, he was around to Alma's door, swinging it wide as he stood, she almost imagined, at attention.

"Ma'am, do you want me to leave or to stay?"

Stiff with the long ride and with the protests of aging joints alike, Alma put her feet on the pavement beside the car, rose, and looked up at the front door, examining it as though it were the battlements of a castle under siege. Except that she felt that it was she herself who was under siege. A preemptive strike, then . . . from someone who had long wished to be done with such things. "I'd like for you to stay, Isaac," she said. "I might have to make a quick getaway. Did you bring a book or a magazine?"

"I'm used t' waitin', ma'am."

"Used to waiting? From your experience as a . . . ?"

He eyed her. "I been around."

"Certainly, Isaac." She smiled, gave him a wink, and went up the steps, taking them carefully, one at a time. To her chagrin, though, in the half minute she waited before the closed door after she had rung the bell, she realized that she had no visiting card: when she had returned to Lee's Corners, she had never intended to make such calls and, therefore, had never thought to remedy the lack. And so she was put in the position of not only having to announce herself to the Negro butler who answered the door, but to do so with an irregularity.

"Alma Montague to see Sophonsiba Gavin," she said, looking up at the man, who was so tall that most of what she could see of his face consisted of chin.

But he did not appear to be concerned by the absence of a visiting card. Instead, he bowed her in, asked her to wait, and himself climbed the wide stairs to the upper floor of the house.

Alma waited. It had been long enough since she had last made one of these structured, rigidly polite calls that she had forgotten whether being left standing alone in the grand foyer of a house was considered proper or improper. But, in the silence, she could hear the pounding and the sawing of construction, the thuds of heavy loads being dropped, and, too, she could smell the odor of plaster dust and raw wood.

"Alma, my dear!"

And there was Sophonsiba Gavin descending the stairs, one hand on the banister for balance against the hazards of heels on marble, the other extended as though reaching for her guest.

Or perhaps for her guest's throat: Alma, schooled by long use in the unspoken language of patients who wished to avoid discussing certain aspects of their lives while, at the same time, they desired with all their hearts for their doctor to know everything, could read Sophonsiba's face even at a distance. A preemptive strike. Exactly. Alma, whom Sophonsiba had wished to relegate to the position of newcomer, had donned her mantle of old money and had so outflanked the upstart.

"It's so wonderful of you to return my visit!"

Alma smiled inwardly. Impressive! "Oh, dear Sophonsiba, I wouldn't dream of troubling you to call on"—Should she? Why not?—"little old me!"

Flank and double-flank. Sophonsiba obviously decided to end the preliminary maneuvering. "You'll stay for tea, of course? You're just in time!"

She had, by then, reached the bottom of the stairs, and, managing to beat Alma to the punch, offered her hand. Alma ignored the hand and instead gave Sophonsiba a delicate little embrace that could not have allowed more than two square inches of fully clothed body to come into contact. "I'd be utterly delighted to, dear Sophonsiba. I'm sure we have . . . *ever* so much to talk about!"

And she must have intoned her last sentence just right, for Sophonsiba Gavin started noticeably, pulled away, and stared straight into Alma's innocently smiling face. "Ah . . . yes. Of course."

The Negro butler was tall, strong, impassive, stolid, and wonderfully deft at creating the illusion that tea—including tiny sandwiches and even tinier pastries—was laid every day at three o'clock in the afternoon.

"Your man there is quite skilled," Alma said blandly when he had left after attending to the needs of the table once again.

"Oh," said Sophonsiba, "James has been with us since before Mr. G died. He *is* quite a find."

Alma hardly heard Sophonsiba's last words. And was Mr. G over *there,* too? And what part of that other Lee's Corners did he inhabit? What part of him made up his memory . . . or his . . .

No. She would not think about that.

"He's . . . he's from Lee's Corners?" she managed.

"James? Oh, by no means. Some more tea, Alma?"

Alma had not touched her tea. The cup was still quite full, so she knew by Sophonsiba's oversight that she still held the upper hand. "No, thank you, dear Sophonsiba. I'm quite adequately provided for."

"It's so hard to find decent help in a place like Lee's Corners," said Sophonsiba . . . with a look at Alma. "Mr. G—before he died, that is—found James up in Memphis."

Alma smiled. "You're from Memphis, too, aren't you, dear Sophonsiba?"

And Sophonsiba sat there with her cup halfway to her lips, unmoving, for several seconds. "Well, *part* of my family is from Memphis, my *dear* Alma. We're related to the Hawkins family down here, didn't you know?"

Alma, granddaughter of Walter and Sinta Hawkins, certainly did not. "Oh!" she said. "How interesting! So you're almost a native of Lee's Corners, then, aren't you?"

Sophonsiba preened. "My roots in Oktibushubee County run deep, dear Alma . . ."

*At least as deep as ground ivy,* Alma found herself thinking. But there she was, brought back to her grandfather once again by virtue of Sophonsiba's fabricated claim to Hawkins blood. *Blithe Spirit* on his headstone . . . and on the bench in the gazebo.

And so what difference did all this present flummery make? The horror of immortality was staring her in the face, and here she was making arched pleasantries with a pretentious vulgaroo who, doubtless, hated her and everything she stood for. (Hawkins blood indeed!)

". . . and I was very, very happy to be able to come back to the place that I've *always* called home."

"Yes," said Alma, smiling. "Of course."

"It's *so* wonderful that we can talk like this."

"Of course it is."

And who cared? And what was it like over there? Were there conversations like this? Were there artful interactions out of which every drop of sincerity had carefully been drained? Did people hate one another because of where they had been born? Did the dead think in terms of having been born at all?

Deliberately, Alma turned away from the thought just in time to hear Sophonsiba say:

"But I'm rather shocked to see you come back here . . ."

Alma noticed that she did not say *to see you come home*.

". . . since, after all, the climate here can't possibly be at all good for your health."

Off in the distance, someone started pounding on something. Loud, heavy hammerblows, like the tread of some advancing behemoth.

Alma carefully picked up her teacup and attempted a swallow of the pale liquid. She was somehow not surprised to find that, like the coffee in that other place, it had no taste. "Ah . . . how so, my dear Sophonsiba?"

Sophonsiba fluttered casually. "Oh, well, you know the heat is *so* utterly bad in this part of the country. And it's *so* sultry. For someone as . . . fragile . . . as you, this must be a great disadvantage." She fluttered some more. "Don't you agree?"

"I can't say I've ever noticed the heat being particularly bad," Alma remarked. "I suppose I'm used to it."

The thudding grew louder.

"After all," she continued, "I was . . . born here in Lee's Corners."

"Indeed?" said Sophonsiba Gavin. "Why, I never would have guessed. You're so . . . so . . ."

"Fragile?" Alma smiled helpfully.

"Yes." And Sophonsiba fluttered a little more . . . projecting, like a magic lantern, a transparent, luminous, and entirely illusory sense of concern for the woman who sat on the other side of the table. "Fragile. One never knows, at your age, what might happen, and it's always best to take care of oneself. The weather here . . . why, it could do almost *anything* to you." She fluttered a little more, smiled helpfully in return. "*Dear* Alma."

Alma sat for the better part of a minute, patiently counting the beats of her pulse while Sophonsiba's smile faded . . . and was replaced with a just barely detectable case of the fidgets. "Why," Alma said at last, "I do believe you're worried I might drop dead some fine day." She smiled with great pleasantness. "I'm so utterly touched by your concern, dear Sophonsiba. You're just like a sister to me already!"

With Alma having laid her three aces and two kings straight out on the table, Sophonsiba had very little choice in her response. "Why . . . ah . . . yes. I'm sure you'd be much more comfortable . . ."

*Dead,* thought Alma.

". . . elsewhere." Sophonsiba sipped at her tea. "Wouldn't you?"

And there it was, staring her in the face. Oh, it was not so much the implicit threat in Sophonsiba's words (though it was indeed a threat). It was, rather, the tedium of senseless, useless circumstance that forced two women who did not even vaguely like one another to parrot civilities while simultaneously maneuvering their way through their agendas. Entanglements and interactions: Alma had left the Northern city and the life she had shorn of all Montague influence in order to escape them, only to find them crowding toward her with her first step off the train and onto the Lee's Corners platform. And now there was the added novelty of potential lethality.

She could return to her birthplace, she could renovate Montague Mansion, she could prepare herself to live out her final years (as she had put it to Mr. Snatcher) reasonably busy and entertained . . . but it appeared that if she wanted to have any real comfort during that time, then she was going to have to deal in one way or another—and once and for all—with Sophonsiba Gavin.

She almost laughed out loud. And how, she wondered (as her silence grew and Sophonsiba fidgeted more and more . . . which was, Alma considered, a possibly dangerous combination, since fear—whether of damnation for a forbidden transfusion, of societal condemnation for illicit love, or of exposure of . . . of . . . she did not know what—could make people do all sorts of things that they, not to mention others, would regret) was she supposed to do that? Should she don a deerstalker cap, have Lucy fetch her grandfather's big magnifying glass from the desk drawer of his study, and begin hunting for footprints around the back of Mildred Riddup's boardinghouse? Should she look very sternly at Sophonsiba Gavin, extract a notebook from her beaded handbag, and say, in a suitably grave voice: "And now, Mrs. Gavin, would you mind telling me where you were on the night of . . ."? How absurd!

The pounding left off abruptly, but in the backwash of silence, she heard feet pattering along the corridor outside the open door. A small boy suddenly rushed into the room, his eyes so intent that they were shadowed, his right hand jabbing spastically at the empty air.

"Pow!" he said. "Pow! Pow! Pow!"

"Ah!" said Sophonsiba. "Here's Magic. Alma, this is my dear little boy, Magic. He came to me so miraculously that I can't but call him my own, and I hope you'll consider him so, because he's so very, *very* dear to me. Magic, sweetheart, do go say hello to Miss Montague."

Magic fell silent, turned slowly toward Alma. His eyes were as gray as a storm front, and Alma noticed that he did not ever appear to blink.

"What do you say when you meet someone, Magic?" Sophonsiba was prompting. "Come on, now. What do you say?"

And now Magic was staring at her, and Alma shuddered at the look in the boy's eyes. She could almost believe that the mother of such a feral thing would have indeed been capable of beating herself to death.

"Come on, sweetheart. What do you say? You say, *pleased to meet—*"

Suddenly, Magic exploded, swinging his stiffened right hand in Alma's direction. "Pow! *Powpowpow!*" he screamed, jabbing his stiffened finger at Alma's face with each shouted syllable.

"Oh, dear! Magic! Now, be nice to Miss Montague."

"Powpowpowpowpow!"

"Benny!"

Heavier footsteps in the corridor, and the sallow youth ran into the room.

"Benny," said Sophonsiba, producing a tiny lace handkerchief and fluttering it at her face, "take Magic out to the garden where he can . . . play."

"Sure thing, Mommy," said the youth in a voice deep enough to make Alma start.

Benny put his hand on Magic's shoulder and expertly caught the hand that swung up toward his face. "Don't give me that," said Benny. "Let's just go out and . . . and . . . and play."

"I want the pow-er! Give me the pow-er!"

"Benny!"

"I told you I got rid of it!"

"Take Magic out of here this instant!"

And Benny, still grappling with the hand that looked as though it were trying to jab its index finger straight into his eye, dragged Magic out the door and down the hall. Faintly, drifting back, Alma heard:

"And you hit me in the nards and I swear I'll tear out your hair!"

Sophonsiba flushed . . . and continued to fan herself with the handkerchief. "I'm sorry, dear Alma. Magic's such an intelligent child . . . but he does get so mischievous at times!"

"Of course," said Alma. She paused for just the right length of time, then picked up the pendant watch she was wearing, flipped open the case, and, while the tiny music box movement played a perfect rendition of a Mozart rondo, made very sure that she looked surprised.

"Oh, my goodness," she said, knowing while she did so that Sophonsiba doubtless noticed that the watch not only had to be at least a century old but was doubtless worth more than all of the ersatz mother's diamonds put together, "where *has* the time gone? I'm afraid I must be going."

"Oh, can't you stay a bit . . . longer, dear Alma?"

But no, she could not. Time, though, was not so much the determining factor as revulsion. But with many expressions of sincere regret on both sides of the exchange, the two women took their leave of one another, and James escorted Alma to the front door.

Alma descended the steps, feeling Sophonsiba Gavin's eyes on her . . . probably from a room on the second floor. Heat? Piffle! This was hardly what she would call heat. Why, when she was a girl there had been a heat wave . . .

Isaac was out of the car and around to her door before she reached it. "I hope you had a pleasant time, ma'am," he said.

"Pleasant, Isaac? I'm not sure I'd call it *pleasant*. I did, however, manage to escape with my life. Which is a good thing. Maybe."

He blinked at her. "Ma'am?"

"Let's go home, Isaac," she said. "I believe I have a ghost to lay."

# Chapter 16

It was Magdalene that had gotten all the immigrants, probably because of Vinty White's decision to put his big textile mill on that side of the county line (and there was a story going around about *that,* too: something about Vinty's ties with the governor and about how the governor had persuaded Magdalene to co-operate fully with Vinty White with regard to a few minor things like tax credits in return for the governor cooperating with Magdalene—or at least with Magdalene's town council—with regard to something else that no one really knew about but which everyone agreed was—hell, *had to be*—something un-ethical and, God damn it, but wasn't that just like Magdalene?), thus attracting a substantial number of those who, having de-parted from Ellis Island with names so mangled, altered, and curtailed that all trace of original nationality had been lost (save in the individuals themselves, in the basic fiber and sinew of human beings who insisted upon being of the wrong complex-ion and speaking English badly or not at all, and who, lured on by typical promises of typically American wealth, journeyed farther and farther into the varied noons and midnights of a country they did not know, their shoes rotten, their pockets weighed down with the new-minted pennies that the unscrupu-lous immigration agents had swapped them, piece for piece, for the gold coins they had, with pains, brought across the ocean, coins from grandparents' hoards in socks and in wooden boxes, coins from the hand of a parish priest passed from a hand that would remain behind to another that would never return—a farewell gift for the proverbial rainy day—coins brought secreted in belts and in hidden pockets, kept from thieving hands and, in fact, from knowledge and even from rumor during that long voyage in steerage, coins valueless now by simple lack of possession, the absoluteness of the immigrants' poverty urging them to factories near and far, to New York and to Chicago, to Pittsburgh and to Detroit, to, at last and at farthest, to Magdalene and to Vinty White's mill), came, all unprepared save for a willingness to glean in the fields of an alien land. But in spite of that, or maybe *because* of that, Lee's Corners, though essentially white (except for the colored folk) and Protestant (except for those few who were not Baptist or Methodist), had come to have one or two citizens who called themselves Americans not by birthright but by naturalization, and Mr. Fiorello, who owned the flower shop just across the street from the railway station (which was the number-one perfect place for a flower shop, because every would-be Romeo running to meet his sweetheart or his wife or even his mother at the station—and running, invariably, at the last minute—who discovered his hands empty of that one symbol of affection capable of melting, without exception, even the hardest female heart, would look frantically for someplace he could buy a posy, or a bouquet, or even (for those difficult cases) a dozen, long-stemmed, red roses and find his glance alighting upon . . . Fiorello's Flowers) was one of these.

A stout, swarthy man with black eyes, black hair, a black mustache that was the terror of the maidens of Lee's Corners and the delight of his wife, and accented but otherwise perfect English that only occasionally (when Fiorello wanted it) tossed up a stereotypical but effective *Mama mia!* or a pejorative *Bastarde!,* Fiorello was everybody's friend, an outspoken and unashamed romantic, a dab of crimson paint on the otherwise drab landscape of Lee's Corners, and an admirable, upstanding, and perfectly honest businessman who could, each year, look forward to a brisk rise in income in the weeks just prior to the Gardenia Society Tea and Cotillion.

True to Fiorello's expectations, the husbands and boyfriends and even (when they thought they could get away with it) the lovers of the women of Lee's Corners had once again begun to present themselves at his counter to order corsages for their ladies, the flowers to be picked up the day of the cotillion. And, again true to tradition, there was a certain amount of rivalry between (openly) the husbands and boyfriends and lovers as to who would present his lady with the largest and most extravagant tribute, and between (clandestinely) the ladies themselves as to whose husband, boyfriend, or lover would gain that distinction for himself.

And then there was John Harlow . . .

Though the fall cotillion was the big social event of the year in Lee's Corners, the Harlows had not attended since Greta had died . . . and not just because there was some doubt in everyone's mind, including the Harlows', about whether anyone at the gathering would actually speak to them. Part of it had to do with money: gowns and long gloves and fine shirts and rented suits could add up to a substantial sum, and ever since he had lost his job at the bank, John Harlow had had little money to spare for anything beyond food, house payments, and the occasional tin toy he used as a bribe for Magic's allegiance. But part of it, too—perhaps the larger part—had to do with Sophonsiba Gavin, the president of the Gardenia Society, whose status and office ensured her a prominent part in the evening's activities, and whose money and standing ensured that her hold on Magic was unquestioned . . . save by the Harlows themselves.

But here was John Harlow in the flower shop, and here was Mr. Fiorello bouncing—there did not seem to be any other way for such a bundle of romanticism to move: certainly any ordinary method of perambulation was out of the question—out from the back room where he had been assembling a large construction of irises, gladioli, and baby's breath.

"Good morning, Mr. Harlow!" he exclaimed. "A wonderful morning, too! *Mama mia,* but I've seldom seen such mornings in this lifetime!"

And when Mr. Fiorello said something like that, one could believe it, but John Harlow was slouched in front of the counter, his hands in his pockets and his shirt untucked, looking most certainly like nothing that belonged in a flower shop or had anything to do with wonderful mornings. "I need a corsage."

"Ah! A corsage!" And Mr. Fiorello winked. "For a . . . special occasion?"

"For the cotillion."

And this caused Mr. Fiorello to stand dumbfounded for a moment, for if John Harlow had told him that the corsage was for the occasion of his wife entertaining the pope at dinner, he could not have been more surprised.

But he recovered in a moment. "Ah! For the cotillion! I have . . ."

And here Mr. Fiorello was doing some rapid, mental calculations, weighing what he knew of his prices (which were quite modest) against what he knew of his customer's means (which were considerably less than modest).

". . . just the thing."

But John Harlow did not appear to be at all interested in Fiorello's calculations. Still slouched, still with his hands in his pockets, he was brooding over the display case behind the counter, where flowers in abundance gathered, spread, and unfurled in chilly preservation.

"I'll want one of those," he said suddenly, taking one hand out of his pocket and jabbing an index finger stiffly, almost spastically, at one particularly exuberant creation.

Fiorello glanced back over his shoulder, turned back to John Harlow, then started, looked again, and gasped.

"Ah!" he said, "Mr. Harlow, you show exquisite taste for beauty and color, but I doubt that your wife would want to carry a wedding centerpiece for a corsage. It's much too big, for one thing, and for another—"

But before he could finish, John Harlow suddenly took both hands out of his pockets and slammed them, palms down, on top of the counter as he leaned toward Mr. Fiorello. *"I said I want one of those, dammit!"* And his voice was neither a shout nor a scream, but more of a strangled cry that, later on (when he had time to think about it) Mr. Fiorello would describe as sounding like that of the trapped rabbit he had seen when he was a boy in Italy and his father had taken him into the hills to inspect the steel, leg-hold traps he had set: muffled and hoarse, holding nonetheless something that was the essence of frenzy, as though the animal, denied the ability to attack its captor, would turn its claws on itself and rend its own skin rather than submit to its fate.

And Mr. Fiorello just stood there, looking at John Harlow. And at last he said,

"Very well," in a very small voice, and John Harlow said,

"How much," and Mr. Fiorello, still stunned, said,

"W-what?" and John Harlow said, or, rather, shrieked again in that voice that not only indicated but embodied and came close to making physical that trapped and hopeless frenzy,

*"I said how goddam much?"*

And Mr. Fiorello, almost unwillingly, named the sum, hoping that the actual utterance of it would either bring John Harlow to his senses and cause him to leave the store (with or without explanations: Mr. Fiorello was not about to be particular in this regard . . . he had, after all, a wife and children, and a grandchild on the way) or prompt such an explosion from him that he (Mr. Fiorello) could legitimately retreat to the back room and telephone for the marshal.

But John Harlow neither left nor exploded. Instead, he reached into a back pocket and pulled out a brown leather wallet so old and worn that it was riddled with deep cracks and held together mostly by heavy green fishing line. "How much did you say again?" And his voice was quiet. Very quiet.

Mr. Fiorello named the sum once more.

But John Harlow counted out bills and laid them, side by side, on the counter; and Mr. Fiorello finally came to his senses enough to open the register and count out John Harlow's change.

"Day of the cotillion," said John Harlow. "I want it ready then."

"Yes," said Mr. Fiorello.

"You have it ready that morning. I'll be in to pick it up."

"Yes," said Mr. Fiorello.

"You got that? In the morning."

"Yes," said Mr. Fiorello. "Yes. The morning of the cotillion. Yes."

\* \* \*

Looking for anything hard enough, one is inevitably found by it, the act of searching turning as though by abstruse and Oriental mysticism into the act of being found. The suitor, pursuing, finds himself caught. The hunter kills not his prey but himself. The unbeliever is felled by a flash of lightning on the way to Damascus. Perhaps it is an excess of hope that accounts for this, that leaves us all vulnerable to sudden invasion, perhaps it is merely a symptom of our innate yearning for surrender to something outside of ourselves, something that will relieve us of the awful burden of conscious autonomy and decision, something that will enthrall us in the most precise meaning of the verb and return us to the carefree dependency of the bright, golden womb.

And so, as Lindy Buck had his God in the image and likeness of himself, and Abram MacDonnell had justice in the image and likeness of God, and Alma Montague had death in the image and likeness of (she hoped) nothing at all, so Greta had her quadroon in the image and likeness of whoever she wanted him to be . . . who found her as she was herself looking for him, found her in Memphis, on Beale Street, where she had gone that day to listen to the music for a few minutes—the jug bands, the strutting, blues screamers, the sultry lady crooners— the long, sustained bass notes of the popular style seemingly uplifting her into the sensual realm theoretically denied her by her clothing and her appearance and even by the paucity of the sum of money with which she had been supplied for the day: the paucity that did not, could not, provide for her son (even assuming for a moment that she could have had Magic with her), that allowed for a few childish entertainments and no more. She did not even have enough for a scandalizing pack of cigarettes.

But she did not need cigarettes in order to scandalize, for she had a colored man for a lover . . . or would have, for there was no question in her mind when the bright, two-toned yellow car pulled up beside her as she stood listening to the music, smelling the cigar smoke and the odor of Negro as thick as a slab of fatback and as creamy as warm molasses all about her; and there was no question in her mind when the driver, who was almost as fair as Greta herself and whose gold tooth added a second wink to his own, leaned across the wide seat and popped open the passenger-side door.

"Goin' my way?" he said.

And Greta said, just as she had seen and heard it done in the movies that Mrs. Gavin had encouraged her to see, "Thought you'd never ask," and, stepping into the big car first with one foot and then with the other, just as Jimmy White had, years before, entered her bedroom, stepping through the open window first with one foot and then with the other, his head bending to clear the sash and the cold April-night air pouring in and her cat up a tree somewhere, yowling, where Jimmy had driven it so that he could come to her window in the darkness and imitate its scratching until she herself raised the sash . . . so that he could say afterward that she had herself let him in . . .

"My name's—"

"Jimmy," said Greta.

He looked surprised, peered at her from beneath the broad brim of his Revel hat. "Why . . . how'd you know a thing like that? 'Course my name's Jimmy."

"It'd be whatever I wanted it to be, wouldn't it?"

A smile. "Why, sho 'nuff. Whatever you want. Where you goin', girl?"

. . . she sat on the leather seat stiffly, her back hardly touching. She was clutching her small, child's purse with both hands, but, without much of an effort, she made herself relax, surrendering to the butter-soft embrace of the tan leather as she would, she knew without question, surrender to the embrace of the man behind the wheel.

"Wherever you want," she said.

When Alma closed the front door behind her, it was nearly midnight, for she had waited for Lucy to leave and for Isaac to be very soundly asleep so that she would not have to deal with any questions on the part of anyone about what she was doing or where she was going. Nevertheless, she slunk through the moonless darkness along the side of the mansion as though she

were a child with a pocketful of purloined cookies or a vandal
with a bucket of red paint, for the base, personal nature of her
inquisitiveness and curiosity and the demands she was making
on her credulity daunted even herself.

She found and unlocked the gate to the gazebo garden by
feel—fumbling in the dark for the key that only she herself
could see even when there was light to see it by, fitting it into the
aperture guided not by her eyes but by the touch of her fingers—
but when, almost recoiling at the preternatural smoothness of
the mechanism and the hinges, she pushed it open, daylight
spilled out at her, for in the garden it was still afternoon, and the
sky over the low hills that lay beyond the gazebo—beyond the
locked gate in the railing, beyond the stile steps that allowed her
to pass that railing without passing through the locked gate—
was bright with that strange, darkling radiance.

It was bright and summery, the sunless sky shining with the
silver effulgence of a blank motion-picture screen, as she took
the road to that other Lee's Corners that mixed so much of the
pasts of others with so much of her personal present; but
today—or was it tonight . . . or was it any time at all: did time
even have meaning here (and she steadfastly refused to look at
her watch for fear that she would find that the hands had stopped
moving or were missing altogether)?—Lee's Corners was quiet,
and she stood on the shoulder of the hill, looking down at the
town of the living and the dead without seeing any movement at
all on its streets.

She turned to look back along the way she had come, but as
she had not seen the black man on the porch of his house near
the road, so she neither heard footsteps nor saw the woman in
the childish frock carrying her son up the hill and down into the
town. Perhaps the souls who existed here only participated in
their anachronistic theater when they felt like it, or perhaps
their memories, having been seen by one of the living, had dispersed like so many uneasy dreams. Or maybe she only found
in this Lee's Corners what she wanted to find . . . or was afraid
to find . . .

. . . or what she needed to find.

But Abaijah Jones was still at the counter of Jamison's, still with the chrome and the lights glinting off the lenses of his spectacles, and she slid onto the stool beside him. "Morning, Abaijah."

"Mornin', Alma."

"*Is* it morning?"

"I'm sorry, Alma. I'm afraid I'm not al—"

"Abaijah," she said, ignoring the formal response, "where is Greta Harlow?"

"Greta's dead, Alma. Died sometime ago."

"How long ago?"

"I'm sorry, Alma, I'm—"

"Abaijah, I *know* she's dead," Alma rushed through the gossamer barricade of his words, "but I know she's here . . . wherever here is."

"In Lee's Corners?"

Alma gave him that wry smile. "I'm sorry, Abaijah. I'm afraid I'm not allowed to discuss that."

Abaijah just stared off. "I understand completely, Alma."

"Can I get you something, ma'am?" said the busty woman behind the counter.

"Coffee and pie," said Alma.

"What kind of pie?"

"What kind do you have?" said Alma. "And don't give me any of that *I'm not allowed to discuss that* stuff."

The woman smiled. "You done sound like you're gettin' the hang of this place."

Alma did not know whether to be flattered or terrified. Again, her flesh rebelled at the thought of existing, even for a moment, among such shades . . . or such memories. "What place *is* this?" she demanded without thinking.

"I'm sorry," said the busty woman with another smile. "I'm afraid I'm not allowed to discuss that."

Alma sighed. "Eatin' pie, then."

"Comin' right up."

Could the coffee and pie of the dead nourish the living? Alma did not know, but she ate and drank at the side of the late friend of her late youth while, behind her, outside the big glass windows with the tracery of gilt scrolling around their perimeters, the streets remained empty. "I know she's dead, Abaijah," she said, "but I saw her last time I was here. She was carrying her boy up the hill outside of town. Then, later on, I saw her leave the train station. Where do you reckon she is, then?"

"She's stayin' with Sophonsiba Gavin."

The casual mixing of the living and the dead chilled her, but she persisted. "And before that?"

"Mildred Riddup's place. You remember Mildred."

"Yes," said Alma, "I remember. We went to school together."

"Wasn't much she could do after old Tony died 'cept open that boardinghouse."

"How is Tony, by the way?"

"He's dead, Alma."

"I know he's dead. How is he?"

"He's fine."

Alma nodded. "And where's Greta going to be after she leaves Sophonsiba Gavin?"

Abaijah picked up his cup and drank his coffee slowly. He set the cup down. The busty woman returned with the coffeepot and filled the cup. "Much obliged," said Abaijah.

Alma waited, wondering whether she were going to hear the formulaic response once more.

"She's with Mildred again," said Abaijah at last, and Alma noticed the casual change in tense that could have indicated the plasticity of memory, a casual familiarity with temporal inconsistency, or even ordinary carelessness.

"Do you want some more coffee?" said the busty woman to Alma.

"Is it stronger this time?" said Alma. "I can hardly taste it."

"Well," said the woman, "you're not supposed to taste it."

"Why's that?" But Alma already knew what the response would be.

"I'm sorry. I'm afraid—"

"—I'm not allowed to discuss that," said Alma. "Thanks. Much obliged."

"Glad to help." The woman smiled, lifted the pot. "You want some more coffee?"

Alma spread her hands, shrugged. "Fill it up."

The coffee *was* tasteless. So was the pie. But Alma finished both. And, *Now,* she thought. *Now I've left a piece of me here, and I've taken more than a piece of here into me. And I don't know what that means, but if I'm coming here in any case, then I suppose it doesn't much matter.*

Delbraith Whittington had never seen Snatcher run. If the bank representative moved quickly at all, it was because he was driving or riding in an automobile . . . never was there any question of him achieving by unalloyed self-propulsion anything beyond the dignified progress commensurate with his opinion of his status at the bank. And yet here was Snatcher coming down the sidewalk, shoes clattering, tie flying, face as close to white as Whittington had ever seen flesh and blood.

And he leaped, positively leaped, the cable fence that encircled the automobile dealership; but though he came down wrong, came close, in fact, to breaking his ankle, something put his feet under him at the last minute (Whittington did not know what it could have been except that same overweening dignity and pride that had precluded Snatcher from ever running before), kept them there, and allowed him to come to his senses long enough to slow to a fast walk as he approached the tiny house that Whittington had converted into an office when he had bought the lot.

But in keeping with whatever business was urgent enough to have propelled him along the sidewalk—and, for that matter, through the air—at such an extreme pace, Snatcher seized the door handle and nearly put his head through the cross-and-bible panels as, in his haste, he tried to enter before he had actually opened the door far enough to do it.

"Was he here?" he said when he had sorted things out and had gotten enough of his head through the widening opening to speak.

"He?" said Whittington. "Who?"

"Who? That tomfool John Harlow, that's who. Was he here?"

"Sho. 'Bout half an hour ago."

"Tell me you didn't sell him a car!"

Whittington stared at Snatcher. "I can't tell you that, Snatcher. It ain't true!"

Snatcher was looking agitated. No, more than agitated. Had Whittington, in fact, possessed any imagination at all, he would have expected the representative's eyes to be bugging out and goggling at him on long, optic-nerve stalks like he had seen the Negro caricatures do in the penny comic books. "And I suppose you'll tell me that he paid cash for it!"

Whittington was unimaginative in all things save automobiles. He was particularly inept with irony. " 'Course he paid cash for it, Snatcher! I wouldn't have sold it to him on credit! My God, that man don't have enough credit to buy a plug of tobacco, much less a new car!"

Snatcher groaned and sat down in the chair on the other side of the desk as he pulled a handkerchief out of his coat pocket and mopped the sweat that was running down his face. "So he just came in here, and he gave you money, and you gave him the keys."

"Well, o' course not!"

Snatcher looked more hopeful. "You didn't?"

Whittington was indignant. "Gotta go through the registration procedures first, Snatcher. State's gotta know who's driving what afor'n they'll let someone out on the road with a car!"

Snatcher groaned again. "That's got to be the end of it, then. Now there's no hope of talking any sense into him at all."

Whittington gradually came to the realization that Snatcher's agitation stemmed neither from whim nor from the exertion of running down the street. "What are you trying to tell me, Snatcher?"

"That jackass came into the bank this morning and put a mortgage on his house. And some other jackass at the bank approved it and gave him the money when no one in his right mind ought to give that first jackass anything more than a quarter in the first place, not to mention if they give him anything they ought to just *give* it to him outright, because there isn't any more use expecting someone with an income like John Harlow to repay a loan than there is expecting him to repay something that's an outright gift!"

It took Whittington a while to figure that one out, but he did eventually. "You mean, he's gone and spent it all?"

"He bought a dress for his wife at Susie McDermot's dress shop, and he bought a suit for himself at the men's store up on Fox Street that he hasn't got any more reason to wear than a 'possum's got to wear a mink's skin. Then he ordered a corsage from Mr. Fiorello that's big enough to go on the front of the mayor's car at the Fourth of July parade, and then he came here and bought a car. And as I got it figured"—Mr. Snatcher consulted a notebook he had extracted from an inside pocket— "he's just about gone through it all by now, when it oughtn't to have been given him to go through before someone had a chance to catch him and talk him out of it. So there's no hope nohow of getting any of that money back, because everyone knows that John Harlow's too poor to afford a pot to piss in or a window to throw it out of, and so how's he going to pay off that mortgage?"

"What'd he want all that stuff for?" said Whittington, who, though he had gotten cash from John Harlow, could dimly appreciate the position of the bank vis-à-vis the repayment of a loan.

"Damned if anyone can figure it out," said Snatcher. "He told Fiorello he wanted that corsage for the cotillion, so I guess . . ."

And he suddenly sat up and thrust notebook and handkerchief away so quickly that both items might well have been smoke scattered by the wind.

"The devil!" he cried. "He's off to buy tickets for that cotillion! I still might be able to catch him!"

"If he don't got much left," said Whittington, trying to be helpful, "it sho don't do any—"

But Snatcher had already risen, and, after nearly braining himself once more by trying to pass through the door before he had managed to get it open, he ran across the lot, vaulted the cable fence once again, and proceeded down the street at the same extreme pace as he had come up it.

Whittington sat for a moment, unmoving, as though Snatcher's speed and haste had, by necessity, to be counterbalanced by stasis on the part of someone else; but then he opened a drawer and took out a wad of bills. Carefully, he counted them, shook his head, and put them back in the drawer.

"Cash," he muttered to himself. "Cash is the way to go. None of this mortgage business. Cash down. Pretty as you please."

# Chapter 17

Somewhere between Jamison's Drugstore and Mildred Riddup's boardinghouse, Alma had gotten lost. She had looked
down at the sidewalk for a moment, wondering, despite her efforts not to wonder (because wondering could not but bring up
the fear once again, the fear of the quick setting foot among the
dead, the tactile, palpable fear of living flesh for the touch or
even the whisper of the nonliving), what she was really walking
on, and the sidewalk had blurred and shifted, as though lights
had been switched on behind a theatrical scrim, and had turned
into bare dirt.

And then she had looked up to find herself on a country road,
with sycamore and oak and sumac on either side, and, up on a
rise to her right, a stand of crabbed and irregular pine. No
shacks. No gates. No paths. No crossings.

What part of death—or memory—was this? she wondered.
And the fear did indeed come to her then, stronger, hanging
about her throat and reaching up to her face with cold, corpse-
fingers. What was she doing here, and what would this intimate
journey into this place do to her living body?

But the way forward and the way back looked essentially the
same, and so, having steeled herself to the shattered limbs and
spurting arteries of the emergency and operating rooms in
which she had once officiated, she steeled herself to her own,
more subtle dismemberment . . . and continued on the way she
had been going. If sidewalks could become roads, then roads
could become sidewalks again, and if Lee's Corners could fade

into a forest that might well have predated the town—or the state or perhaps even the nation itself—then it could fade back into itself again.

So she walked beneath the sunless, cloudless, radiant sky, the trees rising—unmoving, unrustling—to either side of the road, and she kept her eyes on the distance, kept her thoughts from wandering ahead to where she was going or what she might come to or under what roof she might find shelter if night overtook her . . . but then she recalled that there was no night here, and that was, perhaps, all the answer that she needed; but a flutter of something just within the closest trees caught her attention, and since she had been walking for some time without seeing any other change in the landscape about her, she stopped.

There was no breeze . . . but there was indeed a flutter as of cloth caught by the wind. With the fear still palping her face, she left the road and approached the movement.

The corpse lay facedown. It had been a man once, but the back of his head had been crushed by a length of lead pipe that now lay beside the motionless body.

Who was he? Who had he been? But, moreover, and perhaps more urgently, how came this corpse to be in the land of the dead? Alma, a doctor still despite her retirement, creaked down on one knee and touched, examined, felt; but all the while she could not keep the thought away: what was death . . . *here*?

But he was dead, long dead, and the scavengers and insects had already been at the body. Eyeless sockets gaped at her when she lifted the yellowed head, and something skittered off and away into the brush as she felt the strange clothes, clothes such as she had never seen before, not even in the North. Odd fabrics and odd colors . . . and a portfolio made of something that looked like leather but was not.

Feeling unclean, feeling sacrilegious, she opened the leather case and thumbed through the papers, bus schedules, and pamphlets half out of horrified curiosity, half out of an instinctive and surrealistic desire to notify the next of kin. But the letters and numbers blurred into one another, and she could make out only the largest of the boldfaced, black-lettered titles: CORE, SNCC . . .

They meant nothing to her, and she was about to put everything back in the portfolio when her eye fell on a date that suddenly coalesced into something approaching clarity.

A date in the future.

Nothing she had seen, whether in the hospital or in these lands of unreal reality, had prepared her for such a clear violation of . . . of *everything*. Standing, dropping the portfolio, she backed away from the corpse, her mind frozen in the denial of what she had seen until her heels caught on a fallen log and she went over backwards.

Then she was looking up at a street sign, and in the sunless light of the dark but luminous sky, she could read it easily. Hewlitt Avenue. It was the street that Mildred Riddup's boardinghouse was on, and yet she could have lain there—on her back on the sidewalk—for many minutes, waiting for her heart to slow down, waiting for her conscious mind to master a fear that had abruptly been pushed well beyond matters of life and death and straight into a clear violation of the most sacred laws of time and temporality . . . but for another fear—of lying, helpless, in that . . . other . . . place—that drove her to her feet.

Yes, the forest was gone, and she was on Hewlitt, and there, just across the way, in crudely whitewashed clapboard, was Mildred's house, shifting and wavering with the same uncertainty of past and present (or was that memory and reality?) as everything else in these lands. Hesitantly, not quite knowing whom—future shade, present individual, past recollection—she would actually encounter, she crossed the street that was, like the other streets of Lee's Corners today (today?), deserted and still, a tableau of small-town life, a diorama cutout pasted against the glass wall of time.

Mildred was Mildred, and she and Alma greeted one another with a familiarity that came from days in the one-room schoolhouse of generations ago and ignored—at least on Alma's side—the impossibility of their meeting. But . . .

"Is Greta Harlow still living here?" Alma asked.

"Trash is what I'd call her," sniffed Mildred. "Trash and more trash. Bringing that lewd nigger truck into my house. But she's dead and gone."

"How long has she been dead, Mildred?"

"I'm sorry, Alma. I'm afraid I'm not allowed to discuss that."

Alma nodded. She had expected nothing else. But there were other ways here. "Greta's been living here since she left her parents' house?"

"They put her out, I took her in," said Mildred without missing a beat. "She's upstairs in the room t'middle of the hall."

Alma nodded. "That must have been quite a send-up to have her folks put her out."

"None of my business," said Mildred. "Long as she's not trashy and don't have no trashy friends, long as she pays her rent and don't bother the other boarders, she can do what she likes."

"And since she ran away from Sophonsiba?"

"Ran away?"

Alma struggled with the indirection of this place . . . and with the lingering shock of the corpse in the land of the dead. And what happened to souls who . . . ?

Was it *not* real, then? Was it indeed only memory?

"Left. With her boy."

"Charity," said Mildred. "Just simple Christian charity I took her in. But the boy's quiet, that's all I can say. Don't say nothin' to no one, not even a please or a thank-you. Broodin' like, if you know what I mean. She's a fallen woman, and that's a fact, but Jesus let a whore wash his feet, and so the least I can do as a good Christian woman is to let her stay here for a while. At least so long as she ain't trashy and she don't bring no trash with her."

"But she's dead."

"Dead for some time now, that trashy whore . . . bringing a nigger into my house in the middle of the night. Think of it! A nigger with a lewd black butt and a gold tooth in my house! But I showed him a thing or two."

"How long—"

"I'm sorry, Alma. I'm afraid I'm not allowed to discuss that."

Faced with a brick wall once again, Alma passed a hand across her face, considering. "Thank you, Mildred. May I see Greta's room?"

"You lookin' to rent?"

"No," said Alma. "I'm looking to lay a ghost."

To her relief, Mildred appeared to accept her explanation without further question, and Alma followed her up the stairs and down the hall to a brown door, which Mildred unlocked and swung open.

Alma stifled a cry . . . but only just barely. The room beyond the door was in utter disorder, with tables toppled and chairs overturned, lighting fixtures half ripped out of the wall, curtains pulled down, and a thousand things—figurines, postcards, pictures, magazines, perfume bottles, clothing, shoes, stuffed animals, and more—littering the floor as though a hundred closets had been picked up, shaken, then upended into the room.

But all that was nothing compared to the sight of the lifeless body lying atop the debris, one so blackened with bruises and reddened with raw, split wounds that for the first moment or two Alma had not recognized it as a body at all . . . seeing it, in fact, as no more than a garishly patterned bedspread until the two glazed and staring eyes had caught her own.

Mildred seemed unaware of either the state of the room or the presence of the body. "This is it. Stayed here until I found her that night, after I showed that fast-talkin' nigger with the gold tooth the business end of my shotgun. He's settin' heavier to this day than he ever did before, I warrant. But that just goes to show you that trash is trash, and all the Christian charity in the world can't help people who are bound and determined to be trash. And that's why I told her she had to leave."

"You don't see her body there, do you?" said Alma.

"I'm sorry. I'm afraid I'm not allowed to discuss that."

But Alma had already gone forward to bend over the mutilated corpse that lay, clad only in panties and a filmy nightgown, on top of a heap of clothing and shattered vases; and, as she had with the corpse in the forest, she was examining, touching, looking for . . . something.

There were hardly words fit to convey the state of Greta's body. Repeated, blunt impacts had broken bones, split skin, removed pieces of scalp, and yet, for all her medical training, Alma was not a forensic specialist, and though she doubted that the verdict of suicide in this case was at all accurate, still she could not say with complete and absolute certainty that Greta had not taken her own life. For that matter, neither could she say with absolute certainty even that this was Greta's real body, for she had seen Greta on the hill above the town, climbing to the crest and then descending. And she had seen her, later on, leaving the train station with her son. And, in fact, Mildred, standing in the doorway, did not appear to see the corpse at all.

Memory?

Yet Alma was touching dead flesh, just as she had touched the dead flesh of the anachronistic body in the forest. And she was seeing wounds that could not be more than a few hours old. And—

"What about Magic?" she asked suddenly. "He didn't see her like this, did he?"

"See who like what?" said Mildred.

Deliberately, Alma rose, turned away from the corpse. It was there for her. It was not there for Mildred. She had to remember that.

"When Greta was found—"

"You mean, when I found Greta?" corrected Mildred. "There wasn't nobody else here but me. I found her. Then I called the police, and Otis York came out."

"All right," said Alma. "when you found Greta . . . where was Magic? He didn't see . . ." She looked over her shoulder. Greta's staring eyes and battered face were turned directly toward her, and with a shudder she realized that it would not be at all out of keeping with this place if her corpse suddenly and spontaneously reanimated, rose, and spoke.

And what about the living Greta she had seen? Would *she* know the truth?

"Surely he didn't see his mother like this . . . ?"

"Magic wasn't here."

"He wasn't?"

"Nope. When I found her, Magic wasn't here at all."

"Was anyone here?"

"Just me and Greta."

"And you called Otis York, the . . . the . . ."

"Deputy marshal," said Mildred. "Called him right away. Called him 'fore I did anyone else. I'm a fine, Christian woman, and I know the place of the law in my life."

Alma looked over her shoulder again. "How long . . . how long has she been lying there like that?" she asked without thinking.

The response was immediate, unhesitating, formal: "I'm sorry. I'm afraid I'm not allowed to discuss that."

Revisiting the scene of an old police incident, MacDonnell thought, was something like revisiting the bed of an old lover. Not that the marshal had ever had any lover save his wife, but he was not an unimaginative man—had his circumstances been a little different, had his capacity to believe in the indomitability of the human spirit been a little larger, he might well have been a poet—and so he could conjure up mentally the idea of what it would be like to enter a bedroom in which he had once had a claim, and he could liken it in an abstract and oblique fashion to his arrival in front of Mildred Riddup's boarding-house. Like the boudoir of a onetime paramour, everything here was the same . . . and yet it was not. And all was familiar with the unfamiliarity of passed years, acquired knowledge, and the polish and lacquer applied to memory by simple duration.

Otis had arrived first, he recalled, going over the events in his mind, ticking them off one by one. And Otis had called the office (which was foolish, true, because it was late enough that MacDonnell had been at home and in bed; but given the state of Greta's body, the marshal could well believe that the deputy had been rattled enough to forget that), then MacDonnell's home, and MacDonnell's wife had caught the phone almost before it had begun to ring—May was like that—and it had been necessary for MacDonnell to listen to Otis's voice for no more than a moment before he was swinging his feet out of bed and into the trousers that his wife was already holding out for him—May was like that—and within two more minutes, he was in his car.

It had taken no more than a quarter of an hour, he estimated, to cross the town and arrive at Mildred Riddup's boarding-house, and in that time, as he now knew, Otis had found and had been persuaded to dispose of a brand-new, unmarked, unblemished, unbloodied axe handle. Which meant that Sophonsiba Gavin had been nearby, and that was itself something he had not known or been able to infer until he had dragged Otis's confession out of him.

But who had notified Sophonsiba? And when? And why was he now so sure that a death that had been ruled a suicide by the duly certified and appointed representatives of medicine and the law was no more a suicide than a gangland execution in Chicago?

In contrast to his state of mind when he had paid his visit to Alma Montague, MacDonnell, though he did not know what he would find out on this visit, was very sure of what he *wanted* to find out and of why he was here today. For a few minutes, though, he looked—just looked—at the boardinghouse, examining it as he had examined many things during his terms as marshal in Lee's Corners: looking for the past, to be sure, but looking beyond the past, running the motion picture forward as the cliché pages might fall off a calendar to indicate the passage of time.

The same . . . and different. New coats of paint. New siding. Nothing overt, though, that would indicate that any kind of large infusion of money had come Mildred's way. Which was not what he had been expecting at all—surely there would have been *something*—but then, he had not been expecting Otis's story about the axe handle, either.

At times, MacDonnell wished that he smoked, and this was one of them. It seemed appropriate, somehow, that the moment of his decision to end his reflections and begin his actions should be marked and punctuated by a final meditative exhalation of smoke and the stubbing out of something hot and glowing.

But he did not smoke, and so he left his car and went up the walk to the boardinghouse door without any sort of prefixed or accompanying gesture . . . save that of his right hand, which, he found, was lying firmly on his mustache as he knocked.

Mildred Riddup was a spare woman: spare in height, spare in girth. Her hair was thinning and had been since she had come into the world, and her face always seemed to MacDonnell to be lacking in some way, as though the invariably threadbare quality of her housedress and apron had, somehow, infused itself into her physical being, as though even in her grave the woman would be characterized not by her presence but by the absence of something. Wiping her hands on a dish towel, she examined MacDonnell for a few seconds after she opened the door.

"Morning, Mildred," said MacDonnell. "How are—?"

"Is this official, Marshal? Now, I want you to know that I can't think of any official reason you'd be here besides looking into any trashy people I might have. But I want you to know that I don't allow any trashy people or lewd behavior in my house. That's the way it was, that's the way it is, that's the way it always will be until Gabriel's Trump. And I don't have no niggers in my house. Lord knows, they carry on all hours of the night, and I won't have them disturbing my other boarders, and I certainly won't have them disturbing my neighbors, and . . ."

MacDonnell had been nodding at her speech. It was Mildred's way, and one just had to go along with it the way one had to go along with a riding mule that had taken it into its head to charge forward straight through a patch of brier. But: "I recollect you showed Greta Harlow's nigger about that rule, didn't you?"

Which brought Mildred up short for a moment, and before she could go on:

"I wonder if I could take a look at that room Greta had the night she was . . ."

MacDonnell caught himself.

"The night she died."

Mildred looked at him, then back over her shoulder . . . though not as though anyone were standing behind her. At least, MacDonnell thought, not as though anyone *physical* were standing behind her. "That room's empty," she said, turning back. "I just had it painted. Ain't nothing of Greta's in there, if that's what you're lookin' for."

"Ain't lookin' for no such thing," said MacDonnell affably. "I'd just like to . . . refresh my memory."

Her eyes narrowed. "How come you want to do that?"

He smiled, and, as usual, the expression stopped just south of his nose. "Sentimental reasons?"

"Sho," she said in a tone that indicated anything but belief.

But she led him back into the house, up the stairs, and down a hallway to a door that MacDonnell remembered . . . except that he remembered it as being brown. It was beige now.

"Here 'tis," said Mildred, and, taking a key out of her apron pocket, she unlocked the door and pushed it open.

Again, perhaps because of the miserable excuse for coming that he had drummed up for Mildred, MacDonnell was reminded of the old lover. He recalled this room, but only in outline, for outlines were all that were left. Greta's body had been cremated years ago, which was probably for the best—no undertaker MacDonnell had ever heard of could have made anything respectable out of that corpse—and her belongings had been dispersed, whether to Sophonsiba Gavin, her parents, or to the municipal dump. And, yes, the room had been repainted. But that was all right: MacDonnell had not expected anything more from looking at the room than the immediacy of environment that would refresh his memory of that long-ago death, its discovery, and its aftermath.

"So Greta was stayin' in this room when she came to live with you the second time," he said.

"She didn't live with me," Mildred said flatly. "I run an honest house. Honest and aboveboard. Ain't nothing trashy 'bout my house. I take in boarders, and they live in their rooms, and there ain't nothing trashy 'bout them, either—leastwise if I can help it. What they did afore they come here is their business, and what they do after they leave is theirs, too. But they don't do nothin' trashy when they're here, and they don't live with me. They just rent my rooms, and if they pay me to, I feed 'em."

MacDonnell had been examining the room, hardly hearing Mildred beyond her first words . . . which were all he really had needed in any case. "So Greta stayed here that second time she boarded in your house."

"Sho," said Mildred. "And if I'd a known that she was goin' to have that lewd nigger trash of hers creeping in through my windows at night, she woulda been boardin' somewhere else, too."

"Sho," said MacDonnell. "I can understand that. Was he creepin' in through that window, there?" And though he knew it was not so, he pointed to the single window the room possessed.

"That one there is over the big rosebushes," said Mildred. "He couldn't get in there. He came in the window at the end of the hall, just like this was some kind of trashy shoutin' bar up in Memphis with niggers goin' in and out every which way."

"You saw him, Mildred?"

Mildred was undeterred. "No, I didn't. But there wasn't any way he coulda got in besides that. That window there don't look out on anything 'cept rosebushes, and the other boarders were in their rooms, and that don't leave any windows unaccounted for except the one at the end of the hall and the ones that look into my part of the house." She fixed MacDonnell with her gaze . . . MacDonnell noting that even her eyes had something threadbare about them. Scrimping and making do: and what could she have profited? "And if you're thinkin' even for a moment that that nigger came in through one of *my* windows, then you start thinkin' elsewise, 'cause there ain't no trash come into Mildred Riddup's room, 'specially black trash, 'cept it goes right out again with a behind full o' buckshot."

MacDonnell nodded. "Which, I hear, is what happened with Greta's man."

"That's no lie, Marshal. I heard him chattering away upstairs in Greta's room, and he was yellin' up a blue streak—"

"You 'member what he was saying?" MacDonnell asked casually, again wishing that he smoked so that he could emphasize just how casually he was asking by taking out a pack, tapping a cigarette free, and lighting up. Casually.

"Now why would I be payin' a hidee-hoe to anything that some nigger was yellin' at some trashy white girl?" Mildred demanded. "I got better things to do than to listen to that truck. No: when I heard him a-cussin' and yellin' up there—"

"Was Greta yelling back?"

"Why she was . . . I mean she wasn't . . . I mean . . . I don't 'member."

MacDonnell nodded. "Go on, Mildred."

"So I heard him yellin', and I grabbed my shotgun 'cause I was a-figurin' that he was fixin' to thieve something from my boarders. But then I got up the stairs and found him a-comin' out of Greta's room. And he must have come in that window, 'cause he sure knew his way back to it . . . leastwise he 'membered real good when he saw what I was totin'."

"The shotgun."

"What else you think I was totin', Marshal?"

"And then you fired the shotgun at him. Right, Mildred?"

"That's right."

And as though to show off her prowess, she grabbed Mac-Donnell by the jacket sleeve and took him out and down the hall to the window.

"There," she said, pointing to the paint that, though relatively new, was dimpled with the depressions of the holes over which it had been applied. "There's the ones that missed. There and there and there. But there was a right bunch more in his black behind when he went out that window."

MacDonnell nodded, suitably impressed. "And that's when you went to tell Greta that she had to leave."

"That's when I went and told her that I don't 'low no trash in my house, and that if she was taking up with niggers, then she was trash, and lewd trash at that, and she had to go."

"And she was alive then?"

"Sho, Marshal. Why would I be talkin' to a dead woman?"

MacDonnell ran a hand over the dimples in the paint. "You sho know how to fire a shotgun, Mildred. Lot of women would just plain lose their heads seeing a strange colored man in their house. And you just took a good aim and let fly, didn't you?"

"That's right, Marshal."

"And after you told Greta that she had to leave . . . ?"

"Then I went downstairs and fixed myself a toddy." Mildred suddenly blushed . . . sparely. "And I won't have you thinkin' that I just fix myself a toddy whenever I want to, Marshal. I'm a fine, Christian woman, and I only fix myself a toddy when I need one to settle my nerves. And that kind of lewd, trashy behavior always unsettles my nerves on account of the devil is behind it all, and seein' it and all is like havin' him come up and tug at your sleeve."

MacDonnell, nodding, removed his hand from his mustache. "You're a fine woman indeed, Mildred."

"And so I settled my nerves with that toddy, but all the while I was frettin' 'bout that trashy girl up in a room in *my* house, and 'bout how that nigger would come back—they always come back, you know . . . always—when I wasn't lookin', only now he'd have a behind full of buckshot and he just as likely want to slit my throat with one o' those razors they always carry. You know how niggers are: always carryin' razors and dice and other inst'm'nts of the devil."

MacDonnell just nodded.

"And so's I just kept frettin' and frettin', and after an hour or two, I decided that I sholy didn't want no trash and no niggers in my house, and I'd go and tell Greta that she had to leave right then and there, because my reputation in the community—my reputation as a good, Christian woman—was at stake, and I wasn't about to have that reputation b'smitched."

"B'smitched . . . ?"

"B'smitched!" repeated Mildred with emphasis. "And so I went back upstairs to tell her, and I saw her door open, and that's when I saw that she'd showed herself just the kind of trash that I thought she was after that nigger went out the window with his black behind full of buckshot, just the kind of trash that'd make everyone come and see my house and stop in front of it and point at it and say to each other *that's where Greta Harlow kilt herself*. And they would. And I *knew* they would, too."

MacDonnell was nodding. "And so that's when you called Sophonsiba Gavin."

And Mildred got one syllable out before something caught in her throat. And then she just stood there, speechless, looking at MacDonnell with that spare, threadbare gaze.

# Chapter 18

*He is waking up, and his wife is making breakfast. He will have pancakes and eggs and bacon this morning . . . and coffee, too, just as he always has pancakes and eggs and bacon and coffee in the morning. He will sit in the kitchen that he and his wife painted a pale yellow, and they will smile at one another, and she will tell him that she will take the streetcar across town today, and she will visit their son and his wife, and she will play with their granddaughter in the living room of the small, sunny apartment, and she will tell the girl stories and read to her from bright-colored, cardboard-paged books while he himself is—*

And there it always ended.

Alma lay in her bed with open eyes, looking up at a ceiling that, six months before, had been a dusty, patched thing, pocked with cracks and fallen plaster and stippled with mildew. Not so now. It was a clean, even expanse of plaster and piped florals and hand-painted borders, fit for the glory of the Montague household, past or present.

*While he himself is—*

She shut her eyes, drowsing in the haze of weariness that had possessed her ever since she had climbed back over the stile steps and into the sunlit gazebo garden. Though fatigue appeared to be unable to follow her into those other lands, it had been content to wait, gathering itself, biding its time until her return to the same Mississippi midnight from which she had departed eight or ten—or, at least, what had seemed to her to be eight or ten—hours before. And so she had come home, had let herself into the house, found her bed, and . . .

*While he himself is—*

Why this inability to settle upon an occupation for her boy? With her imagination, she had gifted him with school, adolescence, and manhood. She had provided him with a wife and family, a home and children. She had gone so far as to create, *ex nihilo,* lives and careers for those children. And so deft had she been with the minutiae of his existence that she could even contemplate what he ate for breakfast.

Why, then, should she quail at his work? Why should that one facet remain uncompromisingly nebulous?

. . . slept. Slept for hours. Dozing now, she sensed that more than a day had gone by, recalled Lucy looking in on her, remembered her own voice sleepily but firmly reassuring the colored woman and sending her back to the kitchen.

A day? Two days?

Dimly, she heard the back door close. Lucy. Yes, it was morning, and that would be Lucy arriving for the day. And she was probably arriving a little early because she was still worried about her employer.

Perhaps, Alma thought, still drowsing, still drifting, she could not fabricate his occupation because that omission was the only accuracy in an otherwise fantastic and improbable collage of fragments clipped out of imaginary magazines and pasted on a background of guilt and regret. Everything else she had dreamed for him carried with it an implicit admission of its true status—passing it was, but passing openly: hair unconked and diamond-set tooth flashing—but the matter of his occupation could not, would not be pinned down, because it conflicted so absolutely with the reality of what he did that the mere existence of that reality—known or not, perceived or not—blasted her feeble attempts into tatters and strewed them on the fluttering wind.

A knock came to her door. "Miz Alma?"

The sound brought her back to herself, back to the room, back to the absurdity of her thoughts. His occupation was nothing. His occupation was that of a corpse. He was dead. He had been dead for a long time. He had died even before his lungs had filled with air for the first time. "Come in, Lucy," she said. "I'm all right."

The look on Lucy's face when she opened the door indicated that she did not believe Alma in the slightest. "Can I get you some breakfast, Miz Alma?"

"Yes, Lucy, you can. I'll come down in a few minutes." She stared at the ceiling of the room—her old room—as she had stared at it on the morning of her departure almost sixty years before. Then, she had looked forward to a clandestine escape, a walk down the road, a ride on the train. Today she would rise and eat breakfast: challenge enough for an old woman with too many memories of the living and far too intimate a knowledge of the dead.

Lucy nodded and started to withdraw. But then:

"Do you want me t' call Dr. Wyatt?"

As though someone had waved a bottle of ammonia—or a syringe full of strychnine—under her nose, Alma was awake instantly. "No!" she said quickly, loudly. "For God's sake, *no!*"

She sat up. Lucy was examining her from the open door. They looked at one another for a long moment.

"All right, ma'am," said Lucy, reverting to formality.

"Thank you, Lucy," said Alma. "I'll get into a robe and be down in a trice."

"I can fix a tray and bring it up, ma'am."

"No. I'll come down. It's time I got out of bed and did something useful. My visit to Sophonsiba Gavin was a little too tiring, perhaps, but I'm fine now."

Lucy did not look convinced. "Yes'm."

"What . . ."

But Alma stopped. She had almost asked what day it was. She could find that out from the paper. There was no sense in prompting Lucy to think again of calling Wyatt.

Wyatt. And that brought her straight back to the ghost that she had, so far, failed to lay.

"Did the newspaper come?"

"Yes'm."

"All right, then. I'll be down shortly."

Lucy nodded, withdrew, closed the door behind her.

Alma rose and, true to her words to Lucy, shrugged herself stiffly into her robe, tying the thick sash about her waist as though the softness of the fabric and the allure of the design had indeed been made for the bent body and withered dugs of age. But instead of going directly to the kitchen, she padded in slippered feet down the length of the hallway, taking a turning into one wing, then another, stopping, finally, before the door to her grandfather's office.

No rustling greeted her when she opened it. Nor was there a gap-toothed smile of a missing volume from the bookshelves: the Joinaud had been returned to its proper place.

She did not quite know why she had come to these rooms this morning. She had, after all, been through the drawers and the cupboards many times in the course of the restoration of the house, and she had found exactly nothing that would tell her anything about the gazebo garden or about the lands that lay beyond. If her grandfather had kept a journal of his journeys beyond the Veil, it had been buried with him . . . or perhaps Wilfred had found it and burned it.

"And then that would be the end of it, wouldn't it?" she murmured. "How very like Wilfred . . ."

Hands in the deep pockets of her robe, she wandered past the shelves and through the inner doorway to the room with the old man's desk, gazed down at the brass paperweights, the antique fountain pen, the miniature telescope that he had carried in his pocket all the days that she had known him. By her standing orders, these rooms were cleaned and maintained, and everything was dust-free and precisely arranged, as though waiting for the sound of his footstep in the hall or his hand on the doorknob.

And yet, despite Wilfred's probable attempts to extirpate all signs of the heretical philosophy that had once dwelt in this house, her grandfather had still managed to leave her a sign . . . by the simple expedient of leaving it in a place that Wilfred could never know about.

But why *Blithe Spirit*?

Struck by a thought, she returned to the outer room, dragged a chair over to the tall bookcase, and, balancing precariously, reached up and extracted the volume of Joinaud from the shelf. Descending, then, she took the book to the desk, held it—upright and balanced evenly—on its spine, and then abruptly released it.

The book fell open, as she had hoped, to an oft-read page, and her eye was pulled, as though a pointing finger had guided it, to a faint pencil mark that bracketed a paragraph on the verso:

> *Nor is the medium's talent the sole wherewithal by which these illuminated realms may be interviewed; for as is well-known to the various mystical organizations and brother-hoods to whose vigilance the care of these material planes (q.v. Neshamah) has been entrusted, there are, ordained and preexistent to any of the workings of mankind, portals that allow access to the inner planes at sundry levels, depending for their efficacy in no little part upon the skill and develop-ment of the aspirant, for as pearls are not thrown before swine, sherds are not forced upon angels, and as the pre-Socratic philosophers have so ably demonstrated, this exclusionary and selective process is as rooted in preexistent natural law as the portals themselves, for* ʻοδος ανω κατω μια και ʻωυτη: *the way up and the way down is one and the same, and the way in and the way out likewise. But perhaps also as an illustration of this very point, these same portals can, by means of techniques hinted at by the teachings of the great fraternal organizations of guardianship or, indeed, in extremi-ty, by simple desire,* be created where previously they were not, *and they will resemble in all ways and forms those pre-existent to human history, yet will manifest themselves in ac-cordance with the wishes and desires of the aspirant who called them forth.*

She read the words, read them again. Analyzed carefully, they made no more sense than the Delphic pronouncements of the white-faced mediums who had stayed up into the summer nights with her grandfather while unseen hands played instruments in the dark and roses fell from nothingness onto the dining-room table. Or, rather, they made precisely the same sense.

Yes, the old man, as though divining the future straits of his granddaughter, had indeed left a message for her, attempting, in his own way, to give her hope, or maybe belief. But Alma was no Spiritualist. She was a doctor, and the physical, whether it manifested itself in bones, blood, a baby's scream, or stillbirth, was all to her. And so, unlike her grandfather, she saw nothing more in the Joinaud than the maunderings of a mind lost in metaphysical mazes of its own construction. Even Joinaud himself had hinted that one found what one wanted to find.

She closed the book, stood with her head bent. And yet . . .

. . . what if . . . ?

"Portals, Grandfather?" she said softly. "Or mirrors?"

The book was silent.

*"Which?"*

When Lindy Buck was well enough to leave his bed—or, rather, when he was well enough that his language toward Sipsey Dewar became so abusive that she categorically refused to set foot in his house ever again, even if he were sick unto death . . . and so he *had* to leave his bed in order to cobble together his meals of corn bread and fatback (and had to eat them half-cooked for the first few days because he got dizzy before they were finished cooking) he stayed home for a week; but, for the same reason that he had to leave his bed, he eventually had to leave his house, too, because he had to buy food, and there was no one in the world, not even one as good-hearted as Sipsey Dewar, who would do it for him save himself.

There was little enough for him to do, though, besides totter to the general store and add to his furnish bill. It was August, and the cotton was ripening, but it would be another few weeks before he had to worry about picking it . . . or about having the strength to do so. If it needed to be done, he was sure that he would find the strength somewhere, whether in his own arms and back or in those of Sam Libbeldoe, whom he was equally sure he could convince, blackmail, or extort into doing it for him.

Not that he worried overmuch about making his crop. Cotton grew. One planted it, and it grew. It was the way of the world, and it was God's will, he was sure, to see that he, Lindy Buck, always had a crop out of which to pay off his rent and his furnish . . . even if by so doing he would be contributing to the comfort and wealth of a landowning, nigger-loving, whoring Jezebel like Alma Montague, who did not even have the decency to keep her abominable vices private but, rather, had felt compelled to announce them immediately upon her arrival in Lee's Corners.

No, what occupied his thoughts was neither his crop nor even Alma Montague (for she would get what was coming to her soon enough), but, rather, the question of what he was going to do about that shambling, tongue-wielding Dark, who was—now that Lindy was well enough to take up once again his loiterer's place in front of M'Creed's Hardware—a physical, daily reminder to Lindy not only of his violation but of the revenge that he had determined to exact.

It was a white man's plan, a white man's revenge, and Lindy, squinting at Dark through the noon glare of the sun (while, inside the hardware store, M'Creed, in turn, squinted at Lindy through the plate-glass window, wishing heartily that the heathen Presbyterian would go away and damning him heartily in his prayers), turned it over and over in his mind, dwelling on it, looking for loose ends that could trip him up (for, mindful as he was of Dark's tongue, he was also mindful of MacDonnell's warning), and, when he found them, tucking them in or tying them off so that they would not ravel. He had, days ago, decided that he needed not only an intimate knowledge of Dark's movements—particularly his movements after nightfall—but also a certain amount of privacy, whether that privacy came from a deserted road or from a lock on the door of a back room. But it was not until he saw John Harlow pulling around the corner in the new car for which he had mortgaged every scrap of his house (Harlow himself wearing a suit that must have cost over a hundred dollars, and his wife, sitting uncomfortably beside him, her face set rigidly forward and a new black eye shining out of its paleness, clad in an equally expensive dress) that Lindy recalled hearing how Snatcher had caught up with Harlow just as he was climbing back behind the wheel of that car after purchasing two tickets for the annual cotillion, and how Harlow had ignored him, shifting into gear even as Snatcher was grabbing for the door handle . . . leaving the bank official sprawling in the gutter as he drove off.

And that recollection fixed all but the last detail of Lindy's design. The cotillion was held every September just before the cotton was ripe enough to pick, and everyone went to it, whether as guests who had paid steep prices for tickets or as hangers-on who stood outside on the sidewalk, watching the guests come and go in their fine clothing and listening to the music that drifted out through the open windows . . . Negroes and whites alike standing elbow to elbow in contemplation of splendor that was not quite as artificial as they sincerely wished that it was.

Which meant that, for the duration of the cotillion, the streets of Lee's Corners and the roads leading into and out of the town would be essentially deserted, the bright pools of the street-lights sparse and intermittent, and the stretches of darkness be-tween them wide enough for a nigger to be taken undetected . . . and wider still the darkness of the back ways and rutted roads of Oktibushubee County, where that nigger would suffer the con-sequences of his sexual crimes and proclivities . . . undetected.

The cotillion, then. It would be the night of the cotillion. But the cotillion was hardly more than ten days away, and that left Lindy little time to determine where Dark went after sunset: where he lived, who he visited, what he did, which windows of which white girls he crept into, what whores from what city he received money from.

"He prob'ly don't got a schedule," he muttered to himself as he watched Dark come out of McCoy's Soda Shop with his usual dish of vanilla ice cream. "He just goes where he wants and comes when he wants."

Drooling, almost slobbering, Dark contemplated the tiny dish of ice cream as though it were the ivory-colored body of a white slave. And then his blub lips curled up at either end in a travesty of a smile as, with a large, thick-nailed hand, he seized the spoon from the dish and scooped up a lump of the dessert, his mouth yawning wide and his tongue probing out as though in anticipation of the yielding sweetness that hung before it.

Lindy shuddered and, involuntarily, looked away. But when he looked back, he saw Alma Montague standing before Dark.

And there was, once again, that damnable fluttering in her breast at the mere sight of the man, but this time Alma was ready for it, and so she did not have to stand, stricken, like some girl feeling her front and finally realizing what it was she wanted, with her hand pressed to her chest as though to cover what she felt. No, she could maintain the illusion of dignity that age conferred (even though she had long ago realized that age conferred nothing at all save aches in one's joints and a tendency toward dyspepsia), and she could offer her hand as befitted a proper Montague.

"Good afternoon, Mr. Dark," she said.

He was on his feet in an instant, taking her hand, bowing deeply, doffing his hat. "Good afternoon, Miss Montague. I trust you're well."

She had struggled with this meeting for two weeks: whether to see him or not, whether to ask the questions that were churning within her or not. She had even, for the space of six hours, considered leaving Lee's Corners altogether, though the thought of the victory she would thereby give Sophonsiba Gavin (as well as her own conviction that the ghost, left so unlaid, would pursue her regardless of where she went) made the thought, in the end, so unpalatable that she had utterly rejected it.

Which led her to this: her final decision to see him, to ask her questions.

"May I join you?" she said.

Another bow. Yes, indeed, he might have been a knight out of an old book. "Need you ask? It's my pleasure, I assure you."

Courtly still, he held the chair for her, but no sooner had she settled in and set down her purse than Willie McCoy burst out of the door of the soda shop. Ill-suited waiter that he was, his white apron, stained with butterscotch and chocolate and a dozen fruit toppings, flapped against his knees and was echoed by the flick of his untied shoelaces and the untamed cowlick that hung over his eye. "Mornin' . . . I mean, afternoon, Miz Montague. Can I get you somethin'?"

And he stood there, shifting his weight back and forth from one foot to the other, looking so charmingly and masculinely ill at ease that Alma, who had not intended to order anything at all, came up with, "A glass of soda water, please."

"Yes, ma'am." And he was gone, apron, shoelaces, cowlick, and all.

Mr. Dark smiled. "I see you've become known in Lee's Corners."

Alma gave him that wry, despairing smile that suddenly

seemed to her to be so utterly inadequate to the task of conveying anything of what she felt. "It wasn't my intention, I assure you."

His eyebrows lifted. "No?"

"I'd wanted to come home to Lee's Corners," she said, wondering why she was telling him, "but I wanted to stay up at the house. To be alone."

And, bursting out of the door again, Willie was back, with the soda water, a tiny paper napkin, and, for some reason, a spoon that—after he had set down the glass, caught himself, picked up the glass and replaced it with the napkin and set the glass down beside it, caught himself, picked up the glass, moved the napkin over to where the glass had been, and settled the glass on top of it—he could not figure out what to do with.

"Thank you," said Alma.

"Pleasure, ma'am," said Willie, still staring at the spoon in his hand as though convinced that a woman who was about to drink a glass of soda water should really have *some* use for such an implement.

"Oh," said Mr. Dark. "While you're here, Willie: I do believe that Miss Montague could do with a spoon."

The spoon was duly placed beside the napkin and the glass, and with a look of unutterable gratitude, Willie retreated into the soda shop.

Mr. Dark dipped into his ice cream. "A terrible thing," he said while his own spoon was on its way to his mouth. "To be alone."

"You think so?" said Alma, keeping her eyes on the glass of soda water.

"I believe we're . . . social beings, Miss Montague."

Faced again with the problem of how to broach a subject that still smacked to her of derangement, Alma was quailing. Did she really want to know?

Out in the street, an obviously new, very shiny automobile came into view, its windows wide-open because of the heat. Alma had heard of John Harlow's purchase, and even had she not, she would have recognized his set face—and the equally set face of his wife—behind the windshield. It was a strong reminder of Sophonsiba Gavin and her tacit threat, of Dr. Wyatt and his fear, of the shattered, staring gaze of Greta's corpse.

Did she really want to know?

She did. She had any number of reasons now.

"My grandfather, Mr. Dark," she began, "how well—"

But just then, Willie McCoy bustled out of the door of the soda shop with a fresh napkin. "I'm sorry, Miss Montague," he said, flustered, "I got your napkin all soggy with moving it around s' much as I did. So I brought you a new one."

"Thank you," said Alma.

And Willie, encouraged by her words, made a great show of lifting her glass, removing the soggy napkin, setting the new napkin in its place, and replacing the glass.

"Willie, you're a true gentleman," said Mr. Dark between spoons of ice cream.

"My pleasure," said Willie, and he gave a kind of nervous bow before retreating back into the soda shop.

"You were saying, Miss Montague?" said Mr. Dark.

Alma tried again. "How well did you know my grandfather, Mr. Dark?"

Dark frowned and set his spoon down. "I didn't know him at all in life, Miss Montague. He died before my time."

Alma persisted. "But you know him in some way."

He looked at her. She felt the absurdity of it all, and she felt the entanglements growing. Yes, she had come back to Lee's Corners to regain the sense of place that she had lost in the Northern city, but she had intended to regain it in isolation, to remain an outsider, as though a house and gardens—renovated or not, ravaged or not—could make up for the complex warp and weft of interaction that was life . . . that was, in fact, that sense of place itself.

But despite her efforts, the weave had been growing, first with Uncle Buddy and Lucy, then with MacDonnell . . . and then the floodgates, it seemed, had opened, unleashing a torrent of faces, names, suspicions, fears . . .

. . . everything she had tried to escape.

"Know?" said Dark.

"Well . . . knew, then." Though she was not at all sure that the past tense was necessary, seeing as how everything—past, present . . . even, apparently, future—lay *over there,* inextricably mixed together with an undeniable logic that ceaselessly confounded her.

And then she recalled that not once while she was in that other place had she lifted her eyes to the hills above the town where stood Montague Mansion, and the thought of what she might find there (and that was, doubtless, why she had not looked) made her hand shake as she reached for her glass.

"Are you not well?" said Mr. Dark kindly.

"You're playing with me, Mr. Dark," she managed after a sip.

"Playing with you?"

"You know—or knew—my grandfather. And you know about the garden."

He eyed her.

"What *is* the garden? What is all of that beyond the stile steps?"

"You've been across, then."

"Yes, I—"

And, once again, Willie bustled out with a glass and a napkin in his hand, his apron, shoelaces, and cowlick flapping in unison. "I thought you might like a fresh glass, Miz Montague," he said, half-stammering. "They get awful warm in this kind of heat awful fast."

"That's very considerate of you, Willie," said Mr. Dark. "Thank you."

"Mor'n welcome, Mr. Dark," said Willie, repeating the ritual of the napkin, the glass, and the napkin once again, this time with the added complexity of a *second* glass and a *second* napkin. Alma was sure that she would have shrieked had he brought another spoon as well.

And when Willie had once more retreated, Alma struggled, with only partial success, to pick up the thread of the conversation . . . and the courage she needed to pursue it.

Mr. Dark dabbed at his mouth with a paper napkin. "I'm very glad to see that the Montagues are being accorded the respect they deserve."

"Mr. Dark, you're not helping me at all!" she found herself exclaiming.

He put down the napkin and looked genuinely concerned. Yes, everything that Mr. Dark did—his expressions, his words, his gestures—were undeniably real . . . so real, in fact, that they made the maundering interactions of life as it was usually lived—day to day, hand to mouth, half-attentive, ignorant—seem as dreamlike as the actions of those who dwelt beyond the stile steps.

"I'm sorry, Miss Montague," he said. "I'm truly sorry. You have indeed been across, then."

"Yes. And I found . . ." She sat there, now feeling utterly old, utterly deranged. Midnight forays into a sunlit garden, somnambulistic entities who knew more than she did and who would not tell her why or how or what, decaying corpses from the future, staring corpses from the past . . .

Perhaps Wyatt's syringe was the best thing after all.

"No," said Dark quietly. "You're not mad. Not at all."

"What . . . what is it . . . over there?"

But though still he looked concerned: "I'm sorry, Miss Montague. I'm afraid I'm not allowed to—"

And Willie came bustling out of the soda shop door again. "Miz Montague," he said, "I'm real sorry. I forgot to bring you another spoon."

She sighed, passed a hand over her face, feeling the sharp peaks and papery skin of an aged visage. "Thank you, Willie. Thank you very much."

"My pleasure, Miz Montague," he said, laying down the spoon and retreating.

"A fine young man," Mr. Dark remarked, looking after him. "He'll probably be back with another napkin for you in another . . . oh . . . two minutes or so."

"Mr. Dark, can we go someplace where we can talk? Uninterrupted? This is rather important."

Mr. Dark considered for a moment, then extracted a pocket watch from his vest. "It would be my pleasure, Miss Montague," he said, consulting it. "But at present I have a rather pressing appointment that I can't put off."

"Will you come to dinner at my house, then?"

The words were out before she realized she was going to say them, and the flutter in her breast made itself felt a fraction of a second too late to save her.

He looked at her. She felt herself blushing.

"That would indeed be my pleasure," he said. "I'd be honored to dine with you, Miss Montague. When would you like to see me?"

And the thought of having it known in the town that such a young and handsome man was coming to her house to dine alone with her nearly made her look for a way to back out of the invitation. But she persevered . . . and she suddenly recalled the upcoming cotillion. The whole town would be at the cotillion, either participating or watching from without.

"A . . . a week from this Saturday?" she said. "At seven?"

"But that's the night of the cotillion, Miss Montague," he said. "I hardly consider myself sufficiently interesting to cause you to miss the cotillion."

"I assure you, Mr. Dark: I've had no intention of attending the cotillion."

"Then it's a done thing," he said, rising. "I shall call at your door promptly at seven."

She offered her hand, and, ever the gallant courtier, he took it lightly as he bowed. "I must be off, then. Good-bye, Miss Montague."

"Good—" Still that fluttering in her breast. "Good-bye."

And then he was a dark shadow moving along the sunlit street, striding away. For a moment, though, fear caught at her, brought her to her feet.

"You'll be there?" she called.

And he turned. "The night of the cotillion, at seven," he called back, his voice carrying cheerily. "My pleasure, I assure you."

# Chapter 19

Greta did not tell him about Magic. She did not tell him much of anything, in fact, save when he could expect to see her again. And this appeared to satisfy him perfectly, for he was, she knew, not at all interested in facts or backgrounds, but only in the body that she bared for him in his walk-up apartment north of Beale Street, that caught its breath time after time as his fair but colored arms wrapped about it and his lips sought its breasts, that enthusiastically (and, though he did not know it, calculatingly) opened itself to receive him and his attentions.

And as she told him nothing about herself, so he left his own life bare and empty to her, a blank canvas upon which she could sketch her own details . . . just as, at their first meeting, she had sketched—and he had accepted—the primary determinant of his name. But this was satisfactory to her, for she was not interested in what he was or where he had come from or whom he might have slept with before he slept with her. No, not at all. She was concerned only with the future: what he would become, what she could make of him, how soon she might be sure enough of his attraction to her that she could begin to plan her—and her son's—escape from Mrs. Gavin.

But, in fact, she was already planning that escape, already beginning to execute her plan. After all, she now had Jimmy, and she had her increasingly passionate meetings with him, and she had her undeniable woman's sense that his possessiveness toward her and his appetite for her company were both growing steadily. He was a fair-skinned Negro with all the status among those of his race that lightness of hue could offer, and he craved a white woman on his arm and in his bed as another man might crave an expensive automobile or a gold cigarette lighter or a deluxe watch. For him, Greta knew, she was evidence of having arrived at the pinnacle of the colored hierarchy, a position from which he would not willingly depart; and for that reason, she would eventually be able to count on his cooperation with perfect confidence, knowing that, regardless of what she might ask of him—a nocturnal rendezvous at the outskirts of Lee's Corners, a quick relocation to another city, even an acceptance of the continuing complication of a child sired by another man—his need for her and her white body would be great enough to remove any objection on his part.

Adversity had made Greta practical: she had not imagined a colored savior, but, having found herself in his bed, she recognized the utility of the match. Committed to her choice, then, she tolerated the annoying inconveniences of miscegenation that barred her from appearing in his company outside of the Negro district and that even occasionally drove both her and her man from colored nightclubs with the hissing of outraged Negresses loud behind them. She treated him well, better than she might have treated a white man, in fact, for not only did he represent to her that slowly opening door that would lead her and her son to cities and towns far beyond the reach of Mrs. Gavin, but he had also become for her (and this she recognized only dimly, feeling it most strongly when she was least thoughtful and most instinctive: in her clenching of his body to hers, in her sensation of replete fullness when she had enveloped him, in her hoarse shrieking aloud of her sexual climax) a force that lifted her up out of the suffocating and enforced childhood with which Mrs. Gavin had surrounded her. In Memphis, in his arms, she could set aside the tiny, infantile purse, cast off her child's frock and shoes, and become the woman her body insisted that she was, simultaneously defying the sterile, pallid matron who had given her that purse and that frock as a deceptive and barbed mess of pottage with which to separate her from her birthright son. It was a rehearsal, a dry run of the future defiance that would take her and Magic away from Lee's Corners, away even from Memphis; and as much as she threw herself into her instinctive passion, screaming her shuddering loins into the close air of his apartment while he, moving above her, grinned his approval and his triumph, so did she, unconsciously, fling that passion at Mrs. Gavin, inwardly daring her to contradict her pleasure or interfere with her future escape.

While in Mrs. Gavin's presence, though, she was, outwardly, still the child. She wore the frocks. She carried the purse. She donned the shiny, strapped shoes with no heel to speak of, and her face was bare of makeup or cosmetics of any sort. And if she was now going more willingly to Memphis, and if her stays in that city now lasted longer, it was because (as she dutifully told Mrs. Gavin, who was dutifully interested) she had found other children with whom she shared interests, friends with whom she could stay overnight and in complete, childlike innocence.

Perhaps Mrs. Gavin believed in Greta's submission. Perhaps she only *wanted* to believe in it, since Magic was thereby implicitly yielded to her without objection or question. Perhaps it was merely a utilitarian compromise on the part of the older woman: the longer Greta was away from Lee's Corners, the longer Mrs. Gavin could have Magic to herself. Regardless, Greta found that Mrs. Gavin approved of the increasing frequency and length of her Memphis trips, so much so that the older woman not only encouraged them with small gifts of extra money—just a little something to see Greta through, something which to treat her friends to ice cream—but, more importantly, with a complete lack of questions about Greta's friends or her pastimes in that city.

Greta could not blame her for snatching at such an improbable straw: she was herself tired of the constant strain, the deceptions, the unconscious calculations necessary to balance her plans for escape with her loyalty to Magic. She could well believe that Mrs. Gavin's tacit complicity with her trips to Memphis stemmed from the same need for relief, the same desire to believe that the struggle was at last over. It did not occur to her, however, that as Mrs. Gavin's actions were, possibly, predicated on illusion, so her own actions and plans regarding Jimmy might well have been similarly based; that Jimmy, in fact, had, with regards to her, his own agenda, one that had nothing in common with hers. And so it was without any premonition of disaster that, on a Sunday morning in Memphis, with the sun streaming through the window of his stuffy apartment and his pale arm cast carelessly and sleepily across her belly, she waited until he was awake enough to talk and then said:

"You ever thought about leaving this place?"

"Mmm? Get some oth'r rooms?"

"No. Leave Memphis. Leave Mississippi."

He laughed: slow and deep. "Now, where would som'n like me go?"

"Not you," she said. "*Us*. And we could go anywhere. Up north, maybe. Chicago. Maybe New York. What do you think?"

He sat up, looking at her as though she were a stranger. "You's serious, ain't you, girl?"

"Yes," she said. "Real serious."

Smoke was still seeping from the belly of the overturned truck when MacDonnell pulled up in the police car. He parked on the shoulder and shut off the engine, but though Hap Hayes, the sheriff, was waiting a short distance up the highway from the wreck, his short arms folded just above the hemisphere of his belly, MacDonnell did not get out immediately. Rather, he sat for a minute, staring with his cold gray eyes at the sun-drenched highway and the cotton fields that bordered it, thinking about what he had been thinking about all during the drive out from Lee's Corners: Mildred Riddup and Greta Harlow. And Sophonsiba Gavin having tea with Alma Montague.

He had decided from the beginning that he trusted Alma Montague, and the matter of the tea had not changed that. But Alma was independent and strong-willed, and there was every chance, he guessed, that, intrigued by the Gavin-Harlow affair—and possibly piqued at Sophonsiba's forwardness in calling upon her (May had explained it to him)—she was starting to make inquiries of her own. Whether that was good or bad or entirely neutral MacDonnell could not be sure, but if Greta's death was *not* a suicide, then MacDonnell was very certain that—good, bad, or neutral notwithstanding—making inquiries was a dangerous thing for Alma Montague to do.

And what about her comments about Dark? Wanted to thank him? Phooey!

He rubbed at his forehead. It was all insoluble, just as insoluble as the original question of what had happened during a certain one or two hours in a certain room of Mildred Riddup's boardinghouse. That Mildred had called Sophonsiba Gavin was, perhaps, not as suspicious as it sounded: everyone knew that Greta and Sophonsiba were connected by something that was a little less than blood and a little more than money, just as everyone knew that Greta's parents had put her out. Who else would Mildred call? Who else was Greta's next of kin? Who else was so obviously willing to take in her bastard child?

It was the silence, he decided, the damned silence that had sifted down like ash from a crematory, descended like a funereal curtain—or a thick layer of dollar bills—over the events of that summer evening, leaving unanswered questions . . . or, rather, in MacDonnell's case, complete uncertainty as to whether there were actually any questions to ask in the first place.

He could only keep looking, watching the town go about its business, peering through the interstices of daily life as he tried to fathom the lights and the shadows that semaphored their cryptic messages at him. Somewhere in there, he was sure, there was meaning; and if there were questions at all, then, somewhere in there, there had to be answers.

"You gonna stare at the cotton all day, Abe, or you gonna come out here and he'p me keep a-holdin' up this piece o' sky?"

Hap Hayes had been waiting patiently, waving the occasional dawdling automobile past the wreck . . . but that had happened, MacDonnell realized, two or three times in as many minutes since he had arrived. Roused by Hayes's words, then, he got out of his car and approached.

"Afternoon, Hap."

" 'Noon, Abe. Lord, but you must have summat on your mind to be lookin' like a squirrel with his nose stuck up the business end of a shotgun."

"Always do, Hap."

Hayes nodded, and, "Thought you might like to see this," he said, freeing an arm from its resting place on his belly and indicating the smoldering truck.

MacDonnell examined the truck. From the tracks and the footprints in the soft ground, he judged that an ambulance had come and gone sometime ago. "Looks like he rolled."

"Rolled?" Hayes's belly shook a little as he chortled. "He rolled the way a young'n rolls when he goes down a hill on his side. Musta looked like one of those whirlagig things they sell at the fair."

"What you think happened?"

"Dunno. Mebby he spent too much time on the road and fell asleep tryin' to get down to Biloxi. I think that's where he was goin'."

"He didn't say?"

"Not much o' him left to say anything with," said Hayes, waving another car by. "Go on, you walleyed, rubberneckin' horse thief," he roared at it. "Go on and get to wherever you got to get to."

The car pulled by, white faces pressed against the windows. MacDonnell admitted privately that it was indeed an impressive wreck: though the truck lay essentially in one piece, that piece had been so thoroughly shaken and dislocated that it seemed less a truck and more a heap of vaguely related parts. Still, though: wrecks happened all the time on the county highways. Why had Hayes made a point of having a deputy call into the Lee's Corners office with an invitation to come out and see one?

"I—"

Hayes's belly was still shaking. "You want t' know why I called you out here, don't you, Abe?"

"I wouldn't say no to that."

"Check out the license plate on that rig."

MacDonnell looked . . . and then he understood. "You think it was him?"

"Pretty much so. Plate number matches that partial we finally pried out of your folks in town. Found a cheap gun in the cab, too. Same kind as would throw those bullets Doc Wyatt pulled out. The amb'lance crew—they came down from that colored hospital in Memphis—didn't have much to put on a stretcher, but what they had was pretty big. I think it was your boy."

"Dead, then?"

"If he wasn't, he sho woulda wished he was."

MacDonnell nodded. "Well, I guess that settles that."

"Guess so. But now I'll never know."

Smoke continued to rise from the truck. Burning oil. Soon, a wrecker would come from wherever Hayes had summoned it, would extinguish the last of the fire, would haul the remains of the machine away for scrap. If the company that owned the truck was lucky, someone would notify it of the accident.

"Never know what, Hap?"

Hayes's belly had stopped moving, but now it started up again, shaking with the sheriff's deeply buried laughter. "Now I'll never know if I'd a pinned a medal on that nigger for shootin' that li'l rattlesnake of a Lindy Buck, or put him in chains for not havin' killed that li'l rattlesnake outright."

MacDonnell nodded.

Hayes fished inside his jacket and came up with a short cigar. He bit the end off and spat the fragment into the grass, then shoved the roll of tobacco into his mouth and lit it with a kitchen match he ignited with a thumbnail. "You want a cigar, Abe?"

"Don't smoke, Hap."

"Mmmm . . . that's right. I forgot." His eyes mirthful slits in his pouchy face, Hayes puffed on the cigar, sending up white smoke to mingle with the black. "You really ought t' do somethin' 'bout that, you know?"


Alice Harlow had not asked her husband where he had gotten the money for the new car and the new clothes and the tickets to the cotillion and the gasoline that he was burning by the bucket as he drove, every day, up and down the streets of Lee's Corners with no goal save the next turning and no destination save nightfall. She did not have to ask. She knew. But she did not know what it was that had finally turned him into a silent, brooding man who would mortgage his house for the sake of appearance and who was more likely to indicate his wishes with a fist than with words. Somewhere between one day and another, as she had lain sleeping by his side, something had changed in him, and just as he now drove the new automobile that was the product of his relinquishment of any and all claim to ownership of his house (for Alice knew, just as Snatcher knew . . . and, probably, even as John knew himself, that the mortgage could never be paid off, that the inhabitants of the clapboard house with its powdering and mildewed paint would now be—and could never be anything other than—tenants in a building owned by someone else), so was he himself driven, guided down the streets and roads and byways of his mind by a hand even stronger, more determined, and more implacable than those of flesh and blood with which he gripped the wheel of his automobile.

But she did not argue, and she did not question. She wore the dress he had bought her, and she sat on the seat of the car beside him as he ordered her to, and she watched as, chin jutted forward defiantly as though to prove to Lee's Corners in general and Sophonsiba Gavin in particular that he was a man who could gather enough resources to do anything, whether it was buying an expensive automobile or snatching his grandson back from the arms of an interloper, he motored through the town, repeating the pattern of drive, turn, and turn again endlessly throughout the day until night fell and hunger finally forced him to park the car in front of the house that was no longer theirs. Then they would go inside, and they would exchange their finery for plainer dress, and she would put dinner in front of him. He would eat silently, and he would go to bed; and after that she would sit up into the night, fear and humiliation keeping her eyes sleepless and her face turned toward the dark rectangle of the front window.

There was nothing else she could do, for protest, whether against Sophonsiba Gavin, the town, or her husband, was a habit that had been thoroughly broken. And yet a vestige of her common, female practicality remained, urging her toward common, female concerns: food, clothing, shelter, children. Whether her husband believed it or planned for it or not, Magic would eventually be returned to them—without warning, true, and only for so long as Sophonsiba Gavin willed it, but returned nonetheless—and some provision had to be made for him. Then, too, there was the matter of the supper that she was tasked with preparing when hunger drove her husband to put aside his obsessive motoring: day by day, there was less that could be considered food in the house, and, as she well knew, less money with which to buy anything more.

It was beans and the last scrap of bacon when she finally ventured to speak. "I can't go out with you tomorrow," she said. "I've got to go to work at the diner. They said they'll fire me if I miss one more day."

John sat in silence, mumbling his beans, the scrape of his spoon on his plate the only sound besides that of his hoarse, regular breathing: a sound so distinct that he might have been making each cycle of inhalation and exhalation a conscious, defiant effort.

"So you'll have to go alone tomorrow."

"No."

She just watched, waited.

"My wife doesn't have to work," he said. "We've got money. We've got money enough to show that bitch that she can't take a man's grandson away from him."

Protest was alien, protest was unthinkable: her eyes still hurt from where he had blacked them—one at a time—in the course of the last week. But: "Maybe I don't have to work," she said, "but we got to eat. And Magic will have to eat, too, when he comes back."

"We've got money."

"We won't have it for very long."

"We've got money."

And he sat there with his smeared plate before him and his spoon in his hand like the scepter of a kitchen god, while outside the crickets chirped and the cicadas buzz-sawed their way through the steaming night.

"We won't for much longer," she said, forcing herself to utter the words. "We're putting the last of it in the gas tank of that car, and if you aren't working, and I'm not working, then there won't be any more."

And then she noticed the whiteness of his knuckles, and how the spoon he was holding was starting to shake. Nothing much. Just a small tremor, like the rattling of the weight on the lid of a pressure cooker.

"You're coming with me tomorrow," he said.

And still with that female practicality gnawing at her like termites within a silent house, she was thinking ahead. How long would the food last? Two weeks, maybe. She might be able to stretch what was left in the house that long; and on the morning of the cotillion, while he was up at Fiorello's picking up the corsage that she dreaded seeing, she might be able to sneak out and buy some groceries with what she could salvage the night before from the loose change in his pocket, but that would be the end of it. It was as though he expected time to stop with the cotillion, with what he intended to be a glorious arrival and entrance that would spite Sophonsiba Gavin and match her, elegance for elegance. After that, it seemed, he had decided that they would not need food or money or anything else. After that, there was, would be, nothing.

Nothing. She shut her eyes, clenching them, feeling the pain of the bruises that cupped them. She could not contemplate nothing, could not accept it even as an interim placeholder for the future. Her very body, made and conditioned by breed and birth, cried out against such surrender, for she had brought Greta into the world, and Greta had brought Magic, and there was future and continuity in that. But Greta was dead now, and Magic was essentially gone, and now John was not only driving his automobile but driving her, too: toward an ending beyond which he saw, *could* see, nothing.

*No. No.*

"We'll have to—" she started . . . and then she stopped, looking at the hand with which he was clutching his spoon. The evening had brought shadows to the kitchen that could not be dispelled by the single electric lamp, but there were darker shadows between his fingers, shadows so dark that they looked black, shadows that grew and welled up and pooled and trickled down the back of his hand until they puddled on the tabletop in a sticky blot.

And still he sat there, his knuckles white where they were not streaked with blood, the spoon shaking with that small tremor.

She rose, slid her chair back, and went into the living room, there to spend the rest of the night staring at the darkness outside the windows. It must have been well after midnight when she heard him go upstairs, but she did not expect that he would sleep, either . . . no more than he had any of the previous nights.

In the world she had created for herself—a world of new paint, new paneling, constantly renovated rooms, and the endless, youthful presence of children—death had no place. Death had, by her fiat, been banished long ago, and so thoroughly had she altered her surroundings that no hint of that entity's existence was visible within Gavin House.

She had purged herself, inwardly and outwardly, of such associations, her task made easier, perhaps, by Mr. G having conveniently not died in the house or even within the boundaries of the county: he had met his death in Memphis, in a brothel just off Fourth Street, where an enterprising whore had taken him a bit farther into ecstasy than his liquor-saturated heart could stand. And Greta, too, had been found . . . elsewhere, thereby keeping at bay any morbid associations that might, under other circumstances, have attached themselves to a particular bed, or to a given room, or even to something as ephemeral as a quality of afternoon light on the windows.

Caught up in the ambiance of youth and life that she had striven so hard to foster within the house, then, it was perhaps understandable that she did not notice the dark figure standing at the side of the road outside the front gates of the drive until it had been there for several days.

"James . . ."

He appeared in a moment. As his black skin and his black livery might have been contiguous, so his existence might have been one with the interior of the house. "Yes'm."

"Who . . . or . . . or *what* is that out there in the road?"

He looked, bending a little to see out the window. "I believe it's Anger Modestie, ma'am."

"Anger . . ." Her voice trailed off.

He misunderstood. "Modestie, ma'am. The one who—"

Cerements. Rot. Withered hands. They were suddenly very near, pressing close. "How . . . how long has she been there?"

"Just a few minutes, I believe, ma'am."

"No. I mean, for how many days has she been coming? It *has* been days, hasn't it?"

James was tall, straight, formal. "I believe so, ma'am."

"How many, then?"

"Two or three, ma'am. I don't quite recall when she first appeared."

The dark figure had not moved. "Go out and see for sure if it's Anger," she said.

"Yes'm."

And he was gone, leaving her to stand at the window, peering out through the sheers at the dumpy, fantastically clad being that had planted itself before the gates of Gavin House so as to look—just look—in through the wrought-iron bars.

In a moment, James appeared below, striding out along the drive toward the gate. The figure did not move at his approach. Even when he reached the gate and stood just on the other side of the iron, it might as well have been a bundle of rags (which, indeed, was what it looked like from the upstairs window) for all the mobility it demonstrated.

And then James was coming back, the figure still unmoving and outside the gate.

"Yes'm," he said when he reentered the room. "It's Anger Modestie."

"The one who . . ." She found that she could not utter the words.

Again, he misunderstood. "Sings people to Jesus," he said. "Yes'm. She said—"

She spoke quickly, hastily, loudly. "I don't want to hear what she said! What she said makes no difference to me! What she said *could* make no difference to me! Do you understand?"

James blinked . . . and then his gaze reverted to deferential and straight ahead. "Yes'm."

"Why hasn't she left? Did you tell her to leave?"

Caught firm in the meshes of race and occupation, James was keeping his gaze fixed. "No, ma'am."

She struggled to keep her voice even. "Why not?"

"I'm sorry, ma'am. You didn't ask me to."

Still struggling, she managed: "Go back out and tell her to go away."

"Yes'm."

His steps were steady and even on the carpeted stairs down to the foyer, but by the time he came into view once more, striding down the driveway, her gaze had returned to the dark figure outside the gate.

"You can't have him." She was clutching at the sheers as though she would pull them down. "You can't have my Magic. He's mine. Do you understand me? Mine!"

# Chapter 20

Lindy had a two-foot-long strap of thick leather that he had doubled over and filled with buckshot, and the device stretched Mr. Dark out on the ground facedown, the only sounds having been the muffled thud of impact and the soft, susurrant crunch of concussing skull.

A short distance away, Sam grinned in the deep twilight. Lindy could see his teeth, but not much more. "Looks like you 'bout got him all right! Huhuhuh!"

Lindy straightened up from the follow-through, hefting the bludgeon with a twinge from the scars in his chest and a shade of regret that he had not thought of such a weapon on another occasion when he had been called upon to defend the morals of Lee's Corners. Compared to the sounds the stick he had used at that time had produced, this blow had been utterly silent. But that was all in the past, and Dark was what mattered tonight. And, in fact, Dark lay unmoving before him, the back of his woolly head matted with a seep of blood where the scalp had split.

"Gimme that lantern," he said.

"Huhuhuh!"

He whirled on Sam. Here, just within sight of the lights of Montague Mansion, speed was important if they were not to be seen by that whore in the house or by MacDonnell or one of his hired eyes. But it was important, too, to have a good look with the lantern, to make sure that Dark had been sufficiently subdued. It would not do to have him suddenly caterwauling.

"Where's that lantern?" Lindy hissed.

He could see the dark shape that was Sam fumbling about. "I've got it. Right here. Huhuhuh!"

"Well, bring it on over here."

"I will. Just a second."

Dark mumbled something indistinct, and Lindy had to reach down, feel for his woolly pate, and hit him again to make him quiet. Another thud, another crunch. "Ain't you got that lantern lit?"

"Oh, yeah. It's lit. Just a second. Huhuhuh!"

But, as Lindy found when he groped his way to Sam's side, the lantern was certainly *not* lit.

"You—!"

"It just went out! It was lit, but there was a wind, and it got blown out!"

The September night air was utterly still, the lantern was stone cold, and the chimney creaked up only with an effort. Muttering, Lindy fumbled in his pocket for a match. "You got those chains I tol' you to bring?"

"Sure! Huhuhuh!"

It was immediately obvious to Lindy that Sam most certainly did *not* have the chains.

"Damn you for a horse-assed slubgullion! Where'd you leave those chains?"

"They're right here. Huhuhuh!"

"Where?"

"They *were* here. Right here! I had them!"

Lindy's jaw clamped, compressing his lips to a thin line. In the darkness, though, the expression was lost on Sam. "The wind blew 'em away, I guess."

"I *had* them! They were right here! *Right here!*"

Dark began mumbling again, and Lindy, caught between Sam's continuing protests and the need to keep Dark quiet, gave up on the lantern and the chains for the moment and started to feel his way back to Dark's side. His arms, however, were extended out just beneath the level of the overhanging branch that struck him soundly on the forehead.

"That must have been a big one! Huhuhuh!"

Lindy reeled, felt the trickle of blood start down his cheek, and looked for something he could blame. He settled on what was defenseless and close at hand. "You damned, faggoty whore of a nigger! You hell-bound, p'verted son of 'n unrighteous drab!"

Dark moaned in response, and, judging from the sounds he heard, Lindy understood that the Negro was attempting to crawl away.

"Sam! Dammit! Where's that light?"

"Right here! Huhuhuh!"

It was clear, though, that Sam was nowhere near the lantern—which was still unlit in any case—and Lindy swung rapidly from glaring at his invisible assistant to lunging for the invisible Dark; but a clump of grass caught his boot and he toppled face forward. The flare of a match that Sam conveniently produced just then allowed him to see that Dark was now faceup and grinning . . . and that the treacherous clump of grass was sending him, arms flailing, straight down on top of him.

"Looks like you sho tryin' to fly, Lindy! Huhuhuh!"

The match went out, and Lindy fell into the darkness. He landed on something big and warm, something that smelled distinctly of Negro.

"What de damn hell's goin' on here?" said Dark. "Why dun did ya' hit me? What de hell's ya' tryin' t' do?"

Lindy flailed, remembering Dark's probing, inquisitive tongue. "Git away from me, you p'verted nigger! Git away and shut up!"

"You really outta t' tell me whut youse tryin' t' do, dude."

Dark's voice seemed loud enough to be a brazen trumpet of doom, and Lindy, having dropped his bludgeon somewhere between Dark and Sam, lashed out with his fists, pounding repeatedly and desperately at the invisible, negroid features as Dark's protests first grew louder, then slurred and intelligible, then fainter . . . and at last faltered into silence.

Exhausted already, frightened at the thought that someone in the house had heard or that MacDonnell's spies—or even MacDonnell himself—might even now be watching, Lindy took a deep breath in order to settle his nerves, letting it out slowly as he unthinkingly allowed his head to drop forward . . . at least until he felt the touch of moist, battered flesh and the flick of an inquisitive tongue.

And then the lantern came on, burning much brighter—so it seemed to Lindy—than it had to. Before his face was the ruin of Dark's features, pounded by his fists into a mass of bruises, broken cartilage, and swollen knots. But, even so, the Negro's pale, probing tongue was still extended, as though, even in battered unconsciousness, he was still attempting oral copulation with his attacker.

For a moment, Lindy blinked at the tongue, worried that he had seen it tremble as though in preparation for an offensive thrust. But then he recalled the light that was illuminating the entire area with what seemed to be the equivalent of noon sunshine. Surely someone in the house would see something that bright! Levering himself off Dark's inert body, then, Lindy pumped his arm, palm down, at Sam, who was standing a few feet away and holding the brightly burning lantern up so that not only Lindy could see it, but probably most everyone else in Oktibushubee County.

"That thing's brighter than a se'chlight, Sam! Turn it down!"

"You can see him real good now! Huhuhuh!"

"Turn that thing down!"

And, rising in the effulgent flood, Lindy grabbed the lantern away from Sam and turned it down. As he turned the small knob, though, he overestimated, and the flame promptly went out, plunging all three of them into darkness again, one made deeper by the light that had dazzled their eyes for the better part of a minute.

"Tarnation!"

"Whatsamatter, Lindy? Can't make up your mind? Huhuhuh!"

"*Shut up!*"

Frightened by the volume of his own outburst, Lindy stole an anxious glance at the house, but he saw no movement and no sign that anyone had noticed anything. This far from the mansion—just where the drive came out from under the trees and began its leisurely circle up to the front steps—there was a good chance that they were reasonably safe, he guessed, from anything but chance observation. Unless, of course, they made some . . .

"Huhuhuh!"

. . . colossal blunder.

"We don't need th' lantern no more, Sam," he said. "Fergit about the lantern."

"It was lit! The wind blew it out!"

It was more than Lindy could stand. "I don't give no good God damn about wheth'r the wind blew it out or not! We don't need it no more!" He struggled, mastered himself. "Never you mind. Just help me git those chains on him."

And then he recalled that Sam, through his exuberant affirmation that he had brought the chains, had indicated, unequivocally, that he had *not* brought the chains.

"Huhuhuh!"

Again, Lindy mastered himself, keeping back the words that he wanted to shout at Sam. "A'right, then," he said at last. "You help me pick him up. We'll carry him back to the wagon without the chains. He ain't gonna give us no lip now."

"Huhuhuh!"

"Just you grab his feet and help me git him to the wagon."

Together, they lifted the insensible Dark and carried him down the road. Behind them, off in the warm night, on the far side of the circular drive and just beyond the borders of flowers that Isaac had managed to coax out of the feral and unrepentant ground, Montague Mansion glowed warmly, its well-lighted windows looking out as though welcoming the evening into its genial, Southern embrace.

Alma had entered the garden, circumvented the locked rear gate by climbing the stile steps, and crossed into the other lands once again, looking one last time for a confirmation of her belief . . . or, rather, a confirmation of her unbelief, for she still wanted nothing less than a flat denial that there was anything in that place in which to believe.

But belief, unbelief, denial: all hid themselves from her the moment she set foot on the road and walked the impossibly short distance into the Lee's Corners that shifted and blurred like a reflection in an uneasy pool.

It was the Fourth of July this time, and Jefferson Street was filled with the orderly randomness of a parade. From the top of the hill, she saw soldiers in uniforms that had rotted on corpses for generations, who marched beneath a flag that did not have anywhere near enough stars. Others had fallen in behind them wearing defeated colors, and still others proceeded in silence, wearing the shadowy hues of liveries as yet unthought-of. Streamers fluttered from rooftops and from windows over their heads, and on either side of the street, figures in costumes as varied and sometimes unsettling as those of the marchers watched, waved, cheered with the muted enthusiasm of this place.

She should have expected it. Here, there was no time. Here, all was contiguous, shades of the past and the present and even the future mingling without contradiction or disharmony. And even if what she hoped was true—that these were shades of recollection only, wandering somnambulistically through streets and shops and gardens that owed their existence only to the shifting memories of the living—still there was no inherent contradiction, for there were memories of the future just as there were of the past, and where one living soul might dream of the departed, another might well imagine the unborn.

Defeated once again, inclining more and more toward the admission that her own endeavors could gain her nothing (and, therefore, placing ever more hope in her upcoming interview with Mr. Dark), she started to turn away, to turn her back to her own garden and the life that she lived on the other side of the locked gate and the stile steps; but curiosity held her, forced her to turn back, her gaze drawn beyond the parade, beyond and up . . . to the white mansion on the hillside above the town. The other mansion, a different mansion from the one she had left a short time ago in darkness and secrecy.

And now she could not turn away. She could not go back until she had traced—or, perhaps, retraced—the road that led from the town into the hills and up to the broad, circular drive before the wide steps. Unwillingly, then, yet with a desire that she recognized as half of hope and half of fear, she descended toward the crowded streets where the soldiers of past and future glided in stately procession and the crowds that lined the sidewalk looked on with vague perspicacity. But she did not walk among them or join them. No, she avoided Jefferson Street entirely, crossing instead up one block and then another at the edge of town where Mildred Riddup's boardinghouse stood sterile and God-fearing behind its picket fence and the man she recognized as Lindy Buck slouched toward it with a cudgel in his hand . . . turning then, and only then, parallel to but well away from the parade route, making her way slowly, block by block, to the railroad station.

It was as it was and as she remembered it, gas lamps merging unsettlingly with electric lights, sidewalk melded with board-walk. Within, she knew, she might meet almost anyone, but she did not go in. Rather, she approached the taxi that was standing ready outside the main entrance . . . just as she knew it would be.

And that knowledge gave her hope, even as she shuddered at the thought of who was driving and where she would ask him to take her, for if there was volition here, then how could she have predicted that the taxi would be waiting for her? Still . . .

"Uncle Buddy?"

"Why, Miz Alma!" His smile was as bright as ever. As bright as she remembered it. "How are you today!"

"Fine, Buddy. Can you take me up to the mansion?"

"Why, I'd be mo' than pleased to do just that. And you can be sho I won't charge you a red cent."

"Thank you, Buddy."

"My pleasure, ma'am."

"What time is it, by the way?"

"I'm sorry, Miz Alma. I'm afraid I'm not allowed to discuss that."

As she expected. "Perfectly understandable, Buddy. Forgive me for asking."

"Nothin' to forgive if there ain't no offense taken, ma'am."

She got in, and he started the engine and took her away, and it did not seem overly remarkable to her that as he crossed through the intersection of Jefferson and DeWitt, there was not a sign of the parade that had, a quarter of an hour before, filled the streets with a press of people and uniforms.

Dark was still insensible when Lindy and Sam loaded him onto the back of the mule-drawn, flatbed wagon, and at about the same time, Sam came up with the chains that Lindy had asked for, declaring over and over again that he had had them with him all along and that he had just forgot—temporarily—about where they were. This technicality, however, no longer concerned Lindy, for with Dark on the flatbed and trussed up in the chains, his revenge was, after a few unlooked-for detours, now proceeding according to plan.

Squatting beside Lindy on the flatbed, Sam snapped a padlock closed on the chains, then stood up in the dim light of the lantern that Lindy had turned down so that the wick bore more of a resemblance to a glowing coal than to a flame. "He sho ain't going nowhere now! Huhuhuh!"

"Shhh!" They were well away from the house, but they were still just off the long road that led up to the Montague drive, and there was always the chance that MacDonnell . . .

Lindy started, looked up, looked around. Had he heard something? He had the sense that he was being watched, and there was indeed a chance that MacDonnell had seen him drive the wagon out of his yard and into town to pick up Sam . . . and had decided to postpone his attendance at the cotillion long enough to come snooping around Montague Mansion.

There it was again. Cricket or . . . something else? Lindy peered into the darkness that, with the fading of the last traces of the light in the west, had become absolute outside the tiny area illuminated by the lantern, and, taking a step in the direction of the sound . . .

. . . wound up hanging off the side of the wagon by one foot, for Sam had unwittingly closed the padlock on a loop of Lindy's bootlace.

"Huhuhuh!"

Sam's incessant giggle was annoying at the best of times, but at present Lindy found it utterly intolerable. "Hellfire and abomination, you jack-splatted, long-ribbed mule licker! You c'mon and get me down from here!"

But before Sam could move, the insensible Dark—

"What's goin' on here, mah dude? Whut de hell be dese chains doin' on me?"

—or, rather, the previously insensible Dark, dragged by the weight of Lindy's body, slid toward the edge of the flatbed, simultaneously lowering Lindy to the ground. This had the unfortunate side effect of placing Lindy in a less than favorable position when, with a jingle and a thump, Dark fell off the edge and landed on top of him.

"Oh, Ah am so's impressed, Mr. Buck. What it is, Mama! And dun did ya' gots sump'n else in mind tonight 'sides kidnappin' dis hyeah little old nigga' and tyin' him up in chains?"

Cursing about bitchery and abominations, about nigger Jezebels and whoremongers, Lindy was already fumbling at his bootlace, interspersing his abuse with less-than-polite requests for Sam to turn up the light. Which Sam did . . . just in time for Lindy to look up and see Dark's tongue unrolling with inhuman length and speeding straight for him.

"Sweet Jesus!" he cried, springing to his feet, thus bringing his head into resounding contact with the underside of the wagon. The world—what he could see of it—swam in his vision, but the thought of lying unconscious within arm's (or, rather, tongue's) reach of Dark, drove him to his feet again, and he gripped the edge of the flatbed to steady himself.

"Will ya' please let me out o' dese chains! Sheeeiit!"

"Let you out, you unrighteous black demon?" Lindy was holding his head with both hands, but his mouth was still free. "Let you out? I'll show you how I'm a-gonna let you out!"

And, so saying, he reached into his back pocket and extracted one of the razors that Sam had bought in Memphis. Flipping it open and swiping blindly into the shadow cast by one flatbed, he felt his hand graze Dark's face, felt his fingers turn warm and wet.

"That'll teach you, you . . . you . . . you . . . soddymite!"

"Huhuhuh!"

Sam held the lantern over the edge of the wagon, then, and Lindy could see the deep gash he had put across Dark's swollen features. "And that there's just the beginning! You go on stickin' your tongue in where it don't belong, an' you just see whut you get! Abomination! Abomination and bitchery!"

"I duzn't see whut abomashun gots'ta do wid any o' dis," came the reply through blub lips hideously swollen from Lindy's beating.

Lindy's reply was another swipe of the razor, and then, his head having finally cleared, he bent down, grabbed the chains across Dark's chest, and hoisted him half-up. "You ain't done yet," he whispered hoarsely, razor poised to fend off any intru-

sive flicker of Dark's tongue. "You ain't done at all. We got a little cotillion of our own all planned out for you, but we got to get
there first."

"I still duzn't see whut—"

Lindy hit him, but not with the razor. Dark's eyes glazed, and
his head slumped to one side.

"Help me get him back up on the wagon, Sam," he said. "We
got to make some tracks."


Uncle Buddy—so he seemed to be—took Alma out of town
along a deserted Jefferson Street lined with the flickerings of
buildings that had been, buildings that were, buildings that
would be. Through the front window of Jamison's Drugstore,
she caught a passing glimpse of Abaijah seated at the counter as
he drank his coffee and chatted with the busty woman; but, rising from behind Jamison's—or perhaps from within it—was
the shade of another establishment, one clapped together out of
unfinished boards and lit only by the flicker of oil lamps. And it,
in its turn, vied not only with Jamison's and with McCoy's, but
with another that slid into and out of existence as the taxi passed
it by, one with white walls and multicolored signs and a strange,
inner window that flashed and flickered.

"What *is* that, Buddy?"

"What's what, ma'am?"

She recalled the limitations of this place. "Oh . . . nothing.
Never mind."

And then the rolling landscape was about them, and the hills
grew, and Buddy's engine whined with the grade.

"My wife doin' OK by you, Miz Alma?" Buddy asked.

"I've never had a moment's complaint, Buddy," said Alma.
"But, then, you knew that."

He laughed, and had it not been for her distinct recollection
of having climbed over the stile steps of the gazebo garden,
Alma would have been hard-pressed to say that she was *not* in
the everyday Lee's Corners to which she had returned—to
die—after so many years. And perhaps that was what was most
terrifying about it all. Maybe this was indeed what death was
like: a gentle sliding into an existence so similar to what one

had been used to one's whole, breathing life that any differences could essentially be ignored. Or perhaps they were indeed ignored, the soul merging easily and imperceptibly into something that was no more than a simple continuity of all that it had known before.

But . . .

"You're alive, aren't you, Buddy?" she asked quickly.

" 'Live as I ever been, Miz Alma." He laughed. "Now, what you want to go scarin' me with questions like that anyhow?"

"I think you know, Buddy."

He seemed unperturbed. "Well, I reckon I do."

Gliding. Sliding. Living and dead—or living memory and dead reminiscence—mingling seamlessly. "You and Lucy have been good to me, Buddy," she said. "Can *you* tell me anything about this place?"

"Place?"

"Buddy!"

"Wish I could, Miz Alma. But I'm afraid—"

"Yes, Buddy. Thanks." She sighed, watching the trees pass by. The knots of gnarled pines grew thicker, blended together, and were replaced by dense walls of oaks and sycamore and hackberry as the hills rose and they drove deeper into Montague land. "I understand."

"I'm sorry, Miz Alma."

"Don't give it a second thought."

And it *was* terrifying: that thought of sliding from life into death without even a clue—a sign, a gesture . . . not even a gate unlocked that had been locked before—that one had done so. Because then it would mean, without question, that it would all go on forever in a kind of dreamlike illogicality of parades that were there one moment and gone the next, of long-dead heroes helping one up from a stumble on the pavement, of corpses from the future and laughter from centuries ago, and all the little senseless errors and slightings and dashed hopes and realized fears that were inextricably concomitant with all of it.

Now she could leave. Now she could return across the stile steps. But *then* . . .

She shook her head. What lay across the steps in any case? Sophonsiba Gavin and her veiled threats. The madness of

Magic Harlow. The misunderstandings of Abram MacDonnell. The intolerance of Lindy Buck. Go or stay, she was, in effect, right back where she had started from. There was no escape, not even in death. And, in any case, would she even notice?

Her flesh rebelled, and she found that she was clenching her fists. "Buddy, I can't stand this."

He shook his head slowly, sadly. "Lots of things we can't stand in our lives, Miz Alma. Lots of things. But we just *have* to stand them anyway, 'cause there ain't no gettin' out of 'em. And sometimes when time comes 'round to be lookin' back at 'em, they ain't so bad after all. And sometimes they are." He shrugged, easing the taxi around a wide bend as though he were whitewashing a fence with a long, even stroke of a brush. "Colored folk know all about that. We been livin' with things we can't stand for a long time. Some of us turn to drinkin' to forget. Some of us sing the blues. Some of us just work harder. It's all the same."

Alma passed her hands over her face. "Is that a colored heaven or a colored hell, Uncle Buddy?"

"I'd have to say *yes* to that, Miz Alma."

"Just so." She wiped her eyes. "But you're not allowed to talk about that, either, are you?"

He laughed. "Can't talk 'bout what I don't know, ma'am."

She let him drive then, but it was not long before Alma recognized the trees and the rocks and the contours of the road near the mansion with the same instinctual, imprinted response as had struck her when a different Uncle Buddy—or perhaps the same Uncle Buddy all along—had driven her from the railroad station up to the house for the first time. And her flesh might have rebelled once more at that recognition, at the thought that she was, at such an intimate level of fleshly historicity, linked with this . . . other . . . place, but it did not have time, for the trees fell away on either side, and the wide drive opened before the taxi, and Alma could not suppress the scream that clawed its way out of her throat at the sight of the burnt and blackened remains of the mansion that had, when she had viewed it a short time ago, stood proudly and whitely above the town.

Buddy spoke softly. "Oh, ma'am," he said, "I shoulda told

you about this. It been a long, long time since anybody lived
here."

It was not burning. It had burned. It had burned weeks ago,
maybe even months or years ago—if such words meant anything here—for when, tottering as though she had been struck,
she got out of the cab and walked to the ruin, the ashes and
charred timbers were cold, stirred by past winds, matted with
past rains.

She bent, reached, touched. "How . . . how long?" she whispered, the ashes grainy and slick on her probing fingers.

"I'm sorry, Miz Alma. I'm afraid I'm not allowed to discuss
that."

Blackened plaster, cracked stone, charred wood, ashes. The
chimneys were toppled, and they lay like broken spines across
the blot left by the fire.

"I know," she said. "I know."

Numb, all but blind with shock, she waded into the remains
of the mansion, picking her way through the tumbled beams
and the fallen walls. Rooms were but outlines. There was no
trace of furniture. This was the blasted skeleton of a house.

"You be careful in there, ma'am!" came Buddy's anxious
voice.

The humanity and absurdity of his words brought her to herself, and she could not but smile. "And what happens if I get
killed while I'm *here,* Buddy? Do I go back to start? Do I get reborn as something else?"

"I'm sorry, ma'am. I—"

"Don't bother. I know. You can't talk about it."

But a gleam as of gold had caught her eye, and she scrambled
over tumbled brick and scorched plaster until she reached it.
Kneeling then, she extracted from the ashes a small brass telescope. It was identical to the one on the desk in her grandfather's
study.

No, she thought, examining it, her fingers confirming positively what her eyes had only suggested. It *was* the one on the
desk in her grandfather's study.

She stood, then, looking up at the sunless, darkling, brilliant
sky, stricken with the immediacy and the horror of where she
was, of what she was seeing and holding, her logic and sane as-

sumption rebelling against that which partook of neither, their revolt spurred into frantic urgency by the fear that, one day, she herself might—

She lowered her eyes. Off at the edge of the ruins, she saw Buddy waiting for her; and yet she found no comfort in his presence, because he was, in fact, not himself. Or maybe he was. If she wanted comfort, it seemed, she had to believe in the reality of this place. But she did not want to believe, and so comfort was one with the useless and preterit ashes of the house.

But she was looking beyond Buddy, then, looking out across the valley. Below, past the tumble of roiled foothills, was Lee's Corners, and from there the land stretched off and away. Smoky with haze and humidity, lying spread out beneath the shadowless sky, other hills and valleys rolled toward the horizon, and roads cut the land with lines of dirt and concrete, now ruler straight, now meandering like a drunkard's walk.

It was not just Lee's Corners, then. It was bigger than that. Much bigger. It encompassed, quite possibly, everything in her life, every place she had lived, every house and hospital she had visited, every person she had met or would meet or, even, perhaps, could possibly meet. And, though she tried, she could not push away the idea that anything so large as that—so broadly reaching and so firm and utterly material in its expanse—surely could not but possess its own, separate, and intrinsically validated existence.

And if that were so, then she was, truly, lost.

She dropped the telescope back into the grave of the house, and she asked Buddy to take her back to Lee's Corners. He drove her back to the town silently, as though grieving with her, and when he turned the taxi onto Jefferson Street, Alma saw that the parade was still gone, but that the sidewalks were now active again with all the signs of the Christmas holidays: shoppers and packages and lights, cheerful greetings and breaths—did they breathe here, then?—that smoked in the humid cold.

Buddy spoke only once, offering to take her to the edge of town, to the road that she would have to walk alone, but she refused and left him at the railroad station. Again she took the back streets to the edge of town, again she took the road up the hill, again she found the hedge and the steps.

That had been last night. Tonight, now, she had sent Lucy home early, and she had told Isaac to take the evening off and go and watch the cotillion. Tonight, alone in her house, clad simply but elegantly in the frock in which she had faced Sophonsiba Gavin, she was waiting for Mr. Dark. She would feed him the simple dinner that she had cooked with her own hands, and then she would ask him a few questions about matters that had grown increasingly important to her. And after that . . . after that, she did not know.

A knock came to the front door.

# Chapter 21

The hollow could have been more damp only had it been literally submerged. As it was, it might as well have been, for moisture seeped not only out of the quicksand-riddled ground and the clay-slick hills that surrounded the treacherous marsh, but also straight out of the air itself: coalescing in heavy drops on the mats of moss and scum that lapped at the patches of stagnant water, dripping from the outstretched branches of the half-rotted trees that stood lurchingly at the juncture of land and not-land like would-be suicides hesitating before the final, irrevocable plunge, lying low in a thick mist that, impelled by drifting winds or even by the clandestine exhalations of the earth itself, rocked back and forth like chowder in a soup plate.

Here, miles from Lee's Corners, on a patch of ground that was only slightly more solid than the almost-mud and not-quite-water that surrounded it, Lindy stopped the flatbed wagon and listened.

"Huhuhuh!"

"Keep that cake-hole of yours shut," said Lindy. "I need t'make sho there ain't nobody else here but us."

Sam sat up, looked around intently, his lips drawn back to expose his teeth. "But there's somebody else here! Huhuhuh!"

The light from the dim lantern glowed on the spectral trees, fell swirling into the rocking mists. Lindy started at Sam's words. "Who? Who's here?"

A long pause, with Sam grinning at him. Then: "Mr. Dark's here! Huhuhuh!"

And, true, as though taking a cue from Sam's words, Dark began to struggle against his chains, moaning:

"Ah'm . . . Ah'm . . . What it is, Mama! What it . . . it . . . is!"

"You gonna hit him again, Lindy? Can I watch? Huhuhuh!"

"I don't gotta hit him again," said Lindy. "Ain't no one can hear him way out here no matter how loud he yells. This here's where Earl Hogback had his still—you c'n see what's left of it over there. And you know how Earl liked his priv'cy." He spat. "The godless, unjust'fied sinner."

Dark writhed, his plaid suit and two-tone shoes an uneasy stirring in the dim light. "What it is, Mama! What it . . . it . . . it . . . is!"

"Can *I* hit him, Lindy? I can hit him real good! Wanna see how I can hit him? Huhuhuh!"

Sam, excited, was bouncing up and down on the board seat, his thick, womanish thighs smacking again and again onto the wood, rocking the wagon back and forth on its rusty springs.

"An' . . . an' I got my *razor*, too! Huhuhuh!"

"You jest hush up."

"Thought you said there wasn't nobody around! Huhuhuh! Did I scare you, Lindy? Did I? I'm real good at scaring people. A-and you wanna know something? Some people will give me *ten dollars* just to scare them, 'cause I'm so good at it. And . . . and guess what? I—"

"I'm saying hush up. So *hush up*!"

"Huhuhuh!"

"What it is, Mama!"

With an uneasy look at the roiling mist—as though unsure that Sam's joke had been entirely a joke—Lindy jerked a thumb at Dark, who was now rolling back and forth, the chains that bound him clanking dully in the wet air. "Let's git him down . . . and then we'll git him *up*."

Sam understood. "Huhuhuh!"

But Dark had been bound with several lengths of unmatched chain that Sam had linked together with a number of padlocks, and Lindy discovered, upon climbing onto the flatbed, that Sam had used one of the padlocks to secure Dark to a ringbolt.

Lindy grunted approvingly. "That was a good idea, Sam.

Woulda been no good t'all having him roll off the wagon halfway here."

"Huhuhuh!"

"Gimme the key to this lock and we'll string him up on that tree over there."

"Huhuhuh!"

Lindy suddenly felt uneasy. "You got the key, don't you?"

"Sho! Huhuhuh!"

"Well, then, give it here."

"Just a second. I've got it. I've got it right here. Huhuhuh!"

Dark rolled back and forth. "Oh . . . oh, what it is, Mama!"

Lindy lifted a foot and kicked the bound man. "Shut up, you godless, whoring nigger!"

"Oh, Mama!"

"Where's that key, Sam?"

"Huhuhuh!"

And Lindy, standing on the flatbed above the stirring, moaning Dark, passed a hand across his face because it was becoming obvious to him that Sam had no idea whatsoever where the key was. "God damn it, Sam! Where's that key?"

"I got it . . . right here. Huhuhuh!"

"O Gawd . . . O Lordy . . . the decent doodad t' do would be t' let me go," said Dark, writhing like a fish within his rusty skin of chains.

Lindy kicked him again. "You just shut up! You're gonna learn a lesson tonight 'bout stickin' your tongue where it don't belong. And you're gonna 'member it for a long time!"

"Huhuhuh! A long time! A real long time!"

With his goal in sight, and with Sam seemingly frustrating his progress toward it at every turn, Lindy fought to stay calm, even though a veil of rage was threatening to creep across his vision. "You shut up, too, Sam! You jest shut up! You hand me that lantern, and you go and get some wood and pile it up under that tree over there! This nigger here's gonna get hisself some schooling tonight!"


True to his word, Mr. Dark was at the door . . . and it was precisely seven o'clock. Down in Lee's Corners, the yearly Gardenia Society Tea and Cotillion would be well under way—dances and refreshments, the men formal in suits that they wore only once a year, the women resplendent in gowns and flowers—but here in Montague Mansion, there was a sense of uneasy restraint and simplicity, as though Alma's long sojourn in the Northern city had colored the exuberance of her Southern hospitality with a touch of the cold, withdrawn, Yankee winter that was, even now, beginning to seep along the streets and into the bricks of that metropolis.

But there was nothing restrained about Mr. Dark's smile: that same inextricable blend of the bitter and the sweet, overlaid now with a sense of obvious joy at seeing her (as though any young man, black or white, could look forward with enthusiasm to a tête-à-tête with a woman as old and dried up and, yes, underneath it all, despairing . . . as Alma). He was indeed the courtly knight again.

And Alma's heart was fluttering.

"I hope you'll not think me presumptuous," said Dark. "I brought wine."

Alma held the door wide for him, noting that he had not only brought wine, but also a small bouquet of flowers. "I believe you're psychic, Mr. Dark. I'd completely forgotten."

"Psychic? Oh . . . I suppose that fault could be laid at my door."

But here he was now, in her house—willingly—and here she was . . . awkwardly facing him in the entry hall after she had swung the door to, awkwardly taking the flowers from him, relieved that, with Lucy gone for the evening, she would legitimately be able to turn away from him for a moment while she went to find a vase. Still, though, there was the dinner that she had prepared—like the evening, simple and restrained, as she suspected he would prefer—and now that she was within reach of the opportunity to ask her questions, she was, once again, more and more uncertain of her ability to ask them.

"My word," she said, looking at the label on the wine bottle after she had settled the flowers, looking for something . . . else . . . to talk about. "I'm . . . I'm afraid I'm not offering you much to go along with this, Mr. Dark."

"Much?" he said. "Supper made with your own hands . . ."

*How did he know?* she wondered.

". . . in such a magnificent setting as Montague Mansion . . ."

*The colored people. They all talk. Lucy must have told him.*

". . . and with such splendid company as yourself . . ."

He was sincere, and she knew it. *But, then, Lucy didn't know, either. Nor did Isaac. How . . . ?*

". . . and you say you're not offering me much to go with the wine!" And he laughed.

She laughed, too, in spite of her increasing uncertainty. "But where on earth did you find something like this in Lee's Corners, Mr. Dark? I'm no connoisseur, but even *I* can tell—"

"Oh, as I've said before, I've been all over this sad old world of ours, Miss Montague. I have . . . ah . . . connections . . . almost everywhere."

"But this vintage is a hundred and fifty years old!"

He beamed. "And wonderful stuff it is, Miss Montague. I urge you to try it."

And she did. And though she was strangely reluctant to admit it, the magnificent old wine with its subtle aromas and tangs was a perfect companion to the unadorned fare she put before him: simple broiled chops, a few vegetables . . .

"I confess there's no okra," she admitted. "I've never been enthused by okra."

"Nor have I," said Dark. "I'm very much of the opinion that okra could have spent some additional time in beta test."

"Beta test?" Alma blinked at the outlandish expression. "I'm afraid that—"

He made an indefinite gesture, laughed. "A quaint turn of phrase I picked up somewhere."

. . . and fresh fruit for dessert. And so the two of them sat at the small table in the alcove off the dining room, drinking wine and eating, the candlelight mixing with the incandescents, and the flowers in the crystal vase that had come down to her from her great-great-grandmother—the flowers he had brought—seemingly glowing softly, glowing with the same kind of muted color that she had seen . . .

. . . elsewhere.

She stopped, staring at the blooms. Yes. Exactly as she had seen . . . elsewhere.

"I must say you've done a magnificent job with your house, Miss Montague," Dark was saying. "It's utterly lovely."

"Thank you," she said, deciding suddenly, in the face of what she read in the flowers, to be forthright. "I wanted to be comfortable . . . in my last years."

And she let the final syllables fall heavily, heavily enough to convey exactly what she meant. He had been looking down to spear a piece of sweet potato, but her tone made him look up. "Last years?" he said.

"You're being just a little disingenuous, Mr. Dark."

"Oh, my! Is it showing again, then?"

And they both laughed at that, and he refilled their wineglasses. "Then you did indeed come home to die," he said.

His phrasing was strange, but she answered. "I did. Yes."

He looked at her for a long time. Down the hall, the old Regulator clock chimed. Half past eight. She could not help but wonder what was happening at the cotillion . . .

. . . and that took her back to that evening, long ago. Her father had ordered the surrey built just for that occasion, and the best matched pair of horses had come out of the Montague stables to draw it. She in her gown, and he in his most formal and severe attire, they had taken the road—her father driving the team himself—to the cotillion, and, in the best Montague style— a moneyed but restrained ostentation that had descended from and been refined by generations of wealth mixed in with a piquant sprinkling of speculators, gamblers, and one or two outright thieves—they had arrived at the hall. Negro grooms had held the horses as he had helped her out, and she had entered on his arm.

Everything had been proper, Southern, in its place: a cathedral of propriety offering itself as a testament to the human condition rendered immutable by wealth. Externals might change— gas might give way to electricity, surreys to automobiles—but stretching into the future as it stretched into the past was, would always be, an unbroken line of fathers bringing their daughters to cotillions, colored men in livery murmuring "Sir" and "Miss," flowers and dances . . . all leading—perhaps all designed for the express purpose of leading—to the eventual trip to the church for a formal ceremony that would legitimize the union of clan with clan via the agency of juxtaposed reproductive organs and shared germ plasm.

Yes, it was at the cotillion that it had all fallen on her. Even before Vinty White had assaulted her in the upper hallway it had fallen on her. Leaning on her father's arm, wearing the gown and gloves and shoes that proclaimed her essential adulthood—or, at least, womanhood—she had looked into the future and had seen the subtle bars of custom and coercion that would hold her in Lee's Corners, that would constrain her marriage to this or that man, that would keep her in house and with child, that would relegate her to managing domestic affairs that, while important in their own way, were not to the taste of one who had run wild and barefoot through the woods and who had peered through her grandfather's telescope at the wonders of stars and nebulae.

And from that moment, she had striven against her ordained fate, first physically with Vinty White, and then verbally and emotionally with her father. And though her arguments with her father had quickly degenerated into alternating shoutings and silences—neither of which promised any sort of victory for either side—she had, throughout it all, maintained that striving that was as one with the force that had broken Vinty's ribs in that upper hallway. And when failure had seemed most tangible to her, she had (eighteen years old and with one hundred carefully saved dollars tucked into her purse) walked away from Montague Mansion, declaring herself—in words louder and more defiant than any she could speak, shout, or even scream—alone, independent, and without family of any kind.

Would it, she wondered through the candle flames, have been that much different had she remained in her proper place and fulfilled the pattern of matrimony and breed that was the Montague dispensation? Her flight had been, in essence, a quest for freedom, for autonomy, and yet here she was: returned to Lee's Corners and to a mansion she had insisted upon restoring to the same condition it had been in when she had left it, returned weighed down with the burdens of decades of interactions, choices, and regrets . . . and no more free than she would have been had she remained here all along. Oh, true, her present guilts and sorrows were more exotic then they would have been otherwise, perhaps, but exotic or not exotic was merely a distinction of quality . . . one imperceptible, in any case, to anyone who did not know the exotic in the first place.

She came to herself, realizing that Mr. Dark was looking at her. And she knew without a doubt that he had followed her memories and her thoughts.

"So, you see, that's it," she said. "That's why I came back. There was nothing here for someone like me, and it turned out that there was nothing out there, either. Remember Marley's Ghost?"

"Dickens," he said. *"A Christmas Carol."*

"Yes. He was in chains, and he dragged them about with him wherever he went. But we're all chained: every single blessed one of us, whether we've done good or we've done bad." She sighed, offered her wineglass. Dark refilled it. "I've just noticed the chains a little more than most people, maybe. Or maybe old people notice them, and there's some kind of tacit agreement not to talk about them"—she eyed him—"so as not to frighten the youngsters."

Mr. Dark smiled. "I assure you, Miss Montague . . ."

"Call me Alma, please."

"Very well, Alma. I assure you, I'm not at all frightened."

"You're very fortunate, then."

"It's not a question of fortune," he said. And there was his smile again, as joyous and as grief-stricken as she had ever seen it. "But tell me: is there nothing . . . uplifting . . . to balance the weight of your chains? Nothing hopeful? Nothing that—"

She shook her head. They had finished the meal, and she had, really, not tasted a bit of it. Dessert was waiting in the icebox in the kitchen, but she was not inclined to rise to get it. Chilled fruit and a dab of sherbet seemed paltry things with which to interrupt such a conversation. "Most women have children," she said. "They stare death in the face . . ."

Dark smiled.

". . . and go *pffft!* . . . because their children live on. I have no children." She shrugged. "Well . . . none that are real."

She had never told anyone about the boy. He existed, fully fleshed—as fully fleshed as she could make him—solely within her own mind. It was as though she, in living, had been pregnant with the whole, entire, unfulfilled life of another . . . and had never given birth by uttering a word about it.

"None that are . . . real?"

She was suddenly uncomfortable. Why had she mentioned children? Why had she tacitly mentioned *him*? "It's a little hard to explain, Mr. Dark."

"Alma, if you insist that I address you by your Christian name, then I must ask the same. Call me Primal."

The uniqueness of the name cut through her discomfort. "Primal. A strange name, if you'll forgive me saying."

He laughed again. "Well, you know colored people. If it's not biblical, it must, by necessity, be unique."

And then it hit her, like a great wave rising up just offshore— all unlooked-for—and sweeping across the land in a heartbeat. She froze, for it was as though that boy out of her past, the one she had gestated and nourished for nearly fifty years, had become real. "Primal."

He nodded.

"Forgive me . . ." She rose, turned away from the table, turned to the window and looked out, surreptitiously dabbing at her eyes with her linen napkin so that he would not see her tears. "I . . . I knew . . . I mean I know someone by that name. I mean . . . I . . ."

He remained at the table and did not speak. She sensed his silence behind her as much as she heard it: a presence as dark as his name or as his skin, a depth into which all sound was absorbed, captured, shut up.

"He's my child," she said. "The one who's not real. That's his name. Or, rather, that's what his name would have been . . . had he lived."

A long silence, deep and palpable. Then: "He . . . died . . . then."

"Almost before he was born." She bent her head, wiped her eyes again. No genteel, ladylike weeping this: these were real tears, deeply welling tears, tears that hurt, that tore at her as they brimmed and escaped. She had kept the knowledge of him and of his life to herself for so long that she had not known how much it would hurt to speak of them. "It's . . ." She laughed with self-deprecation. "It's a rather sordid little tale. I'm sorry I'm inflicting it on you."

She glanced at him over her shoulder. He was still sitting at the table, and she wondered whether his eyes, too, were damp. But no: that would be her eyesight. She was old, and she had been—still was—weeping. Eyes were deceiving things. They might, for example, perceive a dry-eyed man to be crying, or even read a lifetime of love and cohabitation in the face of a woman who had probably never desired either.

"Not at all," he said. "Tell me."

She turned back to the window, for she thought that it would be easier to speak if she were not looking at him. "I was an intern at the time," she said. She thought about excuses: a woman in medical school was a pariah, the harassment—psychological and sexual—had been constant, she had been working thirty- and forty-hour shifts, she had no staff backup. But there was no excuse, really. Or, rather, excuses were, in light of the event, such trivial things that they hardly deserved to be thought of, much less mentioned. "I was in delivery. Maternity."

He nodded. "If this is too painful for you . . ."

But she had already committed herself. "No. I'll go on. White people had doctors. Colored people had interns. This patient had me. It was a difficult birth: preeclampsia, the baby was in distress. And then the mother had a seizure on the delivery table and started to hemorrhage."

"I've heard the condition is often fatal for both the mother and . . . and the child."

"Not always. With vigorous intervention—" She was still looking out the window, out into the night. Down there was Lee's Corners and the cotillion, the lights of both twinkling, mingling. And Anger Modestie was down there, too. Was she singing tonight? Alma could hear nothing, but the window was closed, the distance was great, and the wind and weather on that April evening might have been just right. "Listen to me," she said. "I'm talking like a doctor."

"You *are* a doctor, Alma."

"I was . . . once. Did you ever hear the proverb: *Physician, heal thyself?*"

"Tell me."

"I called for a transfusion, but, as I said, colored people had low priority. If I wanted blood, I was going to have to get it myself. But the woman's husband had heard me, and he came into the delivery room, shouting scripture passages. I can't recall which ones now. The couple was apparently of some sect that did not allow transfusions."

Mr. Dark was silent.

"And so she died. There on the table. Bled gray. Her baby died, too."

"Their religion—"

"Shouldn't have made any difference," said Alma. "Not to me. I was a doctor. I was there to save a life, and to bring one into the world. I could have ordered the man out—"

"He would not have gone."

"Maybe not. But I could have tried. I could have tried." She bent her head, looked at the even, white layer of paint on the windowsill. "But I didn't. I was . . . I was cowed."

"He might have hurt you."

"He might. But I would have tried, nonetheless. If the woman and the baby had died, it wouldn't have been without a fight. But instead . . ."

She turned around to face him: she had realized that in keeping her back to him, she was hiding. "The woman had made her own choice," she said. "She'd married the man, and she'd stayed married to him, and she would have protested the transfusion herself . . . if she'd been conscious. The baby though . . ." Her hands came up, gesturing helplessly. "It was a boy, their first. They were going to name him Primal. And he didn't have a choice. He didn't have a choice—or a chance—at all. And so . . . I've . . . I've carried him throughout the years, dreaming about him, imagining what his life would have been like, where he would have gone to school, who he would have married, what his children would have been like. If he'd lived. I couldn't save his life in reality, so I made one up for him. It wasn't much, but it seemed the least I could do."

And then her resolve broke, and she was crying helplessly, crying openly, crying like the old woman she was: a cracked, wheezing sobbing thing whose fragile body was so racked by

her emotion that it had to grip the windowsill with both hands
so that it would not fall.

But Dark had risen, and he came to her, and then she did not
have to worry about falling, for he put his arms about her and
held her while she wept, the darkness of his skin and of his presence blending with the darkness behind her clenched eyes . . .
leading, finally, to a deeper darkness, one of utter exhaustion.

It was a white man's revenge. No shouting, hollering, or
dancing here, no rolled eyes and no ecstasy: just a calm, me-
thodical proceeding from kidnapping to vengeance, as a boy
might draw a line in the dirt with a dry stick.

Which was not to say that there was not rage behind it. By no
means. It took rage to drive a man to kidnap the object of his ha-
tred, just as it took rage to make him pick up a stone and batter a
padlock into bent, yielding metal when he could not get it open
in any other fashion, and it took rage—vast amounts of rage,
rage pent-up for weeks and focused with single-minded intent
upon a given goal—to make him suspend another man from a
tree branch and set fire to the pile of brush and sodden deadfall
beneath him.

And Dark swung slowly, a living pendulum, back and forth
as the deadfall steamed out its moisture and the smoke thick-
ened. Eyes rolling, blub lips smacking repeatedly at the taste of
the burning, he gibbered at Lindy, moaning and calling upon Jesus and the saints to save him. Finally:

"Look, Ah know you've gots sump'n against me, but dis be
no way t' deal wid it. Ya' dig?"

Lindy stood a dozen feet away, feeling the growing heat of
the fire on his moist face. "Shut up."

"I mean, it plumb stands t' reason—"

"Shut up!" And Lindy was finding, curiously, that this was
not enough. The smoldering fire, the moaning, the raving . . .
none of it satisfied him, none of it made up for or took away
even the smallest particle of the sense of the unclean that had
possessed him ever since he felt the intimate, lingual probing
from between those negroid lips pressed full upon his. And
now, to hear the moaning and the raving set aside, and to be ad-
dressed directly with calls for reason . . .

He had looked forward to screams, to the cries of a trapped animal, to harsh and guttural and near-incoherent pleas for mercy. And Dark, stubborn and vulgar Dark, was denying him what he wanted and what he needed in order to cleanse his mouth of the abomination that had been forced upon it.

But he had, perhaps, half expected that. In fact, that was why he had asked Sam to buy the razors, why he had planned this elaborate theater of kidnapping and transportation when a single shotgun shell or a few additional blows of his bludgeon would have been more than sufficient.

"You see. Sheeeiit, dude—"

But Dark had no chance to say anything more, for Lindy, striding forward and extracting his razor from his back pocket, had, with that intent and single-minded concentration that was so utterly violent that it had become, at once, its exact opposite—a calm, unblinking commission of an act that was no more than casual and offhand—seized the faintly pneumatic, protuberant lips of the Negro and slashed quickly, letting the severed flesh drop into the growing flames that were now licking at his own boots.

Dark stared, his yellow and uneven teeth exposed where they were not dripping crimson, his jaw moving in startled, spastic convulsions.

"He smiles real good now! Huhuhuh!"

"Shut up, Sam."

But though the fire was growing hotter, larger, steam and smoke rising as one, Lindy braved it still, letting his razor work as though it were guiding itself, gliding of its own volition through the sweat-slick flesh of the Negro and leaving behind the glistening and knotted movement of exposed muscle, the yellow rings and striations of fat, the heave of tongue and limbs that had lost all connection with the volition of their owner. Methodically, and with a growing sense of intent excitement, he watched the gleaming metal dive into the blackness of black skin and trace out dark upwellings of blood and gapes of deep-furrowed tissue, and he knew that Dark, in turn, watched him, feeling every stroke, every cut, every severing plunge.

When he was done, Dark's face was mostly skull, and Lindy

contemplated the lidless and staring eyes not so much with satisfaction as with relief, a cleansing wash of expiation for his own failure to guard his purity and masculinity against the violation of an unguarded moment. Dark could see him—he knew that Dark could see him—but the glibness and reason of his tongue was gone along with the tongue itself, and the cut that Lindy had put through his voice box ensured that no sound beyond the harsh breathing of an open trachea would issue from the suspended thing that was increasingly less a man and more a lump of butchered meat.

And Lindy, with a sigh, a sense of relaxation as of a hand letting go of his heart, stepped away from the twitching, smoking Negro flesh, stepped back onto his bootlace that was still flopping loose after he had broken it when extricating himself from the padlock, tripped, and sat down hard on the moist soil.

"Looks like you got your pants dirty, Lindy! Huhuhuh!"

But Lindy hardly heard. He was looking at Dark's dying body swinging back and forth, the flesh blackening and curling with the incongruous odor of frying bacon and the fire hissing and spitting with the steady patter of oozing fluid.

Then, with a sudden crack, the limb of the tree, unsound to begin with and weakened by the heat, gave way, sending Dark's body and its imprisoning chains straight down into the fire. Branches, sticks, dry leaves, and grass . . . all exploded outward in a puff of combustion, sending Lindy, who was still tangled in his bootlace, scooting back on his rump while, from within the blazing heart of the now-augmented flames, there came a sound of rending, like a dropped squash.

"He . . . he just went and split right open!" And so astonished was Sam that his nervous giggle was, at least for that instant, silenced.

Lindy squinted into the crackling light from beneath singed eyebrows. Sam was indeed right. Heated, smoked, and slashed, what was left of Dark's flesh had given way with the impact, and the remains of the Negro lay like a torn and deflated balloon amid the glowing cinders.

"Well . . . that's just well and good," said Lindy. "He'll burn real good that way, and we'll just come back in the morning and pick up the—"

The flames suddenly hissed, lowered, and went out.

"What in tarnation?" Loosing his bootlace at last, Lindy scrambled forward to find that Dark's body had released the last of its fluids into the coals. Combined with the general sodden nature of the ground and the air above it, that had been quite enough to quench the burning fuel beyond any hope of reignition.

"Damnation!" Lindy poked at the ashes and the wet wood, his finger coming away cool and slimed with Dark's remains. "God-damn damnation! Of all the stupid nigger tricks to be playin' on us right here at the end, if this don't take the whole cake!"

"I betcha he's just tryin' to spite us. Huhuhuh!"

"Puttin' out that fire! Well, I never! God damn, worthless nigger that never went and did a day's honest work in his life! So full o' moonshine and cum that he been a-savin' up for white girls that he went and put the whole thing out!"

And, getting to his feet, Lindy aimed a solid kick at Dark's blackened head. But he caught himself just before he delivered the blow. He had been relying on the fire to consume all evidence of the murder, but that was now impossible. So, if he wanted to get rid of Dark's body—and thereby remove all possibility of MacDonnell or someone else finding it—he would have to do it manually, and in one piece.

MacDonnell. In the silence left behind by the fading hiss of drenched embers, Lindy felt once again as though he were being watched, and though he reminded himself that Sam's comment upon their arrival in this hollow had been a joke, his fear of observation had been rekindled by the unexpected collapse of the tree and the fire. Once again he was staring into the dark, looking and listening for movement.

"You see anything, Sam?"

"Huhuhuh!"

"Shut up and look!"

"I don't see nothin'. Huhuhuh!"

Which meant nothing. Trying to shake the fear, then: "There's a big piece of canvas under the wagon seat. Get it."

Unmoving, Sam stared at him. "Why?"

"Just get it, you tomfool! We got to wrap that body up and

sink it in the swamp so that no one'll find it. Is that good enough for you?"

"Why?"

"So MacDonnell won't try to haul us in for murdering this nigger!"

Sam was suddenly defensive. "It ain't my fault! I didn't do nothin'!"

"Is too your fault!" Lindy was shouting without realizing it. "You're in this just as deep as I am! You helped me, and that makes you an accessee-ree!"

"But—!"

"And that's even worse, 'cause you coulda gotten out of it, and you didn't, so you got no defense."

"But—!"

"You just go get that tarp. Scurry! We'll wrap him up and we'll sink him in that hole around t'other side of the swamp. It's big and it's deep. No one'll ever find him there."

# Chapter 22

Lukie Fisher played first horn in Eddie Brigham's band, and he could tell that the bag of jello over at the side of the dance floor was dip-o-roony even before the yearly shindig that the richkins of Lee's Corners put on had got to first base. He even mentioned it to Brownie, who was in the middle of beginning what the boys all called his "foreplay before sax," stroking his worn blowpipe and fingering the keys and mouthing the reed as though his mind were on matters worlds away from music, but Brownie just rolled his eyes behind his thick glasses, stared at the feep for about ten seconds, and:

"Skogs," he said.

"Skogs?" Lukie had never heard Brownie say anything like that before.

"Skogs," repeated Brownie. "Real skogs. Real far skogs."

And then Brownie went back to mouthing his reed, his tongue working in a way that always made Lukie a little queasy.

But the richkins all wanted to start getting down just then, and Eddie, as always, was all jerked off on his short hairs because he thought that the band was not ready, when, in actuality, they had all been ready (with the exception, maybe, of Brownie, who was *still* working his tongue around on that reed in a way that Lukie did not like even to *think* about, much less look at) for the last half hour; but it was Eddie's band, after all, and this gig paid more for one night of banana oil and jive than all the others in the rest of the year put together, and so Lukie figured that Eddie had a right to be jerked off on his short hairs; and as he raised his horn to start "Mood Indigo," he reflected that he

had a bit more of a stake than usual in the goings-on tonight, because his girlfriend had just had a baby, and she was saying that
it was his, and she was starting to skank him about money, and
while Eddie *was* a musician, his mother had raised him to believe that there were certain things in a man's life that he had to
be up-front and responsible about, and babies were one of them.
And so jive and banana oil or not, he was going to blow his horn
tonight like his life depended on it.

Which was a bad way of putting it, he realized, because right
after "Mood Indigo," they went into "Avalon," which had just
come out that year and was big hotcha-hotcha stuff up in New
York and Chicago, and all through "Avalon," Lukie found himself staring at the bag of jello, who was looking less and less
like a bag of jello and more and more like a nutcase the way he
was slouching around at the edge of the dance floor, leaning
against the columns that held up the balcony like he was convinced that the whole hall would do a walls-of-Jericho routine
if he left them even long enough to take a leak, or like he was
trying to turn himself into another coat of paint or something
like that.

"Say . . . Brownie . . ." he whispered while Eddie was intro-
ducing the band between dances.

"Skogs," said Brownie. "Way out skogs."

"Yeah. Right."

"Skogs, man. Ab-so-lute skogs."

So it was a big doughnut and a half of a relief to Lukie when,
at the start of the second set, he took his place on the risers and
discovered that the nutcase was gone. There was no sign of him
anywhere. And, about midway through the second set, he had
just about managed to convince himself that old wacko-butter
had left the hall entirely when he heard the shots from upstairs.

As the night advanced and the air cooled, the moisture in the
hollow increased, and the mist that rose up from the quicksand
and the marsh expanded like bread dough, filling the broad, low
place with a gray, sullen fog. Slouching on the seat of the
wagon, Lindy peered ahead, trying to distinguish between road
and suckhole through an atmosphere that was doing its best to
keep him from seeing even the behind of the mule that was

drawing him while, at his side, Sam rocked back and forth, idly flicking his unblooded razor open and closed and singing under his breath.

"Cut that out."

"Cut what out?"

"That singin'. This is impor'n't stuff here. Ain't nothin' for you t'be singin' 'bout."

"I wasn't singin'."

"You were, too. So stop it."

"I *wasn't.*"

"Well, put that razor away 'fore you hurt yo'self."

"I ain't got no razor."

"You—'

"I *ain't.*"

And, convinced by now that any contradiction would merely cause Sam to repeat his lie with greater and greater conviction, Lindy let the matter drop. It was not overly important, anyway; MacDonnell was, doubtless, far away at the cotillion, and once they transported Dark's mangled remains to the deep hole on the other side of the hollow and pitched them in, that would be the end of the matter. Even if the marshal had some suspicion that Dark's disappearance was something other than natural, there would be not a shred of evidence left to show that the man had ever walked the earth.

But Lindy suddenly lifted his head, tugged at the reins, brought the mule to a halt. "What's that?"

"What's what? Huhuhuh!"

"That sound?"

"What sound?"

"Kind of a thump. You hear it?"

"I didn't hear nothin'. Huhuhuh!"

"I heard it two or three times now. You *sho* ain't heard it?"

"Huhuhuh!"

But something made Lindy tie the reins, set the wagon's brake, and turn around on the seat. And then he saw that the canvas in which Dark's mangled remains were wrapped had come loose on one side, and that a half-burnt arm was dangling free of the cloth.

"Jesus, Sam! I tol' you to wrap him up good! I don't want

no parts of him danglin' around and leavin' blood anywhere that MacDonnell can find. And I'll tell you: *you* don't want it either."

"I wrapped him up good! I *did*!"

"How you 'splain his arm hanging out, then?"

Sam was unfazed. "I *did* wrap him up good! He was all wrapped up when I put him on the back of the wagon!"

Lindy sighed. "Well, we're gonna have to wrap him up *agin*, then. I ain't gonna have him drippin' all over the road."

But when Lindy got down from the wagon and loosened the edge of the canvas so that he could tuck the arm back under the wrappings, he realized that cutting Dark up so badly might have been a bad idea, for the Negro's body had turned into something resembling a large, lumpy pudding, with limbs and organs and bones all swimming around in a sort of a gelatinous stew that was given cohesion and shape only by the surrounding canvas . . . that was itself turning slimy and wet with the moisture of the air and the corpse.

"God-damn fornicatin' whore of a nigger," Lindy mumbled. "Puttin' out the fire, and then he just goes and turns into jelly on me. You'd a-think he wanted to git even."

"Tol' you he was just spitin' us. Huhuhuh!"

"Just you shut your mouth and git down here and help me," said Lindy, feeling suddenly uneasy, as though he were missing something obvious about the situation. "You make sure that other side is tucked in good." And he went back to mumbling to himself about whoring niggers, wagons that he was going to have to scrub clean with sand and hot water, and the difficulties with which a laboring man was faced when he tried to provide for himself like a decent, God-fearing, white man.

"God damn it, Sam! I said *hold that other side*!"

"I am! I'm holding it real good!"

"You ain't holding nothin'!" And Lindy, his anger increasing, thrust the arm back up into the folds of the canvas, only to feel his own arm sink into something warm and wet, something that yielded for a moment, then tumbled forward, smacked him in the chest, and oozed down the front of his overalls.

"Huhuhuh!"

And Lindy, instinctively recoiling from the organ, once again caught his foot on his loose bootlace and sat down hard, feeling the—liver? spleen? stomach?—squish under his weight while Dark's loose arm, freed from his grasp and now quite loose within the folds of the canvas, slithered out, swung loose, and smacked him in the face.

"Huhuhuh! Looks like he's still gettin' his licks, don't it, Lindy! Huhuhuh!"

But though Lindy's temper had flared, he was distracted from venting it at Sam, for a chance thinning of the mist behind the wagon had given him a glimpse of the pale and bare dirt road stretching off and away, curving gently to the left as it rounded the treacherous swamp, its preternatural blankness broken by a series of irregular splotches.

"Christ Jesus! There's pieces o' him all over the road! God damn it to hell, Sam! I tol' you to tuck in that canvas!"

"I *did* tuck it in!"

"Sho you did, and I 'magine he just crawled out all by his lonesome! Jesus Christ, I ain't never *seen* such an idiotic set of mule apples as you, Samson Libbeldoe, who can't even tuck in a piece of canvas to save his Christian soul!"

And, just then, something else slid out of the slimy canvas and fell into Lindy's lap.

"Oh, Jesus . . ."

"I tucked it in! I *did*!"

"Jesus . . ." Muttering now, he picked up the nameless things and shoved them and the arm into the gelatinous mass that was quivering under the thick cloth. Snatching his hand back, he stuffed the edge of the canvas under the heap and grunted when it held. "We're gonna have to go back and pick up all that truck that fell off the wagon," he said. "And I want you to be watchin' this here canvas and makin' sure that nothing *else* goes fallin' off. You understand that?"

"Sho! Huhuhuh!"

Feeling as though he were depending on a burnt-out match to light his stove in the middle of a blizzard, Lindy climbed back up onto the wagon seat and, after glancing sidelong at Sam to see that he was at least giving the appearance of being watchful, he carefully backed the wagon to the edge of the road, turned it around, and started back toward the splotches he had seen . . .

that seemed to be even more visible now than when he had first noticed them.

His loathing for Sophonsiba Gavin had so expanded that, when he saw her at the cotillion that evening with Magic at her side, he could no longer perceive humanity, but only the strain of taut, animal bucks and locomotions against the imprisoning formal gown and tight stockings, the heave of paps too large to suckle anything but swine or bulls or other snorting things, the tottering shuffle and click of hooves strapped into the absurdity of high heels, and the blind gesture of forepaws. And yet it seemed that no one else at the cotillion could see what she was save himself, who stood at the edge of the dance floor and watched as she led his grandson about as though her own animal flesh had birthed him. And that, too, was a prod and spur to his emotions, for as his grandson was the offspring of his daughter who, in turn, was the offspring of himself and of his wife (despite the latter's final rebellion of a few hours before, he would not deny her that status), Magic's tacit and accepted denigration to the level of leashed and exhibited pet was an abomination of such massive proportions that he could not understand why public outrage did not immediately put an end to it and return that so-called woman to a quadrupedal existence in the fields.

But she had mastered them. Every one of them. Whether with money, or with influence, or with calculation, or with a bestial, snakelike hypnosis that had come upon them all while they slept, she controlled them in thought, word, and deed. And she, brute and husbandless, and childless even when she had possessed a husband, had no master. Indeed, her lack of offspring was a salient ensign of her defiance of convention and of propriety, for she carried not a solitary mark of subjugation to manhood, and so she had not only broken free of her paddock but had gathered to herself the temerity to fly in the face of the established sexual order.

Leaning against the fluted columns that supported the balcony of the hall, he watched her ape and shamble among the guests—lowing praise, grunting approval, snorting flattery— and he watched his grandson brought forward for display when it pleased her and put away when it was convenient for her. She did not dance, though. He was glad that she did not dance, for the sight of such hideous unnaturalness would, by necessity, have moved him either to instant laughter or to a confrontation much more immediate and public than he had planned . . . and such confrontations, as he had found out earlier that day, were apt to have unexpected consequences.

And so, watching, waiting, he bided his time there by the white columns until he saw her leave Magic in the care of May MacDonnell, the marshal's wife, and start upstairs, her thighs and hams heaving fattily, straining the seams of the human garb she wore: abundant, unmastered, bovine flesh that begged for confrontation and compulsion.

The gun was heavy in his pocket as he followed her.

To Lindy, it stood to reason that cooked meat was more cohesive than its raw counterpart, and so he was unable to explain this almost total liquefaction of Dark's body, which was rapidly assuming all the amorphous and amebic characteristics of warm jelly. Nevertheless, he and Sam managed to collect the squishy, dropped organs that littered the dirt road and to force them back into the seething mass of slime within the enfolding layers of canvas, but when he turned the wagon back in the direction of the deep, marshy pit that had been his original destination, he found that he was jumping at every sound, whether it was the croaking of a frog, the lingering plaint of a whippoorwill, or even the beating of his laboring heart.

"What was that?"

"I didn't hear nuthin'. Huhuhuh!"

He looked over his shoulder at the back of Sam's head. Sam was still playing with the razor. "I tol' you t' keep an eye on that there body and make sure it don't go runnin' all over the road."

Sam looked up and, too late, Lindy read the silly grin on his face and realized that a joke was coming.

"But he's *dead*, Lindy. He ain't doin' no runnin' no more! Huhuhuh! Huhuhuh!"

"Just shut your mouth and watch that canvas. If MacDonnell finds out what we done tonight, you'll be in trouble."

Sam blinked. "Me?"

"Didn't I tell you before that you ain't got no excuse? You watch that canvas and quit playin' with that razor."

"It's *my* razor."

"No it ain't your razor. I paid for it , so it's *my* razor."

And, realizing that he was now *arguing* with Sam, whom he was coming to truly loathe, Lindy swung around to face the road again just in time to keep the wagon from running off the edge and into something dark that could only have been water and mud and who-knew-what-else.

But still . . .

"What *was* that?"

"Nuthin'."

"You sure?"

"It wasn't nuthin'. Huhuhuh!"

This time, though, Lindy stopped the wagon and got out to find that one edge of the doubled canvas had again come loose, and a glistening thread of elongated and disintegrating organ led off the edge of the flatbed, down to the dirt, and away into the distance behind the wagon.

He could stand it no more. "You yellow-toothed, lyin'-mouthed, mule-brained excuse for a lick-spittloon! What're you goin' on tellin' me that you been watchin' this nigger's body when you ain't been watchin' anything but that razor you been playin' with?"

"I *was* watchin' it!"

Lindy took off his hat and wiped his face with his sleeve, discovering, as he did, that when he had thrust Dark's arm back into the mess of entrails under the canvas, he had succeeded in smearing himself up to the shoulder with mucous horror.

"Damn this to hell," he nearly shouted, passing a hand over his face to find that parts of Dark had thoroughly slimed both his cheeks and his chin.

"Huhuhuh!"

"We gotta go back again and pick up what you let fall off the wagon—'

"I was watchin'! I *was*!"

"—and we gotta do it quick. I don't want to be stayin' out here all night."

Sam grinned again. "What's the matter, Lindy? You skeered o' the dark? Huhuhuh!"

"Shup up and start lookin'! And mind you: you find *everything*. We don't want no pieces of this nigger out here for MacDonnell to find. You understand what I'm sayin'?"

"Huhuhuh!"

"And put that damned razor away 'fore you hurt yo'self!"

"Huhuhuh!"

MacDonnell, who knew trouble when he saw it, had been watching John Harlow from the beginning. Though it did not take much watching at all to see that John Harlow was trouble, even discounting the fact that after ordering an entirely inappropriate bunch of flowers that could no more be called a corsage than could a Rose Parade float (and Fiorello was *still* talking about it), Harlow had arrived at the cotillion alone, unaccompanied by anyone or anything save a fixed, hostile expression and a weight in his suit pocket that MacDonnell hoped was something innocuous . . . without much belief that it actually was.

But Harlow appeared content to stay by the pillars beneath the balcony and watch the dancers . . . or at least to *look* as though he were watching the dancers, for MacDonnell knew that his gaze was fixed entirely on Sophonsiba Gavin, and it was probably a good thing that Sophonsiba had a good constitution (MacDonnell assumed that she had a good constitution: she had, after all, buried her husband, and what he had done up in Memphis was well enough known throughout the town that its periodic effects on Sophonsiba could easily be guessed), or else she would more than likely have been burned up on the spot. Nevertheless, there was not much that MacDonnell could do, for no city or county law made it illegal for someone to look at anything that he or she wanted to in any manner that he or she wanted to. And so if John Harlow wanted to glare at Sophonsiba Gavin, that was his affair; but it seemed to the marshal to be a pathetic waste of money to go and buy a ticket to something like the cotillion just for the opportunity to glare at someone when one could stand on the sidewalk and do it for free.

Still, there was that weight in Harlow's pocket, and so when

Sophonsiba put Magic's hand into May's hand and told them both that she would be right back after she freshened up, and when MacDonnell noticed that John Harlow appeared to decide that he had to freshen up at about the same time, he told his wife that he needed to stretch his legs a bit and started across the floor, curiously glad of the weight that he himself carried tucked into a holster at the back of his belt.

The band was still playing as he climbed the stairs to the second floor of the hall where the rest rooms were located, and as the drummer they had down there was an enthusiastic gent who seemed intent on beating his instruments flat as pie plates, MacDonnell could not hear anything from the floor above (and he guessed that no one else could either); but there was a thump in the middle of it all that did not appear to go with the music, and it made MacDonnell climb the second half of the stairs considerably faster than he had climbed the first, which, as it turned out, was a good thing, because he reached the upper hallway to find Sophonsiba Gavin pinned up against the wall by John Harlow, who had torn her gown from one shoulder and thrust his knee between her thighs, forcing them open as he bent her back over a table.

"Jehoshaphat!"

MacDonnell realized that it was he himself who had uttered the exclamation, and he cursed inwardly at his lapse as he rushed forward, for though Sophonsiba Gavin had been so thoroughly frightened that she had fainted, John Harlow was now aware that he had been discovered, and he dragged Sophonsiba off the table and backed down the hall with his forearm cinched up against her throat.

"Get back, Marshal," he said. "Just get back."

MacDonnell swallowed, cleared his throat, thanked God that the upstairs hall was otherwise empty, and prayed that it would remain so for the next minute to two. "Mr. Harlow, I think you need to put Mrs. Gavin down now, and you and I need to go have a little talk. I 'magine you're a bit upset—"

"You bet I'm upset, Marshal. And I'm just as upset at you as I am at this pig here." And Sophonsiba moaned hoarsely as he jerked his forearm tighter against her windpipe. "You haven't been doing much of a job here in Lee's Corners if you let pigs like this go stealing a man's grandson from him. You and every-one else. You just let her come and go as you please, soiling the lives of good, decent people like—."

"I think you'd better put Mrs. Gavin down, John," said Mac-Donnell quietly. "You're in 'bout as deep as you can get. I reckon you don't want to get in any deeper."

"She's going to learn not to take my grandson away from me! He's my daughter's son, and he's mine!"

"I'm sure that—"

And there MacDonnell hesitated, for he was suddenly awash in thoughts of Greta, of her supposed suicide, of Sophonsiba Gavin's presence at Mildred Riddup's house within minutes after Mildred had discovered Greta's body, of Sophonsiba's deal with Otis to dispose of a certain piece of evidence that did not sound, in the end, as though it had been much of a piece of evidence at all.

But he struggled on. "I'm sure that Mrs. Gavin wants nothing more than to see you and Alice just as happy as clams with Magic."

Harlow was not convinced. "She doesn't want anything of the sort! She wants Magic! She wants to own him!"

MacDonnell felt the sweat starting out on his forehead, wondered how long Sophonsiba Gavin's windpipe could hold up, wondered, too, how much time he had before someone else came upstairs and touched off the powder keg that John Harlow had become. "You just let Mrs. Gavin there go, and you and I can talk about it tomorrow," he said. "What do you say to that?"

"I say go to blazes!"

He was feeding on himself, MacDonnell realized, madness and obsession leading to more madness and obsession.

"You just stay there," Harlow was saying. "You just stay right there." Dragging Sophonsiba, he began backing down the hall toward a pair of doors at the far end. "I'm going down these back stairs, and this pig and I are going to go someplace quiet where we can have a talk about my grandson."

"I'm not letting you go down those stairs," said MacDonnell, taking a step forward.

And then the gun was in John's hand. "Yes, you are," he said. "You stay right there."

By then Harlow had reached the double doors, but in order to open them and keep his gun trained on MacDonnell at the same time, he had to lower Sophonsiba to the floor. Dazed, half-choked, she slumped immediately to one side, leaving Harlow entirely exposed, and when his hand closed on the door latch and found it locked, his surprise distracted him just long enough for his eyes to flick away from MacDonnell and down at the un-cooperative latch.

It was all MacDonnell needed. He dropped full-length on the floor, one hand catching his fall while the other went to the holster at the back of his belt. Two shots, and John Harlow was down, his pistol clattering to the floor, his blood smearing the treacherously locked doors behind him.

MacDonnell got to this feet as footsteps came running up the stairs behind him. "How loud was it downstairs, Otis?"

"I think they're all figurin' it was firecrackers, Marshal."

MacDonnell's eyes were on Harlow, looking for any sign of movement. There was none. "Was it you locked those doors?"

"Sho," said Otis. "I saw Mrs. Gavin go up, and I saw John Harlow go up, and I saw you go up, and then May poked me and said I really ought to go and do some of that lawman stuff."

MacDonnell holstered his pistol, settled his coat over it. "I'll forgive you for that axe handle, then, Otis."

"Much obliged, Marshal."

MacDonnell had his hands under Sophonsiba's arms by then, and he was pulling her gently away from Harlow's body. She was still moaning, but she was breathing, and he could tell that she was more frightened than she was hurt.

He sat her up and propped her against the wall. "Mrs. Gavin?"

She just moaned.

"Otis, you go downstairs and get May to come up here and help with Mrs. Gavin. Tell her to bring those smelling salts she keeps in her purse."

"You want Doc Wyatt?"

MacDonnell reflected that he would rather put two rattle-snakes together than bring Wyatt and Sophonsiba Gavin any-where near one another. "No. The less folks we get involved in this, the better. At least for tonight. Just get May. But first off you put Fiorello and one or two of the other men at the bottom of those front stairs so no one else comes up until we get this body out of here. No sense in riling everyone and spoiling the whole dance over this. Time enough to sort it all out tomorrow."

Sophonsiba Gavin moaned a little more, then gave a small shriek. Her eyes flew open.

"Just rest easy, Mrs. Gavin," said MacDonnell. "You're safe now." He felt unclean, as though he had just done a great injustice. Though he could not say exactly how he had done it or what it was.

Otis was turning away to follow his orders, but:

"One more thing, Otis," said MacDonnell. "We got to go out to the Harlow place sometime tonight."

Otis stopped, turned. "What for?"

"We got to go pick up Alice Harlow's body."

Otis just stood there.

"Run and get May, now. And get those stairs blocked soon as you can."

They found pieces of Dark's body strewn along a mile and a half of road, and Lindy made Sam pick up every one of them himself, muttering inwardly that he would be perfectly justified were he to demand that Sam pick up every one of them in his *teeth,* for having been a stupid, infantile-minded shirker who could not be trusted with even the simplest of tasks without being distracted by the simplest of amusements.

"Put it in with the rest, Sam."

They had run rope through holes that Lindy had bored along the edge of the canvas with his pocketknife, thus turning it into a kind a shapeless pouch, and it was into this that he was making Sam scoop the semisolid body parts.

"Did you get 'em all?"

"Yeah! Huhuhuh!"

"Get 'em all."

"I did!"

"I said, *Get 'em all.*"

"I did. Well, I mean, I got *most* of them."

"Get the rest."

And so they proceeded, picking their way along into the early hours of the morning, Lindy holding the lantern, Sam bending, stooping, scraping chunks of glistening jelly from the road.

"You mean to tell me that you didn't even notice his *head* fallin' off the wagon? Why, you stupid—"

"It was there! It *was*! It must have just fallen off now!"

"Just . . . just . . . just get it."

But as Sam bent to retrieve the nearly fleshless head, the skull suddenly gave way, and something dark slipped out and thumped down onto the road.

"Now what the hell was that?"

"Nuthin'! Huhuhuh!"

Lindy leaned closer with the lantern. "God damn you for a goose! That's his brain! His God-damn brain fell out! Pick it up!"

Sam hefted the organ in his large hand. "You wanna play catch, Lindy? Huhuhuh!"

"Put it in with the rest!"

By the time they reached the deep hole on the far side of the hollow, both Lindy and Sam were thoroughly smeared with Dark, the canvas pouch was brimming and gurgling uneasily . . . and it seemed to Lindy that there *had* to be more in that pouch than could be accounted for by any single body; but he supposed that he could put that down to a need for completeness: portions of dirt and mud had, by necessity, been picked up with the scattered and viscous body parts, and therefore the contents of the pouch could not but be steadily augmented.

"Stupid, God-damn nigger. Going and turnin' into jelly on us. Ain't that just like a nigger?"

But here, finally, was the hole, and it was with a sense of relief that Lindy, his barely healed wounds and scars twinging mightily from the labors of the night, tied off the pouch as tightly as he could, and with Sam's help, muscled it from the flatbed wagon into the deep, swampy hole. In less than a minute, the water, the mud, and the quicksand swallowed it up, and the treacherous surface resumed its lethal placidity.

Lindy stood looking at it for several minutes, feeling the pain in his chest subside, letting his breathing and his heart slow. Eventually, though, a rhythmic sound caught his attention, and he looked up to see that Sam was back to playing with his razor.

"Lemme see that razor of yours, Sam," he said.

"It's *mine*! I bought it!"

Lindy was not inclined to argue. "Just let me see it for a minute."

Reluctantly, suspiciously, Sam handed it over. Lindy examined it. "Sorry you didn't get a chance to use this, Sam."

"Can I have it back now?"

"In a minute. Pick up those chains. I don't want MacDonnell finding them here."

Sam bent, gathered, picked up the heavy lengths of chains; but as he straightened, hugging a pile of metal links, Lindy moved. Flicking the razor fully open so that the back edge lay along the knuckles of his hand, he struck out and up, slicing through Sam's throat so quickly that there was no time for a sound, whether scream or giggle.

For a long moment, Sam stood there with this throat gaping and frothing—still holding the heavy chains, still half grinning as though Lindy had just proposed some new game for him to play—but then his eyes started to glaze. As he started to topple, Lindy gave him a small push, and, with a splash and a sound as of quiet sucking, Sam followed Dark into the quicksand, bleeding himself into unconsciousness even before the muck closed over his head.

# Chapter 23

Mr. Dark drove north, peering over the steering wheel of the big gold convertible as though his thoughts were already well beyond the horizon. But the goggles he wore masked the expression in his eyes, just as his driving coat and rakish cap kept Alma from examining the set of his head and shoulders. In essence, then: utterly unreadable, no more knowable than he had been over the dinner table when she had seen—or, maybe, had *thought* she had seen—tears in his eyes.

But there had been tears enough in her own for both of them, for after decade upon decade of holding herself, of denying any outlet to her inner world beyond that wry, despairing grin with which she had faced, continued to face the abyss, she had collapsed . . . into tears, into arms. Indeed, she had fallen so far that she had actually fainted, as though the inner, emotional walls that had held her upright had worn so thin that the abrupt removal of the strain that had so worn them had prompted their disintegration.

She had to come to herself quickly, but that one breach of her will and resolve had been quite enough, and so it had not surprised her when he had taken her hand and drawn her up from the big chair in which she had fought to recover both her senses and the inner bleakness that sustained her. "Come," he had said.

"Come . . . come where?"

"I want to show you something."

With her collapse—brief though it was—their relationship had changed. He had held her, and, regardless of youth or age, or of the color of his skin or of her skin, he had, for those few moments, been no more than manhood to her womanhood: supporting her, caring for her in a fashion that was even more ingrained in the stereotypes of their age than the shuffling darky of vaudeville, that could not but give him a claim to further support and further caring. And so as she had not been surprised when he had taken her hand and raised her from her chair, so she had not been surprised when he had led her—and she had allowed him to—out of the house and through the warm, close velvet of the Mississippi midnight to the locked gate of the gazebo garden, nor, after she opened the gate, when he, with sure steps and without any sign of surprise at the gazebo, the fountain, or the magnolia tree that was always in full, summer sunlight and bloom, had led her to the stile steps beside the locked rear gate. But at the sight of the automobile waiting in the road, with coats, hats, and goggles for Mr. Dark and herself folded over the back of the front seat, she had faltered.

"We'll be driving north," he had explained.

"North?"

And beyond the bittersweetness of his smile, there had been something else. Something that had given the bitterness the ascendancy, as though, in light of what he knew—or what he felt, or saw, or maybe . . . maybe simply what *was*—the sweetness had to take its leave for a while. "North. I want . . . I need . . . to show you something."

Having yielded to herself, it seemed, she must now yield again. To him. And so she had donned the coat and the goggles, and with Mr. Dark's help she had climbed up into the passenger seat of the high automobile with its broad running boards and its bulbous fenders and its whitewall tires and its spoked wheels. Mr. Dark had started the engine . . . and then they were off, wheeling northward along the dirt road, leaving behind a smoking trail of dust that drifted across the fields beneath the muted sky.

This country—this . . . other . . . country—was indeed bigger than Alma had thought when she had first taken the road to the Lee's Corners beyond the garden. It was even bigger than she

had thought when, from the brow of the hill beside the burn
ruin of Montague Mansion, she had seen that it stretched broad
and wide in all directions, that highways led off into the dis
tance, off to rolling hills and rivers, for even then she had as
sumed that it was no more than a reflection of herself, of her life
and of her past. Or perhaps—perhaps more likely—she had fer
vently hoped that it was so, for such an intrinsic limitation upon
its expanse and duration could not but confirm that it wa
memory and nothing more.

But as Mr. Dark drove, and as, first, Lee's Corners and, then
Memphis rose up and fell behind (rising and falling faster than
would have been possible in the realm of living breath), it be
gan to occur to her that this place obviously encompassed
memories that did not, *could* not, belong to her, that its vastness
could not but be contributed to by the memories of others whom
she did not know, that it was, in fact, a repository and a reifica
tion of *all* memory . . . possibly of all dream.

Or else . . .

Mr. Dark was not looking at her, but she turned away any
way, turned away to landscape that simultaneously rushed by
and rushed away from her, that stretched off into the distance
like a painted canvas unrolled out to the edge of the world.

And then she saw it.

"Stop!"

Had Dark not stopped, she might well have swung the door
open and stepped from running board to rushing road withou
thinking. But the automobile was motionless and on the shoulder by the time her foot met the hard ground, and she pushed up
her goggles as she tottered to the edge of the broad lake, stopping beside a green-metal post on which sloped a corroded
penny-a-look telescope.

Glass-smooth water mirrored a blank sky. And, off in the distance, visible as a thick dark line on the shining surface . . .

There was not a breath of wind, and she heard the crunch of
Mr. Dark's shoes as he came forward to join her. "Do you want
to look?" he said.

She hardly understood his words. She was straining her eyes
at the distant island. She thought that she could make out the

faint, vertical lines of trees so green they were almost black. And—maybe it was her imagination, maybe not—the outlines of rocks. Maybe more.

"Allow me."

She was steadying herself on the telescope, and she felt the barrel move under her hand and heard the clink of a coin in a slot. She turned to find Mr. Dark removing the cap on the eyepiece. He let it fall, and it swung back and forth at the end of a short length of rusty chain.

"Look," he said, gesturing. "That's why it's here."

He, also, had pushed up his goggles, and his eyes were both quizzical and kind.

"Here for me?" she said. "Or here for . . . others?"

His eyes did not change expression. "I'm afraid I'm not allowed to discuss that."

"Even you, Mr. Dark?"

"Me more than anyone else, Alma. And"—he smiled—"I believe I asked you to call me Primal."

And maybe it was his smile that allowed her to swing the telescope's eyepiece toward herself and to train the instrument on the distant island. At first, she saw only her own eye staring back at her, but then the view cleared and the scene from beyond the objective swam into focus, pouring through the tube in muted detail. Yes, it was all there, just as in the painting: the cypresses, the enclosed harbor, the cliffs with the hewn windows . . .

*I want to go there. I want to go there when I'm done here, and I want to think for a long time. It looks like a good place for thinking.*

"Is it a good place, Grandfather?" she found herself whispering. "Is it good for thinking? Is it—?"

And then she pulled her eye from the telescope quickly and turned away, because something had moved out there on the island, and she did not want to know whether it was him.

She heard Dark put the cap back on the eyepiece, heard the shutter within the telescope close as the time ran out. "It could be anyone out there." she said. "It doesn't have to be him. And this could . . . could be any one of a hundred or a thousand or a million lakes and islands just like this, where people who

looked at that painting and longed for a place to go and think . . .
could go and think. For as long as they want."

Dark was silent.

"I mean . . . wanted."

Dark was silent.

"Isn't that right, Primal?"

"I'm—"

"You can't talk about it, can you?"

"No."

"Where are we going?"

"The past."

"My past?"

"Yes."

"Why?"

"I need to show you something. Something that will . . . that
will . . ."

She turned back to him. His eyes were clenched, his mouth
drawn as though he were fighting himself.

She understood. "Don't," she said. "Don't. You'll hurt yourself. You're not allowed. I understand that."

"Something . . . that will give you hope," he managed at last.
"That's all I want to do. I can't stand to see you without hope."

"You can't . . ." She stared at him. Hope? What hope was
there? Hope that, though these lands were real, they were,
nonetheless, capable of offering something of solace and peace?
Hope that these lands were, as she so fervently desired, no more
than evanescent memory and fading dream? But perhaps it was
something broader and more general—and, at the same time, infinitely more valid and more powerful—that he was offering: a
hope that stretched not forward into death, but back into her life,
reaching, perhaps, *between* the griefs and the disappointments—
into those unlooked-for and unremembered spaces of common
humanity that had been, after all, what had drawn her back to
Lee's Corners in the first place—anchoring itself, rooting itself
into commonalities and thereby turning itself into something with
which she could meet her final passage with equanimity . . . regardless of where that passage might lead.

It was this last that he was referring to. She was sure of it. The very fact that he—forty years her junior and a stranger to her up until a few months ago—was offering hope at all told her what it was and where it came from better than any words he could have used.

*I can't stand to see you without hope.*

"But . . . why . . . ?" was all she could manage, but his expression told her that, no, he was not allowed to discuss that, either.

Greta did not know how she managed to convince Mildred Riddup to let her stay in her house a second time. Perhaps Mildred needed the money that Greta—thanks to Jimmy's support— had to offer her. Or perhaps not even Mildred Riddup's sense of morality and public outrage could stand against the desperation that Greta was hearing in her own voice.

Yes, she was hearing it. Ever since she had left Gavin House in the early evening for a walk with Magic—no different, on the surface, than any of the other evening walks with Magic that she had been taking for the last two weeks . . . taking so as to lull Mrs. Gavin's suspicions (assuming that there were any suspicions left to lull)—she had felt detached from herself, as though she were, in fact, floating behind and above her body, listening with detachment to her words as they came forth glibly when she said good-bye to Mrs. Gavin or pleadingly when she spoke to Mildred Riddup, watching objectively as, in her room at Mildred's, she had put off her childish dress and had donned more mature clothing while Magic played with a few wooden toys on the threadbare rug.

And that, she supposed later, should have warned her, for as the lithe, pliant girl became the young, earnest mother—even down to the stockings and the spare gray hat with its touch of fashionable netting—and as the mother sat on the bed and watched Magic play in childish innocence at her feet, she knew without a doubt that Jimmy would hardly recognize her.

She had never mentioned Magic to him, had, in fact, always spoken of their flight in terms that implied only two, trusting that his attraction to her would be sufficient to surmount the impediment of Magic's eventual presence. But, looking at herself this way, seeing at last all the maturity and maternity that simple survival had forced her to suppress up until now, she felt the growing hollowness of doubt. No, of certainty: she had, really, no doubt whatsoever as to his perception or his reaction. And it was perhaps just then that she felt the first, cold touch of lethality seeping into her.

Shivering, she went to the window, pushed back the curtains, and looked out. The evening was far along, the chinaberry and magnolia trees on the far side of the street floating like smoke in the light of the streetlamps. Sidewalks lay like pale ribbons. Crickets chirped hesitantly.

A shadow on the far sidewalk. Greta stiffened, and perhaps she was thinking of another window at which she had stood, years before, when she had seen a different shadow, one much closer to the glass, one that had come, in the end, closer even than that: putting out hands to the sash, lifting it beyond the eight or nine inches that she herself had raised it, following the spill of the streetlamp inward . . . into her room, into her bed, into her body.

But this shadow was short, squat, dumpy, and was surmounted by a fantastic, flowered hat. It was Anger Modestie who was passing by on the other side of the street, bound for someone's bedside.

Shivering, Greta pulled back from the glass, but when she looked again for some sign of Jimmy, she saw that Anger was standing, still and silent, beneath the corner streetlamp. And her reclaimed maternity possessed her then, forcing something that was almost a hiss from her clenched teeth. "You can't have him," she whispered. "You can't have him. He's *mine*."

And just when Anger, as though hearing her whispered words through the glass, through the air, through the distance, turned to continue her journey into the dark, Greta heard a knock and swung around to find that the door to her room was already opening. It was Jimmy—she guessed that he had either sneaked in through a side door or climbed in through a window—but he was not looking at her. Or maybe he was. Maybe he had already seen enough in her adult attire and the demeanor of motherhood in which she had wrapped herself that he could now look at

Magic (single-mindedly playing with his wooden toys) and still be cognizant of her.

His lips were flat. His jaw was clenched. He lifted his eyes to Greta, and she saw something in them that she had seen many times before, but had willfully ignored.

"Yeah," she said. "He's mine. He's coming with us."

He just stood there, framed in the doorway, his hat pulled low and his shoes polished as bright as the gleam of gold in his mouth. Finally, though, he came to himself enough to step forward and close the door behind him; but she had to turn away from the look in his eyes, she had to face the window once again as though what she had just said was nothing out of the ordinary, was something that he had known for weeks—of course he had—from the very beginning, in fact.

Down in the street, she saw a squat shadow. She tensed, for she thought that Anger Modestie had returned, but then she saw that it was not Anger, and she let out the breath that she had caught.

"He's . . . yours?"

"Yeah," she said, relaxing. "Don't you remember?"


It was as though, in being driven farther and farther away from the garden and the stile steps, Alma was also distanced from the present, and when the first indications of the Northern city appeared, they did so solely in accents of the past: faded signs advertising obsolete products for extinct species of female beauty, agricultural engines of uncertain function idle in the cryptic desuetude of half-tilled fields, well-traveled roads showing only the marks of iron-rimmed wheels and the prints of horses and mules.

But the land did not change—even here the land did not change—and Alma recognized it and knew where he was taking her.

"Why?" she said.

Mr. Dark drove on, his goggles and cap dusty. "I said I wanted to show you something."

Had her tone not carried over the sound of the rushing wind and of the tires on the rutted road? Or was he merely ignoring

it? "Here?" she said, "*Here?* Of all the things you could show
me . . ."

He pulled over and stopped, moving the heavy gearshift lever
to neutral, but leaving the motor running. His black cheeks
were powdered with dirt, his black eyes unreadable behind his
goggles. "It's important," he said.

"To *whom?*"

"To me."

Alma pushed up her goggles and wiped at her eyes. "To . . .
to *you?*"

"Yes."

His words—his admission—went against everything she had
supposed about him. But she realized that, in supposing anything at all about him, she had been fooling herself. She did not
know him at all. A black man in a little town in Mississippi. A
black man who ate vanilla ice cream every day at noon, who,
despite his denials, either had known or (more disturbingly)
*knew* her grandfather, and who had given to her the key that unlocked the gate of an impossible garden.

Facts. Bare facts. But there was nothing beyond them, no
unifying thread that brought them all together and made of him
a person with understandable likes and dislikes, with wants that
could be understood and a future that could at least be partially
intuited. And he must have seen the question that was forming
within her then, for without her having uttered a word, he said:
"I'm sorry. I'm—"

The formula broke the spell that had sustained her silence.
"*I'm* sorry. I don't want to hear it." She replaced her goggles,
settled back on the hard seat. Hope? Yes, of course. Hope. Hope
for *him.* And how many other illusory and incorrect things had
she supposed about him? And now she was here, in this place,
barely holding in check the panicked flight of her flesh, with no
way of returning to her home and the lands of normalcy save by
his grace and cooperation. "I've heard enough of that. It's important to you. All right. Drive."

He sat, half-turned in his seat, still facing her. "It . . . it might
be important to you, too."

"Yes, I know. Hope. Just drive."

He drove, and the signs of industry and habitation grew about them. Yes, she knew what was coming: the old highway led into the city, and the streets turned shabby and narrow as he guided the big car north and east. The skies were still muted, but now they held a sense of cold, as though all the winters she had spent in the living counterpart to this place, whether in a basement room with pipes clanking and condensation dripping from the ceiling or in an uptown house empty save for herself and the fine furniture she had bought, had taken their bleakness and their smoky, early dusks and had painted them onto the sunless luminosity, veiling it thereby, marking it with a desolation that, over the years, she had recognized as being compounded equally of the hearts of those forced to dwell in the blank sterility that came from too many people in too small a space—for even two was one too many when it came to questions of heartache and sorrow—and from the loneliness that had no cure save in company . . . which was, in the end, no cure at all.

Alma had not seen the hospital in years, but it was as she remembered it from her first days there; and in much the same fashion as the hills and trees about Montague Mansion had reached within her to find something that resonated with their image and their presence, so, too, the brown, spare outlines of this dirty building with its blank rows of dark windows and its cheerless doors that beckoned the sick out of the cold.

Dark pulled the car to the curb in front of the building. "Do you want to go in?" he said.

Alma turned her gaze away. "No."

"I'm sorry," he said. "I'd intended to give you—"

"Hope?" she said without looking up. "This is a strange way to do it."

Dark shook his head, pulled off his cap and laid it on the seat behind him, pulled down his goggles until they hung loose about his neck. "Maybe hope." He tipped his head back to look at the muted, luminous sky hedged in by brown buildings and smoke as the subdued, gliding rattle of the street—wheels, footsteps, distant voices, ragged people in ragged clothes—went on about the big gold automobile. "Maybe just . . . just vindication."

It was a seductive word to one who had lived so long with nothing, and it made her straighten. "Vindication?"

He was looking at her again. She could see his eyes plainly now, and she could read them without effort. Earnest. Painfully earnest. And pleading. "Will you go in with me?" he said. "Please. It's not just me. It's you, too. I think you know that."

Yes, she knew. And though she thought of Greta's corpse and wondered what it would be like to see once again the grisly failure that was considerably more intimately connected with herself, "Yes," she said. "I'll go."

He offered his hand, but she did not need to be guided: even after so many years, she knew where he was going and what he wanted her to see. Indeed, she suspected that she knew better than he did, for while his prompts and leading seemed to come as from someone whose knowledge was but indirect, secondhand, hers were immediate, visceral. Here was the brown-linoleum floor, the fifty years of chipped paint on walls that no paint in the universe could make anything other than drab and cheerless. Here were the thick, slab-varnished doors of her internship, the frosted-glass panels glowing dully with gaslight and smudged with countless fingerprints. Here were the hushed, moist echoes that were the hallmark—inarguable as the sign of plague—of underfunding.

"Up one more flight," she said to Dark.

He looked up the twisting, iron-banistered stairwell. "I . . . I don't remember."

"How could you?"

"I should remember." He was ahead of her on the stairs, and he did not look back. "But I was young . . ."

She stared at his back as he ascended, wondering at his words . . . wondering that she needed to wonder at all.

They came at last to the door, and Alma heard the voice she remembered, the voice that had haunted her for over five decades. This time, though, it was muted, distracted, seemingly coming not just from the far side of two inches of oak, but from across an all-but-limitless abyss. She would not, in fact, have been surprised had she swung the door open to find a kind of tableau chipped out of cold marble, the Bible verses emanating remotely, lifelessly, from the fabric and shellac horn of an old Victrola.

But she did not swing it open. Instead, she turned away from the door, from the voice, put both of her hands on the stair railing and looked down. Below, a nurse in garments a generation out of fashion when Alma was born was descending the stairs carrying a tray with what looked like a glass of lemonade on it. "I can't go in there. *I'm* in there. I could face him . . . now. But I can't face myself."

Behind her, the voice went on. Muted, almost unintelligible. She was glad that the wood appeared to be blocking the strangled gasps of the woman who was dying in labor or the entreaties of the intern who could not summon the will necessary to attempt intervention.

"You don't have to go in," said Dark.

"Why did you bring me, then? Are you trying to show me what it's like over here? That I'm going to have to revisit every single place where I ever failed . . . and do everything over and over again until I get it right?" She was glad she was facing away from him. "Please . . . please just tell me that there's nothing, that I'll soon be done with it all."

"I can't tell you that."

"I know." Her tone hovered between acid and resigned. "You're not allowed to discuss it."

Below, the nurse continued to descend. Behind her, Alma sensed that Dark was moving, stirring within himself. "I said I wanted to give you something," he said at last. "That's what I'm doing."

She did not look at him. Below, the nurse reached a landing and vanished down a hall. A memory rose within her, and she suddenly wanted to flee.

"What is it, then?" she said. "Tell me. Just tell me . . . and then let me go home."

And then, impossibly, a child began to wail from the far side of the door, and as muted and distant as had been the Bible verses of the father's jeremiad, this sound was bright, vibrant, immediate, and it pulled Alma around as though it had grabbed her hand and turned her.

"That's . . . that's not right," she said. "That didn't happen. The boy died before he . . . before he could even . . ."

But Dark shook his head. "The child," he said, "was born. On that day. Denied life, he entered the world by death."

Alma was still staring at the door. From within, the cries of the child continued. The jeremiad had faded completely. "That can't be. That . . . doesn't make any sense. Not even here."

"There are all kinds of birth," Dark said. "Birth into life, birth into death."

"You can't be born into death!"

He simply looked at her, and there . . . there was her own expression come back at her: that wry grin, so innocuous to the observer, the origins of which were rooted not in any humor at all, but only in the surety of despair. "That's what you did, Alma," he said. "There was death in that room that day, but by your resolve, you took him into yourself, and you sheltered him, and you birthed him into your inner world." He pointed at the door. The child was laughing, as though someone (and Alma did not want to know who, was afraid she knew nonetheless) was rocking him, tickling him, making faces at him. "You gave him a life. You gave him a reality. He's grateful."

Alma was staring. She did not have to ask. She could read it in his face, in the bitterness, in the sweetness, in the wry despair. "You're . . . you're not talking about *him,* are you? You're talking about . . ." She could not finish.

"Me," he said. "Yes. *I'm* grateful. I've been grateful for a long time. That's why I came to Lee's Corners for you, and why I made sure that you got hold of the key to the garden your grandfather made when he wanted to know this place better. So that you could know it, too. So that you could find some hope. Because you cared about me there at the very beginning. Because . . . because I knew you'd need me when you finally showed up."

He had been waiting for her, then. All along. All the years that he had been in Lee's Corners eating ice cream there on the corner. Waiting. For her. And, yes, she had indeed needed him. She had, in fact, come to Lee's Corners looking for him, pawing through the interstices of life and living, searching for a glimpse of him to let her know that he was near, but, in the end, seeing neither hope nor him, seeing only the confusion of humanity, the confusion she longed to escape. "How . . . how did you know I'd need you?" she managed.

"I know when everybody needs me. And you most of all. It's my job."

His job. The one she had never been able to fantasize because she had known intuitively that any imagining on her part could not be other than utterly inadequate. But now . . . now she knew the reality, and the inadequacy of her imaginings left her reeling— she had envisioned coffee and pancakes in the morning!—and her flesh, held in check for so long despite its growing, instinctual terror of such proximal and embodied dissolution, finally rebelled and sent her stumbling down the stairs.

"Alma!"

Her mind was all but blank, and her body, left to its own guidance, struggled to continue: step after step, flight after flight, descending much, much farther than she had ascended, much farther than the living counterpart of this building had ever allowed, descending until her old knees so ached with the strain that she had to stop at last, teetering at the brink of yet another flight, staring down into the square, banistered abyss of encircling and receding steps, realizing despite herself that the same dumb, mouthless emotions that had leached away her hope and optimism had also subverted all Dark's efforts, for what he wanted to give her, what he had tried to give her, what he—God damn them both—had *succeeded* in giving her was precisely what she had all along desired to be untrue, for whether in the lands of the living or in the lands of the dead, vindication and hope were equally false in that both implied some continuation in which to realize and reflect upon them.

*Come on in.*

"No."

*The water's—*

"No!"

"Alma!" Dark's voice echoed down the square stairwell.

But there he was: up there, physically present, *alive*. Or something like alive. He existed. He worked. His work might terrify her, but it was work nonetheless . . . possibly the only work available to one as irrevocably marked by the circumstances of his birth as he was by the color of his skin. His life might be incomprehensible to her, but surely it had not been wasted: despite the fanatic idiocy of his parents, he had endured, and even her own failure might therefore have been justified. What, beyond that, could she have ever asked for?

When she lifted her eyes, Alma found that she was looking at her.

She was as Alma remembered. Blond hair, white starched cap and bodice, pale face at once expansive and reserved. Odd: Alma had forgotten her face over the years, for the ceaselessly flowing memory of her retreating form had washed out most everything save the physical memory of that single touch. Even that look they had shared—that long look—had been so eroded by the years that Alma had come to half disbelieve in it and in everything at which it had hinted.

"You've come," she said.

"Yes . . ." said Alma, realizing that she still did not know her name . . . and realizing that now it did not matter. "Yes . . . I've come."

She nodded, looking beyond her, looking off into . . . someplace else. "That's good," she said. "I'm glad you did."

Alma had expected nothing of the sort from her. What about her husband? What about the violence that had taken her after so many years of abusive marriage? How was it that she was at this hospital, seemingly waiting for Alma's arrival, and glad of that arrival when it did come? "Can you . . . can you talk about it?"

She smiled slightly. Or maybe she frowned. It was hard for Alma to tell. The light here was uncertain, at once clear and obscure. "You mean, am I allowed to?"

"That's all I hear from everyone else."

"You ask the wrong questions. Maybe . . . maybe you ask questions, period." She shook her blond head as though to dismiss a trivial subject. "That doesn't matter. You're here. That's good. You went up to that room up there."

"I didn't look."

"You heard. That's good enough."

Her sentences were brief, clipped, almost brusque. She might have been preparing a balky patient for an enema. Was that, Alma wondered, the way she had always been? She struggled to remember, but the recollections fled: the communication that had passed between them had been wordless, gestureless. There had been no exchange, no revelation of personalities, only the vivid immediacy of hypothesized love.

"What—?"

"Don't ask. I'm not allowed to tell you that. But I'm glad you escaped."

Alma blinked at her. No, this was nothing like what she had expected. But, then, neither was what she had heard behind the door. Doubt fluttered within her: dream or reality? Did dreams so mutate? Could reality offer such predestine volition?

"Escaped?" she said.

"Escaped. Like that kid in that room up there." Her eyes had come back from the distance, and now they were looking at Alma. Seeing her. All of her. "That's what happens to the innocents . . . if they're lucky. That kid was lucky. So were you."

"I don't understand."

Her eyes. Seeing her. Seeing everything. Like Dark's. "It could have been both of us," she said. "That's all. It's enough. It's enough for me, anyway. Maybe it's enough for you."

"But . . . but what—?"

A shake of her head. "I'm not allowed to discuss it."

And then she was gone, her footsteps clicking down the dullness of the hospital corridor.

And Alma stood there—not calling out to her, not screaming, not even weeping—just looking . . . at what she knew to be her past—perhaps her future—walking away as it had walked away fifty years before.

*Maybe it's enough for you.*

When she turned away from the bleak corridor and climbed the stairs, she found that a single flight took her to the street level. Muted light came in through the dusty windows and fell across the streaked floor, while, sitting in a corner, a man in a bathrobe and thin slippers held his arms across his chest and shivered: all that he could find to do—or to remember doing—here on the other side.

Out at the curb, Dark was waiting by the car. He held her coat and the door for her, helped her to arrange her goggles over her dry eyes, then climbed in himself.

"It's a short trip back," he said.

"I know," she whispered. "But it's more than enough."

# Chapter 24

"Pow! Pow! Pow!"

She had managed to get through the rest of the evening, refusing both help and a ride home from May MacDonnell, refusing even the warm, alcoholic comfort of a toddy (Mr. G had been fond of alcohol, and she was not about to start emulating him) from Mrs. York (and she never *could* remember that woman's Christian name). No, she had started the evening as Sophonsiba Gavin, president of the Gardenia Society, and she would end it the same way, and nothing that John Harlow had done would keep her from doing that.

"Pow! Pow! Pow!"

"It was just firecrackers, sweetheart," she said. "Firecrackers. Some bad boys were outside with firecrackers, and they were setting them off. You don't want to be a bad boy like that, do you?"

"Pow! Pow! Pow!" And Magic, staring even more fixedly than usual, staring out the front window of the big automobile as though he had, somehow, actually seen MacDonnell and his pistol and had thereby had his mania for guns reinforced tenfold, was jabbing his finger at the road ahead as though to lay waste to streetlamps, stop signs, mailboxes, late pedestrians walking through the warm, autumn night on their way home from the cotillion, automobiles that, like great, lurking fish, swam up and then out of view in the beams of the headlights.

And so, all through the evening, she had smiled and she had offered her hand, and she had beamed at the fresh young things

that had been brought before her for confirmation of their entrance into the society of Lee's Corners. And then—and only
then—as the guests (all unknowing of anything regarding John
Harlow's assault, his death, or the stealthy removal of his
corpse down the back stairs of the hall) were departing, had she
forced herself to daintily hug her especial friends, to compli-
ment Tiffany on how nice she had looked that evening (though
she was noticing that the girl was ... well ... looking not
overly much like a girl anymore, and that meant that she would
soon have to go), and to take her leave, with slow, perfectly
steady steps, of the cotillion that she had supervised as she had
supervised it every year for the last two decades.

"Pow! A pow-er! It was a pow-er!" Magic's forehead was
pressed against the windshield, bumping loudly and hollowly
with each roll and wiggle of the car, his stiffened, almost spastic
finger at a level with his chin, pointing ahead into the night.

"They were *firecrackers,* sweetheart," she said, but even she
herself heard the edge in her voice, and she knew that Magic
knew that she was lying.

"Pow! P-p-pow!"

And as she guided the car along the dark road out to Gavin
House, with Magic twitching and, in his mind, killing over and
over again beside her, she found that she could not distance herself from what had happened in the upstairs hall that night, and
the memory of John Harlow pawing at her, pulling her gown
off her shoulder, forcing his knee up between her thighs (dear
God ... had he intended to *rape* her?), clung about her like the
stench of rotting meat and prickled like heat rash within her
throat, turning the darkness that pressed close on either side of
the road into not only a visible memory of her loss of consciousness during that minute of terror before the hot blast of Mac-
Donnell's revolver had ended it all, but also a reliving of those
weeks and months after that first conversation with Greta ...
when everything, *everything,* had seemed old, decaying, dead.

"Pow! Pow! Pow!"

Magic was sitting back now, his arm and finger extended,
taking careful aim at his targets. Killing.

"Pow!" His voice was high, loud, abrupt: an ear-stabbing
shriek.

She stopped the car in the middle of the deserted road and grabbed him by the arm. His eyes—shadowed but dark, seemingly looking at what was not before them—met hers.

"Pow!" he screamed in her face. "I want my pow-er!"

And the evening came up on her then like a hot flame—John Harlow and the thrusting of his knee and the sharp, brisk reports of MacDonnell's pistol—and she shook the boy by the arm. "Stop that!" she cried. "Stop that right now! There wasn't any pow-er! There isn't any pow-er! It was firecrackers!"

He struggled in her grasp, writhing, spitting. "Pow-er! I want my pow-er!"

She let him go, then, and as though a taut rubber band had been cut, he snapped back to the slender view of the world visible to him in the headlights, methodically pointing his finger and uttering his ejaculation at every distinguishable feature of landscape.

*It's not his fault,* she told herself. *It was that mother of his.* His mother: with her petty deceptions (not that she herself had been taken in for a moment by them: quite the contrary, in fact) and her overwrought plans and her idiotic and misplaced trust in a colored man. But she herself had seen through it all, and she had made arrangements. Nonetheless, she had been pacing back and forth along the length of the upstairs hall that night when the telephone had rung, and she had snatched it up herself (leaving James standing there with his arm outstretched for the receiver and obviously wondering how to gracefully withdraw from his mistake) to hear, not Sam, but rather Mildred Riddup blubbering something about a body and Greta and Magic . . . the three subjects so jumbled up that there was no sorting out who went with what until she herself had driven out there to find Magic running about in the street and Greta dead of a beating and Sam behind the tree by the corner, giggling, with that axe handle in his hand.

So Magic was safe from Greta, and that colored man had his back to Lee's Corners, and all was well . . . until John and Alice Harlow had decided that after throwing their daughter out into the street as a whore and a slut, they really, without any doubt, had to claim their daughter's son. But John had taken care of himself tonight, and Alice would, doubtless, be little trouble now, and so . . .

"Pow! Pow! Pow!"

. . . she would have her (*her!*) little boy to herself henceforth, without interference, without anything unexpected happening, and once Benny got rid of that gun once and for all (she supposed she could have James go through his room tomorrow until he found it), her little sweetheart's mania would eventually subside, and he could grow up into the sort of child that was always a cause of joy to her: tractable, sweet, winning, innocent.

"Pow!"

"Just firecrackers, dear. That's all."

"Pow! Pow! I want my pow-er! I want my pow-er!"

She was staring ahead just as intently as Magic now, her hands tight on the wheel. "Just firecrackers!"

When she pulled up in front of Gavin House, she discovered that she must have been tensing her arms and legs during the entire drive from the cotillion, for they were stiff and sore and heavy now, so much so that she could barely move. James came down the steps and opened the door for her, and though he offered his hand when he perceived her state, she ignored it and pushed herself up out of the car.

"Magic . . ." she started, but the boy had already swung his door open and was running up the steps to the open door of the house and the yellow light that spilled into the evening.

"Pow-er! Pow-er! Pow-er!" his words drifted back, fading as doors and walls interposed themselves.

She leaned against the car for a moment, then: "Take the car around to the garage, James, then turn down my bed."

"Yes'm."

On her own feet, then, she climbed the steps to the door of her house and passed first into the front hall, then into the sitting room. The chair by the window was soft and inviting, the darkness outside as deep as if the glass had been backed with velvet, but she did not sit immediately. Instead, she remained standing, looking out into the night, examining from her distant vantage the twinkling lights of Lee's Corners.

She was apart from them . . . and she controlled them. She had managed the cotillion once again, and not even John Harlow had been able to stand in her way. And now John was gone, and Alice would be gone soon enough, and Magic—

Footsteps clattered down the stairs behind her. "Pow!"

"Thank you, Magic," she said. "It's time for you to go to bed. When James gets back from the garage, have him—"

"Pow! Pow! Pow!"

Something—some tone in the boy's voice, perhaps—made her turn around, and she saw that Magic was holding Benny's pistol. His arm was still extended stiffly, but instead of a finger, it was now the barrel of the weapon that was pointing.

The prickle of mortality was in her throat again. "Magic," she said, "put that down. Don't point that at me. It's not nice."

"Pow!"

"Magic . . . please put that—"

"Pow! Pow! *Pow! Pow! Pow! Pow!*"

The moist hollow where Earl Hogback had once kept his still (and where Primal Dark and Sam Libbeldoe now lay concealed in the fetid embrace of chains, body parts, and swamp water) was a long way from Lee's Corners, and there was only an hour, or perhaps two, left before dawn by the time Lindy Buck turned the flatbed wagon onto the lumpy and grass-grown track that stretched from the main road to the packed-earth yard behind his shack.

The waning moon, just risen, gave no more light than the lantern that he had kept turned down to cigarette-coal dimness, for he had never been able to shake the feeling that he was being watched . . . followed, actually. It was, he suspected, quite possible for MacDonnell to have been out there in the darkness all along, methodically taking notes (how he hated the godless, unrighteous man!) and keeping just out of sight behind the last rise. What was, after all, the life of a nigger to MacDonnell? Oh, the marshal said all the right nigger-lover things, but when it came down to brass tacks, when it came down to laying those cards on the table to see who had the kings and who had the treys, the marshal, Lindy knew, was perfectly willing to watch Dark be gutted like a catfish right before his very eyes if so doing would allow him to get something he wanted.

A snap, like that of a twig, out in the yard beyond the reach of the light.

Lindy stopped the mule and listened, realized that the hoarse sound that was getting in the way of his listening was actually his own breathing, angrily controlled it until he nearly fainted from lack of air, and finally gave up. If MacDonnell was out there, it appeared that he was content to keep biding his time, and Lindy was not about to give him the satisfaction of watching the man he was watching get all nervous about being watched.

He unhitched the mule and put it in the shed he used for a stable, leaving the wagon standing out in the yard. But then he decided that he had better move the wagon, since what with Dark's slobbery remnants all over the back, it would not only become quite fragrant with the morning sunshine (and Lindy was determined to sleep in late), but anyone passing by on the road might see the stains and wonder what they were. And as he did not want to harness the mule again, he took hold of the hitch himself and succeeded, despite the tearing pain of the scars on and in his chest, in moving the clumsy wagon so that it was completely hidden by the house.

And there was that snap again, like a twig cracked by a boot, out in the direction of the road.

Lindy rounded the corner of the house and stared into the darkness. "That you, Marshal?"

Silence.

"Well, if it *is* you, you just come on down here like a man and tell me whatever it is you want to tell me."

Silence.

"Damnation," Lindy muttered. "Ain't nothin' there at all."

He was tired, sore, and hungry. The tiredness could wait a bit, he reasoned, and there was not much he could do about the soreness, but he would sleep better with some breakfast tucked under his belt; and so he blew up the coals in the stove, and he pushed in sticks until he had enough of a blaze to do some cooking. And when the fatback was frying in the pan and the corn bread was baking, he started to feel much like himself, as though just the very *odor* of the food was nourishing him, even before he put it into this mouth, nourishing him and returning to him his sense of justification, for he had, by his actions that night, cleansed himself of the touch of polluted, Negro lips just as he had, years before, cleansed the entire town of Lee's Corners of the whorish presence of a polluted, white temptress; and now he could face the future and remain satisfied and equanimous all of his days.

And from the back of the house, somewhere near the window, came the unmistakable sound of a leather shoe scraping on the dirt.

Lindy was at the window in a flash, his head thrust out into the night. But there was the wagon, and there was the shed with the mule in it . . . and not a sign of anything else. No shadow. No movement. Nothing.

He squinted into the darkness. Silence.

"MacDonnell?"

Silence.

It must have been the mule, he decided. That was it. From the distance, the sound of a hoof scraping along the side of a stall would sound very much like that of a shoe on the dirt. The mule. Nothing more than the mule.

The odor of smoke distracted him, and he pulled his head back inside to find that the corn bread was starting to burn. Cursing loudly and righteously that worries about evil men like MacDonnell should keep him from enjoying his breakfast, he dumped the corn bread onto a tin plate, then slid the fatback on top of it and carried the mess to the rough-hewn table he used for eating when he used it at all.

But there was something about eating breakfast like this—windows still dark as pitch, his overalls and even his face smeared with things he did not like to think about—that made him pull his chair around until he could see both his front door and his back window without turning his head, and in such a fashion did he start to spoon up his greasy meal.

But while he was looking down at his plate, he heard it again . . . only this time it was not a scrape, but the same dull, sticky sound that Dark's liver or spleen or whatever it had been had made when it had tumbled out from under the canvas and slid down the front of his overalls. And, raising his head at that moment, he saw a blurred motion at his back window, as though something that had been there had just then moved out of sight.

Shoving his plate away, he leaped to his feet, and the chair toppled backward onto the floor as he scrambled for the window. But, once again, there was nothing to see. The yard was empty and still, and the shed and the wagon stood shadowy in the light of the waning moon.

"MacDonnell, if this is your idea of some kinda damn joke . . ."

But Lindy did not really think for a moment that MacDonnell was out there. Nor did he think that anyone was playing a joke on him, particularly when he lifted his hand from the windowsill and found it stained with the same sort of dark stickiness with which he had become very familiar in the course of the night. In fact, the entire sill was covered with a thick, mucous coating of half-congealed blood.

He backed away from the window, wiping his hand on his overalls, until he bumped into the table . . . or, rather, until he thought he heard the door creak, though he could not be sure because his nudge had scraped the table across the dirt floor at exactly the same moment. Nevertheless, still wiping the stubborn jelly from his hand, he circled the table and, his heart laboring, pulled the door open.

Silence. Darkness.

Sleep and hunger were both out of Lindy's mind now, for he could not sleep with the sound of something moving about outside his shack, and he certainly could not eat with that abomination on his windowsill. And so, with the pain from the scars that had formed around the last of the bullet fragments raw in his chest; he got his lantern and lit it from the stove, and this time he turned it up until the flame was like an automobile headlight. Thus equipped, he went out the door and into the yard.

Silence.

The mule in the shed was drowsing, and, worn-out from the evening's travel, it did not stir when he unlatched the gate and peered in at it. Nor did his crisscrossing of the dark yard with his bright lantern turn up anything at all beyond his rusting farm implements and the muted glow of burst bolls in the cotton fields a short distance away. And yet . . .

. . . and yet, it might have been the hour—the predawn blackness that gave no hint of the approaching morning—or it might have been some lingering fear that MacDonnell was somewhere out there . . . biding his time, but Lindy could not shake the feeling that he was not alone. Somewhere, just out of reach of his lantern, he was convinced that there was a shadow duplicating his every movement. Several times, in fact, he turned suddenly, hoping to see what it was, and several times he thought he might have seen something flit away just out of the range of the light. But he could not be sure. He could not be sure at all.

Finally, fatigued beyond his ability to imagine and the scars in his chest straining terribly, he gave up and went back into the house, muttering to himself that any fool could see that there was nothing and no one in his yard that could trouble him. And if, despite his surety, he propped a chair in front of the door and closed the window (putting a nail through the sash to keep it shut), that was no one's business but his own.

Satisfied, then, he dragged a box up to the table and sat down to finish his cold fatback and corn bread, methodically spooning it up although it was horrible and congealed into a whitish mess. It was food, though, and it was *his* food, and he had resolved that no unrighteous lawman with delusions of power was going to keep him from it.

And then he felt the hand on his shoulder.

It was not just the hand. It was the heaviness of it, and it was the moist, clinging sense that told Lindy that something was oozing out of it and was soaking into the fabric of his shirt. And, too, it was the sullen, damp presence behind him that itself appeared to be oozing, dripping, spreading a puddle on the ground about itself that was not of water or whiskey or anything innocuous, but of something much more viscous and slow.

"MacDonnell?" he said. But he knew that it was not MacDonnell.

Slowly, he turned his head. The hand on his shoulder was hardly a hand at all, really, for its flesh had been so charred and cut that it resembled a broiled steak more than any human appendage. Bones protruded from the blackened knuckles. Bones, in fact, protruded everywhere, and as Lindy tried to shrink from beneath its touch, he saw that it was, actually, more bone than anything else. But though Lindy moved, it followed him, keeping and maybe even increasing its grip on his shoulder.

"That was a sorry way to repay a favor, Lindy," came Dark's voice.

Lindy's chest felt as though strands of barbed wire had been wrapped about it, and the pain of his scars turned stabbing as his breathing turned frantic and deep. Despite his wishes, his eyes insisted on traveling up beyond the hand, up along the twin bones of the forearm arrayed in their shredded and blackened flesh to their juncture with the glistening cartilage of the elbow, and then even farther. Up a surprisingly sound upper arm to a shoulder nearly burned through by red-hot chain, and then . . .

The eyes were about all that was left of Dark's face. Lidless, lusterless, dry, they looked at him out of charred sockets, their muscles jerking and twitching like red ribbons as they tracked Lindy, who, half-falling, half-scrambling, fled across the room to the door.

"I saved your life, Lindy," came Dark's voice again. "I started your heart when it had stopped, and I put air into your lungs when you needed it most. And then you went and treated me like that."

Bobbing, trembling, the naked larynx rose and fell in Dark's gaping throat, sending up liquid rivulets that streaked down the bare, white ribs of his flayed chest and dripped into the growing puddle at his feet. Lindy's throat was full of screams, but he could not get them out, because something in his chest had grown so large that it blocked their escape. And, too, his hands had grown unaccountably clumsy, for though he had reached the door, he could not seem to get the chair away from it.

The stumps that were all the fire had left of Dark's feet streaked the black puddle of blood and bile across the dirt floor as he came toward Lindy, and Lindy, falling back, could only look up at the fleshless face above him. Eyes, larynx, and a tongue that fluttered behind the even, white rows of teeth . . .

"I try to take people easy, Lindy," Dark was saying. "I try very hard. It's my job, but I can be merciful. But you . . . somehow, I just don't feel like being merciful to you at all. That's why you're seeing me like this. I'm going to take you hard."

And Dark leaned forward, and as Lindy saw that burnt, fleshless hand coming closer and closer to his face, the great swelling in his chest grew and grew until it finally burst. And then he was

creaming, screaming, screaming . . . until his voice turned
oarse and he tasted salt and he felt that trickle of blood grow-
ng at the corner of his mouth.

The house was full of light when Alma opened her eyes.

At first, she did not even know where she was, but then the
vening came back to her, doled out in dribs and drabs as her
memory roused itself. There had been the evening, and she had
een waiting for Mr. Dark to arrive, waiting with thoughts of
sking him about the other lands. And then there had been diner, and she had hesitated and had managed to fumble her ques-
ions out only indirectly, obliquely, leaving Mr. Dark—no, it
vas Primal now, was it not?—to answer just as indirectly, just
s obliquely.

But the thought of Dark's first name led her to the hospital in
he Northern city, and to her confession to him and then . . .

She lifted her head. She was in the big wing chair into which
e had put her after she had fainted, and she was still wearing
he dress she had worn for dinner. It was morning, she was in
he chair, and the house was full of light.

No, more than light. There was a luminosity that was new to
er, and the windows were glowing, streaming, radiant with
unshine, expansively brilliant as the illustrations in a child's
airy book. Everything within and without the mansion was de-
ailed and fresh, not as though the workmen and the renovators
ad just finished their work, but rather as though their work had
ot even begun: as though the mansion in all its former glory
vas still a distinct and detailed vision in the mind of the re-
torer, one uncompromised by physical realities or materials or
mpossibilities.

And there was movement, too. The light itself seemed to move,
nd the air, though still, seemed to move also, carrying with it
riftings as of voices, laughter: a kind of universal bemusement
hat flowed with great and lively quiescence throughout all the
articles of substance that made up Montague Mansion . . . and
hen continued on beyond that, continued through everything
bout the house that was not physical at all, all the past happen-
ngs and the dreams and the hopes of everyone who had lived in
t or ever would.

And then Alma recalled the burnt-out ruin of the mansion that she had seen once, and, too, the drive to the Northern city or, rather, to the Northern city as it once had been, as it existed in the dynamic stasis of the lands on the far side of the locked rear gate of the gazebo garden. And she rose in the luminous voice-filled morning to find her purse in her lap and a card in her hand:

*Come on in. The water's fine.*

Her grandfather's writing.

"Grandfather?"

A trickle of laughter—or maybe a sigh—streamed through the room and out through the French doors and into the overgrown garden.

But the garden was not overgrown. Somewhere between one day and another, Isaac must have worked miracles, for the grounds of the mansion were full of flowers, the boxwood sculpted into precise topiary, the grass paths vivid, verdant, trimmed.

She stood in the doorway, her hand to her head. She did not recall the drive home. Mr. Dark—Primal—had said that it was a short way, but she did not recall the drive itself, or having crossed back over the stile steps, or—

And where, in fact, was Primal Dark?

"Mr. Dark?" she called across the flowers. "I mean: Primal?"

Still the moving, stirring silence.

And then she wondered where Lucy was, and where Isaac was. She called them both, but though it was late in the morning, they did not answer, and as she passed through all the rooms of the mansion—kitchen and dining room, bedroom and parlor and drawing room—she found no sign that anyone else was there, save in the soft, playful voices that always appeared to drift faintly from the next room over, and in the impeccable order and arrangement of everything she saw. Clothes were folded and hung neatly, dishes were put away, papers were ordered, table and figurines were dusted.

It was all perfect, all still, all moving with the movement that appeared to be going on just under the surface, all radiant a though with an inner light that hovered just beyond the full perception of her eye.

And finally, when she was satisfied that the house was empty, her steps took her outside and to the gate of the gazebo garden. But though she had apparently lost the key—for it was not in her purse when she looked for it—she discovered that she did not need it, for the gate was already open.

Within was the grassy path and the magnolia tree and the ever-brimming fountain. And the copper roof of the gazebo shone so brightly in the sunshine that it hurt her eyes, and she had to lift a hand to shield them from the glare until she had approached and climbed the steps into the little building.

From there, she looked out beyond the railing and the hedge onto the same wide vista of sunlight and corn and cotton that she had looked out onto when she was a child, when her feet had been bare, when she had run wild in the woods with not a thought about family strictures or about what she might, someday, come to know of entanglements, despair . . . and love stripped away to leave only mute survival behind. But closer than the gay, glad fields, much closer, in fact, and just as she remembered, was the rear gate of the garden—standing unlocked, open, and inviting—and the road leading off and away toward Lee's Corners.

# INTO THE FIRE

Book Two of the *Hèl's Crucible Duology*

by Dennis McKiernan

# FLESH AND SILVER

by Stephen L. Burns